Beauty and Ashes

Susan Anita Jones

" ... Can I mature beyond

defining my SELF by someone

else's response to me?

I am stretching towards the hope of an identity

I do not have to guard and protect ... a Self

Both strong enough and flexible enough to remain

PLANTED amongst the STORMS, FLOODS, BATTLES, ... and DROUGHTS too ..."

"You are a tree replanted ..." Ps.1

"Beauty instead of Ashes ... Oaks of Righteousness ..." Is.61

"I am the VINE, you are the Branches

... Remain in My Love." John 15

"The leaves of the trees are

for the HEALING of the NATIONS." Rev.22

No part of this publication may be reproduced in whole or in part, or stored in a retrieval system, or transmitted in any form or by any means, electronic, mechanical, photocopying, recording, or otherwise, without written permission of the publisher. For information regarding permission contact Cadence Designs at jonessa@shaw.ca

VISIT website: http://beautyandash.weebly.com

Text copyright © 2017 by Susan Anita Jones

All rights reserved. Published by Susan Anita Jones. jonessa@shaw.ca

Title: Beauty and Ashes

Government of Canada ISBN 978-0-9959996-1-9

To Michelle!
So awesome that you have my book — what a sweetheart! :) Enjoy the read!
All the best,
Susan Jones

"... Beauty instead of Ashes ..."
Isaiah 61

*Thank you to my family
for your stories*

Upper Silesia
July, 1944
Chapter One

The young man would have been cautious, judging when it was time to break his shadowy scrutiny of the old man. Although I wasn't present at that first encounter, (it seems another lifetime ago), I can imagine how it must have gone.

He viewed the flat landscape with dull eyes and felt confident he had lost his own trackers, those who watched him for different reasons than he watched the old man. As he was sure no one was following him, he approached the grey-haired man, the one who seemed to be in charge, whose wife was not the nagging sort, whose children were not hanging around him. His focus was absolute as he strode toward the old man standing alone at the edge of the road near a copse.

"*Sind Sie Deutsch?*" he asked in German.

"*Na, ja,*" replied the old man. He viewed the tall slender man before him, assessing whether he was a German.

"*Grüß Gott,*" he ventured cautious hello.

Social conversational niceties still hold strong even in

gruelling days. The expressions of goodwill came and went, but they were exchanged with no more than the feel of a breeze across a calloused skin.

"Some here say we are Ausländer," the old man's voice trailed off.

The spell of mystery was broken: another wanderer, the symbolic refugee.

"A long way from home …"

The older man sniffed, "Yes, a long way from home." His sense of personal history made him swell his chest. His simplicity became an epic. His refugee flight became a soul-searching trek. He gave an expansive sweep of his arm toward the country that had placed him in a precarious marginality. "You, who are you?" the old man asked.

"Nobody in particular," he replied warily, lest the introductory conversation should become a lecture.

The older man raised his eyebrows. He found unanswered questions perpetually annoying incidences of conflict. "It's a difficult place to be, being a nobody." The old man sniffed curtly and spat on the ground. "It is wrong not to belong to this family, that village or this country. Here I am treated as an inferior, tainted."

The young man noted the bitter turn to the personal and resigned himself to waiting.

The old man grumbled, "The government even thinks it can do what it wants with you like a lump of dirty wool the dogs have dragged through the farmyard."

Apparently, the older man spoke of someone else because his angry demeanor indicated it was not he who was lost. Not he, with a personal sense of family history and seventeen remembered treks across the Lowlands, Prussia, the Russian Ukraine, and now back to *Oberschlesien*, Upper Silesia. Not he with his finely tuned sense of achievement even while currently landless. Confused man. Exile, even a welcome exile, with its change of social status, loss of community and belonging, and possible loss of legality can make each of us comes apart when our worlds are in pieces, even if just a little. For it is not land, wealth, achievement or even status that makes you somebody; it is your sense of belonging, your sense of connection.

Well, he would not be belonging for long, no matter what he thought, if he didn't learn to keep his mouth shut. You would think the older man would know better at his age. Years of communist suppression honed unease, keeping people from ever speaking against the government — any government.

But there was always a careless man, like this one, the one who would disappear in the night.

"I am from here, from the village of Boleslawiec, but it is of no consequence," the young man replied staring off toward the horizon.

If he had watched the older man, he would have seen the slight start the elder gave at the mention of the village and the renewed interest he showed toward his new companion.

"Come. Join us for *Faspa*. Not much, but enough," offered the old man trying to sound casual. Having tea together was a small affair. So small that the older man extended the invitation without any chance of fulfilling the offer.

"*Nein, nein*, I must be on my way to see my *Tante*. My aunt is not far from here." He tilted his head to the side. "Where are you headed?"

"Almost there, I go to the refugee camp in Zator. It is not far, approximately five kilometers. Zator is a town here in the Oshpitzin district, lying on the left bank of the Skawa River. You know it?" The older man thrust his chin out in the direction of the road. "They say there is a castle," he barked in disbelief. "I will be staying in a five-hundred-year old German castle!"

"So, you are staying in a German castle?" The younger man knew Zator had been incorporated into the Kraków Voivodeship of Lesser Poland in 1564. Two hundred years later, most of Silesia was seized by King Frederick the Great of Prussia in the War of the Austrian Succession; consequently, Silesia became part of the German Empire when it was proclaimed in 1871. However, by 1919, Zator, with its majority ethnic Polish population, again belonged to Poland. The Zator castle, actually a palace, belonged to the aristocratic Potocki family, a Polish family.

The older man shrugged and made a face.

"How long will you stay here, in Silesia?" It was a good question posed to the old man who, the younger man now knew, was of German descent.

Silesia was among the first regions invaded during Germany's 1939 attack on Poland. Dressed in German uniforms, thirteen German convicts were driven ten miles west of the

German-Polish border on August 31st. There they were shot dead and arranged on the ground to suggest they were advancing into Germany. The spectacle was immediately broadcasted on the German radio as an attack on Germany.

"The Germans say we are German," the older man shrugged again and stood taller as if to cast off a possible contradiction.

"The Germans say many things," the young man said quietly. He knew the truth about the Germans. He recalled the radio station broadcast in the Polish town of Gleiwitz, six German soldiers with a German convict in tow, seized a radio station. One of the soldiers broadcast an inflammatory statement in Polish announcing that Poland was attacking Germany and called Poles to join in the fight. A fake scuffle with much shooting was staged in front of the open microphone, and the dead civilian-clad convict was left on the studio floor to impersonate the Polish broadcaster. The sinister broadcast reverberated in the world like a scream in an empty church. World War II had begun.

"We Mennonites have emigrated seventeen times over the centuries, but we certainly had more than here …" the old man complained.

Lebensraum, the first objective of the official Nazi policy, was to settle the area with German people and that policy was definitely in effect. The second objective was to rid the area of the Polish and Jewish populations. Two thousand Polish intellectuals, politicians and businessmen were promptly murdered in the *Intelligenzaktion Schlesien* as part of the Germanization program. The area would one day again be part of Poland. However, at the present time, the Germans called it Schlesien, Oberschlesien or Upper Silesia.

"Ah, yes, Mennonite ..." The Mennonites, who followed the teachings of Menno Simmons, a sober, peaceful, and evangelic preacher, were an Anabaptist sect originating in Friesland in the sixteenth century.

"But the West is where the opportunity is. We move west," said the older man.

"You are a man of opportunity?"

"I have thought so," agreed the older man, turning to stare across the wild pasture where the river made a winding streak of silver under skinny trees rapidly losing their few leaves. His stare paralleled the automatic assumption that the conversation was drawing to its tedious conclusion.

"Can you give me the opportunity to create an opportunity for you?"

This was an unexpected direction.

"Perhaps," supposed the old man, trying to hide his surprise.

Beguiled by nature in the sweetly cool atmosphere of the evening, they both paused with anticipation. The dull land hung flat along the horizon. The ducks sat so still, so still in the clear river, while hunters waited. A huge black crow flapped overhead, croaking mournfully before disappearing into the muted grey of the sky.

"Mmm, I must visit my aunt, but would prefer not to carry a bundle with me. I could reclaim it in a few days ... at the camp?" There was an air of geniality about the young man, a pleasing, boyish quality in his smile.

"Perhaps," mused the old man with an assumed air of indifference. All the while his pulse took a leap, shocked into wondering how better fortune might be achieved. Nevertheless, caution enveloped the old codger.

The sun disappeared behind the singular trees and the chill

in the air was almost immediate, like a deliberate descent into a tomb echoing with the din of massive precision raids due to the sound of hundreds of aircraft. The unending war hovered in the air. The immediate surroundings drifted from twilight into darkness. The transition was complete.

He spoke casually to the older man as if his own personal matter was of no serious consequence. "It could benefit you. I know many people around here. Possibilities could come your way. I would be willing to compensate you for your help, but if you would prefer not, it is no large matter." He turned nonchalantly to go.

"Yes, yes, as you say it is a small favour to ask. Leave the item with me. I am Gerhard Wiens. You can pick it up from me later, at the camp. Yes, it is good to help each other," the old man encouraged.

And so, the small brown satchel with the dream inside was handed over. It was a strange business that was conducted, but desperate times call for desperate measures.

The older man held the satchel in his hand. *Ya, old man, well done.* Gerhard Wiens congratulated himself as he watched the other depart. His tongue flicked over the slight grin growing on his lips as he gazed down at the satchel.

No one could possibly know the catalyst this small event would be. One just cannot know how links are forged in our chains, can you?

Besides, stupidity gives remarkable assurance.

Zator, Upper Silesia
Sunday, July 23, 1944
Chapter Two

The breeze outside gained force as it snivelled its way into the mistreated Zator castle through the hole in the roof. I could identify the rank smell of unwashed bodies covered in dry sweat; the constant odour of a people in flight. A new family had arrived late in the night. Under the dark tent of the heavens there was plenty to listen to as people stirred in their self-made nests, complaining of discomfort with a cacophony of snores, whistles, and elongated moans. Others comforted or grunted to take advantage of each other as fragility and vulnerability became confidants. A child cried out from the floor below; another nightmare was speedily silenced by a harsh whispered reprimand.

As my son, Abraham, lay next to me, I could hear his desolate voice say, "I am nobody here." A sniff escaped from Abraham's mouth. It was not only that he had lost his home; it was the despair of loneliness when surrounded by people. His most faithful companion was depression. No wonder he kept it close. It weighed upon me that all this happened to my son.

The door to the room had the faintest slit of pale yellow underneath, a sliver of a distant glow. I could hear his mumbling about the light and asking where the key was. Abraham must be having another nightmare. Dread. I knew it laid its hand on his chest and pressed with a force that made breathing difficult. It was a gale force wind holding him down, causing tears to stream down his face.

Abraham moved closer to me, his mother, his *Mutti*. I longed to comfort him, but at the same time I felt afraid that my compassion would make him weak. So, I held my tongue and held back my embrace.

"We are all afraid of something," Abraham whispered. He was awake now.

I tried to watch Abraham out of the corner of my eye, but the night was so dark I could just see the window. He seemed to be staring, trying to stop the agitation in his brain. He was a ghost hovering above the broken wood floor. Any respite from sleeping swiftly dissipated. He scratched at his clothing. The itch and constriction of his clothing contributed to his perpetually discomfort. I could see him searching the wall for the glass window, almost a miracle in these circumstances of constant bombing and air raids. I wondered if the lifeless inner wall of the large room made him feel insignificant and unwelcome, similar to the time when he confided in me about a visit to his cousins. They had refused to open the door of their home even though they knew he was there; they ignored him.

    I brushed his hand lightly. The chill in the air made Abraham's slight hand outside the cover of the dirty blanket feel raw. I knew his body and soul were at their lowest ebb. The church bell next to the castle chimed to note the melancholy hour. The cold castle walls pressed my family together. The smudge from the spot where someone had previously built a fire inside, on the wooden floor, soiled our clothing. I whispered to my two-year-old Heinchen, who lay beside me on the right. Beyond, on the same side as Heinchen, was Abraham's older sister, Susannah, who was sixteen, and Tante Anika, my sister. Beside him was *Oma*, my children's grandmother and my mother. I was "Mutti" to my children and Eleni to the others. We were bound to sleep in cramped quarters in the same way our meager existence had been bound to the earth in our village, Chortitza. I could feel the ache of misplaced sentiment as I remembered the tidy rows of the Ukrainian village. I could still see the river, the houses one after another with gardens, and the wide, dry, dirt lanes. Our house had belonged to our family, and when we had moved in that space, we had been real. All our lives we had lived there, on that hill, beside the river.

The darkness upset my children. I could see Susannah was awake as well.

Perhaps she thought it was on a night as concealing as this one that Papa had been taken by the Russians — before we fled the Ukraine. Although she had not witnessed the event, she had heard the story on many occasions as I lamented, and shared the tale to whoever would listen.

"It was in the middle of the night ..." Susannah would hear me begin the story Papa's abduction. The Russians always came in the dark. They burst in through the door and grabbed my husband from his sleep. My pain, longing to be heard, would lament about what I could have done. The only thing I could do for him was grab some bread and shove it into his hands while sobbing his name. *Heinrich. Heinrich.* The Russians took them all, all the young men in the village. The men went like sheep. They knew nothing about politics. Nothing. They were farmers. They were sheep.

Susannah would make vague reference to my recollection of events, so I knew she often thought about it. What I didn't know was that she knew the story was actually a little different. I had not even been there, but Abraham had. The Russians came with trucks in the dead of the night and banged open the door without ceremony. The soldiers had brushed by my ten-year-old Abraham as if he had been invisible, and his *Papa* was taken in silence. In shock, Abraham had stood dumb. Both of them had been too terrified to offer resistance. Not a word had been exchanged, not a goodbye. My version recalled the fear and Heinrich's single utterance of goodbye. I did not know how often Susannah wondered if there had been a small gesture of the hands, some words perhaps, between Abraham and his father. I did not know Abraham confided in Susannah, and I thought there had been, at least, a fleeting touch. Afterwards, he had stood in the cold empty room, and then … Abraham had laid down on the bed, alone.

I believed, as did the family, that Heinrich was in the prison, but no one ever got past the prison gate. My freshly baked bread would be left with the guards. For months we went to the prison, daily. Other families in the village did the same for their men. The Christmas Heinrich had been taken even Oma had baked *zwieback* and taken the soft buns to the prison. Every so often, the Russian guards even gave a slip of paper saying the package had been received.

Betraying the rules was what the Russians did. We assumed they didn't. It showed how naive and oppressed we had been and still were to even think there was an etiquette to abducting people in the middle of the night.

"Life is different when survival is at stake. People are different when they are starving and desperate. Morality is a luxury. It needs to take a long winter nap and wait for spring." I would say, because I knew. I knew how to survive.

Those were the reasons Abraham and Susannah had to steal, a necessary circumstance with disastrous consequences.

Zator, Upper Silesia
Sunday, July 23, 1944
Chapter Three

"Don't be so sensitive, Eleni," my mother would often chide me. "You're behaving like a child." But, I feel things deeply like a storyteller and in a way, a storyteller is like the child of all humanity. There is a type of self-absorbed and singular perspective. We are made out of our stories. The potential exists for us to be open to stories not our own even though we live in such different worlds from each other. How we think, how we behave, and how we spend our time can be so different. Certain accounts are shared, others are not. We forget many stories in our lifetime. Some stories never existed. A few of our stories are lies we tell so often we believe they are true. We accept these stories in our youth and these must be distinguished from the stories we create as adults.

Seize the opportunity to enter the stories of the world, a voice murmurs to me, *to be heard, to be remembered, bearing witness to what is invisible to the eye.*

The child in me asks, "Why am I me and not you? Why am I here and not there?"

If I watch a large crowd, my attention will be drawn to one or two people. They catch my eye and I am held. I watch from a distance to see how they move and how they speak. There is an absolute wonder that I am not that person, and I ponder what their mysterious and enticing world is like. I want to control what they share. I want to stare and adore and imagine. Then, I can create a perfect story. I love things to be perfect. All they must do is look beautiful and beguiling and keep their mouths shut, so they do not ruin the picture.

But narratives are full of contradictions, seemingly black and white at the same moment. Several of those tales are amazing and unbelievable. Yes, unbelievable ... yet true, continues a voice.

Especially narratives chronicling recovery from trauma which are journeys of small increments and despite the foibles of storytelling, we magically heal ourselves by being together. It is the feeling of being home. That never grows old. I need that story. But, the journey home is often complicated. It is like a tall fence erected around a field blocking the path where a short cut used to exist, a fence that goes right up to the edge. Now I must go around that fence, thrash through the forest gully and the brambles, and wade through the pond to get home. That is how stuck feels. I want to go home. I want to be safe. I want to live and love and be happy, but I can't. I can feel the urgency of the desires fill my lungs and my heart. They consume my thoughts and direct my actions. Let me go home.

That fence. It keeps things in ... and out.

I journey on. It becomes treacherous as if I am riding my beloved horse on a more dangerous route because I cannot take the shortcut; yet, I must reach my destination. I absolutely must arrive ... there. I might not make it and the thought drives me to ride hard. My horse gives me his heart, but he cannot make it. You see, it is a longer route. It is a route where he dies. Everything dies. That is the story. Well, at least that is how it feels. I hoped my growing fear would simply be that my mounted companion would become overwhelmed but still carry me through. But no. I hoped I would underestimate him. That was not to be either.

I found out I would have to make the journey through my trauma on my own. To begin feels like the end of experience, the end of memories; it feels like the end of everything. I feel the solitary pain and the lonely fear that I might not be enough. I feel the overwhelming panic of a possible repeat. I am terrified I will be hurt again, that I will have to laboriously reorganize and reframe experiences into a positive interpretation over and over when I know there is so much anger and bitterness out there to be endured.

A voice agrees. *Our stories illustrate how we try to achieve passion and hold onto balance. There is no formula.*

But there are stories. I envision the commanding and invisible phenomenon of God placing me in the universe to receive the illuminating framework and texture of my life necessary to invite me into the story. I forget that I live in God's country and I am not the lead character in my life story; nevertheless, I still need to hear myself define who I am by declaring I am here. I belong to the world's beauty and happiness; the world belongs to my pain and sorrow. How simply stated; yet, the more I try to improve my situation, the worse it becomes.

For example, here I am with my family in the Zator refugee camp, a dead end. I try hard not to turn the corner into a pit of negativity where I forge a link in a chain that says every bad experience in my life is typical. Paradoxically, I know so many of my actions, even though the motive is good, are resented. Criticism and reprisal can be so scathing. It feels like vomit dripping off my body after every encounter.

Trauma leaves a certain perception of a besieged human spirit. It goes deeply inward. The work of recovering is slow. A voice conveys how much is needed.

It is in those depths I search for one exception, just one exception is needed. One small gesture of caring, from a child even, one to help turn the day around. I am so tired of conflict. It makes it tempting to submit and betray my ideals. I admit my morals slip. Each time, the conflict disfigures my confidence. Perhaps if I were grateful, grateful that the sun rises, grateful that it's raining and cold again, grateful that I have dreams, still. I could be grateful for the pain. Joy and despair make for such drama! I suspect those occur in the search for fulfillment although that is not what all of us experience. Sadly, certain people live in misery, but I am determined to survive, to live beyond misfortune.

Hate, anger, and feelings of entitlement are so exclusive and love to live on their own, as you will see in your story, speaks a voice.

I am so exhausted from living in perpetual fear. There has to be another way. I will find it. After all, I am a master at survival. Where does this story start? It starts where I begin to tell it, which is sort of in the middle. But I am wandering, as so many in my life have ... and I hear them all speak, not at the same time of course as that would be weird, but they speak to ruin the picture.

Zator, Upper Silesia
Sunday, July 23, 1944
Chapter Four

Tears rolled down Susannah's cheeks. *I will get caught. I know it.* Susannah spoke the words slowly to herself. The consequences of capture made her throat constrict and her body freeze. She did not know if she would be able to fight her way out to escape. Susannah imagined she would collapse, succumb to her terrible fate and become one of Mutti's two line stories. *"Ja, ach, ja*, I remember that Schapansky girl; she was raped by the Russian soldiers. She was never right after that," Mutti would always say. It was a tale Susannah did not understand but dreaded nonetheless. If she were caught, she would be shipped back in the direction they had travelled from or even further to Siberia!

Her terror made her struggle to bury any awareness of its existence. *What if I am caught stealing?* she moaned silently. *They will say the girl has no right to live. I will be an epitaph after only sixteen years and nowhere near the active front of the war!*

Abraham turned to stare at her and motioned with his finger to his lips, signalling her to be quiet. Susannah knew the recurring nightmare he had told her about was so vivid that Abraham doubted he was living only one life. In his nightmare, he was at home in the Ukraine and when he gazed outside the window, he saw a world soft and green and loving. Outside these castle windows was another world, barren, wet, and suffering. At times, when Abraham looked, his imagination would present him with an image of a black and darkened face, split with despair and hate, and alone that face would wait its fate.

The memory of those nighttime excursions would stay with him the entire day. He would exist as if in an empty trance. If his tears were emptiness they would be faithful confidantes in the company of despair, disappointment, distance and death. For him it was about the capital letter D. He would remember over and over the life he had lost.

"There is nothing to look forward to in the coming day," Abraham lamented in the direction of Susannah. "We get up and make it through the day. At night, we lie down and try to sleep."

She could hear the war around her. The "oil war" had moved into Upper Silesia, a major German synthetic-oil industry based on vast coal resources. The British-based U.S. Eighth Air Force and the Royal Air Force increasingly bombed the eight important oil plants clustered near the Zator refugee camp and the neighbouring Auschwitz concentration camp. The landscape shook under the impact of tons of high explosives.

But this was irrelevant to Abraham who felt strangled by being alive. Susannah his elder sister, functioned better. He was dark-haired with thoughtful black eyes that reflected Papa. Susannah had conveniently decided her reddish blonde hair must be a throwback to a distant ancestor, for she had noticed she did not have any of Papa in her, nor Mutti for that matter.

Papa had disappeared, so Peter Wiebe slid into Papa's place and became *Vater*. After all, Mutti was without a man and Peter always made sure to benefit from every opportunity. Interestingly, he always managed to effectively avoid any of the authorities, Russian or German, when the situation became difficult. Divorced, unmarried, widowed? What was that when there was a life to live! Peter and Eleni, Susannah's mother called Mutti by her children, had come together during the chaos in the Ukraine. When weren't there years of chaos? Then baby Heinchen arrived. He was as different as Abraham and Susannah were, yet Mutti declared he was

Papa's son. He was a German who would make Hitler proud, pure blonde and blue-eyed.

"I am German," Susannah declared. "My *Personalblatt* confirms it, one hundred percent."

Susannah was obsessed with her heritage.

****

I had registered the family at the *Einwandererzentralstelle,* the immigration office, in Silesia and shown Susannah the stiff thick brown paper document. The four digits of her *Umsiedler Nummer* were large and clear at the top middle of the document. Her *Abstammung* was *Deutsch,* German, her *Deutchstammigkeit in Prozenten* was indeed 100%. Below that notation, in tidy little boxes, her grandparents were also noted on the document. It clearly stated German 100%, for no one was tainted with other blood from different races. We had solid German names and heritage, or so we had thought. There was a hesitation with one name — Abraham. Immigration officers could find it too Jewish and demand it be changed. One officer had asked if Abraham was named after his father in heaven. Abraham had laughed giddily and said no, his uncle. The officer found it a good joke and had let his name stand even though the *Herkunftland* was noted as UdSSR. Indeed, the summary at the bottom of the page stated: "*Familienabstammung: Deutsch* 100%." Susannah thought she was a perfect German. But I knew the German nation was not moving towards perfection; instead, it distorted reality by always searching for more — an ideal, a master race. It was a sickness; that's what it was.

But I kept these thoughts to myself for that document didn't define me: Mutti, Eleni. I have my own personal narrative that begins way before my birth and will not end with my death. I am a wonderful contradiction. On one hand, my self-knowledge brings a consistency to my life that not everyone obtains. I feel sure of that coherence. Only when necessary do outsiders find a place in my interpretation of life. But, on the other hand, I confess, I lose my way dreadfully. Events are outside of my control. I hate to feel like I am irrelevant and it can engulf me in a thick murk. I always fight to reverse the direction into desolation, to halt the descent, for I am filled with passion to be better, to be the best. I try to make it the dominant state of my mind because one day, I believe, it will be true.

Little did I know back then that years later my children and I would be seen as the living legacy of displaced and dishonorable populations of nations gone wrong. I could hear Susannah mumbling about her heritage with Abraham. Our kind would be academically studied with fascination and curiosity. But now, Abraham's basic despondency about the upheaval plunged him into an unfathomable intensity where the emotion made no sound. I could see the effect of the turmoil of our lives on his face.

I turned my attention from my two children to the glow of light breaking into the darkness outside. The workers and the visiting director of the *Einwandererzentralstelle,* or EWZ camp, who had settled themselves into the cozy warmth of the outbuildings beside the five-hundred-year old castle, already stirred. These camps were established to handle the thousands of evacuees attracted to the magnetic core of the German nation. Zator, with over forty refugees, was one of the many branch offices. Roving teams of forty to seventy staff members moved from refugee camp to refugee camp processing individuals. A panel of six to nine workers interviewed the folk. The length of the interviews could be a couple of hours or a couple of days. Families, mostly women, youth, and children, were usually processed together except for those above the age of fifteen who were registered separately, hence the reason for stating that Susannah and Abraham were one year younger than they actually were. The majority of male refugees were elderly men, men with broken bodies or those devious enough to somehow escape the gathering net of the Russians. After obtaining a family history, testing for fluency in German, passing a health examination and having a photograph taken, racial examinations based on anthropological evaluations of physical attributes were conducted. In addition, this particular camp housed patients in the small hospital clinic.

These people were part of the National Socialist plans for Germanizing the frontiers of the Reich. The EWZ processed about one million repatriated ethnic Germans up until 1945. The headquarters, the central German authority for the immigration and naturalization of qualified ethnic Germans for citizenship in the Fatherland, were moved several times before locating in Litzmannstadt or, as it was known in Polish, Lodz.

I watched a relief worker come into the neo-Gothic palace.

The light beams from the single oil lantern wavered against the Italian designed stucco and marble fireplaces as the worker picked a careful path through the throng of bodies wrapped in their filthy clothes and dark grey wool blankets. A hacking cough resonated from the jumble. My world. No one had personal space. Cultures collided as we huddled together to fend off the perpetual winter which kept its grasp on us. What to do? What to do?

"Oh, it's Susannah, isn't it?" whispered the worker as he leaned over Susannah's sitting figure. I contemplated his face in the jumping light and recognized him as Bruno. With his young handsome smile, he continued the one-sided conversation. "Last evening, I played briefly with your baby brother, Heinchen." He was alluring. His looks were gentle and masculine with firm cheekbones and a chiseled jaw.

I glanced beyond them to Isaak and his wife, who had been wealthy private landowners for generations in our village of Chortitza, in the Ukraine. Life became especially difficult when the communists overthrew the monarchy during the Russian Revolution. After the collective farms were established in 1928, the wife had to milk their cows now owned by the state. One day, a

Russian official decided she needed more than just cow's milk, and the youngest of the boys had been born after that vicious rape, nine months later.

Children are a gift from God. The verse popped into my head. Really?

"That is the eldest son, Helmut." Susannah said to Bruno pointing at an ugly five-year-old. "He thinks pinching the girls hard and running away is the best joke in the world. He is a brat and he will end up like my uncle," she whispered to Bruno, who was trying to follow the thread of her conversation.

I mused about this touching of young girls and wondered about Helmut. Raised by an unyielding hand, Helmut would be driven out of paradise by the fierceness of his upbringing. *It is for his own good*, his parents said.

Close to Bruno were my brothers-in-law, Susannah's uncles. *Onkel* Reinhard always greeted her with a hug that lasted too long and ended with the back rub that went too far down her torso before he let her go. Then there was old *Onkel* Jasch, who believed in a good handshake but would crush your fingers so you could not use them for the next hour. Susannah always tried to escape the embrace of Uncle Reinhard and pull back her hand as Uncle Jasch closed the vice on it. That way, only her fingertips were mangled. Regrettably, polite behaviour to Uncle Reinhard and Uncle Jasch was a must.

Bruno nodded at Susannah then raised his voice to stir the crowd. "May God bless this day! There is clean drinking water by the relief tent. Please remember to use the designated latrine areas. The worship service will commence at daybreak."

I could see dawn was imminent. Susannah lay back down to wait for the day to start.

"*Steh auf, steh auf, die Sonne ist auf,*" someone chanted by the cooking fires outside. The sun was rising.

"No use, Susannah." I nudged her. "You are not allowed to linger behind."

The smoke already drifted into my nostrils as we searched for our shoes. Susannah had received her shoes from a kind old woman who had given Susannah the shoes off her feet and now didn't own any footwear except for the wood strapped to her feet. The black laces were frayed and Susannah had worn the soles of the shoes almost through. Soon, she might have to go barefoot, the way the children regularly did in the summer. The soles on Abraham's shoes were bound together with wire. When Abraham had asked the director of the relief agency if there were any shoes for him, the director sent him away with a vicious retort and chose to give the available shoes to someone else. I knew the director made a great fuss about his actions and thought he was magnanimous, but he was re-gifting. On the other hand, it had cost the old woman a great deal to give Susannah her shoes, but she had done it anyway. True generosity.

The cold night air nipped my toes, fingers, and nose. As we shuffled outside. Susannah caught Vater's eye in the early morning light. I could tell by his mannerisms that he was hyper-vigilant and irritable. He was so defensive too. He gestured toward a couple talking to Bruno. In the grey light Susannah and Vater had noticed Gerhard, who had arrived the previous evening, carrying a brown satchel. It looked like it contained potatoes and maybe even a *Wurst*. In these days of starvation, potatoes and sausage were certainly too much food for Gerhard.

****

Susannah smoothed her hands down over her wool skirt. She would have to separate Gerhard from his satchel. Susannah's imagination was flooded with unwanted images of Mutti separated from her wedding ring back in Chortitza, as was her grandmother when Communists had gone through the village plundering and raping. These were the stories that Susannah had heard all her life of the marauding Machno gangs, who had freely roamed in the Ukraine after the Great War had ended in 1918. She imagined those gangs creating anarchy in every tidy German Mennonite village: a great-uncle brutally attacked; his daughter, six years of age, pleading with the gang to stop; her head split open like a watermelon with an axe; the mother, Susannah's great-aunt, sliced up trying to protect the child in her arms. In the gang's wake, they left not only trauma but typhoid fever. Despite brutal intergenerational victimization, the survivors endured. For the next generations, Susannah and her family, life in the Ukraine continued to be remorseless. She tried to concentrate on today, but the old stories kept flooding her mind.

Susannah had observed how the Russians came into the village whenever they wanted. If they came in automobiles, it was real trouble. If they came on foot, they would come marching eight across the street, carrying their rifles. Once, the mayor thought he would greet them. If he was nice to them, then the Russians would be nice to him. The mayor got dressed up in his best complete with a gold watch and chain across his chest. He went up to the Russians and extended his hand. *Guten Tag. Willkommen.* The Russian soldier hit the mayor across the face with the back of his hand and grabbed the gold watch and chain.

Now we know, thought Susannah, who had seen the whole episode.

"Ha!" she whispered to herself and shook her head. She sweated in the cool morning air and felt short of breath. *There is not enough food and no money. There is nothing to buy anyway. You live in a world of nothing. Get used to it. You will starve. You will die an unhurried death.* Susannah's lips curled, and her gut growled angrily at the contemplation of food. The repeated struggle to fight temptation ended as it usually did, with giving in. She knew she would steal.

Vater came and stood beside her. "This is essential for survival, for us. Stop thinking about your Sunday school lessons," he hissed in her ear and moved away.

Essential for survival ...? They were safe in a camp. Here there was at least food. Susannah argued with herself about Vater's ridiculous comment, but his excessive planning of every possible outcome had made him change his belief about the way one should live. He had not always been that way.

"I am thinking about how to manage it," Susannah grumbled at his retreating back. *What if I'm caught? My family would be humiliated or worse. Who would tolerate thieves? The decision of the relief agency executive would be unyielding. They would no longer help us even though there seems to be a preference for ignoring our requests.*

A peal of merry laughter broke the morning.

"Listen to Friedrich," someone chuckled.

Friedrich retold his joke to the group nearby. "I was driving down the village lane one day with the ox cart and knocked over two Russians," Friedrich stated, his feet and floppy hands moving around like a puppy, a big floppy puppy. It was difficult not to laugh at the man, never mind what he was saying.

"What's funny about that?" an irritated reply came from

Gerhard.

Friedrich grinned. "I drove into the field to do it."

Susannah watched the group laugh with glee and pull blankets and coats around themselves as they moved off to conduct morning necessities. She kept her eye on Gerhard, and when he moved toward the common ground for the Sunday morning message, Susannah's entire family fell in deftly behind him.

Zator, Upper Silesia
Sunday, July 23, 1944
Chapter Five

Up until now, Abraham's smaller size had been an advantage and made him a notable provider for the family. However, his most recent adventurous raid through a barbed wire enclosure had left him with significantly cut palms. Today, therefore, it was Susannah's turn. My family passed by the three-room hospital clinic to the open space used for Sunday service. Vater made especially sure we loitered near the newcomer, Gerhard.

Susannah give a small yelp. Helmut's thick-lidded eyes and fat lips stretch into an impish grin. He had pinched Susannah in the back and jumped out of her reach, laughing. A practiced hand grabbed Helmut by his left ear. As his father turned it sharply. Helmut squealed as the *Ohrfeige* accomplished its purpose. I never laid a hand on my children, but this accepted form of cruelty was masked by the honorific term of "parenting." Others near me nodded with approval and contained laughter so as to not spoil the Sunday morning seriousness.

Abraham mingled into the shuffling congregation and stamped his feet on the ground to generate warmth. For him, I knew, the sound triggered the memory of shuffling, stamping army boots, slurred soldier voices, and the shouts of German officers aimed at keeping the lines of regimented bodies moving as one. Abraham was one of the thousands of German-speaking Mennonites in Ukrainian villages who had greeted the soldiers as saviours. Many would recall their elation as Army Group South, mobilized under General Gerd von Rundstedt, entered one village after another.

To be sure, it was startling news there were German soldiers, several arriving by horse cart, in their Ukrainian village. Naturally, there was initially great apprehension. They were, after all, soldiers and Hitler's anger drove him when he sent his soldiers marching toward the Ukraine. Operation Barbarossa began on June 22, 1941, a glorious date. Three million men divided into three army groups were installed along a 3,200-kilometer front to achieve a speedy victory before summer's end.

Not knowing what to do, my family had simply sat in the front room looking out the window, waiting. Two dusty soldiers stood at our door on August 18, the first of their kind, arriving on a motorcycle with sidecar. They asked in the Russian language, *khleb*, making the outline of bread with their hands. They did not barge into the house, and so everyone had answered them politely in their native tongue.

"Sie sprechen Deutsch!" The soldiers were thunderstruck to hear the German language. The sound of their mother tongue made them weep with gratitude.

Immediately liberated from feelings of distress, we eagerly fulfilled their request. The soldiers only wanted bread! When the German supply trucks and panzers caught up, they commandeered the village school and a few residences. A repair facility was immediately established. Wires were strung from building to building. The German's did not evict everyone, but they did take a house close to our home.

The commander of the unit had stated to our family when he passed them in the street: "I am German. Germans like to live comfortably. I feel this village is my home." He paid me particular attention. I was flattered, but Abraham instantly detested him.

By July, the German army had already advanced across the southern wheat lands, crossed the Dnieper River, and was headed toward the industrial centre of Kiev. Many villagers found the

German army remarkable. Large trucks and panzers were like beasts ingeniously concealed under trees. No one paid much attention to us Mennonites. Soldiers stood around and chatted. One night they brought out a movie projector and we sat on the wooden benches in the school yard watching the film on a white bed sheet. All I remember of the movie was that it was strange, and a line from it stuck in my head. *Jetzt wenn wir tanzen, kann ich dir sehen von forne und hinten*; now when we dance, I can see you from the front and behind. It made no sense to me and I laughed. But, for the few Soviet Russian inhabitants of the village, the table was now turned. The Russian men, fathers and older sons, disappeared into the night.

Even though the Russians had blown up the bridges, pontoon bridges went across the Dnieper. One of the first to be constructed was south of Chortitza, near Kakhovka. Ultimately, the evacuation of Odessa was only possible via the sea. Keen to face Marshal Semyon Budenny, the Germans neatly trapped 100,000 Russian soldiers and 317 tanks near Kiev, north of Chortitza. Around our little German villages, the Ukraine succumbed after the loss and capture of 665,000 men. The Germans triumphed after forty days of bloody combat.

The commander, Lieutenant Strauss, seemed to be ever-present in our home. I was not oblivious to the fact that Abraham abhorred him. Abraham had questioned me as to why I didn't tell the lieutenant that his constant visits were unwelcome. His anger disturbed me, but I allowed Lieutenant Strauss to come anyway.

I knew bits of information came to Abraham from talk. None of us, even the men, who constantly debated the war, fully understood the scope of what had happened. In retrospect, the amount of time it took to turn the table and put the Germans on the defensive was very short. In the larger theatre in the war, the attempt by the Germans to take Kursk required 900,000 troops. Von Manstein's call for more troops to fight on the western front meant the German soldiers pulled out of our Ukrainian village but to no avail. The carefully gathered troops were wiped out in the fighting. On July 13, 1943, the last major German offensive on the Eastern Front ended as a costly failure with the loss of over 550 tanks and 500,000 men killed, wounded, or missing. It was a major disaster for Germany.

I kept an eye on Abraham this morning. He seemed to be daydreaming again. *Thank God the Germans had come! If you put a cat in the oven, it did not come out a bun. It came out a cat. We were German. We always would be German, Germans from Prussia.*

I scanned the Mennonite congregation gathering for the Sunday morning sermon. *Look at them. They are sheep.* I didn't believe in relying on the Germans or on God but on oneself. God gave us brains to use! It would be a deliberate insult to the gifts God gives us to try to get through life without at least trying to figure problems out, and why would one want to purposely offend the Lord? It's true, I don't want to know the answers. I don't presume to have a special relationship with God or even to assume that I am an instrument of his will. How can I? How can I presume to know the full character of God? God is busy enough with other people. I am busy with surviving. I have concluded one has to make the best of situations.

The crowd shuffled closer to the makeshift platform that was the pulpit. Casper, the camp cat, rubbed his way between our legs. His friendly presence was accepted by nearly everyone without question.

"Life is one constant effort to be fought for every day," the lady next to Abraham complained. "It's easy to be good on a full stomach when your feelings match your convictions, but I am hungry now."

"Change your feelings to match what your mind knows is right and be quiet!" her husband snapped.

****

Susannah stared nervously from side to side like a stray cat and smoothed her hands on her skirt. *Four dead birds are worth two packs of Trommler or Sulima Record cigarettes,* she thought to herself erratically, *but I don't smoke.* She could feel Abraham watching her. *He's probably thinking I shouldn't stand around like a moron.* Susannah made a face in his direction. Susannah knew Mutti valued surviving. She valued life. Susannah was here, alive, because of Mutti. Where were the others? Their neighbours from Chortitza? Probably dying in Siberia. To honour God was to honour life, an accomplishment Mutti admired. Yet, Susannah was not interested in admiration nor in receiving one of her pats on the back along with a whisper to get on with it. Mostly, she felt foolish and ill at ease as she did in any conversation where the adult always had the advantage.

Life has a huge unfair advantage over me, Susannah moaned. All she could see was a shapeless mass of dingy browns and greys. She struggled with the absolute interpretations of the Biblical word. *Thieving is a sin. Jesus is going to be disappointed in me if I steal. I will probably, definitely, end up in hell like a Catholic.* However, she was more afraid of hunger and Vater's intense anger than distant Purgatory. Any bits of food were nuggets of affluence. She tried to focus on what she needed to do now, not on what might happen. The indistinct early morning light would help hide her movements from the white-haired Gerhard and his wife.

Everyone in the camp was at the morning service, sleepy but chatting and greeting one another. The evils of the war seemed to be far away. Here was safety, compassion, a chance for affiliation, fulfilling the need to belong. Here people could feel they counted. Through those budding relationships, many felt they were capable of surviving the war. It gave them a small sense of achievement that they had made it this far.

Gerhard stood beside a family fully clothed in new second-hand clothing right down to the functional pair of shoes from the relief agency. *People here seem sympathetic.* Surely there was no one who was secretly delighted when others who had more wealth slid into the mud. That was such a mean thought. *We have so many barriers to overcome,* Susannah concluded. *Even in periods when there is no war.* She began to second-guess herself, but the look in Vater's eye quickly put an end to that.

A girl of about Abraham's age stood next to Gerhard. Carefully, Susannah stood behind the old man. The satchel was on the ground. She tried to make herself invisible, but to her chagrin, the girl smiled at her and nodded her head as if they were conversing. Susannah wondered if the girl would remember her among all the youth in the camp.

As *Prediger* Wiens stood upon his box, the gathering fell silent, respectful of the minister. Another religious service. Yet, little rituals give life its texture. The service was held outside, not inside, the Polish church. Susannah had never seen such grandeur inside a church. The churches in Chortitza were bare benches and bare walls. During the week, the room was the school. But here, the

Gothic and neo-Gothic elements made of brick and stone were outlandish. Peering inside, for she would never enter, the fifteenth century bronze baptismal font, the bells, numerous epitaphs, fragments of murals on the walls, and the Gothic altar alarmed her.

None of the gathering knew how near they were to the sarcophagus of Princess Apolonia Poniatowska. People rubbed their faces with their dirty hands. Others scratched at the lice in their hair or popped the lice in the seams of their clothing, a never-ending task. Under the church, in the crypt, no one knew that General Stanislaw Wasowicz, who had served as Napoleon's I aide-de-camp, slumbered on in eternal sleep through another war.

The minister began his sermon. "People think the Mennonite faith teaches us that we must be passive, maybe even deserve our fate for misfortune and suffering are divine judgments. Although our faith does not promise escape from these woes of life, it can help us walk through the valley of deepest darkness. Life is full of contradictions."

People bowed their heads with an ache in their hearts. Religion and tradition work hard to connect people spiritually, but in the Nazi state, this was denied. Religion became a perverted idol.

"Without God, everything is permitted."

Susannah was in a tangle, a complicated knot involving a mass population capable of great love, yet, capable of inflicting great unkindness. There are some types of inflictions, when we are cruel to one another, which ignite the outrage of church and state — but not this state, not Hitler's state. The Nazis would laugh and admit to a lot of unkindness, saying it was called discipline, the natural order of society. The Nazi party gave the attractive messages of the importance of the Germanic heritage, the joy of quality teamwork and the bonds of family. Specific roles in the family were celebrated with the utmost respect, especially the father. What a contradiction for a generation who had lost their fathers in the Great War. What a tasty package to sell — but inside a demon was hidden. One only needed to ignore what God placed inside the heart and live only on the outside. It was such a subtle illogicality. If you can confuse people enough, there will be no connection to what is true but merely to what is false. They will not know what is deep inside.

Minister Wiens continued. "Faith offers us an identity. Exploring *who* we are means being aware of our values and purpose in life. How do we relate to the world around us? Here we are. We are a community. Balance the challenges of the world with your inner spiritual journey. Long for truth. Long for justice. God has a purpose for each one of us, although we may not embrace it. Trust each other. If we can't trust in others, we will have a difficult time trusting God. God created us to be responsible choosers. We can choose to defy God or turn away from God altogether. Both choices leave us empty."

****

I could feel Susannah's hopeful gaze linger on me. I was sure Susannah wondered what I was going to make of the content of this sermon. I smiled to myself. I was astonishingly adaptable which was a constant source of amazement to my daughter. I was good at separating interesting ideas from necessary actions. One time, a dour and totally unimaginative guardian of the Relief Agency Library had given me a stiff rebuke about the literature I read. Susannah had commented that *Mirabell Der Roman einer Frau*, the German romance novel about a Catholic Austrian Bishop and his mistress, did not go over too well with the more pious in the

Protestant Mennonite community, even if it was written in German. The obdurate opinion was that inappropriate works would excite people into unwanted conclusions and undesirable behaviours. Such a ridiculous attitude. I intended to donate the book to the library collection, but I kept it. Such shabby thinking makes me shake my head with disdain and disbelief. *To heck with others.*

I recognized how Susannah felt the war was a great adventure. It was true. There was an irresponsible freedom, a type of primal feeling generated by the demands of daily living during wartime. Abraham, on the other hand, was on the verge of drowning.

The sermon went on. "We are not yet the people God wants us to be. The person we are is given to us, not invented by us. We must accept this each day and not connect it to the Past. Choice makes life genuinely different. It is the answer to despair. Accept the genuine unpredictable Future. Exist today in God's love and be the bearers of eternal life. We are eternal because of our connection to God. Let us pray." I shut my eyes and bowed my head.

****

No one noticed Susannah deftly pick up the satchel, slide it under her grey wool clothing, press it tightly to her body, and rise to slip between the virtuous. As soon as the brief prayer was done, from the front of the assemblage came an exclamation. Susannah could not see but she deduced there was a special presentation today. A murmur of "chocolate" rippled through the shifting crowd, which pressed Susannah between the girl and Gerhard. The sweat poured down her body, and her breath came in short little gasps. The crush of people made it impossible for her to escape.

The girl held the cat, Casper, who was as squished as she was and she giggled to the people around her, "We both need help!"

Susannah's horrible imagination kicked in. She saw the dreaded disappointment on Mutti's face. She saw her baby brother screaming in agony. Her thoughts of them dying in the cold filled her head. She stared toward the minister and members of the organization who held boxes of candies that had been sent to the camp. Beyond them moved the orb of the sun above the tree line of the surrounding forest. To Susannah it was a judgment shedding light on everything.

Gerhard was pressed close to her.

She squirmed in embarrassment and panic so much that Gerhard nearly lost his footing. She was careful to keep her head turned away from the old man and the girl. In dismay, she shoved her way out of the crowd. Her reaction offered a release from her feeling of panic, for which she was truly thankful. The initial excitement of the crowd was replaced with resignation as they understood that the sweets would not be given out until the evening.

She pulled the satchel out from under her clothes and shoved the bag toward Vater. He snatched the treasure and turned away slightly as he peered at the contents. He nodded and passed the satchel to Mutti, who hastily tucked it into the folds of her clothing.

"No more of that foul grey broth they call soup tonight," he hissed. "Stop breathing so hard. You look sick!"

If Susannah had not had an empty stomach, she would have been.

"It's better if the old man does not see you though," said Vater. "We will leave the camp right after the service in order not to attract attention. We'll stay in the woods briefly before moving on to another village. We can go back to the camp in Kutno. We have to keep moving." The constant dread of capture by the Russians hounded us.

Susannah was so relieved the situation was now Vater's responsibility that she forgot to regret the chocolate she would be missing in the evening. It was a treat never experienced, only talked about.

"A girl saw me, not take it, but she saw me there." Immediately, Susannah regretted saying this and steeled herself for the wrath that was sure to come.

"You worthless ..." Vater's dark yellow teeth leaped into her face.

Susannah took a step back. "She tried to help me. She did not see. I am sure. She wanted to see what was happening up front I mean. The old man was close to me ..." Susannah's words tumbled out of her mouth. Her spittle flew onto Vater's pants.

"What?" His face held a look of disgust. He gasped, "He saw you?"

"No, no. He never saw my face. No. I kept it turned away," exclaimed Susannah as she turned her head away from Vater's glare, but he was numb to her anguish.

Mutti tried to calm the situation and hushed, "Peter, it's …"

Vater said, "I told you she couldn't do it."

Zator, Upper Silesia
Sunday, July 23, 1944
Chapter Six

Everyone in the family was fractious this Sunday. Gerhard complained, "I never wanted to come to the relief camp."

Mika soothed, "Someone will hear you."

Elias walked along beside them. He did not count. They would have been astounded if he had contributed to the conversation. He was fifteen, a year older than brother, Dietrich, but, to his continual vexation, he was reminded daily that he was smaller and weaker than his younger brother.

"Get out of my way." Uncle Gerhard could not hide his irritation that Elias seemed to be forever in his way and unable to measure up. He made a derogatory comment. "Are you complaining of exhaustion again even before the sun reaches noon? You need to work hard. Get tough." Under the guise of what was good for children, such abuse flourished as Mika and Gerhard's own need to exercise power over a child went virtually unhindered. Uncle Gerhard, having lost his own three children, took a particular interest in the two boys.

"We are a little tired today, *ja*?" Tante Mika made the situation worse by trying to manage her nephew Elias when he became upset and moist-eyed. She thereby drew even more attention to the already embarrassed youth whose emotions ran so close to the surface.

"Where's Dietrich?" Uncle Gerhard demanded, excessively proud of his second nephew.

Tante Mika would offset Gerhard's praise by scolding Dietrich for being blockheaded. In many ways, it was true, for Dietrich showed an immense lack of self-awareness. He never identified the manipulation and abuse. He did not know it could be any other way. He never contradicted his aunt. Yet, he was savvy and attentive to those little details that bullies pick up on. The authentic ones balk, the clever ones give in, waiting for retaliation. Dietrich's anger burned. Deep.

Back in the Ukraine, Dietrich had enjoyed taunting his older sister, Renate and her friend Sabina. He had told Sabina never ever to walk by his house. Silence, denial, and taboo are central themes in repression. Dietrich used intimidation to perfection. Instead of learning the lessons of kindness, Dietrich learned about hate and indifference from the suffering people around him. And Sabina suffered. She was so terrified of him that she would walk around the entire village rather than pass by his house. That meant everyday going for a long trek because Dietrich was a neighbour.

Sabina's personal silence became saturated with feelings of insecurity and inferiority without even understanding why she felt the way she did. She became consumed by a kind of toxic guilt and shame. It carried such power. She was at the receiving end of hate, defenceless against a message that was felt rather than spoken. Dietrich's hostile approach bewildered her. He whispered he would report Sabina's parents to the Communists if she walked anywhere near his house. His lies would carry weight because the Russians would believe anything. She was petrified. She never told her parents. Did her silence equal ignorance? Was she morally weak?

No.

It was sheer terror. Powerlessness and silence go hand in hand. Sabina never told anyone, not even her best friend, Renate.

There was no doubt about it, Dietrich was clever. On this day, his illustrious past behind him, he barged into the line for lunch rations the way big nasty boys do. It was meagre enough, but it was food. People complained at his rudeness, along with their other irritations, to one another.

"The bedbugs torture me."

"It is futile to get rid of them."

"We wait in line with our ration cards for lunch. We wait for everything."

"What are we having today, a ration of cottage cheese or grey broth? If there was a thin slice of bread, a chunk of potato or maybe a mouthful of meat that would be a wonder …"

It would have been a wonder indeed. Rations basically provided a diet based on poor quality bread and vegetables. By the end of the war, the cards allowed for a daily ration of 40 grams of meat derivatives, 15 grams of lard, 3 grams of tea or *Ersatz* coffee, 40 grams of sugar, 250 grams of bread with 13 grams of jam, and 30 millilitres of milk. Potatoes and vegetables could be obtained without a ration card, and half a pack of cigarettes, occasionally a whole pack if you were a lucky adult.

Elias kept the cigarette packs, empty, of course. He even had a Memphis 1939 Austria ten pack, *Tabakwerk. zehn Stück.* Since the word Österreich was banned by the Nazis in the year of that country's annexation, the company simply used the English word for Austria. The cigarette packs came from different places, Hamburg or Dresden, sometimes Munich.

"*Tee oder Prips?*" the relief worker joyfully asked. "Sticks from the old raspberry cane make our tea today and our coffee, the *Ersatz Kaffee*, nicknamed Prips, is from ground rye is hot at least! *Tee oder Prips?*"

"This is it!" complained Dietrich as he raised his eyebrows to question the beverage.

The relief worker leaned closer to the youth. "In my day, we took what was given, whenever, wherever," he advised, giving Dietrich a knowing look.

Apparently Dietrich was the new generation, for he sneered, "What ever." His disgruntled attitude was readily apparent for he complained again with the expression he wore when he wanted to be elsewhere. Nothing could please this boy.

"Why don't you shut up and be grateful," was the next suggestion from the annoyed worker. "I am the one dishing out the food. You might consider using better manners toward me?" He smeared the *Griebenschmaltz* a little bit thinner on Dietrich's slice of bread.

When a look of sheer stupidity met that idea, the worker started a conversation with the next person in line, giving them helpful suggestions.

"Boiled water and chemicals fail. Those demons live in the wooden walls of the building and cannot be reached."

"Get your sores treated at the clinic."

"It takes a while to heal."

"I am always in pain."

Down the line, Friedrich sidled up to Gerhard, "Not the same as when you had land and food in Chortitza, *ja*?"

Gerhard looked around in irritation, "The Communists came to take it all."

But Friedrich continued with glee, "*Na ja*, but the generations that followed that magnificent revolution …"

"… made us scrape together what we could and toil away at a meagre life!" snapped Gerhard.

Friedrich could tell he had him now. He pressed the irritation, "*Ja,* but the crops were …"

Gerhard turned to face him fully. "The crops we grew, and

the milk and the eggs were the property of the Communist state, to be bought back later, at a higher price, to feed the family!"

"Well, if you were not smart enough to hide ... " Friedrich poked Gerhard playfully.

Gerhard slapped away his hand. "There was no hiding anything! There was no place that the Communists couldn't see! The children worked hard too," Gerhard gestured toward Renate. "When she was four years old, Renate was placed on the plow horse. Her father ordered her to stay there to make sure the horses plowed up and down the field. She stayed," Gerhard finished the tale with an approving nod. Of course he had not noticed that she cried all day but even at that young age, Renate was instructed to be tough, to carry out her duty gladly, to be obedient, and to have no inner Self. The next day, she did not cry. After all, being emotionally stunted was for her own good.

"During the more violent stretches, we instructed Elias to take the plow horses to the gully and stay there until the marauders passed through. They were beautiful creatures, one chestnut and one bay," Gerhard said loudly.

Elias shrunk down as the conversation continued. On that

day, the horses were restless, stamping their feet and blowing air loudly out of their nostrils. Alas, the horses would not be quiet, and Elias had been discovered. The family's livelihood was seized by the Russian army. There was nothing he could have done.

Later, Gerhard won the ensuing argument with the help of Elias's failure. He persuaded the family to honour their German connection, to gather their few possessions into packs and pull the wagon themselves as they walked out of the village they had known all their lives. Mika had been so distraught that she rushed back to the door of the abandoned house she would never see again, making sure it was locked. For Elias, leaving was a happy moment, but nevertheless the journey had been difficult.

Gerhard unconsciously stroked his chest with his thumb where up until recently his supposedly secret papers had made quiet crinkly noises. Elias pretended not to notice the gesture, but he knew Uncle Gerhard had transferred the papers and a precious letter sent by a relative who lived in Boleslawiec, into the satchel he had recently acquired and was usually carrying around.

The food line moved slowly as there was warmth near the oven and the fire pit.

Mika, tired of waiting in line, said crossly, "You would think the director would ask us to join him for breakfast. After all, he is married to your cousin."

Gerhard replied, "If you do not want this food, the war will not care. We can always leave, head west and stand in another line." His voice hardened and his toes curled around the mossy clumps on the ground. He spat on the ground while they stood reluctantly and listened to the varied but chronic topics of conversation around them.

"There is always the lice bringing affliction."

"In Lemberg, they deloused us. I thought we had left those buggers in the Ukraine!"

"The roads to the camp are trackless quagmires."

"I feel I am pursued all the time; we are helpless; we are victims, old women and small children."

Previously, the dreaded anxiety of hostilities escalating nearly sent people over the edge because the world was ending but now that war was happening, people spoke of it in everyday tones. Familiarity is often mistaken for safety. Threats were real and familiar, like old and dysfunctional friends. How dangerous.

Elias noticed the sunrise and the changing colours of the morning light creating dapples on the headstones in the nearby nineteenth century Jewish cemetery. He had searched through the cemetery when they'd first arrived, discovering that half of the inscriptions were in the Hebrew language. The place touched his heart, and because of that, he managed to listen to most of the sermon. The dawn had caressed faces, hands had caressed loved ones, and the mist sparkled in a gentle wakening. Elias enjoyed the prospect of chocolate in the evening but due to the constant nagging conversation around him, he lost his reverie.

Mika whimpered, "We cannot leave here Gerhard. We have no food."

Elias dreaded the prospect and the labor of travel. Dietrich had finally noticed the sparse layer of lard and cracklings on his slice of bread, staring at it with defiance.

"We can and we will!" Gerhard pronounced as he looked for the satchel. "It's gone!"

Zator, Upper Silesia
Sunday, July 23, 1944
Chapter Seven

Everyone in the camp looked on, except Mika who felt her misery rising rapidly. "It can never be replaced. We are lost, lost."

Gerhard searched the ground and retraced his steps back to where he had stood during the service. He bellowed with outrage. He glowered. His grey hair fell on his forehead. His face contorted into a snarl. People backed away to give him room. The line went quiet with foreboding.

An angry man is a dangerous creature; a desperate man is lethal.

Mika grumbled, "You were probably robbed during the service."

Gerhard figured she must be right. In the dim morning light, people had been stealing more than secret caresses. "It's … it's profanity, blasphemy!" fumed Gerhard, gnashing his teeth.

"I bet it happened during prayer." Mika's suggestion made her sniff as if she had discovered a long-lost secret. "The crook slipped the satchel away then."

"The thief must be discovered!" Gerhard cried out.

The young relief worker, Bruno, heard the commotion and came toward them.

"What has happened?"

"Thieving! That is what has happened, you fool!" Gerhard spit aggressively at him. "My satchel is gone, stolen!"

"Was there anything of importance in the bag?"

The question caught Gerhard by surprise. What could he say? To divulge that the *Wurst*, the sausage, he himself had recently stolen was wrapped in papers given to him for safekeeping by a wayward stranger was not an option.

"I am sorry this has happened, *Herr* Wiens. Perhaps it was mislaid. At any rate, I will inform the director immediately."

"Yes, yes ... there was a ... a ..." Gerhard searched for an explanation. "... a letter! It is not right this stealing, not here when we are together as a congregation."

"Mr. Wiens, we can search the camp," Bruno offered, eager to calm Gerhard and the people who were listening. "For your letter," he added. "It is of utmost importance to us to find it." Social lies are so easy and so loud.

To Gerhard that was a ridiculous suggestion. How would a satchel be found? The director could not check all the people coming and going. Gerhard was not placated, for he was a dark wolf at the beginning of a hunt. The first few moments were not his angriest. His anger grew slowly upon reflection, brewing as the implications sank in. He exploded. "*Scheissehund*" he menaced in an even more provoked tone. The angry swearing served no helpful purpose except to disfigure him.

Bruno waited and spoke calmly, "Meanwhile, perhaps you, your wife, and your brother's family could come to the front of the line and sit there at the table?"

Gerhard was diverted and grunted with pleasure, but the anger simmered deep inside. Elias knew that to be singled out and allowed ahead in the line to sit at a table while the rest of the people scattered themselves on the ground was to be granted a special status. Many said his uncle was an intelligent man, a man of note. He had sat on many committees back in the Ukraine, in the Mennonite village. Their family history allowed them to be held in great esteem. Yet, Gerhard was unlucky, more than everyone else. He had no living children. Instead, he devoted his time to success.

The centuries had refined a strain of Mennonite people who were aggressively assertive, class-aware, and motivated, all within God's will, of course. Gerhard's dream of grandeur was the source of his success with his peers and the source of his conflict under a system of Communism that encouraged mediocrity and apathy.

The crisis seemed to pass; yet, Elias could not release the tension from his body and pulled at his dark hair. He knew better than to assume that Gerhard's anger was appeased. Gerhard turned sharply and sent Elias to the church service area. Elias walked around the fringe and to his astonishment discovered the satchel tossed behind a bush.

While Elias was searching, the relief workers brought the bread and hot tea to the bench and Gerhard's family was served first. The bread was stale, but at least it was not moldy. The raspberry tea, although hot, was barely discernible from water. Dietrich, who did not understand the family crisis, spoke excitedly about the chocolate candy in the evening. However, the steely silence greeting his statements was enough to shut him up. The paltry meal was hastily concluded.

"Where did you find the satchel?" Gerhard inquired when

Elias brought it to him.

"There on the edge of the meadow." Elias pointed, eager to please.

He grabbed Elias by his collar, pulling him close. "Not that an empty satchel does us any good now."

Elias was crushed. His face went red and he could feel his tears welling up. His desire for positive affirmation was boundless, an emotion Gerhard vehemently denied.

"This is useless. It does not help us, you fool." Gerhard threw the satchel into Elias's teary face. "Boys do not cry!" As a child, Gerhard had experienced discipline, the early brutal conditioning considered good parenting, making it impossible for him to even understand what had happened to his emotional register, but the suppression of the entire spectrum of emotions cannot be denied forever. Rage survived.

Elias was taken aback. "Perhaps someone else noticed …"

He did not have time to finish his sentence before Gerhard spun around and struck him across the face. "Perhaps someone should only speak when spoken to."

Mika stepped in. "Let the boys go. Perhaps they can

discover a clue."

Gerhard looked away into the distance, absentmindedly stroking his chest with his thumb. "Dietrich, yes, but Elias will probably spend his time reading or drawing. That boy thinks he is an artist. Ridiculous!"

Elias held his face. It was true; he felt he had artistic talent. Literature and sketching were dear to him. In his valued possessions were two of his recent pencil sketches, one of Schiller and the other of Goethe, whom he could quote by heart.

"I wonder if anyone has *Schnapps*?" growled Gerhard.

"Away you go, Elias." Mika dismissed him. "Take your brother Dietrich with you. Look after him." She wanted to get the boys out of the way if Gerhard started drinking.

"Ha!" ridiculed Gerhard. "It is more likely the other way around."

Elias's face stung. Uncle Gerhard had no idea what went on. Elias could look after himself, but Dietrich always got into trouble. Still, Elias knew better than to cross his uncle again in his aggravated mood, so he left without replying. He was chained to his brother in their exclusion. Dietrich dawdled behind him.

The clouds threatened to become slanting squalls of rain, but behind them the sky was light as if glowing with promise. The final raindrop that brings a flood of water does not necessarily bring catastrophe; it brings an entirely new perspective and a new beginning. It would be wonderful to say this was true for the boys and that they left with a spring in their steps and a song in their hearts, but this was not the case. In fact, it was the exact opposite.

Elias and Dietrich trudged toward the forest as if the perpetual and sheer embarrassment of being alive was too much for them. Elias felt trapped. He resented his brother. Dietrich returned the favour. He silently glowered and grunted in hostility behind him. Dietrich's world was wrong to his teenage mind, quite wrong, and all because it failed to understand how important he knew he was.

In the time it took to walk through the camp to the trees at the bottom of the gully, the October afternoon sky rapidly change from ominous to a promising stark blue. Just as fleetingly, fortune or misfortune can enter. Elias, brooding and carrying the empty satchel, attracted the attention of the other children.

"What's in the bag?"

"Did you get a bit of chocolate already?"

The effect of chocolate in the evening had rippled through the camp. Such a luxury had been unheard of in the village. It was like a banquet day. They crowded around him leaving their game of *Dombrat,* which was played with a checkerboard drawn in the dirt and stone pieces. The boys looked eagerly at him, a few of the girls looked coyly at him, and others ignored him altogether.

"Where did you get that from?"

Elias recognized the girl who had stood near him during the morning service. They must be about the same age he calculated. Her clothes were not as threadbare as his, and certainly a lot cleaner. She wore a fetching necklace of colourful wood beads. Elias usually found girls silly. But this one looked at him openly with a gaze he liked.

"I found it." Elias wished it held chocolate, for he had a sudden urge to give her some. When you want approval, giving makes you think you will get it.

"What's in it?"

Elias laughed, shrugging his shoulders. "Nothing."

The girl laughed too while the crowd of children dispersed

with disgust. One of the little girls began to cry.

Ignoring the crying child, Elias asked, "What's your name?"

"Klara. Klara Doerksen. Yours?"

"Elias Wiens." Elias pushed pack his cap, scratching his head.

Klara placed a hand on the crying girl's shoulder. "It will be okay. My, my, look at those big tears," she spoke gently.

The little girl gulped and continued to cry. She looked lost, like a goldfish that has made one turn in a bowl and no longer knows where it is.

"Let's count how many tears you have," Klara said sweetly. "That will tell us how many friends you have."

The child's response was to wail louder.

"Listen," Klara said consolingly, "think of right now, not yesterday and not tomorrow." The child stopped crying to look at Klara curiously. "I have a secret to tell you." Klara leaned over to whisper into the child's ear.

With a quick glance at Elias and a grateful smile to Klara, the little girl ran back to her card game of *Ärgert dich nicht* or *Schwarzer Peter.* Perhaps that was what had upset her. No one wanted to be caught with black Peter in their card hand. The other small children were making bouquets from fistfuls of wild foliage. Slights and disappointments were already forgotten. Little children move on quickly in contrast to adults who can cultivate hatred for generations.

Elias took a stone out of his pocket and flipped it in his right hand.

"What are you going to do with that?" Klara asked

"Oh, practice. You know, the way the guys do over by the tree. I am a pretty good shot myself," Elias bragged, his confidence mounting as he spoke with Klara.

"They won't let you have a turn," his brother jabbed.

"Of course, they will. Why wouldn't they?" Elias shot back, irritated by his brother's interference. "That is stupid, Dietrich. You don't know." But even as he spoke, Elias knew the older boys might push him around, making him the butt of their jokes.

Klara looked at him expectantly. Elias moved to where the youths cheered wildly whenever anyone managed to hit the knot in the middle of the trunk with a stone. He recognized one of them, an athletic boy named Matthew Petkau.

Matthew noticed the stone in Elias's hand and spoke to him in a friendly voice, "Did you want to throw, too?"

Elias scuffed his foot on the ground. "Maybe. Yeah, maybe I will."

"Hey, Erik," Matthew said to the boy next to him, "he wants to hit the mark."

Erik, a stout fellow with a cunning grin, gave Elias a once-over, saying nonchalantly, "He's too small. He'll never be able to even hit the tree much less the mark."

"That might be," Matthew said softly, "but it's not like we're fighting the Russians."

Erik looked up and smiled mischievously, "He couldn't anyhow. He's a Mennonite, a pacifist. You know they do not even get angry." He swiftly moved toward Elias who instinctively backed away. "See, they never defend themselves," Erik laughed as he turned toward the tree.

Jakob Gunther called out, "We are ready. Matthew, you go first." Matthew's tall frame moved up to the dirt line on the ground.

Jakob observed Elias for the first time. "No little boys," he barked.

"What? I can do this!" exclaimed Elias.

"Whatever you think you can do does not matter. Get lost!" There was a yelp of laughter. A few of the boys snickered.

Two red spots appeared on Elias's cheeks. "Give me a good reason why I shouldn't be allowed a turn."

"I don't need to give reasons to babies," Jakob stated. "Come on, Matthew, are you going to take all day?"

Elias was humiliated. Dietrich had been right and now whispered loudly, "Told you."

Elias turned away from the tree. "Shut up."

"You cannot make me or do you want to try?" Dietrich was gaining an audience and bravado. His well-honed anger leaped to the surface with an ease that only practice could perfect. "Go on. Say it. Get it over with!" Dietrich taunted as his body went rigid with expectation. His sullen face stared at Elias. "Do not even touch me," Dietrich challenged. His past hurts were cloaked with the defense of meanness, and he used it with a mastery that confused Elias.

Elias sighed. He could see fighting Dietrich was only going to make him look more like a weakling and a fool. Dietrich was younger but stronger and surprisingly well developed for his age. Elias remembered another lesson handed to him by the bigger boys. It was his own personal swimming lesson in the Dnieper River. They had dismissively thrown him in the water.

"You could go somewhere else, Elias, and find your own tree with a mark. I am sure you could do it. We could go a little bit further into the forest," Klara suggested with confidence for she felt at home and loved walking among the trees. The compliment surprised Elias but had a marked effect; his chest swelled with pride as he grew in stature.

Their parents had expressly forbidden them to go into the woods. There was a war going on, who knew what might be hiding in there? Anyone could be killed, and there were worse atrocities, parents hinted. Even if they managed to be lucky and avoid such outcomes, Uncle Gerhard would surely take the belt to him. Yet, Elias felt defiant after his brother's challenge and Jakob Gunther's disregard.

"They do not deserve to share in our fun. Fine. Let's do that," he said swiftly. "We will make sure no one sees us."

Zator, Upper Silesia
Sunday, July 23, 1944
Chapter Eight

Klara slipped into the forest along a faint trail. Elias followed her quick steps and quickly felt confined. Dietrich was tagging along, but Elias knew there was no point in speaking.

"I know a good spot." Klara laughed openly. "I love the woods! I have never seen a real forest like this in the Ukraine where we had only willow trees and fruit trees!"

It was magical to take one step into the forest and disappear from everyone. The soft sounds of the woods echoed around her, a busy place. There was so much to experience. She had exclaimed with dismay to her mother that the forest was dying, but her mother explained to her those where Larch trees that shed their needles every autumn. She was relieved for this forest gave her a place where she could escape from the world into her own personal space.

For Klara, true happiness was being home in the Ukraine with her gentle family sitting around on long tranquil summer afternoons. The forest was a good substitute and deserved to be christened happiness. Why not? Take it! Make the most of it! Klara could cherish the moment forever, for it created a memory lasting longer than the moment itself.

Elias felt a twinge of apprehension and chastised himself for his foolishness. Yet, he could not turn around; Dietrich would never let him hear the end of it. Elias could see a quiet opening up ahead. Klara froze.

She spoke in an urgent whisper, "Quick, get behind these trees! Someone is coming."

Elias could feel his heart pounding. All he could think of was why he was so stupid. Dietrich was making noises, and Elias realized that Dietrich was even more frightened. Klara shushed Dietrich into silence.

A second later, a girl came onto the path. Klara pounced out and tackled her. The girl shrieked. Klara clamped a hand over her mouth, telling her to be silent.

Elias and Dietrich were stunned at the spectacle. They stood and stared.

"We're going to get into trouble. Why are you following us?"

"I wanted to see about the chocolate. I wanted to get some!"

the girl sobbed.

"I know you. I saw you this morning in the service — you were right beside me. We nearly got squished like bumblebees," Klara said to her in a gentler voice. "Okay, don't cry. We're not that far from the road, don't panic. Besides, I didn't hurt you. What is your name?"

"Susannah."

Elias, anxious not to leave her to the terrors of the woods, declared, "You'd better come with us. You might not be able to find your way back to the camp."

Elias was mollified as the three nodded readily. It was not often his suggestions were heeded. Klara explained to Dietrich that they were not lost. She knew exactly where they were and they were helping Susannah.

"There isn't anyone else in the forest," Elias said hopefully. He meant to encourage Susannah, but he knew anyone else they met would certainly be up to no good. He gave himself a silent pep talk about that unlikelihood. They walked into the small open meadow. Elias called out with relief, "This is a good place to look for a tree and a mark. There that one."

He pointed to a broad trunk on the edge of the clearing. Elias paced the distance out and took aim at the tree. He threw as hard as he could. The stone fell far short of the tree, not even touching it. He was stupefied.

"I need to warm up a bit," he mumbled as he looked around for another stone. On the second try, the stone went a little bit further and bounced up onto the trunk.

"At least you touched it," snickered Dietrich with raised eyebrows, wiping the snot from his upper lip.

The third try was better for distance, but Elias missed the tree completely. He was extremely embarrassed.

Klara took it in stride and did not seem to notice. "Let me have a try."

"Girls cannot do this," sneered Dietrich as he moved his stout frame in front of her and stepped up to the line.

Elias could see how Dietrich balanced himself and judged the distance to the tree. He adjusted his aim too, but seemed to get the knack of it better and sooner than Elias. The second throw hit the tree dead on with a force that far exceeded Elias's ability. Dietrich used his entire body in one fluid motion. Why did these talents flow from his brother when Elias had to plan each movement? His brother could not even follow a conversation.

It was obvious Dietrich had a natural eye and could aim well beyond anything Elias could ever hope to achieve, even with hours of practice. Elias was envious, although he would never admit to it. He longed to be athletic, bold, and swaggering, garnering his Uncle Gerhard's praise, but he was physically slight. It made him dejected when he realized he would be hopeless at anything physical in a world where physical prowess was the measure of a man.

In the awkward silence, no one spoke.

A man yelled. Elias sprang to his feet, his heart pounding against his ribs. He heard another yell, another enraged voice.

There was more than one stranger in the forest. Alarmed, they trembled, silently listening. Twigs snapped. Birds flew in fright.

The sound of frantic running through the forest was coming toward them.

Klara spoke first, "Quick, hide in this thicket." She was flat on her stomach as she crawled inside the bush. Susannah followed. Dietrich, never one to follow orders, ran behind the bush. Elias was halfway in when he realized his cap was on the path. He pulled himself back, grabbed his hat, and dove into the thicket.

Before they saw the man, they heard his laboured breathing. He was running for his life. He was followed by an outcry from his pursuers. Elias remembered Klara stating that they were not far from the road. A second later, the man exploded into the meadow. His body heaved for each gasp of air. He was young, in his twenties, with a rifle in his hand and a dagger attached at his waist. He stopped with his back to the oak tree, holding his rifle like a club. He faltered and dropped to the ground, putting one hand to his neck in an odd motion.

Klara's spontaneously moved her hand to her neck. She moved jerkily in the thicket as she felt the empty space of where her coloured bead necklace had hung. "I've lost my necklace!"

"Stay still!" hissed Elias desperately as he peeked at his companions.

Klara's face was pale and she had her clenched hands by her throat. She shook her head back and forth in a tiny motion. Susannah cast her eyes down to the ground and smoothed her hands on her wool skirt. Dietrich was crouched as close to the thicket as he could get and was peeking through the bush with rapt fascination.

For a second, the man stared in their direction. Elias felt he must know they were there. Elias's muscles ached with tension. Out of the corner of his eye he saw the slow movement of Dietrich picking up a rock from the ground. Violently, the two pursuers smashed their way into the meadow immediately beside the thicket where the four of them were concealed. Elias could feel his stomach heaving. He struggled not to be sick. The pursuers abruptly halted when they saw their quarry. Like the men themselves, their clothing was severe. The stark black SS uniforms contrasted with the soft stillness of the forest.

The three figures paused. The one nearest to the thicket spoke, "Over many days we have tracked you from Wolfsberg, Reiner. Your escape was clever."

The young man stood up, let the rifle fall to the ground and turned his palms up in a conciliatory manner. "You mean Wlodarz, don't you?"

The use of the accurate Polish name nettled them. "You confused as at Wüstewaltersdorf and again at Fürstenstein," the

German spoke emphatically.

"Pleased to make your acquaintance again," Reiner spoke in an easy sarcastic way, with the slightest hint of a mocking bow.

"You cannot evade us. There is no escape now," they bragged.

Reiner moved slowly away from them, but the SS soldier nearest the thicket snatched the hilt of his dagger and the edge of the blade arced toward Reiner. Dodging aside but not fast enough, the dagger rapidly connected with Reiner's left forearm, slicing through his coat and sinking into his flesh. He gasped in painful surprise. His assailant stepped back. The two SS were strongly built and carried their undrawn Vis pistols on their hips.

"We want the documents. Give the blueprints to us, Reiner, and you can go free." The soldier laughed, turning slightly away from Reiner. Every detail of the soldier's face had been carved by wild winds and tempestuous rains. His voice cracked, "Then we will not toy with you."

Reiner chuckled to himself, showing an astounding composure. Elias was sure the two men would kill him.

The soldiers watched Reiner cautiously despite the fact that they obviously possessed the upper hand in numbers. Their eyes locked.

"What could the *Waffen-SS* possibly want with me?" Reiner taunted. "Since you know me so well you must know that '*meine Ehre heisst Treue*,' as your honour is loyalty as well."

Elias saw Susannah raise her head at the moment of action. Together, they watched Reiner's figure move, silhouetted against the dusky light in the forest, a chiaroscuro effect. Conjured up in their minds were large creatures that howled and tore at their prey with fearsome fangs. Behind them the sunlight and sky stretched up into emptiness, fading into a starker blue.

They saw it all as the pistol left the holster.

Danzig, 1788
Chapter Nine

Bernhard held a copy of the Czarina's Manifesto in his hands. Catherine the Great of Russia was determined to see her grand political ambition aimed against Prussia and Poland take shape. She observed the qualities of the hardworking German-speaking Mennonites and she made the offer to settle them on land in the Ukraine.

He nodded to his wife but without commitment. "We are not going yet, Katharina.

Here in the Manifesto, they say 'as a great extent of the lands of our empire is sufficiently well known to us: we acknowledge that not a small number of such regions still lie fallow, that could be advantageously and easily most usefully utilized to be populated and lived in ... the same are richly provided with woodlands, rivers, lakes and seas ...' It is an enticement to foreigners who might desire to settle in their Empire."

Bernhard gazed up at the sky and mused, "Catherine the Great is still German at heart. That is why she wants us there."

Belief can lend purpose to decisions. The active aim of the

Czarina's program was twofold. First, the Russians wished to create agricultural superiority in Europe, and second, they wished to ensure that the Polish state, which had been divided between Prussia and Russia in 1772, would stay that way. It was a policy that garnered much hatred toward Russia by the Prussians, Austrians and the Swiss.

"We will have all we need there, Bernhard," Katharina implored. "We will live in freedom. No one will tell us what we can or cannot do."

The soft heat bounced up from the ground, warming the soles of their shoes. Shafts of sunlight filtered through the leaves of the trees and the magpies' feathers shone like mauve and lilac jewels in the massive oak tree.

"It is an enormous venture, Katharina," argued Bernhard. "Do you know how far it is to New Russia from Prussia?"

"A distance, yes ... but our great ancestors emigrated from Friesland across to here. We can continue the tradition ... of moving toward freedom to practice our faith."

"We would never return here to Danzig. Once we make the decision to go, it is final."

"What will your mother say, Bernhard? Will she wish to come with us?"

"No, no, I am sure that Mother Lena is content to stay here."

"*Yo,*" she agreed in her smooth droll *Plattdeutsch*. Her low German dialect was soft and musical. "She is a Morgenstern, and she will stay here. This is her house and her home," Katharina agreed but remained dubious.

"The promised land is a fertile tract near Berislav. The Dnieper River flows nearby and to the south are the Crimea and the Black Sea. There is talk of calling our village Catherinenhof."

Katharina hooted and slapped Bernhard on the arm with a laugh. It was not that funny, but it was her idea of a joke.

Bernhard peered at her sideways and shrugged a shoulder. "Schönhorst is a nice name for a village."

"The Czarina has promised free board and transportation from the Russian border to the land. We can settle in the part of the country that Jakob and Johann have seen with their own eyes. There will be a loan to build houses and acquire farm tools. There is talk of establishing factories."

"Yes, it does sound promising. The land should be good,"

speculated Bernhard. "I have heard that it compares favorably to the lowlands here near Danzig. There will be opportunity for growing grain and raising cattle. They say the green grass underneath and the air above stretch from the earth to the heavens."

From the beautiful and perfect form of a nearby flower, the perfume floated around them. The delicacy of the flowers kept the bees coming and the buzzing murmurs held that happy sense of warmth underneath the expansive blue sky.

"There will be exclusive fishing rights. Certain islands heavily covered with shrubs and trees will be set aside for the exclusive use of the Mennonites. Houses already in Berislav will be made available and lumber for new buildings will be waiting along with 160 acres per family."

"One hundred and sixty acres!"

"Upon arrival in Berislav, the government will issue the strictest orders for the protection against injury, insult, harm and theft. There will be an exemption from military and civil service. It will be real, not like here." Bernhard spat on the ground, "with Frederick the Great of Prussia requiring our annual military contribution of 5000 Thalers toward the maintenance of the Culm

Cadet Academy."

"Religious tolerance can be bought. But still, there will be exemption from taxes." Katharina continued the thread of encouragement. "We will be free to practice our own religion, and we'll have the right to build and control our churches and schools."

"They say we can proselytize the country's Mohammedan population, even enserf them ..." Bernhard nodded.

"But not the Russian Orthodox Christians," Katharina added. She had never seen a Mohammedan, but she suspected that the Russian Orthodox were just as heathen.

Katharina could see Bernhard's outlook begin to brighten with the challenging opportunity before them. She gazed thoughtfully at her husband. He did not have too many of the copious sins of husbands. He did not drink too much, become violent or look at other women. And the little sins? Men all had those. It was always those husbands with the least sensible opinion that made the loudest noise, but Bernhard was more inclined to say less and avoid more.

Katharina is not me, Bernhard realized. *We are two separate people. Between us there exists an otherness. It is a place where we are not together, but we are not ourselves either.*

The white shape of the Mennonite church, its high windows catching the warm sun, reflected the shimmer of a blue silver and white sky. They were on the edge of a new idea.

Bernhard felt his individual yearning call him into himself — and out of himself. He was a spiritual person characterized by direction and purpose in his life, by searching for meaning and thereby securing an identity. Bernhard was becoming comfortable with the idea of having a future filled with uncertainty. Adventure could take him many places but never beyond himself. This quest was directly tied to Bernhard's spiritual quest to live life aware of the reality of the presence of God and thereby be fully human. It is where he belonged. All that was required of him was to allow himself to be in the presence of God and then God would let him know what he should do … or, at the very least, his wife would.

Katharina ventured cautiously, "Bernhard we have nothing here. We cannot buy any more land here. The government has not allowed it since 1773."

The Prussian army's strength was based on land ownership and its resources in manpower and horsepower connected to it.

Since the Mennonites were granted religious freedom and exemption from military service, it became increasingly worrisome to the military that Mennonites kept increasing their land holdings. The canton system was seriously affected by a decreasing military land base. Each canton was responsible for its own regiment. The king had agreed to the suggestion that the land holdings of Mennonites be frozen and issued an edict that regulated and limited Mennonite land ownership.

"Do you think the Blocks will go?" she pressed the topic.

"*Donnerwetter,* woman! Why would they leave? They live like kings," exclaimed Bernhard. "Besides, the government has prohibited home and property owners from emigrating. The penalty is severe. I am not even sure if they will let us leave."

Katharina nodded her head slowly in agreement. She looked up into his face. "But we have no future here, Bernhard."

"If we settle there, we will have the right of local self-government once agricultural communities are established."

"Will we go?" Katharina pressed him again.

A great flock of birds that had alighted in nearby trees rose up in a cloud and wheeled and dipped through the sky. Behind the small cluster of houses, the gulls dipped in the air before perching on the wall. Their mews were sharp and strident, protesting injustice.

"Come let us sit here under this oak tree." It was a symmetrical and majestic specimen, the pride of nature in its shape emulating mathematical precision. The acorns that fell from its boughs embodied life and immortality. It was truly a noble among the lowly, rising above the mundane and ordinary, spreading its shade in an act of benevolence.

"Come. Sit beside me. I will tell you," Bernhard answered evenly.

Zator, Upper Silesia
Sunday, July 23, 1944
Chapter Ten

As soon as I had left the camp with my family an argument escalated. Susannah immediately stomped off into the forest, and now Peter and Abraham were looking for her. Frustration made me shake my head and angst gripped my stomach. Peter was as unpredictable as Susannah. I sat down and leaned my head back against the wide trunk of the tree by the road to wait with Heinchen. My body longed for real warmth even though it was the way life had always been. I endured the cold clinging to my skin, moving inward to my bones, but my fearful memories went deeper into my soul.

Life is hard, I spoke wearily to myself. *Find the easy way, Eleni. The difficult, that comes on its own.* I had certainly experienced difficulty during the starvation years of the 1920s in Russia when all we had to eat were beets, beet stew with beet bread, and beets, again and again. Times had been lean. Times were always lean. Yet, in our shared scarcity and hardship, my parents bound our family together with love.

I made a memory by opening and closing my eyes and taking in the information from every one of my senses and then by reviewing it, I remembered it precisely. I could now see the intricate spider web in my mind, outlined with droplets pushing the stanchions askew; there was the sound of a hawk circling high above; I imagined the caress of a long-lost love note in my hand. Remembrance, where everything meant love, something I wanted to keep. I felt it completely.

My warm breath made little white clouds in the brisk air. The canopy of leaves on the trees, once green, would soon be the dirty yellow leaves of a finished life lying on the ground around me. I watched as one leaf, a persistent survivor through two seasons, finally twirled and danced its way to the ground. The smell of the forest was moist and earthy. The scent brought back a memory of farm life and the heavy smell of the damp cold dirt floor in the village houses. I love to dance. In my younger years that was what broke the endless drudgery of life and brought together, in Aganetha's tiny kitchen, the few young people who lived in the village of Chortitza.

We would get together when someone would say, "My

parents are going out. Come over and we can dance."

When the evening came, it was always me and one other dancing. Young men played the balalaika and the mandolin. My friends would mostly sit and listen, rarely dance, but we loved it. We were never allowed to dance in the *Gross-stube*. We always danced in the kitchen. I remember Martin's strong, hard arms around my shoulders. It still brings a smile to my face. He was a kind man, extremely patient, and an ordinary dancer. I was better. We would move forward, back, and to the side with complicated steps. We laughed and bumped into everyone as they clapped and sang. There was such little space, but it didn't matter. Not many people could perform a whole dance, but we could.

At one wedding, the older people were dancing in the barn and the young people were outside watching. Then the older people invited me in to join the dance. *Die Eltern* were surprised that the youth could dance — and better than them!

Those times would never come back.

One night though, I miscalculated. I had danced late into the evening knowing angry parents would rebuke me. Our two-room wooden house was on the other side of the orchard and I took the final distance through the orchard at a sprint with my hands thrust deep into my pockets. The wind blew across the land, hard as a slap, and my thin coat was no protection. That night, the Communist Russians did an unexpected sweep of the village. It was always trouble for the Mennonite men in the village. My father managed to hide in the barn and have one of my sisters sleep in the same bed as my mother to cover up the sleeping arrangements in the house.

In the small house, what was there to search? The Russians stomped over the floor and sneered at the washed and knitted cloth menstrual pads that hung behind the stove. What could we do except avert our eyes and keep our heads down? From the orchard in the dark of the night, I witnessed the search. When they were gone, I leapt inside. It was not much warmer than outside and I shook with cold, taking a minute to catch my breath. I hurriedly moved to get on to the blanket-covered straw that made my bed in the pull-out drawer with my three sisters. I tucked my frozen hands under my armpits and snuggled under the wool blanket. Often, despite the cold, my face would still be flushed, my brow still damp from the dancing, except that night it was not the dancing that made me sweat.

It was a brutal existence, filled with constant terror.

My mother would often repeat the old village saying, "Blessed is she who expects the worst for she will not be disappointed." On the other hand, tiny Tante Jutta would always say, "I always expect the worst and when it does not happen, I am pleasantly surprised and happy." That was fine and dandy, but Aunt Jutta lived in fear too.

There were many things I wondered about. Many have criticized me for analyzing too much, but I see there are no simple answers. Life is a puzzle that only completely fits together if all the pieces are available at the same moment. It is tricky, making it work in harmony, an intricate dance. If you do not follow the precise steps, it is chaos. Certainly, you could make your own dance, but you would be dancing alone. *Like I am sitting here alone,* I thought with annoyance. *Where are they? Surely, they have found Susannah by now.*

My thoughts drifted back to what I did know. Fruit trees. Mulberry trees. Each tree was planted in the village to form a small forest. Willow trees were used to weave baskets and the wood was crafted into wooden shoes. The Acacias grew with a powerfully aromatic scent when in bloom. They offered excellent shade although the thorns were decidedly unpleasant. I loved the broom tree the best, for it burst into a brilliant yellow at the earliest sign of spring.

My father had been an agronomist. Born in Omsk, he had studied at the university. Fruit trees. Mulberry trees. Apple trees. Pear trees. Plum trees. The women would collect the wild apple seeds and plant them in the rich black soil. Each tree was planted near the village to form a small forest. The next year, usually in July or August when the bark slipped easily and the buds were well grown, they would begin the topworking. Budding part of another tree on to the saplings was delicate work but necessary work because the wild trees did not bear fruit. My father showed them how to use the twigs, scions, from the fruit bearing trees and cut a T across the bark. Then, with a knife blade, they would lift the corners and carefully loosen the bark. The ebony knife was razor sharp with a very fine tip. It was quite the tool. They would slip the scion in, just so, wrap it with cloth, and leave it. The following spring, they would cut off the original sapling above the bud and be left with a strong fruit bearing tree. My father planted hectares of fruit trees and shipped them all over Russia. Only fruit trees though, not grapes. Grapes wouldn't grow in our area. The climate wasn't right even though the black earth was two feet deep.

Brought on by idyllic memories, I felt the protection of the fantasy from the harshness of government powers that dealt massive blows of betrayal and injustice upon me because they thought I did not matter. But those memories were always intruded upon. My father had received an award from Moscow for his work. The Russians gave the certificate to him the year before they shot him.

The Communists shot everyone that was educated. That's what they did.

Heinchen stirred in his sleep at my side.

"Hush, hush." I gently cradled my small boy. "What is wrong? Are your feet cold again?"

I fiddled with the child's tattered shoes. "You are my Heinchen," I cooed gently and nuzzled his nose with mine. I remembered the contents in my worn bag. "There is so much paper here." I pulled the sheaves of paper from the bag. The wurst we had already eaten. Hurried sketches of various buildings and numbers written as a schedule greeted me. I could not make sense of the documents.

"This can keep your feet warm." I rammed a number of the papers into Heinchen's oversized shoes, shoved the bag back underneath me and leaned against the tree.

"You are by the road and alone, why?" came a call from the road.

I jumped. "Oh," I whispered and motioned to the sleeping child.

It was Margarita, a woman I had seen around the camp but never spoken with. She chose to ignore the niceties of social etiquette and loudly demanded again to know why I was sitting by the road. Margita, of course, recognized who came and went from the camp. She looked at me the way one looks at a fish and true to her reputation for surliness and self-absorption she apparently was not interested in my answer.

"It is good to get away from them." Margita's head flicked in the direction of the camp. She sat down on the ground beside me. "You are from?"

The Mennonite name game took off to discover how we were very, very distantly related. Once that was done, Margita soon recalled her bitter life in Russia. "How our ancestors thought inclusion into the Russian Empire would be the answer to our dreams! What a decision they made to leave Danzig and move to the Ukraine! Here we are. Nearly back where we started over two hundred and fifty years ago! And we have even less now! We had a Jewish family in our village. Oh, they were happy to be part of Russia where they thought they were safe."

I shrugged. I wasn't particularly interested in the notion of a circular path in history. "Safety. Belonging. You are right about the Jews, but the Russians soon sent many of those Jews to Siberia."

"Yes, the promises did not last long, did they? No! If one would not join the Communist party, that was it! Shot or off to Siberia." Margita gave a flourish with her hand gesturing high above her head. "The Russians came after those of German origin in our village. We left when we could, in '41, but I heard how women who gave birth to babies saw their newborns thrown out of the windows during the train journey to Siberia. People with tuberculosis and diseases rode in the same car. Dying people lay in freight cars without straw, and once dead, they were thrown away on the railway embankment!"

The German Russian conflict had been obvious for years. In the immediate diplomatic prelude to the war, a secret German-Soviet non-aggression pact had been signed before the invasion of Poland in Moscow in August 1939 by the foreign minister of the Union of Soviet Socialist Republics, Vyacheslav Molotov, and Nazi Germany's Joachim von Ribbentrop. The Molotov-Ribbentrop pact divided Poland between Germany and the USSR and thereby handed over most of the Polish-ruled Ukraine in the name of national liberation.

The Ukrainian question was an important factor given that Stalin was concerned about a possible alliance between Germany and Ukrainian nationalists, who wanted to liberate the Ukraine from Soviet rule. Stalin knew that the famine-genocide and terror of the 1930s alienated those living in the Ukraine from his regime and they would welcome a German invasion. The secret pact lasted twenty-two months. Personal observations of atrocities against German speaking citizens coincided with intelligence reports indicating the Russians had been well aware of the plans to create a pro-German Ukrainian state under Operation Barbarossa.

If you complained in the communist Russian Ukraine, you

were gone. There was no freedom. I knew the lesson. In 1941, the village realized the Germans were advancing, and I can still hear Herr Letkemann commenting out loud, "I hope it doesn't take the Germans too long to get here." In the dead of the night, the Russians took him away. In the morning, no one spoke of the incident. No one.

Another time, Uncle Jakob broadcasted to a group of men standing in the village, "I wonder if Stalin's pipe is shaking now?" That night he was gone. In the morning, everyone went about their business. No one talked about it. No one asked. That is what governments did. There was no freedom. You lived their way or you disappeared. You did not speak. You did not think.

"In our village the Russians made everyone leave before the Germans arrived. Can you imagine how many people that must have been!" The forced mass evacuation of villages was close to 700,000 people.

Margita nodded in agreement. "*Dummheit!* Just before the German army came is when the Russians started killing. It was a massacre. You know, they killed the people in the prisons too, even if they were in there for petty crimes or no crimes at all!"

I knew. "The Russians were not going to leave scores of Germans in villages with the German army rapidly advancing. Oh, how they tried to tempt me into the Russian Youth movement. 'Won't you wear the red scarf, Eleni?" I exclaimed with indignation. "Their eyes would search mine but I would be careful to say nothing."

Margita listened closely to me.

"Never, never, would I speak of what my parents thought of those politics." I pressed my lips together and thought of my wonderful, pacifist parents.

"Present circumstances will change." Margita nodded in her confiding, insinuating way. "Watch carefully, things will change."

"Never would I say that at home there was a Bible on the shelf and a few letters from Canada since we would then be called enemies of the state. We would simply disappear in the night. I kept my mouth shut and shrugged my shoulders." My face wore a determined look.

Margita eyed me warily and ventured a comment, "Yes. I never wear red clothes, not even now."

"My father hated the colour. To the Russians everything was

red. The scarves symbolized the blood they were going to shed they said. They did. Stalin is still killing."

"How could life there be anything but vicious?" Margita questioned with a curious self-satisfied but shallow air. She was intelligent and crafty.

"*Gott sei Dank* the Germans came to save us. Do you know in our village, the Russians announced the German Nazis were going to invade the Motherland? They proclaimed the Hitlerites had violated the peaceful life of the Soviet people."

"Yes," whispered Margita. "They said the Germans would conduct mass executions and atrocities, but it would not break the spirit of the Russian people."

"Near Chortitza, the Reds gathered the Russian young people with great speeches about the glory of the previous generation and their grandfather's accomplishments, and with that rallying cry, the youth went to fight and to die. Dead, the whole bunch of them."

"That was in 1940 or 1941. I cannot remember, but it was close to the date when the Russians sent out letters to warn us."

"We were to go further to the East," I threw both my hands

into the air above my head. "The Russians drove us in wagons to the railroad station in Konstantinovka. Everything was made worse because we had not eaten well for a long time. My sister Anika, Oma, my three children, an aunt with her children, and myself were loaded into passenger cars." I pointed at myself. "I was wearing a heavy winter coat."

Margita jumped in. "Winter came early in 1941. Temperatures plummeted to almost -40 C."

"That's right," I agreed. "I remember it was a good coat, very warm thick wool felt. I needed the coat for that early October winter when the Russians evacuated every German village and sent everyone east, to Siberia."

"We got out already."

"You were lucky." I became animated as I experienced again a tremendous feeling of loss. My home, my village, my way of life. On the third day of that October, 1941. The first time the train stopped, people ran into the fields for privacy, but they learned quickly that the train did not wait for them to return. The second time the train stopped, people erupted out of the car to do it right there in the open. Dysentery could make you empty your bowels up to thirty times a day. Men ripped the pant seam apart so they would not get frostbite. A real possibility when they pulled their pants down. Others realized the danger of urinating out in the lethal cold and didn't even get out of the train. They shat in the car or urinated where they stood. "Can you imagine making people do that?"

I did not expect an answer. "Abraham sat close to me. I could see how an incredible sadness swept over him. It breaks your heart when you see that in your children. The train flew along the tracks as fast as the conductor could make it go! The conditions were horrendous. There was lice and scabies. People were sick with typhus. There was no place to wash yourself. The journey came to an abrupt halt on the tenth of October. How many days is that ...? Seven days!" I shouted in my excitement. "Nearly three hundred kilometres!"

The train was bombed by six German Stuckas at Puchovka, near Woronezh.

"The humming soon became a thunderbolt directly above us. God's entire creation was a petrifying wail swelling and blaring until it smothered us. I could feel the pulsations in the air as we fled from the train while the children shrieked. After a split second of that incredible noise halting came deafening blasts one after another. There were splinters shooting everywhere. The entire space turned into a blazing mass the whole length of the train. Pandemonium broke out underneath a sky billowing with dark grey smoke as we women stood with our shaking children wrapped in blankets. I thought we would surely die."

The devastation had been horrendous. Nearly all the buildings close to the track were destroyed and massive wounds in the earth's surface were gapping lacerations.

Margita asked in disbelief, "That is over a thousand kilometers from here. How did you get out alive?"

I gave a grim nod. "It felt as if we stood in a massive war with the army's terrible and great eye focused on us alone."

The grey air made us shiver. Our hearts within our skinny bodies pounded at the thought of the journey back. The amount of courage I chose to have was determined by the action I decided to take. I looked west, felt the terribleness of my resolution, and led my family away over the flat, treeless land. Others could not go, for they were in the presence of an absent jailer who mocked them to try. That pitiless grip made them sit down on the ground to wait and be reclaimed. A deep and dark dungeon.

There is no jailer as efficient as the despair stemming from one's own heart, where one can stay shackled without any chains.

Fear can stop us and bind us to inaction, but not me, not this time.

Zator, Upper Silesia
Sunday, July 23, 1944
Chapter Eleven

Many watched my resolute departure but did not comprehend what it meant. I grasped the interlude between the Russians shooting their rifles at the people outside of the train and the strafing attack of the airplanes, and with my handbag full of money, and dragging my children behind me, I ran and ran and ran. My conviction that we must survive overrode all my personal dilemmas.

When we were far enough into the hayfield, I pushed the children and others inside a haystack and waited. As night descended, Tante Anika gave each child one teaspoon of sugar from the little tin she carried. With that, they were put to bed. The bowl in the sky spilled its milky snowy swirls onto the earth. It was nearing the end of October but already unbelievably freezing and severe. That winter was one of the coldest on record in European Russia.

"In the morning, everything was snow covered." I matched Margita's look of incredulity. "Our hands were like stones! My entire body ached. My feet were wedges of ice and did not want to move. Our clothes were clammy and stiff. The children cried. The train was behind us. I headed in the opposite direction, along the railway track."

"What else could you do?" Margita interjected.

"What else, indeed."

Hope and expectation invigorated us. However, soon, too soon, reality set in. Where would we find shelter? Instead there was hunger and fatigue, especially for the children. In no time, our pathetic shoes were sodden and our feet were freezing. It was impossible to walk with any speed since we needed to rest so often. Heinchen suffered the most for his shoes were already too small for his feet. The snow was persistent, and everywhere there were signs of misery and war. Remains of horses lay as ominous lumps along the route. Evil seemed so ponderous that on this scale it far outweighed the good. It would take so much more to ever set it even. It was not safe to travel along the track, and we moved off the railway line to trudge through the snow. The overcast sky hid the sun and our sense of direction was gone. I never lost my head — although the other adults quickly became hysterical.

Margita and I sat in silence. I remembered, and Margita

stared vacantly around her as if forgetting why she had come down the road in the first place. But, I was not finished. Mesmerized and obsessed with my own traumatic story, I felt my truth to be unique.

"This is the way it happened, I tell you. I should know. I was there." I wagged my finger at Margita. "We were a defenseless flock, yet we kept walking." I paused. "I pointed down into the snow. 'Mutti!' Abraham cried with joy, 'there are people near.' But he stopped as he noticed the frozen brine on my red cheeks. It dawned on him as he looked again at the footprints. We were looping around, big gigantic loops. We had made no forward progress, none.

Desperately, I dragged them in a different direction until we came upon a large unharvested field of dried up sunflowers. The stalks stood like outcasts. Susannah, saw a horse and a modest sleigh alongside a shack at the far end of the field. She ran frantically to the entrance, tumbling numerous times in the deep snow, crawling the last few feet. Can you believe it? There was a woman inside who was making borscht! *Gott Sei Dank!*"

I clapped my hands together at this point in the story. Margita nodded.

"Susannah banged on the door with both fists, yelling for help since she could hear voices inside. We carried Heinchen into the dark shack; he seemed unconscious. Susannah was crying. I can still see how the tears covered her face. She could hardly speak. The woman loosened Heinchen's clothing and took the white snow from outside to rub his feet and hands."

Margita exclaimed in interest.

"Yes! She had to get the blood flowing. You could see how badly his extremities were affected by the way they looked. Heinchen was almost gone at that point. He briefly opened his eyes and mumbled, 'Sun's on, on, on. Sun's off, off, off.' The woman gave him warm soup and saved him.

We had only covered a few kilometers. A full day of walking for practically nothing! We could not stay in the tiny hut. I paid a few rubles to the woman's son to take us to the village in the sleigh. In less than an hour we reached the village where we spent the night."

"But ... the train ...?" Margita was puzzled.

"We had to get another train or something!" I slapped my thigh, waking little Heinchen. "Shh, shhh. It is fine now, do not worry." I stroked his arm. For a moment, I did not realize Margita was still there.

I spoke only to Heinchen. "We had to get back. We had to take the opportunity to go west, back to our village, but there were no trains! Yes, Abraham, Susannah, your Tante Anika, your Oma, your Mutti and you. Yes, we walked eight hundred kilometers. Eight hundred kilometers in that weather, on foot!"

I remembered the weather improved a little. There was no additional snow, but the sky was still brooding. We walked along the train track all day and did not see any signs of human habitation. The day drew to a close and silence was descending when without warning, a sharp sound resonated. The sound echoed and vibrated, bouncing over the unbroken snow covered landscape. Where had it come from?

" '*Go,*' I whispered to Abraham. 'Go over the hill and see what is there. We will wait here.' Abraham had nodded and gone alone, for the others were too exhausted. The distance through the snow was dreadful, and I am sure he must have looked back and could no longer see us because he returned before reaching the hill, but we were frantic with fear, so he headed out again. This time he went a little further and saw a light shining in a distant window as if someone were listening, waiting, hoping against hope. A wife, perhaps a mother. He returned promptly, and with the new hope to give us energy, we arrived at a farm house where a disappointed woman stood staunchly at the top of a flight of six stairs, barring the door into the house. It was freezing! The woman was adamant that we would not get into her house."

Margita's nod was almost imperceptible. She would have behaved the same.

"I turned to Abraham, 'Abraham, open the coop in the yard. Let the chickens out.' He did. Well, that woman came flying down the stairs to capture the chickens that had left the little wired coop, and we went into the house. By the time she came back, I had my three children and Oma on top of the oven."

Margita laughed at my cleverness. The ovens were big and flat on top with an opening in the middle to let the heat escape into the house. "We placed our wet clothes and shoes near the opening of the large clay oven."

"She could not kick us out. She was one and we were many." I nodded in satisfaction. "I was desperate. I would do anything. I didn't care."

"After resting, we decided to risk the railroad track again and due to the absence of German bombing raids and the lack of Russian pursuit, we were able to follow the track. One comrade, a farmer, even gave us a piece of pork, potatoes, several loaves of bread, and a bit of tea with sugar. I thanked him and said, yes, *barinja*, for I noticed he used the old Russian greeting and not comrade. Such generosity…"

"Ahh …" Margita understood the meaning. "Did you not try the trains again?" She knew how dangerous that would be since we had lost our papers, but she was curious.

"We did go to the nearby railroad station, but there were no trains except military ones. The station was packed with military personnel and there seemed to be a lot of confusion. I told them we were escaping the Germans. Not wishing to draw attention, we agreed to continue walking along the tracks and veer off when we reached a village. Once beyond the village, we headed back to the tracks. One day, we managed to walk some distance in this manner. A few evenings, we found empty outbuildings with leftover chaff, hay or stubble. Once, we were given a mud hut with a warm fire. I managed to beg a little food from nearby houses. We were sure we would be home soon."

Margita made a little sneezing sound in her nose. She knew the feeling of false hope. "I bet the next days did not go so well?"

I looked at her with annoyance for pre-empting my story. "There was a day the weather was foggy and when we reached the next village, we discovered detonation crews destroying all the railroad connections."

"Of course. Now, you have to try and walk parallel to the track through the fields. This is easier said than done, I am sure," Margita interjected.

"Since the fog prevented us from seeing the tracks …"

"… and explosions sent debris into the air …"

"When evening arrived, we had made a few kilometers through the chaos." I reclaimed my narrative. "It was amazing how they could blow all the railway tracks up. It was cold enough to freeze the fuel in the machinery. German soldiers ate frozen horseflesh because the Russians would find the camp fires … but we were worn-out, filthy, and in dire need of warmth. One more time, a complete stranger, a Russian in a shed behind a house, allowed us to dry our clothes by his tiny fire and gave us a steaming brew. We were fortunate."

Margita's upper lip curled. I could see she was convinced the Russian would have held back on a feast in his stately home and had only been kind for ulterior motives.

"Not unexpectedly, the food I was able to find was terrible. Heinchen was sick of beets. Once in a while we would find potatoes or carrots. A small piece of black bread was a miraculous discovery!"

"Obviously, you decided to walk the tracks again."

"We simply did not have the stamina to schlep across the bare countryside. Heinchen and Oma needed to be helped so much that we practically carried them the whole way. We had to rest continually." I remembered how we shrank in our clothes and looked like walking sticks. The children were especially in agony, even with additional bits of food.

"Yes, you cannot keep going. It is too hard."

"Hard! The railway line was destroyed! The ankle bars holding the rails together had been blown up. The remaining scraps were grey skeletons fighting to the death. The roads were ancient ruts."

"It always gets worse." Margita nodded with satisfaction. In the depths of my mind, a warning flag was waving and I could sense she was someone it was not good to be around, but I ignored the flag. In a way, I couldn't stop telling my narrative even though I knew that the worst bits of my story fit into her established view of a horrible world.

"One afternoon, I spied a timeworn lean-to with broken tools flung on the ground. We stayed for the night because it was large enough. As always, the weather was a cold and drizzly."

We wrenched the locked door open and the earth inside was cold and dry. We discovered a few semi-frozen spuds in the abandoned potato sacks. The grisly food stared back at us, mocking our impending descent into serious ill health and starvation. Abraham gritted his teeth and attacked the loose boards inside the shed. The meagre splinters made a measly fire, barely hot enough to put the potatoes in. The smoke filtered out around the shaky door.

"We took off our sopping wet clothing to dry and sidled up as close to the fire as we could."

Margita nodded. "And you need to check the potatoes

regularly to cook them properly."

"They were half rotten," I said with disgust, "but I turned them anyway with a section of wire and rolled them out of the embers."

"Better than nothing."

I ignored Margita's unsolicited advice and comment.

The decision making fell to me. The others did not even bother to ask anymore, and I did not ask them anymore either. It was obvious I needed help, but from where? I found it difficult to sleep even though the others fell asleep from exhaustion as soon as we had eaten our potatoes.

After this small respite, I pressed them on for two more days in the worsening weather. Most of the places we walked through were in total disarray. Anarchy. No place was safe from the war.

"There was no transportation apart from travelling by foot, cart or sleigh." I looked down to the ground. "The last night before reaching our village, we were in Artemovsk, in a deserted schoolhouse with broken windows and an open door."

Oma, who was always obsessed with the rules, no longer voiced any opinion. She was totally indifferent. When the early morning light massaged its way into the schoolhouse, Abraham was watching and alert. The overcast sky beyond the window reflected grey and somber on the wet ground.

"Only a day's walking distance from home!" There was a note of hope in his voice.

I responded, "Today! We will have a chance to make it if we leave now. We will carry Heinchen and Oma. The rain may be ice again today." I remembered my school days and how I had been pushed away from the warm stove by the bigger boys. Always pushed aside and bullied, and with those life lessons I learned when to fight and when to be quiet. Today, today, no one was going to stop me from doing what I wanted. I was leaving that school, and I was bringing my family home.

My legs throbbed. My empty stomach burned with hunger.

I knew how much I needed my coat to keep me warm. "I had lost so much weight. I thought I would surely die in those final few kilometers. I did not have enough strength left to both walk and wear that heavy coat. I simply dropped the coat right there onto the railway tracks. Nineteen days, can you imagine?" I asked Margita.

Margita gave a polite smile. It looked like she had been

forced to take a second helping of something she detested.

"*Gott sei Dank*. October 22 was Abraham's birthday. His twelfth birthday. Poor child. What gift was there for him when we finally returned home? A few handful of grapes clinging to the vines was all the Germans left! And can you believe it? There was a Russian woman already living in my house!"

"Ahh," Margita shot back, "that I can believe!"

"I said to her, 'Did you sell my furniture too?' and she laughed. The local Russians had plunged onto the house like vermin, and it was empty when she took it! How strange it looked. All my cherished furnishings had been stolen. There was a pathetic table and rubbish for chairs where the old Russian woman sat. She said to me, '*Dorogaja*, when you were sent away, the authorities declared you would never return.' She shrugged her shoulders. It wasn't personal. It was what greeted us when we made it home. Unbelievable! Everything was gone, not an item was left," I spoke with finality.

"Miracles! My Peter Wiebe had gone to Berlin before this happened and now he returned the next day with the Germans. The very next day! What luck!" I didn't mention that Peter and I were not married. "Yes, in those days Peter was … forceful … strong …" I shook my head. "Do you know during that night the Russian civilians brought back everything! All the furniture was in the yard. They were petrified of the Germans." Our small family was the solitary group that had returned from the Russian evacuation out of the entire village.

"But that is still a long way from here?" Margita encouraged the story.

She listened to my story for those bits of information that would be useful to her, for she was adept at latching onto opportunities that came her way. I knew her type. Ironically, she thought people were stupid, arrogant and self-absorbed. She listened because she was waiting to make a point, not a friend.

I didn't care. I was eager to share my story. I needed to tell it. Many of my friends and extended family were lost, caught and shipped east to Siberia on a train. I escaped with the fragment of my family. None of those friends would know about my life now nor would I know about them. I could not tell them about it or put it in a letter. They would never know! Never.

I spoke with defiance, "On the third of November 1941, we

were in the neighboring village of Ebenfeld with our triumphant German liberators. That was freedom! I could take the Bible and go to church. I could speak freely about the Russian Communists. We were ecstatic the Germans had arrived. We were praised for speaking German. Liberated! We moved and found refuge in Waldheim, Colony Molochna but left again in August 1943. The Russians kept advancing and the Germans kept retreating." A sense of hurt came to me from that global level. I tried to push the feelings aside but the space filled with unbidden memories.

"I remember the Germans coming. They sang *Lili Marlene*. We heard that song continuously on the radio," Margarita said.

I wasn't listening to her. *The coat is probably still lying there*, I thought with a sniff. *A great coat.* "I said to the Germans, 'You won't leave without us! And they replied, '*Nein, nein! Niemals!*' I woke up one morning and they were gone! Every single one of them! Gone! They had vowed to never leave!"

I had visions of soldiers trudging on through the death of winter in the Russian Ukraine. I imagined them lying down in the snow due to exhaustion, in their great coats. I reached out again and again with each retelling of my experience to move closer to discovering its meaning. I know people differ in their readiness to perceive a situation as traumatic. The tortured song inside of me hungered to be heard. I felt that each telling would bring me closer to where I could touch the small bit of grace transfixed in each human heart. I believed that. I had to. Grace heals. It would place me where I belonged.

Margita realized my story was not done, but she recalled her task, I guess, which was to go to the train station and promptly return to the camp. An extraordinary number of boxcars on the railway line passed Zator that spring and summer, going west. Margita went to meet the trains in the chance that they carried supplies or new refugees for the camp but there was little of interest at the station today. Without a goodbye, Margita left as abruptly as she had appeared.

Alone again, I absentmindedly took the remaining paper sheaves from the bag and bend my head to inspect the script more closely. *Fürstenstein? These are signed by ...* I scrutinized the signature. Siegfried Schmelcher. *Hmm, I do not know him.* I pressed my lips together and knitted my brow in concentration. *What is this?*

"Geheime Reichssache 91/44! Mein Lieber Gott!" The papers were blueprints of a secret German installation. I gasped, hastily folded the remaining papers and shoved them down between my breasts. Heinchen woke up with all my commotion.

I stared down the dirt road. "How many roads have I walked down?"

Looking both ways, the track reminded me of the road by my father's house in the Ukraine. My father had not been a harsh man, but life had been hard and dry like the road across the village. Yet, my parents, in their own way, showed each other and their children a great deal of love. We depended on each other.

When times are good, why does change happen? the child inside of me asked. Yet, I was never, ever, resigned to the thought that things would not change. I stamped my foot in frustration. Heinchen, the child beside me wailed. "Quiet! Quiet, Heinchen. Nothing's wrong." I fretfully stroked his head, distracted by this new concern. *I do not know how I will manage today or tomorrow; I just do. I do not know what the consequences will be or what form they will take. I will not die, I will not starve. I will survive.* I turned my feet back toward the camp.

How could that *alte Schlor* be missing these? I thought of Gerhard. He was as useless as old slippers. Surely, the papers didn't belong to him. Then who? Fear and opportunity. The enormity of what these papers might mean dawned on me.

It was similar to the feeling I had possessed on the day of my marriage. My heart had felt heavy and light at the same moment. I was married in the church in a terse ceremony conducted by *Prediger* Enns. After, we went to my parents' kitchen. I had worn a veil, and as the bride, I sat in the middle of the room while they took off my veil, put a bow in my hair, and announced I was now a married woman! Not until then, not until that bow was I a *Frau*. We pushed back the table and chairs to celebrate with dance and games. My new husband, Heinrich, and I had waltzed. It had been exciting. There were many dances and a wild one where I jumped high. That was what we did with the little we had.

Heinrich, now my husband, worked as an electrician, hanging the solitary bulbs from the ceiling, running the wire along the wall and fixing the switch on the wall by the door. It was a sparse life for everyone. I never knew if there would be enough food, if any. I never knew what would happen in the night.

Everyone was fearful, nearly all the time.

The memories walked with me as Heinchen and I walked down the dirt track, back toward the camp at Zator. I glanced hastily around me and back over my shoulder. I remembered the night the Russians took six men from the village. I thought the men would come back. No one knew at that stage what had happened to those taken. They came for Heinrich. The communists called him an Enemy of the People — *ein Volksfeind*. That was Stalin for you. It was utterly preposterous. Those men were lambs. They never left the village; they did not know about fighting or resistance. They were German-speaking Mennonites and Pacifists by faith.

What is to become of us? I lamented deep in my heart. *Everything is ruined.* The Russians destroyed every village and every farm. There was no buying or selling; they ruined the market, too. *I was such a hopeful, young bride, naïve.* I nervously patted the papers between my breasts.

After we were married, we lived in the *Sommerstube*. There was no honeymoon. Every married couple lived in the summer room, for a time. It was where my child was born with the help of the village midwife. He was over eight pounds. I named him

Abraham. I loved that beautiful name. Susannah was named after a great-grandmother.

Now as then, the pale afternoon sun shone through a thin layer of cloud and in the distance, darker clouds massed overhead. The day of my marriage to Heinrich was not as cold as the previous year and I had sniffed the hope of spring. As per tradition, on the third day after the wedding, Heinrich came and claimed me from my parent's house. My parents flanked me as we walked across the village to live in the *Sommerstube* of my parents-in-law's house. I took my meagre belongings and two important wedding gifts from my parents, a sewing machine and a single metal bed. I imagined my grand procession might rival the story of my *Opa* who claimed to have seen the Czar. Well, my grandfather had seen his carriage anyway.

Prediger Enn's sermon from my wedding day echoed in my head. *A merry heart is good medicine, but a broken spirit dries the bones.* Unexpectedly, during the symbolic marriage procession through the village, an alarming hullaballoo came from the direction of the river. The details of that day still follow me in my dreams. That day became a memorial of shared suffering.

We had run down to the river to find two young boys on the thawing ice. There was no time to rescue them. We watched with dreadful anticipation. The ice was thin. The two children stood, arms entwined; the ice groaned and cracked as it gave way.

A shot rang out in the forest like the crack of the ice. My head came up with a start, and I left my reminiscences behind. Impossible! Abraham had gone with Peter to watch the road and search for his sister. Had they gone into the forest?

Where was Susannah?

Zator, Upper Silesia
Sunday, July 23, 1944
Chapter Twelve

Dietrich stood up abruptly and in one smooth movement released the stone from his hand. The jagged rock struck the soldier on the temple, leaving a gash. The soldier's hand came up as if to ward off a blow as he staggered and dropped to the ground. The bullet he'd fired had missed its target.

The distraction gave Reiner enough time to react. Dietrich ran, followed by Susannah and Klara. The crack of the pistol shot hushed the forest into silence. Elias stood stock-still. Reiner knocked the remaining soldier to the ground while diving for the pistol, and he tried to take aim but the SS soldier was too quick. He hiked his hand and showered Reiner's face with dirt. Reiner twisted aside as his black-clothed opponent frantically tried to get his own pistol out of the leather holster. Reiner swore with vexation, but he could still see enough, and with an agile right-handed motion he brought the gun up and shot him in the throat. Pure luck. Blood jetted onto the ground. The soldier hit the forest floor with a thump Elias could feel; the blood pumped out of him. Reiner swiftly turned and shot the other fallen soldier in the head.

Done. He dropped the pistol and clutched his slashed left arm. He collapsed, looking pale and faint. Elias was left standing alone with a wounded killer and two SS corpses. He knew he should flee after the others but the revulsion kept him fascinated. He felt no shock. He felt no pity. Life or annihilation. He was overwhelmed by the delicacy and fragility of the human body.

Reiner spoke. "If anyone finds you here, you will be in big trouble."

The imminent life-threatening danger appeared to be over but the word trouble was an understatement. Elias barely nodded.

"I will keep this quiet and to myself, if you will?"

This time, Elias's nod was instantaneous. He was fairly certain the other youths would not divulge the secret either. What would happen to Reiner, who had put bullets into the bodies of the two elite *Shutzstaffel*? The repercussions from such an act would be horrific.

"Help me bind up my wound before I bleed to death, will you?" commanded Reiner. He held his bloody forearm close to his body. He seemed to be able to ignore the pulseless shapes on the ground. His composure was extraordinary. Elias felt his own personal deficit and longed to be as steadfast.

"Well?" Reiner inquired a second time, tilting his head to the side.

"Oh, sure." Elias found it difficult to move. There did not seem to be a path toward the young man that was clear of blood. A complete feeling of fear froze his feet to the ground.

"Take the belt off that one there and wrap it around my arm," instructed Reiner sternly.

His voice snapped Elias back to the moment and he managed to do as he was told. He was determined not to gaze at the face and moved away from the corpse with a speed that was foreign to him. Reiner's clothing was soaked with blood, and the slash on his left arm was a gapping fleshy red mess. Elias felt the bile rise in his throat, but he placed the belt around the wound to pull it closed.

Reiner forced himself to his feet. He looked at the dead bodies. "We'll leave them. We cannot dig graves, and there is too much blood to hide it anyway. Hopefully, the sound of gunshots is not an unusual occurrence during wartime."

Elias stared at him in astonishment. What was Reiner

thinking? He did not honestly consider that Elias was actually going to meddle with the bodies, did he?

"On the other hand, we do not want them discovered too soon, do we?"

Elias did not know what to think. Surely, the risk was over. To drag bodies all over the forest appeared to be a little bit outside the initial agreement. He swallowed and muttered, "Look, I am a little guy, and …"

"We can manage together," interrupted Reiner. "There, over there, where you were hiding, is a good spot."

Elias did not move.

"And then it will be over," Reiner decreed with a grimness that made Elias jump to command. Pulling on one arm each, they hauled first one body and then the other into the tall scrub. "Done," announced Reiner, his face white with distress. He spoke as if he were sinking into a world where no one else could hear what he was saying.

Elias spoke with alarm, "Is there anything I can do for you?"

"My arm is injured, but fortunately the documents they were looking for are with another." Reiner spoke his thoughts out loud.

"There is someone else in the forest?"

Reiner started. "No, no. I met a fellow on the road. I am to meet him ..." Reiner placed his good hand on a tree to brace himself. "I seem to be feeling not well. I'm rambling; never mind what I'm saying." Reiner stared at him with a certainty that made Elias's blood turn cold. "They tried to kill me, and they will kill you. Knowledge puts you in danger. If they can follow me, they can follow you."

Elias was aghast.

"After all, I did not ask you to come into the forest, did I?"

"No," mumbled Elias, wishing with all his might that this day had never happened.

Shakily, Reiner stood up to leave. "I do not mean to frighten you, just put you on your guard." He lowered his voice, as though a fresh thought had come to him in the middle of his comment.

"What is your name?" asked Reiner.

"Elias. Elias Wiens."

"Wiens?" Reiner's pause was lengthy.

Elias raised his eyebrows. "Yes." he replied.

"Remember, not a word to anyone," Reiner stated briskly.

"Be off with you!"

Elias fled. After a short distance, he halted, bent over, and spewed into the green foliage. He steadied himself against a tree, wiped his mouth across his sleeve, and moved toward the road. The other three were waiting for him and moved toward him in one agitated swoop, looking relieved that he was unscathed.

Dietrich was jittery. "The soldier, the one I hit with the rock?"

"He is dead," responded Elias.

"You mean I killed him!" exclaimed Dietrich with wonder.

"No, you idiot," retorted Elias, "The man, the one they were after, did. He shot him and the other soldier too. They are both dead. There was blood everywhere. We dragged them into the bush."

"I'm going to be sick," moaned Susannah.

"We can never, never tell anyone about this, ever," Klara stated emphatically.

"And he didn't kill you? He let you go?" asked Dietrich with disbelief.

"It was murder, and we were there! We have to keep this a secret," Klara ordered. One more atrocity for them to carry as a collective memory. As if the years of terror and multigenerational trauma from repeated revolutions and wars weren't enough.

"I promise," answered Susannah immediately. Her history of unquestioned obedience leapt to the fore. She would continue the legacy of generations cowed into submission by fear.

"Murder is killing in the wrong place. This is war. It does not matter." Dietrich, who was filled with intense unfocused resentment and hatred, quarrelled harshly. He considered international lawlessness repatriation, even though Mennonites from the Ukraine who had come to Germany quickly realized that the ruling Nazi junta was no different from the Russians. Many children, like Dietrich, who had been humiliated and deceived — for those memories never disappear — became transformed into the feral untamed youth of a recreated Nazi world.

"Dietrich!" Klara's hands flew to cover her mouth. "How can you think that?" Klara was mortified.

"I will never tell," promised Elias.

"Me neither," added Klara.

Elias looked at her curiously for she did not belong to the submissive masses, adoring and indifferent or even to those who barely survived. He could tell she was different.

"I swear too." Dietrich mouthed the words.

He was, at heart, a clever and sensitive individual, but he had been molded and dominated. All he could relate to was the power of his destructive feelings. And like many others, he felt joining the German Nazi cause was the least he could do. There he would be valued for his hatred. He had been beaten as a child and told it was good for him. So too was the belief that this continuing domination of the Nazi regime would be good for him.

Now, he would belong to a new people, a new family and he mocked the old with a forced shrug, "Are we allowed to swear? Isn't that against our religion or something?"

"What is the matter with you?" exclaimed Elias.

"What? Nothing. I am the one that saved that man, ya know," boasted Dietrich. For all his bravado and posturing, he still was clearly alarmed.

"Come on. We'd better get back to the camp." Klara was quick to placate.

The afternoon waned and a coppery autumn light slanted across the dirt track. As they climbed up the road, their shadows stretched and rolled over the rise ahead of them like a band of returning warriors.

Dietrich proclaimed, "I want to be a soldier, an elite soldier. No mercy. Take what you want when you want it."

Hitler's pedagogy was hard. He declared what is weak must be hammered away. He wanted the young to be violent, domineering, undismayed, and cruel. They must be able to bear pain. There must be nothing gentle about them. Then he could create a new race. Dietrich was determined to be proud, strong, and without emotion. He would allow himself to be manipulated. In the Nazi ideological realm, those mutilated emotionally and deprived of a moral compass through traumatic socialization patterns and a culture of violence and war become valuable members for a tyrannical regime.

What was it that Hitler once said? "It is good fortune for those in power that people do not think. It gives us a very special, secret pleasure to see how unaware the people around us are of what is really happening to them."

Incensed by Dietrich's remark, Elias retorted, "You have to follow orders, Dietrich." Ironically, following orders always proved to be a difficult task for Elias.

"I know that! You are the one who is too stupid to get it!"

Despite their harsh upbringing, Elias never lost his spontaneity and had retained a thread of his true Self. As a result, he received more beatings than Dietrich. Elias felt it was his job to dissuade Dietrich. "Besides you cannot join the army; you are Mennonite. You can only work in the forest service or as a medic."

"I could too! Others have joined the real army, you know that," Dietrich retorted.

Elias stamped his foot in irritation, "Yes, *Dummkopf*! Czar Alexander drafted men into the army to serve up to four years in the forestry service. Forestry, Dietrich, forestry!"

"No, no. They went as medics. They went as soldiers, too!"

The argument rose to a shouting contest just like the heated discussion in village meetings encompassing the freedom of individual conscience in wartime, the role of faith, and especially, the role of pacifism. But the argument came to an awkward and abrupt halt.

"I could be a hero," Dietrich boasted.

Klara cast him a sideways glance and frowned.

"Hitler is a hero, like in the traditional stories," Dietrich stated with finality.

"What stories?" Elias spat out, "You don't know any stories!"

"I know Hitler has brought *das deutsche Volk* together. *Gleichschaltung*. He has made us one people, all equal," Dietrich proclaimed.

The native Russians looked upon German-speaking Mennonites as foreigners from Prussia who tilled the Ukrainian soil. During the current war with Germany, the Russians wanted to send them to the East, to the very far East. Most of the families in this camp believed safety was the opposite direction — west, and as far as they could go. Germans moving towards Germany. Yet, even under Hitler's master race ideal, the German people considered them *Ausländer*, imported, not real Germans but foreign elements. They were a type of anachronistic surplus evacuated to a strange land, representing the extreme version of an intrusion into the German nation. This was their story, and unknown to them and through their painful experiences, they were creating a history, a place where they belonged, even while in flight.

Dietrich argued, "Hitler saved us from the Communists!"

"Those were not exactly Communists back there," Susannah's small voice whispered.

"Be quiet, Susannah," Klara's voice wavered as she looked at her. "Do not speak of it!"

Dietrich marched along ahead of them. He was typical of someone who has a smidgeon of knowledge and assumes he is now automatically entitled to pronounce with authority on all other subjects. He sniped, "I know some have joined the German nation in its fight against the Russians. They are the 14th *Waffen Grenz* … something or other." He felt that the tie to the former Russian nation that tormented and devoured scores of individuals from each generation deserved no automatic unquestioning allegiance. "Belonging to the new Germany is a new beginning," Dietrich continued with growing conviction now that he was over his fear. "It makes so much sense."

"How could one fight and be a pacifist at the same time?" Elias's question filled the suppressed silence. "Besides, you cannot call yourself a Christian if you are not a pacifist."

But that is the problem with life. We are often unsure of the parameters. And, in any case, the boundaries are constantly changing.

"Why not? Stuff like that happens." Klara's voice was barely audible as she answered Dietrich but she spoke with an astounding certainty. The action of speaking reassured her. "People can love and hate simultaneously, you know. We do it all the time. We love imperfectly."

"Can we hate imperfectly too, then?" Dietrich asked fidgeting from foot to foot. "The forest is a great place. I am going to go again sometime."

Klara's retort came quickly and hit the mark. But for all of that, she felt ashamed and embarrassed after humiliating him, even though it was richly deserved.

The four of them came around the bend in the road. Instinctively, they became silent as they neared the camp. There was no opportunity to continue the argument anyway for Uncle Gerhard was marching toward them.

Zator, Upper Silesia
Sunday, July 23, 1944
Chapter Thirteen

Gerhard faced them with his fists on his hips. "You were gone a long time, all afternoon in fact. What happened?"

When they looked at him blankly, Gerhard clenched his fists and jabbed his finger testily at Elias. "About the satchel and papers, imbecile!"

"Oh, yes. I mean no. No satchel." Elias was overcome by the recent events. His breathing accelerated noticeably.

"There's blood on your clothes, Elias." Uncle Gerhard gestured towards his pants.

"A hare, we … caught a hare, but it escaped," Dietrich offered.

"A hare …" Elias echoed.

"By the edge of the forest and it managed to … we had sharpened sticks … and rocks," Dietrich added.

"There was blood. I had the animal in my hands, but it was squirmy and it was too swift. It got away," Elias breathed out heavily.

Dietrich stood with pressed lips and eyebrows raised, nodding his head.

Gerhard looked from one boy to the other. "You cannot do anything right, Elias. Next time leave the hunting to Dietrich."

"Absolutely," Elias agreed with relief. It must have been the only time he had ever been grateful for Dietrich's ability to lie.

"I cut my finger," Dietrich confided to Elias. "Look. It has bled. I have died a little bit." He nodded with satisfaction. Elias stared at Dietrich in disbelief.

Gerhard turned his scowl on the two girls. "They need help in the clinic. Get going!" he motioned with a quick jerk of his head. His gaze lingered on Susannah.

The nape of Susannah's neck crawled. Unable to make any sound, Susannah imagined a noose around her neck.

"Right away." Klara grabbed Susannah's arm and pulled her toward the building.

That was a smart reply. At least they will be too busy to talk. Elias watched Susannah stumble away beside Klara. *I wish I had the chance to go somewhere else. I wonder if I will see Klara again.*

He and Dietrich turned toward the evening food line. What

was his uncle going to do about the theft of the satchel? Elias watched the grey hair march off toward the road, scanning every face he passed. Searching. Abruptly, Gerhard stopped and with a furtive glance, quickened his pace in the direction of someone who stood there quietly. The familiar figure held his right hand over his left forearm.

Elias gawked in disbelief.

Distracted by Dietrich's complaints about the dinner food line, the second of inattention caused him to lose track of his uncle. Twenty minutes later, his mother came and stood beside him. Her face was still and grey like the walls of the buildings in the camp. His father stood beside her, his shoulders slumped in a posture of defeat.

She whispered. "Your uncle Gerhard says that all will yet be well."

"How is that possible?" inquired Elias. "You know how upset he was about the theft."

"He says it is different now. He spoke to us. Our fortunes are turning."

Elias's father snorted with disrespect, "Yeah, that is what

Gerhard says. He promises a future for us here in Upper Silesia."

"Upper Silesia? I thought we were going west?"

"No, your uncle has a plan.

"What kind of plan?" asked Elias quite bewildered.

"That's not for you to know. Stay out of trouble and do what he says," urged his father who was putting on a brave front, pretending to be encouraged.

"Look, here he comes," she said anxiously.

"Who is that with him?" his father questioned.

Elias turned to see Gerhard approaching with Reiner.

"Brother, let me introduce an old friend, Herr … Grunewald." The pause was barely perceptible. After all, Gerhard didn't know much about Reiner and certainly not his surname, which he had just created. "Reiner, here is my younger brother, Klaus, and his wife, Heidi."

Klaus tried to return the welcome with a damp handshake, but Heidi interrupted by squawking over the state of Reiner's arm.

When Reiner ignored her, looked at Elias and waited, Gerhard insolently added, "… and my nephew, Elias."

Elias was too flabbergasted to speak coherently and merely

mumbled without raising his eyes. His uncle made a noise of exasperation and a look of disgust.

"Where is Dietrich? Bandits are hard at work in the forest. I need someone to take my friend to the hospital to get his wound attended to. Where is my nephew?"

"Never mind, Gerhard," said Reiner affably despite his limp, pallid complexion. "I am sure Elias can show me the way." Although in obvious pain, Reiner's amused eyes met Elias's stricken stare.

Elias nodded and turned toward the clinic. He could hear the crunch of Reiner's boots behind him on the gravel. At the door, Elias shooed a sleeping Casper off the stoop.

Inside the clinic, they were met with the dizzy smell of turpentine, camphor and Lysol. The lazy light of the evening filtering in through the windows gave the place a surreal quality. Dizzy moths awake from their daytime sleep flickered about them. The place was filled with quiet moans, clumsy bandages and the itch of healing skin.

In the next room, Elias could see Klara moving to and fro, and he tried to signal to her. A worker came rushing towards Reiner when she observed he was clutching his arm.

Klara hastily followed. "Is there anything you need?" Klara asked the worker.

"No. Thank you. I can manage the dressing of this wound."

It was a standard answer, but Klara felt maddened by the response every time she heard it. She was relegated to menial tasks and felt denigrated when she was left carrying the buckets. Susannah, who was nearby, was called over by the worker to bring the necessary supplies.

When Klara finally noticed Elias, she stared at him because he was shaking his head like he had had an electric shock. She noticed the paleness of his face. There was the familiar confusion of rising anxiety, and then the reason for his behaviour dawned on her.

Klara held her breath when Reiner conversationally asked Susannah, "What have you been doing this day?" A long silence. The soiled curtain behind Reiner's head billowed out in an arc, and a gust of cold air passed over Susannah's face.

"Watching ... nothing, just around here," Susannah smoothed her hands on her wool skirt. She had not seen Reiner's face in the woods, having kept her head down nearly the entire time. She did not make the connection that Reiner had been in the woods, but, nevertheless, she was frightened he might guess her guilty secret: the theft of the satchel.

"Who is your friend?" Reiner motioned his head in Klara's direction.

Susannah looked at Klara, "Klara. She is helping in the clinic, too."

"That is wonderful." Reiner flirted with her. "But not as wonderful as what you are doing. I appreciate your help." Susannah's confusion burst into a flaming red that covered her entire face, but Reiner had closed his eyes.

The worker said to him, "You must rest. You have lost a fair bit of blood."

Susannah moved quietly away. Klara grabbed her by the arm and pulled her outside. Elias followed, still looking shocked.

Susannah whispered, "What's wrong with you? Jealous because he didn't speak with you?" Even though Susannah was embarrassed by Reiner's brief attention, she was extremely flattered.

"You silly girl!" rebuked Klara.

"That's the guy from the forest, Susannah." Elias sounded

like he was suffocating.

"Are you sure?"

"Of course, we are sure!" Klara snapped. She hated to talk about it. The incident gave her an unnerving feeling that the unpredictable was active and euphorically alive. The possibility that they would be found out petrified her.

"Don't," Elias blurted. "Get control of yourself, Klara."

Klara suppressed a squeal. She made a visible effort to calm down and skidded to an abrupt emotional halt. "If he was going to tell, he would have by now. Besides he doesn't want anyone to know either. He came to tend his arm, and then he'll go. Stay away from him." Klara's hand went to touch her necklace, only to be reminded it was lost in the woods. Her hovering fear turned into a flutter of panic.

"Does he know anyone here?" inquired Susannah with plenty of curiosity.

"You cannot be serious!" Klara's temper shot up again. "He spoke to you for a second. He will never look at you again. He's trouble. Trouble. Do you want me to spell it out?"

Elias stood silently. What was Reiner doing talking to his

uncle? How did they know each other? Elias looked at the two girls he had met today, one with reddish blonde hair and one with dark hair and golden brown eyes. What did he know about them? What was Susannah doing in the forest anyway, and by herself? Did she know Reiner?

"There are rules Susannah, even now," Klara warned.

"Rules drive me crazy," Susannah spoke sullenly. "I can't do what I want."

"Exactly!" Klara said inches from Susannah's face.

Klara had never been in such a shocking predicament, two men dead in the woods, and the four of them might have been murdered if they had not escaped! She wondered why the men had argued. Plainly, it was not about a simple looting. They had mentioned documents, but Elias had said no more about that. He probably didn't know anything, Klara concluded. It was another dangling thread, like her, like her family, like all of them. She felt like a sweater that was unraveling.

There was a familiar stomping step behind Klara and a hollering in her ear. "Bring me water, I'm thirsty!" The man who had hollered continued on his way, waving for Klara and Susannah to follow. His gate was uneven, and he dragged a damaged foot.

"It's my father," Klara said to Susannah. "He always yells." Klara heaved another deep sigh and tried to compose herself. "Don't worry, he's okay."

"What happened to everyone? Where are they? What's the matter, Klara? You have such an odd look on your face." Her father questioned in a warmer voice as his hand lovingly stroked the side of her face. He sat on the ground and ladled water out of the bucket she had carried to him. He took a loud noisy slurp and wiped his mouth on his sleeve. "Thank you, *mein Schatz*."

Klara struggled to keep the recent events in perspective, not letting them create a domino effect, especially not about the loss of her coloured bead necklace. It wasn't working. That necklace meant everything to her. With its wild colours, the blues, yellows, whites, and the surprising reds, it was one of the few innocent and tender memories of 1941. A liberator, a young German soldier, had been so thrilled to hear and meet a German-speaking child that he had given her the wood bead necklace. Fashioned in a twirling pattern, the unexpected beauty of the necklace fascinated Klara and she wore it permanently; even when the soldiers had disappeared in retreat in the summer of 1943. She remembered the young soldier vividly, but was sure he had forgotten her. If she remembered someone, how was it that they could not remember her? An aching heart will often trick the mind.

Don't I matter? Am I that forgettable? We shared the same moment, the same memory, how can it not be memorable to the other person too?

She felt the necklace shared the inconstancy of life and the finality of death with her. The necklace's memories were both precious and poignant.

Remembering is connecting, belonging. If one can still somehow move on, one can recover in a place as real as a living community.

"I loved my home, Papa. I loved my life with my family there," she murmured, the tears welling up inside her. "Ahh, I am hungry, but we will eat soon." She gave her father a beaming smile.

Father and daughter maintained an easy gentle harmony. He was an encourager by nature and withheld his questions. His silent gaze moved to encompass Susannah. Klara was glad not to be the centre of attention.

"I am Susannah from Chortitza," came her cautious response to his expectant look.

"We met today," Klara quickly checked her rising distress about the necklace again. "We are getting to know each other."

"Good." Her father nodded. "I like that. We only have each other in these times. Susannah, we are from the village of Catherinenhof. Mennonites are great trekkers. Soon, we will find another place of peace and quiet, away from this."

He gave an expansive sweep of his hand. His hurts were real and alive, but they did not need to pulse madly through his veins and leave him screaming obscenities at the world. He put those hurts aside and made them wait. When he waited, he could listen. Faith is listening to the voice of God.

"One day we will live calmly, without conflict, without war. We will have all we need, one day. Much can be accomplished with gentleness. We must explore it, express it to one another, encourage each other and learn how to be kind."

Susannah had no idea what he was talking about. Klara responded absentmindedly, hoping to avoid any further inquiries from her father. She considered her new friends. She liked Elias.

His awful brother, Dietrich, was the type whose shallow worldview would fold up and collapse when confronted with Nazi dogma and then as readily accept the new creed. He was that sort, boastful, aggressive and emotionally stupid, but Elias was not.

Klara let her eyes drift over the camp and rest on Irmgard standing under a dying apple tree. Irmgard shone with good grace. Her gentleness and kindness were perfect compliments to her beauty. She had a classic elegant face conveying self-confidence and certitude. Each attractive feature was the correct shape and size in her square face. Her figure was solid yet it was somehow graceful. Her pleasant voice comforted, and her place in Klara's world was upon a pedestal.

Whenever Irmgard was near, Klara would crane her neck to get an extra glimpse for a little while longer. She worshipped the charity in Irmgard. To Klara, she was the most beautiful person in the world. Yes. She was sympathetic and generous. Her good will made Klara feel alive. Klara blossomed in Irmgard's thoughtful presence because she soothed Klara's soul.

Klara determined to be like Irmgard. No problem deterred Irmgard, no circumstance made her nasty; instead, she chose to be kind-hearted. She was a queen even though her life ranged from mundane rituals to unspeakable horrors. Klara wondered if Irmgard's tears allowed her to see the world through diamond cuts of glass. Held up to Irmgard's discerning eye, the world was a sparkling, magical and captivating stillness like a stained glass in a winter window. Her dignity came from her firm grasp on her humanity and benevolence; no one would ever take those away. Irmgard chose the colours and the texture of her inner life. Her days did not always turn out the way she expected, for the length and happening of her days did not belong to her. Yet, she laughed and found a cheerful fragment of life despite all of it because she gave herself permission to be happy. She thrived on sunshine and when it was rainy, she became a kaleidoscope.

  If Irmgard's tears could teach, Klara would learn how to see the world through them and know that life could look better. Any spark in an icy and barren life is so faint, such a little thing. To miss the little things in life is to miss the seed of joy.

  Klara looked at Susannah, who was lean and not pretty despite her beautiful reddish blonde hair. Her used clothes were haphazardly fastened together with string and buttons; indeed, they were rags. Her young face with its tender lips was already imprinted with the harsh lines of her life.

At the moment, her eyes did not indicate much capacity for thought but rather profuse emotions. To Klara, Susannah seemed distant, for her eyes stared vacantly out at the world while her inner eyes saw dreams.

Danzig
1788
Chapter Fourteen

They were like a black and white photograph, stern and serious. Their souls were captured, suspended in depressing hard times. The adults were fat, rotund, even though the children were scrawny in thin clothes and shoeless feet. Generational clothing. Used. The high-collared dresses and long sleeves intimately covered the women's bodies. No extra fabric was to be indulged in for frivolous trims or stylish cuts. Functional. The snug jackets for the men had useful pockets and sparse buttons.

Was the lack of joy in the photograph because their smiles would blur their faces? Was it because life lacked happiness?

How anyone survived was a miracle.

"We will no longer be a part of this country or its people's lives but part of Russia!" Katharina and Bernhard sat as still as a photograph on the bench outside the church.

"Hush, Katharina! Watch what you say!"

"They drive us away!"

Even if it is your home, if you feel you are no longer welcome, every moment takes on such a huge and significant meaning.

There were huge tracts of land in the Ukraine waiting for settlement. The Czarina had abolished the Ukrainian state in 1764 and was determined to settle the area. Her Russia needed the fertile lands. The indigenous people were not entitled to say that their resources were for themselves or that their society did not want foreigners. The Czarina promoted her dubious morality on a grand scale, not concerned about any group of individuals. She doled out her decisions lavishly upon a captive nation. The Czarina was generous. After all, the land was hers to give to the Prussian Mennonites. What could be more morally certain than that?

"Is it a foolish dream to think of travelling to a new land and creating a new home?"

"Katharina, I understand and I am carefully considering everything about staying and about leaving. I am not sure. How will we know this is the right decision? There are hints the future in Danzig will be severe."

"The Russian government wants to destroy any idea of Poland. It wants to destroy Danzig, to economically ruin it. That way we will run to Russia for help." Katharina watched the little sharp-boned alley cat stop, spit and hiss at the world, and slip around the corner of the church. "I don't know either if this is a good idea. It is the steppes …"

"… but the land is good near Berislav, yes, yes." He sighed heavily and looked up to the sky for an answer. Not that anyone else viewed the sky as he did; the sky does not move everyone. "The law forbids the sale of property here to Mennonites, and taxes increase each year to support the army."

"Although we are not required to serve in the army, the price we pay is high, unbelievably high," she vented. "Now the government demands we baptize our babies in the state church. It is the death penalty for those who refuse. The persecution will continue and we will live in agony."

Bernhard pressed his lips together. "Agony is lying on the ground starving in a foreign country, Katharina."

The dilemma plunged him into the ocean of human life, only to emerge and be invigorated. Bernhard's assurance grew. "God will provide."

His habitual optimistic resolve was a way of life passed on from generation to generation, but he did not voice his decision.

Katharina's heavy shoulders gave an elaborate shrug, and she started to speak but checked herself. Her frustration was ready to boil over. Her mind swirled with confusion. She reminded herself that not knowing was acceptable and struggled to regain her calm by breathing in the smell of the earthy leaves.

The birds chirped in the next tree. She felt suspended like a swirling leaf trapped in a glistening web. There she hung, in the sparkling morning air as if wishing to return from where she had fallen and unable to do so. She yearned to return to the past, to the past where she felt she belonged, where she had felt no doubt.

If tears were wisdom, then those pearls of wisdom would help them. Tears, like a raindrop upon the cheek, would instantly signify without question a grand moment of insight. Her mother always said the lingering and troubled past could be healed with a courageous heart and a courageous mind. Do not react with panic or denial because then there is no place for courage to take hold. If she was uncertain, she was to pretend she had certainty. Yet, despite a lifetime of her mother's lecturing, Katharina was close to tears, for some plunge and rise quicker than others.

"When life is hard, you feel it more than anything. I can be determined, and I have strength, Bernhard." Katharina forced herself to speak with what she knew was only outward assurance.

The reward for courage is wisdom, and the blessing is faith. Those inner strengths are much admired in others but often not recognized in oneself. Acquiring wisdom is not accomplishing a new skill but recognizing what is already there. Her mother would have been proud of her.

Katharina and Bernhard were both driven by a well-versed belief that one should work hard, seize opportunity, and not dawdle. Major decisions were made carefully and once decided upon there was no delay, for there was always an opportunity to make it better for yourself and others. Do it, and do it now!

This habit became their character, the character of seven holy virtues, and it became their destiny.

When they were both ready, Bernhard spoke. "We will choose a better way to live. God gives us the means to take care of ourselves. It would be best not to tempt his good grace, but to grasp the opportunity God places before us. The authorities will no longer tell us we do not belong in Prussia, because we have chosen to belong to the future."

They experienced the opening of their destiny while still facing the closing. This was not the time of shadows and inexplicable noises, a time of darkness. This was not the time to be afraid.

The tears on their cheeks were the emotional outpouring of the turmoil inside their hearts. They felt as if they were witnessing a vision from God, where a figure stands silently in the doorway and never speaks a word. They stood in awe.

"The spirit of the living God has come to gaze upon our frightened eyes. He is close enough to hear our tired sighs and comfort our endless cries. Lord be with us until we die!"

"God decides when to bring his creations home, or at the very least the direction he wishes us to take."

"Yes, the Lord's will be done." Katharina turned her eyes toward her husband's face and detected a flicker.

She couldn't hide her relief that he had decided.

"Then we will go?"

Zator, Upper Silesia
Sunday, July 23, 1944
Chapter Fifteen

I arrived back at the camp ahead of Peter and Abraham and immediately saw Susannah. She was watching Bruno attend to the elderly and Margita attend to a group of youth. I knew Susannah had disliked Margita from the first moment. I didn't blame her. Margita was one of those odd people who have absolutely no welcoming skills. She ignored people she met and continued conversations around them or demanded they do some task immediately. There was never a "hello" or "how are you?" from her. Brief encounters had shown Susannah that Margita was clever as well as mean, an unfortunate combination. If she wanted something, she grabbed it. Spite poured out of Margita, from her spindly arms and legs to the tight movement of each step she took. She always gave little sermons to the youth instead of simple answers, preened herself on her wisdom, and feigned humility and good will. She was bound by a harsh Protestant work ethic when it came to cleanliness. Children were severely reprimanded if they urinated in the wrong area.

"My father was one of the first to come to the Ukraine ... blah, blah, blah ... history would have stood still if not for my family. We had many animals ..." Her manner was supercilious. I had overheard Margita preaching her creed about the sin of people having pets when the world was in such chaos. It made me wonder how the abandoned cats and dogs fared after entire villages vacated in panic.

I saw Susannah quicken her step to get by Margita, who was using every well-known cliché to turn her current lecture into a marathon. She followed biblical teachings to the letter and believed she loved her neighbours and her enemies equally. If one asked her who those people were, one would find out they were identical. If she was a man, she would be an overbearing minister, but she did the next best thing and married one. Her pontification for the day was about her coat having a single button.

"Why sew on more buttons when one will do the trick," Margita sermonized on the thriftier aspects of life. The excellence she exhibited by persistently being anal and aggressive could only be accounted for by concluding she pursued and perfected her traits deliberately and with the kind of flourish only she possessed. Far be it for her to have good intentions, genuine concern or honest reliability — absolutely not.

"Why don't you volunteer in the hospital?" Margita suggested to her captive audience. "They will be happy to see you work and you will cheer them up."

I didn't even try to figure out what Margita's true motive was for the current suggestion concerning the hospital. As to what Margita would know about cheering anybody up, I had no doubt the answer was nothing. Margita carried with her an intensity waiting to be sprung.

I bet she thinks it is focus and determination. She is the type that does not realize her presence is unsettling and alarming.

To me it seemed Margita never paused to consider her effect on people. She was oblivious to her own behaviour and rationalized people's negative reactions toward her as personal attacks.

I watched Susannah disappear around the corner of the building. I assumed that Peter and Abraham had not found her and would soon return to the camp.

Bruno came up to me and said, "The food is not great today. All we have is cottage cheese."

He was hungry and I could tell his meal of cottage cheese had not satisfied him. It was his job to supervise the camp meals for the refugees with the cook, check the fresh water, watch as the bread was handed out, and keep track of the supplies. He walked among the throng as they consumed their food. It was a trying task when his stomach grumbled.

I nodded.

"Most of the talk focuses on politics. The news is grim for us regardless," he said.

Yes, it seemed to be true. I heard snatches of those conversations all the time. I wondered if knowing the Mennonites as people of faith made Bruno feel disappointed in himself, somehow. I know the sermons frustrated me with constant references to the failure of mankind and the need for redemption. Always needing to improve, always needing to live the faith as a light to the world was exhausting. I was never spiritually sufficient. I had spent years feeling disappointed in myself, but now I didn't care what others thought.

I looked around the camp and saw anger, despondency, filth, and disease, but the eye of the soul can give glimpses of true generosity and slices of hope. God never promised his faithful would not suffer. The promise was God would be there alongside them when they did.

I nodded again to Bruno and moved on to locate Susannah.

****

A relief worker came up to Bruno and whispered, "Did you notice the young man who came to the clinic this afternoon with a wound to his left forearm?"

"That's interesting," responded Bruno, "but hardly a stunning occurrence during the war, don't you think?"

The novelty of this life had worn off. The repetitive familiarity of the war adventure and the exposure to extremes left him feeling he had no chance to live himself. He had a passionate longing to render himself unique and out of the ordinary.

"The director wants you to come now to the clinic."

Bruno resigned himself to the possibility of yet another thankless task. He arrived at Reiner's bedside to find a pale and exhausted patient.

"This man states he was attacked on the road," the director explained. "He managed to fight off his assailants and make his way here to Zator. He has lost a lot of blood."

Bruno looked at the director's thin vertical face with a lack of comprehension. "Yes. He appears fatigued. He was tended to adequately."

Reiner, silent, looked hastily at the director's face.

"Yes, yes," the director stated impatiently, his rabbit-shaped teeth clicked together. "But he wishes to remain here. He wishes to work at the clinic."

Bruno gave a little gasp. "But that is impossible. He is clearly a man of violence." Bruno turned to face Reiner. "Are you baptized? You are probably not even Mennonite."

"It's not unknown for people to change, to convert."

"That may be, but that didn't happen in your case, did it?" Bruno and Reiner's eyes locked. "I think you flee danger, and you may bring it right into the castle. Who is after you?"

"Bruno! Curb your tongue. That's not the way we work. He wants to help; that's all we need to know."

Bruno turned toward Reiner, but the young man had his eyes

closed and appeared unconscious. Bruno looked back at the director and asked, "Do you know more than you are telling me?"

"Absolutely not! I want you to make sure he is cared for properly tonight, Bruno. Come and see me before you turn in for the night!" It was final.

Bruno was dissatisfied, but it was impossible to argue. The director did not normally worry about the individual patients in the clinic. Clearly, he had a special interest in this one. As the aid checked the bandages on Reiner's arm, Bruno turned away in frustration. His role here was as an errand boy. He had no say, ever.

Bruno lacked depth in thought and feeling, and appreciation. It made him quite ordinary. There is much in life to appreciate and if Bruno had been able to reach beyond his insecurity and discontent, he would have found himself unique and not ordinary. Unfortunately, on the steps of the clinic he met Margita.

Her mouth was tightened in a grim line, "What has happened?" she inquired keenly.

"Why?" asked Bruno curiously. "Have you gone anywhere today?" He picked up Casper, who had twined himself around his legs. The cat purred loudly with appreciation.

"I went to the train station to meet new arrivals." Zator was located about 17 kilometers southeast of Oshpitzin near the railroad tracks of Skawina-Oshpitzin, and four kilometers distant from the Spitkowice railroad depot on the line connecting Skawica and Trzebinia. In addition, it was only a few kilometers from Oswiecim or, as the Germans called it, *Auschwitz*. The rail traffic along the line was virtually constant.

"How many new folks for us today?"

"None. The girls that are already here in the camp," Margita motioned west, "returned back to camp by train."

"Why?" Bruno asked in confusion.

"From Auschwitz, they need seamstresses for military uniforms and … "

Bruno had an ominous feeling about that place, and he gaped at Margita. The leaves seemed to never appear on the trees and the blades of grass never grew at Auschwitz. The birds stayed away, except for the crows, which were too crafty to be caught. The reason for it was beyond his imagination; he was totally unaware the starving inmates ate whatever they could get their hands on.

"The girls work," Margita shrugged. "It is work. They go for the work. What of it?" It was a remark devoid of charity, calculating and icy. It came from a shrunken pit of a heart.

"Nothing." Bruno put the cat down and tried to sound as bland as he could. Although one lives collectively in a certain space and time, responsibility, guilt, and forgiveness are individual. Some deeds are wrong even if the ruling government says it is permissible. It was risky business to help anyone though, for the Gestapo agents frequently went undercover and wore civilian clothes. You never knew who was watching you. In addition, the Kapos, the guards the Jews chose from amongst themselves, always watched. Yet, the Germans in the village defied fear by carefully throwing clothing and food into the trenches by the road where the work gangs of Jews could snatch them. Both the Jews and the Germans took a terrible risk with deadly consequences if caught. Bruno could not shake the feeling of unease, of thinking too much, of knowing too much. He became confused and stopped himself from questioning. He realized Margita's piercing glare was far too often and far too accurate in its ability to inflict hurt.

"I hate cats," Margita stated. There was not enough charity or generosity of spirit in her world. There was plenty of blaming and readiness to punish. Her bouts of melancholy became her aesthetic focus. After all, what could be more savoury than hate and personal tragedy?

"So, you wander around and waste your time?" she jabbed. Was it not better to let such remarks fade away and be ignored?

Bruno pulled himself up taller. "I have many important jobs to do," he retorted.

"Perhaps the director does not notice?" She looked him in the eye and he shrivelled.

He dreaded she would take this line. She was the type of person who always told a bad story about how absolutely everything was wrong in the world. She would tell her tale of woe and it was proof one should always be prepared for the worst, especially the worst in mankind.

"What do you mean?"

"You should let me speak to the director on your behalf. I can sing your praises." She waited for his response. His every gesture was a test. She evaluated every situation on whether or not unspoken expectations and opportunities were met. The only way to leave her school was to drop out.

"Why would you do that?" Bruno asked warily, for he was suspicious of her intentions. What often appears to be virtuous behavior is only a disguise.

"It could benefit us both." She was a prevaricator by nature. "Besides, I am sure he has weaknesses. I can find them out."

Despite his reluctance to be near Margita, he realized the sense of what she said. "That never occurred to me," he granted, nodding his head.

"You have to watch for these openings, the way *der Führer* plans a war." Her resentment could never be contained. When people crossed her or even if she thought they had, she regarded it as an attempt to take advantage of her. She would have none of that. Never. She was always on guard.

"I see that," he allowed, not meeting her eye.

"There can be plenty of opportunity for us," she smiled knowingly. Bruno felt a surge of hope, but he could not imagine how Margita could manage to get them beyond this camp of refugees. "I gave up all I had. Now, I am here and I rely on others." The spleen in her voice soured the air.

Bruno could see the acrimony in the lines of her face,

around her mouth, around her eyes, in her soul. Hard lines were everywhere, and make a person grow old. She was proud of her home and independence. Her family had employed workers and her father was therefore considered a kulak, a rich landowner, an enemy of the communist state. Entire families had been sent to Siberia. A number of them managed to flee; some were arrested late at night. Many left widows. She had managed it all and become a woman of stature. She was the daughter of a wealthy man and the widow of an even wealthier husband. But not now. Now, she groveled as a pauper, worked as a servant and depended on others for everything.

It is amazing how defects, evil passions and moral disease seem to have an almost genetic quality. Mean tendencies are deftly handed down from generation to generation. Margarita's parents and grandparents flashed through her. The hereditary resemblance was remarkable, but it was a learned maliciousness not a genetic birthmark.

"Will the director help you?"

"They try to help everyone, and besides he will need a housekeeper." She spoke with resolve. Her life was filled with work she did not want. She believed she would get ahead, like a card player, by laying down a winning pair of cards. Luck and skill would see that damned *Schwarze Peter* in someone else's hand at the end of the game. She never realized the black card in her heart was bitterness, a constant sense of being wronged while believing others were too fortunate.

After her husband's death, she'd revelled in her ability to be not assertive, but aggressive. She was unnecessarily abrupt and defensive. Was she rude because she did not indulge in idle chitchat? For her, mundane was almost too much to bear. Why did people talk about gardening anyway? Who cared if your tomatoes ripened? Is that what a bitch was—someone who rejects happiness and excitement about cucumbers? She delighted in her quick wit. In reality, she was nasty with her tongue. She laughed when she was called a bitch. She was a bitch. To her it was an achievement and an affirmation that no one would better her. She had it figured out — bitchy, self-absorbed and entitled.

Bruno shook his head. "That work is not enough. You will need money."

"For what? There is little to buy, Bruno. What is needed is a prospect."

They were interrupted by a camp worker who wished to question Bruno regarding the vegetables for the evening meal. It was obvious the worker had no desire to acknowledge Margita, who stood by impatiently. Bruno solved the problem and silence fell between the three of them. It didn't last long and was broken hurriedly as Margita was extremely uncomfortable with silence.

"Okay, okay. It's good you are here Bruno or else no work would get done." Here she was again, unfortunately excluded, listening to a conversation about garden vegetables, one more time. It left her with a dissociative type experience.

She stared directly at the random worker who turned on her heel and stomped away. One did not talk to randoms. Margita gazed calmly after her with satisfaction. She lived on several levels but there was something she missed on the human level.

Bruno waited. There was always that extra comment that came after such an interaction. He waited.

As Margita stood beside Bruno, she stank with antagonism. How dare this person ignore her! She assumed people would prefer to leave her out, but their internal etiquette gauge would be set at rude and they would be unable to function; therefore, she was included. But to be totally overlooked! It was too much. People were mean and unfeeling. Didn't they know how much she sacrificed? Could they not see how hard she worked and how much she deserved?

It did not matter that her words cut, that she slapped small children, and that she swore at their mothers and told them they were cunts and unfit to parent. She had beaten her husband down with guilt and self-doubt, and so he had begun to defend her in the fight against the world. She let everyone know she was a victim. The damage the two of them had inflicted was senseless.

"Bitch," Margita spat.

Yes, there it was. That is what you call follow-through.

Margita watched the worker walk away. The sad fact was Margita wanted to be with people more than they ever wanted to be with her. It embarrassed her. The longing to be accepted, to truly belong and to be loved passionately by a whole group of friends was a secret dream. Yet, when she did spend time with people she was overwhelmed. Margita had long ago come to the sad realization that when people got to know her better they found her wanting. Why was coming to the point directly and probing further such a threat to people? Why were people offended when urged to be organized, efficient, intelligent, concise and explanatory? She lived with passion. She was tired of being misunderstood. People always viewed her as upset and irritated. It was depressing to be constantly told she was difficult and unhappy, that she lacked social skill, and that her presence was a strain.

The constant was herself. It dismayed her. Even though life and joy would fling its arms out to her and tempt her to embrace happiness, it would never happen. Joy would shrink back appalled and in mourning, race to the dungeon of her heart. There it would stay shackled, where it had long been bound.

She had searched and what had she found? She found people unforgiving and always assuming the worst. She became what she had perceived, not what actually was. Her face hardened. She snapped at Bruno, "Everything changes, even if it gets worse. Change will come." Her comment carried no hope.

Frozen thoughts destroy.

Life in Russia had been lived as a shared misery. Hopelessness rends people from their family and from humanity, and those people vanish, never to reappear even though they are still physically present.

Margita prayed that vengeful fate would be her friend. The ugliness crept onto her face, into the thin tight line of her lips, and her eyes shared a bitterness as black as joy was bright. For Margita, resolution and reconciliation meant dry tears and revenge. And here, in the camp, she had begun to truly rebel. It was a delicious feeling. Ignoring morality left her with a feeling of freedom almost wicked in its intensity. She scurried away.

Ill feeling, wherever it exists, is a slow and insidious poison that strangles life.

Zator, Upper Silesia
Sunday, July 23, 1944
Chapter Sixteen

Susannah had promised her friends she would keep the knowledge of what happened a secret, but she needed to account for all those hours away and she was more terrified of Vater than of her friends. She was so disconcerted that she actually told the truth and recounted the whole story to him.

Peter seemed to relish the tale and pressed her for details. His hyper-arousal astonished her.

"Take me there!" he commanded.

It took hours to find the forest location and the corpses in the darkness. Vater was vigilant and immediately searched the pockets, finding a few *Pfenning*. He felt justified in pilfering. "Look at these!" He was thrilled with the daggers. Vater had never acted this erratic before and it confused Susannah. He no longer avoided traumatic scenes as he used to, but appeared to be numb to them. The bodies lay still in their black attire.

Susannah looked upon the scene with incredulity. Her perception of the multitude of horrific experiences that persistently came her way was a struggle. It was difficult for her to draw a breath without feeling a vicious lump in her throat.

"The Vis pistols should be left as they are too obvious to carry," Peter decided. "Strip that one down," he instructed Susannah as he began on the other corpse. "Take off all the clothing! Hurry!" The inert bulks were cumbersome and unfamiliar to handle. "Leave the uniforms." He spoke without any emotion as he wrapped the daggers with the underclothes and the socks into a bundle. "Come on! Hurry! Drag them back into the bush."

He was brash and chatty as they walked back to the camp.

By the wall of the clinic, Susannah found her mother with the boys. Peter grinned broadly, whispered in Eleni's ear, and squeezed her hand.

"Don't let anyone know what you have!" said Eleni.

He lit one of the *Sorte R6* cigarettes from the pack he had taken off the corpses.

Eleni grabbed the pack. "Where did you get these?"

"Relax," Peter snapped and grabbed back the cigarettes. "A little gift from Hamburg. Reemtsma makes a good cigarette," he chuckled.

Eleni shook her head. "I am going to put Heinchen to bed." So, the family would stay at the camp after all. Most of the camp was settling down for the night. It was a type of community despite the hardships and that was more important than people realized. "Come with Susannah when you are done with your cigarette. We have the same spot to sleep as last night." Eleni left to create a nest for her family.

****

Susannah was so weary that she lay down on the ground. Up before first light, she had witnessed, again, a lifetime of drama in only one day. She was asleep as soon as her head rested on the ground but was jarred awake by violent yelling. She looked up to see two black figures walking through the camp. Bruno's hurried steps hopped ahead of them. He carried a lantern. They were obviously looking for someone. She gasped and thought for a second the corpses had come back to life. The two SS stopped before Vater.

"You are Peter Wiebe from Chortitza?" the taller dark-haired one spoke.

"No," Peter lied. "Not me."

The other SS soldier stood with a careless ease that comes naturally when one is young and arrogant. He stood with his blonde head a little bit to one side. His broad shoulders and chest challenged the world. His left arm came forward to draw attention to the swastika in the white circle on the red banner around his upper arm. He hooked his thumbs in his belt and placed his weight on his right leg while resting the other to the side in a gesture of power and privilege.

The dark soldier pushed Peter aside, grabbed the clothes bundle and pulled it apart. The two daggers fell out. He stared at Peter.

In another time, his face would be considered kind with a pleasantly curious and intelligent countenance. His nose was prominent in a Roman type of way. The thin wavy lips, but not too thin to be austere, easily curved into a genuine smile like when you pose for a photograph while holding a soft grey kitten in the crook of your arm. Except, there was no kitten, there was no kindness. The lips became a grimace. "And these are yours, Peter Wiebe?"

"I have never seen them. I do not know anything about

them. I found the bundle on the ground when we were out for a stroll. The weather is changing. It will be winter soon and I thought those old clothes might help in the kitchen."

Too much talk, the hallmark of guilt and stupidity.

He is trying to make them think that all is well. He is a fool to deny it, Susannah thought. *He should tell them the truth. They will make him tell the truth.*

The taller SS soldier spoke again. "You were seen coming from the forest." His voice became a menace. A warning. Trained to be unyielding, all signs of weakness such as tears and pity were suppressed. Psychological death needs the amputation of the soul. For this operation, intimidation is the means and the personal childhood upbringing is the theatre. He didn't care what Peter said. People moved away from the four of them.

"I went for a stroll with my daughter," Peter replied apprehensively.

The soldier nodded. "Yes, she was seen coming from the forest too."

The blonde-haired soldier smiled the entire time, a straight-line smile with the corners of his mouth turned down disdainfully.

The skin of his face was as flawless and transparent as an innocent child. There was not a crease or a wrinkle anywhere. It hurt to look at the perfection of the broad forehead and aquiline nose because the effect was breathtakingly raw and enticing. Here was clean passion in the leopard-like movement and physique. But malevolent eyes never lie.

He moved with incredible suddenness. He grabbed Peter's throat in a muscular clamp and pushed him up against the wall. Someone screamed. Susannah saw the gleam of metal across the man's knuckles. He drew back his arm and struck a vicious blow to Peter's stomach. Peter's face turned white with pain. He would have slumped to the ground but the other SS soldier held him against the stone wall. This time the beating went to his face. There was an unnatural crunch. Susannah wanted to shriek. She had always thought of Vater as omnipotent and terrifying but here he was helpless and defenceless.

The Director appeared with a lantern. "What's happening here?" he asked in a tone of cautious authority.

"None of your concern," the SS replied without looking up. He struck Peter in the back of the head. There was no compassion or control; his behaviour was the *Zeitgeist* of the era.

"Stop! Stop!" the director insisted. His reason and restraint were small barriers for the SS to overcome. Most people lived in fear of being disobedient and were bullied into submission by the brutish Nazi party, but not these two SS soldiers. Under Hitler, no matter what the directive, orders were meant to be obeyed, for Hitler was a protective, competent, even omnipotent, fatherly figure. He had created a public past that would be opposed in years to come, but not now, not in 1944.

The soldier turned. The Nazi machine held him captive and he was totally unaware that the words he spoke were not his own but Adolf Hitler's. "Who do you think you are?" His tone was even, but there was an edge to it.

The director disliked the arrogance of the SS immediately. "I am the director of this camp and the international laws state this brutality cannot go on." His glasses flashed in the light as he turned back and forth between the two SS.

"You should mind your own business as this is the Führer's business." The Nazi genius of Adolf Hitler's *Führerprinzip* rationalized every response. It was ideological trickery, successfully obscuring the crude realities of modern despotism.

Many of the members of the SS came from ordinary organizations such as the Order Police. In Hamburg, the city of origin for these two soldiers, the 500 police members of the 101 Battalion, were recruited from dock-workers, truck drivers, and construction workers, hence, the tragic conformity of commonplace men to do the bidding of the Nazi state.

"I suppose you think you can do what you like while you wear those uniforms," said the director.

The two SS exchanged looks and broke into laughter, "Yeah," they hooted, nodding to each other. "We did in Prague!"

In Prague, the Nazis shot 38,000 Jews and deported a further 45,000 to the Treblinka extermination camp. To persecute was an appeal to the siege mentality of war. Yet, specific police excused themselves by choosing alternate assignments and a significant number were not involved in the shooting or refused to continue. An emotionally healthy adult society does not comply with the execution of atrocities. Nevertheless, the pressure of the peer group set social and moral norms to help enough men complete the transformation into genocidal executioners. Extraordinary

Pacification Action was the Nazi euphemism for mass murder and it was deemed acceptable. Jews were outsiders, like refugees, like Peter.

The director motioned to Bruno. "Hurry and get the baron. If this man is to be murdered, I want a witness to it." His action was a momentary and courageous exception to blind obedience and acquiescence.

The SS soldier spoke softly, "Stop." He put out his hand. The effect was unnerving. "Herr Wiebe has decided to lead us to the place where he found these two daggers. Is that not right, Herr Wiebe?"

Peter did not speak, but his bloody head nodded.

"Along with the daughter who was with him." Susannah's sharp intake of breath drew notice. "This ugly one, obviously." The black clad thug clutched her arm like a vice and drew her to her feet.

The other soldier dragged Peter along. "We will look after them. Do not concern yourself," he said to the director.

The director did not pursue the matter. Despite his attempt to speak up, boldness was not his forte. "Do what they say," the director pleaded as he watched Peter and Susannah being led off to the forest. "We have been dominated by tyrants, monarchs, communists, anarchists, revolutionaries, and now the supreme Schutzstaffel, the SS."

Peter was in no shape to navigate. He moaned like the eerie night wind as the group disappeared into the forest. Susannah could hear him snorting through his broken nose. She prayed frantically that she would find the way again by the light of the lanterns. She did.

One SS soldier pushed Susannah and Peter up against a tree while the other pulled the bodies of their compatriots out from under the bush. "Two dead. This is Reiner's doing."

"Reiner must have the evil luck of a Jew."

Susannah realized the two SS soldiers did not know about her other three friends. They turned to look at her. "Was anything mentioned about a document?"

"No," she blurted. A little hysterical laugh followed. She was close to losing control. "I closed my eyes, down, I mean. I didn't see. I didn't hear. I wasn't listening. I wouldn't listen. I don't know anything!"

"He probably still has it," the man said to his ally.

"We don't know where Reiner has gone."

"We must think of a plan. We cannot go back to Fürstenstein empty-handed. If we don't find it, we'll end up behind a desk."

"A desk?" The response came out as an incredulous snort. "That would be lucky."

There was an abrupt thrashing in the forest as Peter raced away in the dark.

"Forget it, Manfred. It would take too much effort to kill him. He has no meaning now. We can always have fun with him later. He's not going anywhere."

He jerked his head towards Susannah. "What about the little *Fotze?*"

Zator, Upper Silesia
Sunday July 23, 1944
Chapter Seventeen

Gerhard whispered, "There was quite a commotion outside." His eyes narrowed as he watched Reiner. "The SS have given our little camp a visit. It is lucky for you that few people noticed you walk into the camp."

Reiner drew his breath in sharply as he glanced toward the door.

"They've gone now."

"How do you know?"

"I watched the entire incident." Gerhard spoke with *Schadenfreude,* a particular feeling of gladness that bad luck is not happening to you but to someone else. He delighted in Peter Wiebe's misfortune. "I pay attention to what is happening. I am not an idiot."

"Just someone who has lost the documents," Reiner hissed in return.

"They will be found. No one goes far from here. They are here."

"You don't know that!" Reiner's whisper escalated.

"By all that is damned I do know!" Gerhard leaned over Reiner's hospital bed. "Peter Wiebe has information, and I will find out what he knows."

Reiner closed his eyes. His face was white. "Who's Peter Wiebe? What does he know?"

"Peter Wiebe? He's in the camp. He's the one the SS took to the forest. I have a feeling he is linked to all of this. They mentioned Wüstewaltersdorf and Fürstenstein."

"This Peter, he came back from the forest alive?" Reiner countered incredulously.

"Yes," sniffed Gerhard. "He's alive, a little damaged. I saw him running around the camp looking for that bitch."

"I should never have trusted you with the papers." Reiner broke into an unnatural sweat.

"But you did, Reiner, and it was to your advantage that we met on the road. You are ridiculously honest. They would have caught you by now. It was good I recognized your name," Gerhard snickered.

"What do you mean my name? What do you know about my

family?"

"Oh, quite a lot in fact. Aren't coincidences funny? The village you come from? Boleslawiec, wasn't it? Who would have thought your family would be noteworthy? Some of your relatives have already left Germany? Left the motherland, is that not so? You aristocrats are all the same. Traitors."

"What!" Reiner sputtered and yelped as the sudden motion made his wound ache.

"This palace here in Zator, this camp, is not the only castle you are familiar with. I hear that Kliczcow castle is a beautiful place," teased Gerhard.

The light reflected off the dirty windows and sent vomitus green and putrid yellow tinges into the room. It cloaked the two men in paranoia and resentment. Deliberate hate emanated from Gerhard.

Reiner gasped, "You don't know what you're talking about!"

"I am right and you are wrong" Gerhard hissed. He motioned the helper away who had appeared to check that things were in hand.

Gerhard scoffed as he leaned over Reiner. "Watch how you behave! Who's the idiot now? You don't think I helped you on the road because you were lost, did you? People like you can be invaluable when properly motivated. You will be of infinite use to me. You were right. This is a great opportunity for me and for the SS?" Gerhard raised his eyebrows knowingly.

Reiner made a motion toward Gerhard.

"Tsk, tsk, none of that," Gerhard mocked. "You'll hurt yourself." He squeezed Reiner's arm, leaving him gasping with the pain. "It is not only you who had documents worth having. In with your unfortunate blueprints was a valuable letter of mine from Canada via my relative near Kliczcow."

"You have no letter! Those stupid papers aren't that valuable," Reiner spoke with a forced casual effort.

"You think your diagrams of farm buildings and trenches …"

"Farm buildings! Idiot! It's Hitler's new …" He brought himself up short.

Gerhard was indignant at the interruption. "What? What do you say?" Gerhard leant forward. His eyes narrowed.

"What do you mean?" Reiner shifted in his bed. Beads of perspiration glistened on his forehead.

"Yes, strange connection, is it not, Reiner?" Gerhard snarled. "Imagine how a seemingly innocent letter from Canada came to your prestigious home. They are the allied forces now, isn't that the term? Hah! It is easy enough to say my letter that slipped into your papers is treason. Your treason. Everything is treason to this government. Russian or other correspondence, they will not even wait for your explanation, and now you say that you have plans of Hitler's …. hmmm," Gerhard paused for emphasis. "They will hang you with piano wire when they get their hands on everything, Reiner!"

Reiner became apoplectic. "You fool. I have nothing!" Reiner pointed his finger at Gerhard. "*You* have nothing."

"I will get the papers. Your little plan will go ahead whatever it is," Gerhard nodded his head with conviction. "You will pay me for my silence. You will do that, Reiner. After all, I saved your life."

"You idiot!" Reiner hissed. "Have you not heard what happened? The attempt was a failure. Hitler survived and walked on the same day. He believes he is omnipotent and now the SS search far and wide, taking anyone they think is involved." Reiner's breathing came too fast. He gulped out, "If they even think ... you know what they will do ... July 20th assassination attempt was a failure. Those blueprints are a way to inflict wounds on the Nazi stranglehold."

Gerhard pressed his lips together and raised his eyebrows.

"You should think about what you are doing, Gerhard," whispered Reiner.

"Always thinking about what you should do takes away so many opportunities for sweet revenge and delicious greed, Reiner." Gerhard gave a quick nod.

"It was for the Resistance," pleaded Reiner, "for my nation. It is the expression of the real will and attitude of the true people here in this land."

"Bah," spat Gerhard. "You think that? There will only be a nation whose memories are German. There is no legitimacy for your activities. You talk like it is a national identity project. You talk as if it is a universal struggle to fight the monsters of the world, a war between good and evil!" Gerhard laughed.

"People choose evil, Gerhard," Reiner spoke evenly as he

tried to stare him in the eye. "People actually do choose evil. Demonizing those people as simply monsters who commit evil lets them off the hook too easily."

Gerhard smirked.

"I am on the right side!" Reiner tried to sit up straighter. "Resistance fighters will be the bearers of the memory. We have achieved the privileged status of deciding what is to be done, remembered, and what is to be forgotten."

Gerhard could not have cared less for heroics. He actually laughed with delight and mocked, "You truly are idealistic. You are so naïve. You make these sweeping generalizations and think you are ... what?" Gerhard put his weight on Reiner's arm, "that you are attractive and fresh?"

Reiner clamped his mouth shut to hold in the scream of pain.

"I will find those papers, Reiner. Your name is on those papers I believe? Yes?" Gerhard inclined his head to one side. "No? Well, it is a little matter to write it on there ... somewhere. *Ein Hund lebt ebenso lange wie seine Zähne.* How unfortunate ... for you. Besides, I am sure of what I need to do. You will help me find them and I will use my papers ... and yours to make a better life,"

Gerhard stared at Reiner with a grim look. "Yes. You will help me and I will …" He shrugged his shoulders, turned on his heels and left the clinic.

Reiner listened to Gerhard's retreating tread. His chest felt constricted, and the perspiration ran down his face. Knowing he had to survive, Reiner turned away from himself, determined to complete the task at hand, to defeat the Nazis. Reiner's task was to spot the growing edge of the crisis and figure out the possibilities by examining current failures. He felt justified in hating Gerhard and felt no guilt for his loathing. Behind Reiner's wall of frustration lay the path to make his own luck, the way of opportunity.

****

I was anxiously looking for Peter and Susannah when Gerhard marched passed me. Casper skittered under the clinic building to get out of Gerhard's way. I thought it was strange that Gerhard should have a connection with any patient in the clinic. The distant flags of warning in my head waved furiously, but I ignored them, and instead waited until the pounding of my heart slowed. I felt as exhausted as if I had laboured all day long.

"Again, *this* is my life," I murmured to myself. "Take each day, each moment. Life is hard enough, don't think so much." My unwelcome and unbidden memories flooded back to me. "The soldiers always take them away in the night," I whispered peering into the darkness. "If there were enough tears, we would all drown in waves of wretchedness."

I remembered Heinrich, my husband. I remembered my wedding night and how I had turned my face away from the door as he snapped off the electrical light. How was it possible to be close to someone and then lose them? Later, in the dead of the night, the Russians took him away.

I was tremendously relieved to see Susannah back in camp, but someone had said the SS roamed about. Had they taken Peter, too? I slid down the wall of the clinic to sit on the ground in the darkness, I hugged Abraham and Heinchen, who had not gone to sleep, closer to me and remembered the day the village had found out that Heinrich and all the men had been shot. Every single one of them, shot. Shot the day they were taken, outside the village. During all those visits to the prison gate, Heinrich had already been long dead and yet, the Russians had taken the food I'd brought for him anyway. Our family had been utterly devastated. They had even felt betrayed — how skewed was their set of values! Of course, the soldiers took the food when the Russians already knew the prisoners were dead! Of course they would. Our personal shock at the Russians behaviour had been ludicrous in retrospect.

Gobs of sadness engulfed me. I existed and lived where the wingtips of the Past and Future intertwined, the Present. "Life is difficult. Make the best of it. That is all you can do. That's the difficult part," I whispered, gulping down my breath to hold back the tears.

In disbelief, I discerned the limping figure of Peter coming toward the clinic. I rushed to meet him. "Look what they have done to you!"

"I have been around the camp looking for you, Eleni."

"They have beaten you." My body shook from the harsh reality. "Poor man." By prefacing the word, man, with poor, I changed its entire meaning, poor women, poor child, but not poor psychopath. I held no sympathy for the SS, instead, I let out a faint gasp filled with empathy for Peter, a gentle, true response.

****

The door to the clinic closed softly. Unseen, Susannah moved toward the bed where Reiner lay with open eyes.

"It seems safe in here," she spoke with a nervous little laugh. Her memory of the SS snickering, "let the *Fotze* go" and "I wasn't born to rape little girls", was fresh in her head. The man had let her loose and given her a shove, making her stagger and hit the tree. "Run, run," he had laughed at her, adding, "Today is your day of grace, blessing, and luck." The scene spun in her head. She had chased after Peter and nearly beaten him back to the camp.

"You seem upset?" Reiner forced himself to reply; nevertheless, his expression was one of condescension.

It was entirely involuntary, but she could feel the muscles of her face, especially her mouth, tighten to the point of spasm. She could sense there was something odd about him, as it is with people who are wound taut and ready to snap.

"Oh," she responded breathlessly, "I came to see how you were doing. You seem ... are you ... I mean how ... does the arm still hurt?" To her, coming to the clinic seemed a somewhat obvious destination, but now that she was here she had no idea why she was talking to Reiner.

"The arm will heal." The conversation descended into the false giving of information. They were like dancers looking for a chance to hook up with a better partner. Still, they seemed unable to break their connection. Reiner forced himself to speak about the camp happenings and families.

Susannah seemed as agitated as Reiner. Impulsively, she blurted out, "I wish I had never taken that satchel!"

The dim light did not show how his face paled. "Come sit here quietly on the bed," Reiner responded alertly. He took the care now to foster a detailed discussion. But Susannah spoke because she was nervous. She wasn't listening.

"Oh!" Susannah jumped up. "I have to go now!"

"What! So sudden?" Reiner made an effort to smile and took her hand.

"Yes, yes. I have to go," Susannah pulled her hand away, but slowly.

Reiner could see there was no point in pressing her. "Come

tomorrow," he pleaded in a smooth tone that was the total opposite of his initial response to her presence. "Your beauty heals me. We will go out for a walk. I need a change."

Speechless, Susannah blushed with confusion and nodded. Stupid girl. She couldn't see the manipulation of her knight in shining armour, not that it would have mattered. Her inner turmoil would have responded the same way.

The next morning, their black shadows stretched out behind them on the hard and brutalized ground as they walked. Reiner tried for over an hour to bring the conversation around to the topic of Peter Wiebe.

Finally, Susannah broke her silence. "So much has happened and it keeps piling up!" She spoke with an odd little rasp. "Oh, I'll tell you more, Reiner. It has weighed on me. Promise you won't tell a soul. Not anyone?"

Reiner looked the image of innocence and trust. He tilted his head to the side and smiled. He felt close to getting his dream back on track.

"I am looking for a safe place, Reiner. I can't stand it anymore. The world is full of thugs. Why do they hurt people? They should be put away so they cannot harm anyone."

The diversion of the conversation nearly put Reiner over the edge himself. He looked at her, and smiled, and nodded. It took all his effort.

"How can anyone of us help when we feel as if we have been scraped bare?" Susannah moaned.

Reiner took a deep slow breath. "Yes, we should help each other instead … We can make some small things right …"

"It's too hard. I want to live like a happy story in a book. I feel stuck," she groaned.

"That's just it," Reiner leapt at the opportunity. "Let me help you fix that little … incident with the satchel you referred to last night." He could visualize the presence of his precious papers. He forced himself to concentrate on his breathing.

"You won't tell, Reiner, will you?"

Reiner nodded his head to encourage her to continue speaking. It was so intense; it was almost comical. Susannah looked at him skeptically and sighed again. Reiner forced himself to concentrate on composing his face, but his hands clenched tight with frustration.

"I took the satchel Gerhard is always rants about. Vater threatened me. I was terrified. I had to do it. You won't tell, will you?"

Casually, Reiner probed. "The satchel, what did you do with it?" Close. He was close.

"I told you, Vater made me take it." She fussed with her hair, looked absently at the clouds, took a leaf from a tree, and made Reiner repeat himself a few times.

"Your father has it?" Reiner forced himself to walk steadily.

Susannah stared at the huge knots in the tree trunks. They looked like horse collars. They reminded her of the horse collars they used back home in the Ukraine.

"Susannah?" He wished he could put his hands around her neck and strangle her to get the information. He understood how difficult Susannah could be, but he instinctively realized he had to make her feel safe instead. He dug deep to be a safe confidant with the trusting brown eyes whom anyone would fall in love with instantly. He led her thinking and hinted at her worries with sensitivity to help her overcome her doubts.

Susannah hesitated, "No, Mutti took the contents and threw

213

the satchel away. What does that matter anyway? You're not going to tell anyone, are you?"

Susannah's reddish blonde hair shone in the sunlight.

"Of course not, sweetheart," he pulled her close and stroked her hair.

His thoughts spun with the information while Susannah gazed into the distance. She turned her face toward him. At the beginning of every relationship there is a chance things will plunge into a rapid ill-omened descent, and they did. He stood with such a look of hardness on his face that she was immediately filled with fear and dismay.

Dubrovna, Mogliev
1789
Another Dream
Chapter Eighteen

She closed the top of her carrying case. The clasps snapped shut with precision.

"OH!" she gasped loudly; her hands flew to her chest. "I didn't see you standing there." She laughed as her mind whirled, trying to cover.

How can I have missed him?

Had he seen anything? She admonished herself harshly.

Indeed, his bulk loomed outside the bedroom door. He was tilting slightly to his right, leaning his huge frame up against the hallway wall outside the room in a casual and seemingly safe posture. Feet and legs were crossed. He was massive. His head would pass just under the door-frame — had he chosen to come in, but he didn't. He smiled a small, quiet smile. His suspenders stretched from the grey uniform pants up over his stomach and chest.

Who wears a plaid undershirt?

She launched into an animated dialogue in an attempt to

gain composure. His bare arms hung like massive truncheons beside the trunk of his body.

"Yes, yes, all packed up and ready to go in a bit."

She smiled and put up one finger, laughing as she moved toward the door to playfully close it. She laughed again as she shut the door gently with him on the outside. Her panic was barely contained. She shut her eyes and took a deep breath.

No, no. Pull yourself together.

She rapidly forced herself to focus.

You can do this. Keep your wits. Make sure everything is packed. Get it and go. Bernhard is waiting for you to come with everything. You both will make it. You both will be together.

It was a small room with a single bed in the middle. She moved back to the opposite side of the bed. The blank wall was behind her. The suitcase was in front of her on the bed. The suitcase handle faced toward her. She glanced across the bed to the empty wardrobe on the other wall. The door beside the wardrobe was still closed. A slit of light shone on the floor from the hallway. The second bag was beside her on the floor. Opposite the foot of the bed was a curved dresser. It was a quiet room, apparently innocent. She put on a sweater, and over top she put on his dinner jacket. It fit now with the extra bulk underneath.

I must make sure he gets his jacket.

She felt the necessity of not leaving the jacket behind. On top of that she drew on the great coat, which managed now to fit over the wool dinner jacket.

She felt a presence.

He had entered, again, through the door. He was in the room. He stood beside the wardrobe. His massive bulk blocked the light from outside the room. He leered. There was nothing casual about this posture, not this time. She hadn't even heard the door open. In the instant he moved, she moved too but more quickly.

As he moved into the gap between the end of the bed and the dresser, turning slightly sideways, her instinct allowed her to dart through the slit his sideways movement created.

"Oh, there you are uncle!" she laughed and threw the mass a quick smile with a nod. "Can't you hear him coming? He is coming down the side of the house. Great!"

Her ruse caused him to hesitate, and he made no move to stop her flight out of the room. Turn right, two steps down the glass-enclosed hall and out the back door. She ran down the side of the house. She ran across the small front yard. She could feel the house behind her. The front windows watched her.

Run!

Out into the busy street.

Keep going!

Into the traffic and duck behind a tall wagon waiting for the traffic congestion in the intersection to clear. The wagon concealed her. She stopped. She could feel the house desperately scan the direction of her flight, but it could no longer see her. Luck. The wagon moved slowly. She walked alongside it until she got to where the road split. A short distance. She dashed out of the traffic and darted up the street toward the grey stone building.

My luggage, my money, oh, my documents!

She pressed herself against the cool grey stone.

I must get them!

She battled the powerful impulse to return. She peered around the corner of the building. The house appeared to be resting. It looked chaste. Nothing bad ever happened there.

You are crazy. You cannot go back. What if he catches you

inside? You will never get away.

Her thoughts fought a duel.

I need my papers.

Her distress wailed and wailed. Images of imprisonment in the bedroom loomed before her. She could not return. Folly. But she was naked without the travel documents. She stood on the street, in her sweater, jacket, and great overcoat, and waited, struggling to control her thoughts. She had visions of soldiers trudging on in their great coats through the death of winter in the war. She could see them lying down in the snow, in their great grey coats.

Katharina woke with a start.

Dreams can be so real.

She stared at the familiar and decrepit ceiling. Five winter months waiting in Dubrovna, Mogliev! Emotionally, she was in a room that she had entered but was not ready to inhabit, instead she needed to stay in that room for awhile — and not for catharsis either, but to de-reflect, not self-confess. The journey had been so hard. She struggled to be more wise and courageous about their future life in the Ukraine. She tried to move beyond herself the way an accomplished actor does on the stage.

On the day that Bernhard had finally decided, she could still remember the determination on his brow and how he had spat on the ground saying, "We will leave this land and never return, not us nor any of our family."

They left in secret, for the Prussian government had not been in favour of Catherine the Great's plan. After the torturous route from Danzig to Riga, a total of five weeks trekking through the mud, they now waited for the uncaring Dnieper River to take the necessary barges south. Wait they must. Nevertheless, the tightly knit group of Mennonites kept to their plan.

The Russians didn't.

In Kremenchug, the Russian government issued the bad news. The announcement would reach Katharina and Bernhard when they arrived in the Ukraine; unfortunately, it would be consistent with the 34-year chaotic reign of Catherine the Great.

Zator, Upper Silesia
August, 1944
Chapter Nineteen

The group of men outside the clinic stared at the sky.

"The weather is excellent."

"The conditions are nearly ideal for bombing!"

"Nothing will obstruct their view."

"They will be accurate today."

Heavy bombers released destruction, and inevitably, stray bombs struck rail spurs. Whether intentional or not, it made close observation of the severed lines and frequent rebombing by the Allied military necessary. However, efficient rail repairs by the Germans meant the lines and even bridges were often back in operation in three days. From July, through to November, more than 2,800 bombers would hit areas close to Zator.

Reiner's gaunt frame stepped out of the clinic in the late morning. His fever, the result of the terrible infection in his wound, had finally subsided. His ill health gave him a shocking and desperate demeanour that made people avoid conversing with him. The group of men moved slowly away.

Reiner leaned against the clinic wall and lit a cigarette, a German cigarette. He turned it sideways and looked at the slim roll. *Postillion Zigaretten. G. Zuban aus München. Orientalische Tabaken.* The oriental cigarette in the German packaging, probably from Macedonian or Turkish tobacco, made him snort with contempt. He thought sarcastically, *German. Made with quality. Disgusting.*

Up until 1939, he had procured the finest English Dunhill tobacco from von Eicken in Hamburg. The previous year, a royal warrant from King George VI was received by the firm, but the Nazis put a stop to that. Germany declared war in 1939 and Dunhill tobacco was not spared. The store was bombed in 1941. Reiner looked in his pack of ten cigarettes. The last one. He demolished the now empty pack in his fist and threw it on the ground in frustration.

Casper, who had been laying in the shadows, pounced on the pack. Reiner stared at the cat briefly and flicked his gaze up to the sky where American heavy bombers flew.

They rendezvoused at normal bombing altitudes after dropping leftover bombs. Railroads were not the number one target this Sunday in August. One hundred and twenty-seven Flying

Fortresses, escorted by 100 Mustang fighters, had successfully dropped 1,336 500-pound high-explosive bombs on the factory target areas of Auschwitz less than five miles to the east of the concentration camp gas chambers and another six miles from Zator. He could smell the death stench in the air. The German anti-aircraft fire at this hotbed of American bombing activity was negligible. Only one American bomber had gone down; no Mustangs were hit.

Reiner paid slight attention to the minimal flak resistance he heard from the direction of Auschwitz but the cacophony of bombing grated on his nerves. While cheering on the Allies, he cursed his personal bad luck in not finding his documents. He believed the papers were with Eleni or Peter. Hoping helped, just. He barely held on to his dreams.

He tried to encourage himself by recalling better times. *You will succeed. You are wonderful. Kind. Generous. Even in these times, that can be you.*

He grasped the memory of a miraculous moment when he had seen a piece of modern art inspired from watching concentric circles form on the surface of lake water. It was those concentric circles of colour and light that fuelled the creation of masterpieces.

The images could seep into the openings of his soul, however minute, and manage to fill him with satisfaction.

Happiness is not beyond my reach.

Reiner sneered. The aesthete cannot be permanently happy merely by making life a collection of satisfying and best moments.

What I dream of ... the future I dream of ... it will happen.

Beads of perspiration fell from his forehead. In his mind he could see those in the Zator camp, especially Susannah with her guilt, and Gerhard with his hatred and terrifying anger. It was impossible for him to demand the papers back because that would alert Eleni and Peter to their importance. Gerhard was always a nasty consideration. They might play him off against Gerhard. Susannah was tricky; Reiner planned how he would work on her.

I will win.

****

His mind drifted back to his capture at Wolfsberg, to the time before he had escaped and been pursued by the Waffen SS.

Despite the beating from the soldiers, he had avowed with a

steady voice, "I have a task set before me."

The two SS men had raised their eyebrows and snickered in response.

"You Nazis," he had spat, "do not understand. You have discarded freedom. You are an act of destruction turning inward. Eventually, you will succumb to anguish."

Many Germans tried to halt the terrible direction of the Nazi party. In the last free election of 1932, 67 percent of the German people voted against Hitler. Between 1933 and 1945, approximately three million Germans were held in concentration camps for varying lengths of time for political reasons. Confronted by a Reich that knew the true core and avenue of power over others was the political arena, the Munich University students who protested with their White Rose pamphlets were beheaded.

The SS soldier's reply to Reiner's retort had been equally dramatic as if they had parts in a play. "Anguish? I'm not sure that is the right word, but no matter. Whatever you mean, you fool yourself, Reiner."

He had been stronger then and spat back, "Violence and torture! You seek to destroy all that is meaningful and replace it with your definition of reality."

Amused, the SS soldier had announced with certainty, "The German people follow Hitler because he is a father to us all. Hitler knows what is good for us. *He* is our reality."

When a leader emerges and assumes the role of a father, it is no wonder intelligent people trained for obedience and submission embrace manipulation and enslavement. The soldier came from an inflexible family dynamic. Obedience had been instilled in him at the earliest opportunity and was trained generation after generation as the most important virtue. Hitler was the perfect figure to slide into German society and make it incapable of functioning without him.

All types of people became adoring and even infantile in their need to believe Hitler was omniscient. That is the way a dependent child sees his idealized father. No matter how the father abuses the child, the trauma inflicted will go unrecognized. The theatrical way Hitler spoke excited the masses the way small children are enthralled with their father's rants. The dynamics of drama and trauma propelled them and their nation forward, unconsciously.

"Do you see these uniforms?" the proud solider had tapped his chest. "Beware, Reiner, or are you blind? We are *Schutzstaffel*. Our world is the reality."

"I know what is real ... and evil. That is what you are!" he had replied defiantly. "I know who and what I am. My achievements, my actions, and my dreams define all that is right."

The two Waffen SS had been wary of him. Birthed in a Nazi culture where violence and torture were valid, their ethical stance made it impossible for them to even consider another viewpoint and they had become uncertain.

"Well, Reiner, your next action will be your ultimate achievement!"

The other had chimed, "You will lose, Reiner." But the tone had lacked confidence.

Ambiguity, doubt, uncertainty, people would do anything to avoid those. Hitler knew they longed for a leader to tell them what to do. We like predictability and are always satisfied when people behave the way we expect. It gives a feeling of control and power, making the world not so dangerous, but more reassuring and less complex.

Reiner had chortled and smiled sardonically. "How typical. In your Nazi war there is no greater temptation than the opportunity to gain control and establish dominion over the human spirit." His sarcastic tone had confused them. "But not over me."

And he had escaped.

****

He took a deep drag of his cigarette. The drone of the airplanes in the sky over Zator continued.

"I *will* stop Hitler," Reiner whispered to himself.

The news of the slaughter and retribution following the failed Wolfschanze assassination plot against Hitler made Reiner's revulsion complete. The thought of eight German officers hung by piano wire filled him with disgust. Their agony was filmed for Hitler's amusement. Nietzsche had written if you stared into the dark abyss of evil long enough, it would stare back into you; thoughts that control the mind control actions. However, unremitting opposition can see beyond darkness. The light in people was what a frightened Hitler misunderstood. The excessive

Wolfschanze repercussions were proof that fear could control the Nazis as well.

The degeneration of the Nazi state is underway, Reiner thought. *Paris surrendered on August 25th. Soon ... soon ... why did I ever give those documents to Gerhard?*

Reiner went over in his mind what he remembered about the content of his documents. In 1939, a growing number of *Führerhauptquartiere* were destined to be built as more permanent bases of operations. The proposed Arbeitslager Wolfsberg, Komplex Riese, would be a monstrous underground complex under the vast forests of the Owl Mountains, one of no less than twenty Führer headquarters.

The documents detailed everything about the project. The installation would be located on the route to *Kutno ... Schweidnitz, was it? Ahh! I can't remember!*

He kicked feebly at the stones on the ground. It had been so long since he had seen the documents, he forgot what they contained.

Wolfschanze has failed, but we will strike at him again in his lair, Reiner hissed through his teeth as he thought of the

Arbeitslager Wolfsberg where the Nazis believed the strength of the pack was the wolf and the strength of the wolf was the pack. *After the attack in Wolfschanze, he will eventually go there. He must go to Arbeitslager Wolfsberg, Komplex Riese.* Reiner's clenched fists struck his skinny thighs.

The *Panzerzüge,* the armoured trains, needed to have access to a nearby airport and connect to a long-distance communications network. The plans included an underground industrial facility similar to the one in Mittelbau-Dora. The huge complex would cover an area of 194,232 square metres, with the bomb shelter 5,000 square meters. It would shelter command forces, security forces, and 27,244 people in ten self-contained facilities, not including Castle Fürstenstein, also part of the complex.

If Riese is finished, it will be the largest concrete military headquarters anywhere. If ... if ... Hitler is safe! This must not be!

Throughout the summer, rail transports came past Zator and carried tens of thousands of Jews to their deaths in the camps of Auschwitz and Gross Riese. Approximately 9,500 workers would be necessary for the construction of the project, *Organisation Todt.* Managers Speer, Dorsch and Müller estimated the cost for the construction at 130 million Reichsmark, four times the sum invested in the creation of the Wolfschanze. Construction in the Owl Mountains was scheduled to begin this November.

The file "Geheime Reichssache 91/44," compiled by Siegfried Schmelcher, the architect, held data and information on complexes previously built by the Organization Todt, as well as the only single set of blueprints for Riese.

Reiner felt the sun on his face and smiled briefly as Casper stretched in the warmth. *Without those blueprints, the Nazis cannot proceed. I possessed the blueprints once; I will have them again.*

"Trying to get a suntan?"

Reiner opened his eyes in surprise.

Gerhard.

Gerhard put his hand on the sun-warmed wall and leaned toward Reiner. "Well?"

Reiner knew the location of the blueprint documents but was totally frustrated as Eleni never seemed to be alone. Reiner shrugged his shoulders. "You know that family, the one that decided to leave the camp?"

"What about them?"

Reiner shrugged again, "They're good company." He looked around and saw the camp and all who existed in the landscape of war. He realized how different he was and how different life was from the recent past, changed from the way things should be, like coniferous trees shocked naked by bombardments and now standing like skeletons instead of straight, tall and beautiful.

Gerhard looked at him curiously then said with disgust, "The Warsaw uprising was squashed by the Germans. The Russians are outside of Warsaw waiting to pick up the pieces and have been there for weeks."

"I heard."

"Well, you should listen more and find out where those documents are!" hissed Gerhard. "This is your fault. My papers were in the same satchel as your papers."

"I'm hardly to blame for your stupidity," retorted Reiner.

They stared at each other with pure hate.

"I blame you. And you will be the one to set it right or perhaps the director would care to know your real story?" threatened Gerhard. "Find them." The finality in his tone was absolute.

Reiner glared at his retreating back. The planes droned overhead. Reiner felt the weakness in his legs and sank down beside the sunny wall of the clinic. The heat came through the shirt on his back, and he closed his eyes lest his despair escape to consume him from the outside as well. A moan pressed inside him like the beginning of a fissure in a fine porcelain cup. He struggled to feel the conviction he needed to remember who he was! He felt keenly the pressing need to keep all the pieces within himself together. Thoughts of blame and failure nagged at his core.

I could easily kill Gerhard. Even though killing is murder, this is war, this is different, he argued with himself. *Is it ...?*

Reiner moved his head in confusion. *People often fail to achieve their dreams. Come on Reiner ... forget about yourself. You're self-absorbed. Get beyond that! What can you do?* There was such potential in that thought, such meaning.

Yes, and such a huge roadblock because he could be trite, at times. Oddly, it gave him such satisfaction to be small and crooked. It was an accomplishment and no one was going to make him be any different — except himself, of course. It gave him the illusion of being unique. Small is such a tiny place to live. Yet, it felt real, in a tormented kind of way. Each one of us has rooms that are individually unique, cloisters for safety and rooms that are expansive and noble. *Yes, hmmm ...* Reiner agreed with these views of himself, some of which had, unfortunately, led to regrettable past actions.

His actions did speak, but not always of the tremendous conflict or what was genuinely inside. And that was an important distinction.

I fight evil. I fight to survive here on earth. I am aware I possess an intensity that is the catalyst for many of the difficulties in my life, a type of precursor to my most egregious failings. It can emerge in a petty and persistent sort of way; it's, an impossibility to shut off thinking, analyzing, and judging. Reiner opened his eyes and pressed his lips together. *It may condemn me.*

Time was running out. It was war.

On the chessboard, the knight moved.

Zator, Upper Silesia
Friday, January 19, 1945
The Month of Violence
Chapter Twenty

Since *Erntedankfest*, the harvest festival, and the first Sunday of the month in October, Klara and Elias had come to know each other, for they were often together. The January days were shorter, colder, and each was precious to Elias. *How do I stop thinking of somebody whose image keeps coming to me?* Elias thought as he gazed at Klara. *Maybe that person is the only person I want to think about.*

Surprisingly, uncertainty on this topic did not unduly upset him. He wondered about a world he did not understand; yet, he did not even know what questions to ask. So, he thought about Klara instead. His breath shortened with delight when he thought of her. Klara had a pretty outdoor look that Elias always admired. It was an aristocratic look from a pre-revolutionary world when everything was perfect.

He felt drawn to her for all the wrong reasons. Despite her perfection, when he was with her he was trapped in a dungeon. He was in agony. She was competent and athletic; envy fashioned his every response. A warning came to protect himself from the dream of the perfect life because he could feel the longing for that dream to come true descend upon him when he looked at her. It made his eyes water, his throat tighten, making it hard to swallow. He felt the heat rush to his head. A huge sigh escaped from him. The yearning for her screamed it hurt so much.

But it was a dream, and a dream going horribly wrong. Everyday life continued against the backdrop of the war, cooking, eating, sleeping, school lessons, and worries. Would they be late for a meal? Would they make new friends? It was amazing how mundane the day could be amid such chaos. As always, his unhappy memories journeyed along with him. Yet, without his memories, he would be an empty shell.

There is no perfect world and there is no perfect family. Life isn't like that. The real Klara did not fit into the place he made for her in his dreams. He needed to take what the real person, not what the dream person, gave him. He could see her out of the corner of his eye.

"Elias ..." she turned toward him. When she used his name, gratitude welled up inside him. His heart beat harder. A smile grew on his face. She used his name, his name! How fragile he was. He was so hyper-alert that hearing his name called out immediately restored his self-worth and sense of belonging. Without sincere affection every human existence is a blank, for it is the bliss that makes living real and important. When her hand grasped his own, a firm comforting pressure, it caused his pulse to jump and his heart welcomed a trilling shiver of enjoyment. For her, it was a simple friendly gesture. Just friends.

He took her hand. He needed the connection. "If tears were happiness, Klara, I would float in a river of bliss."

She could imagine the gentle image of his face, the cheeks caressed as they turned toward the sunshine. "Yes, Elias, the sunshine would be warm, comforting. It would make me feel carefree." She responded not to him, but to the idea.

"If tears were happiness, I would let them surround me and I would be inside them and they'd form into a perfect … " Elias blushed at his attempt to be poetic.

"If tears …?" Klara looked at him quizzically now.

"But," Elias dropped her hand, "tears are not happiness, and therefore I appear to be stuck." He tried hard to adapt to the conditions of his life and be clever to impress Klara. He desperately wanted to avoid feeling rejected and abandoned.

For him, this relationship counted. It would be the privilege they granted each other and thereby create a hallowed place where he could be transformed and live in a garden of delight. How Elias tried to make that happen! How much he needed to be healed. He looked down to the ground. "This is a dream," he whispered. "If tears were old friends, they'd be close." He kicked the ground. "I don't know. The tears I shed mean I am being molded into perpetual and imperfect misfortune."

Klara stood silently beside him. Some replies are better left unsaid. Quietly, she said, "Oh, Eleni is coming toward us."

****

I moved toward them and spoke to Klara. "Is your father about?"

Elias turned away from me with a confused stare and moved off.

"He's by the tent. Come with me. I was going there," responded Klara."

I could tell Susannah and Abraham were drawn to Klara and

her family since they spent much of their time with them. I didn't mind. Klara's father was kind to everyone. He seemed to orchestrate all the positive notes in the people around him. There was rarely an argument. He conversed well, not about people but about ideas. He solved difficulties by encouraging everyone to behave better; a personal growth he believed could be achieved without hysterically baring the soul. There is nothing enlightening about screaming at the world while your heart shrinks away into a small black pit. Nowhere was he more delightful than with his youngest daughter, Kaethe. Children live with their hearts.

"*Grüß, Grüß,*" little Kaethe said giggling with delight. Little Kaethe's first growth of hair shone in the cold sunlight, gentle and fresh, the soft brown waves curled up on her shoulders. This child's life was beyond precious. There was wonder and love from the family, even in these times. Cherished and protected. The response from the child was so pure and trusting that it elicited a smile of pleasure from all.

Klara's father moved beyond a merely intellectual knowledge of child behaviour, for intellectual knowledge is no guarantee of understanding or tolerance. He understood there would be aspects of his children's behaviour he did not like but needed to accept. He did not demand unquestioning obedience. He was not threatened, nor did he become defensive at their behaviours.

He understood adults and how many of us guard and protect our true heart so much that we no longer live free. Yet, we are spiritual beings who live through our hearts. Those who express their spontaneity are truly alive. The youngest of children can only be who they are. They will suffer and feel many emotions, but when evil is asked of them that is against their true Self, they will be compelled to deny it access. Children are true to their Self and are full of small meaningful requests. Little hands slip into yours, gentle tugs, say "come with me." I loved Kaethe for that and felt how much I needed her! Wonder. How much I needed wonder, delight, and innocence.

And yet people in the camp sent their children to safety. I would never part with my children. Why send them to Lodz? Would they be safer? Safer from whom? The children were safer because they were ethnic German and not Polish, that was true, but still, I couldn't do it. There was too much, too much …

Although I didn't know it at the time, that past summer, ten thousand Jews from the Lodz ghetto had been murdered. In addition, Alfred Rosenberg, chief Nazi intellectual and ideologist ordered *Heuaktion*, the kidnapping of 40,000 ten-year-old Polish children for slave labour in the Reich. Silesia also housed one of the main centers for medical experiments conducted on kidnapped Polish children by Nazis.

> *Stock und Hut steh'n ihm gut*
>
> *Ist gar wohl gemüht*
>
> *Aber Mama weinet sehr*
>
> *Hat ja nun kein Hänschen mehr*
>
> *Da besinnt sich das Kind*
>
> *Kehrt nach Haus geschwind.*

The rhyme stuck in my head, the image of a mother crying after her little Hans. Maybe it was intuition making me keep my family close, or maybe, it was just common sense. I think Klara had the ominous feeling this time little wandering *Hänschen* was not going to return home no matter how much his mother cried.

"What's happening?" Klara asked her father.

"We are in the dark nights of the biblical story, the realm of His story. God's story." Her father took her hand, "Will it get cold and rain? We never know, do we? Trust in the Lord and wait."

"Yes, we must wait and see," I interjected. Many times, I was sure, I had come close to dying. When the Germans first came to our Ukrainian village they hid themselves among our numerous trees. A Russian bi-plane had flown overhead and the pilot dropped five pound bombs, by hand, from out of the cockpit. He flew so close I could see his face! The Germans used their rifles to ward him off, but not before a couple of bombs exploded with a huge noise in the garden right next to the house!

"Truly, I do not know, *Schatz*." Klara's father said. Always trying to be as politically aware as he could be, he took the opportunity to discuss the situation with her. "Last year in 1944, on January 5, the Polish government-in-exile authorized the Polish underground movement to cooperate with the Red Army, but," he raised his finger to his eye, "only in the event of a resumption of Polish-Russian relations. The Russians have not yet recognized the government-in-exile. It is the communist Lublin Committee that they recognize."

"I thought the Russians always tried to outdo the Poles?" Klara turned to her father, "Will the Russians catch up to us? They are close. Will the Germans shoot us?"

"All we can do is wait and think of the years ahead, not dwell on the past." blurted Friedrich as he joined us. I didn't mind Friedrich's company. He was a good sort. Not waiting for a response, he sang about two little stars in the heavens that are always with us and are the last farewell we give each other.

Klara smiled. "Elias told me his constellation was Orion. He observed the stars in the Russian Ukraine and claimed them as his own."

"Now, whenever you see the three stars in the belt of Orion, you can think of him and this moment." I gave both Susannah and Klara a hug.

The girls smiled. The song was a favourite, for it spoke of warm days and roses blooming by the door. Even Casper came from the shadow to join us and jump up onto Klara's lap. Friedrich gave Klara the apple he held, hoping for her applause, but Klara generously gave it to Abraham, who ate the entire fruit, pips, core, and worm. Klara stared at him.

Abraham shrugged his shoulders. "The worm knew it was a good apple too."

"Good for you!" Klara's mother laughed from where she sat on the bench behind them.

Susannah sat beside her and watched how deftly she used the single crochet hook.

"What are you making?" I asked.

Kaethe moved to stand beside her mother. Klara's mother laughed again and shrugged her shoulders, "This? I found string, adequate enough, for idle hands get into mischief." She leaned her head toward Susannah the way adults do when they depart great wisdom. "It will be another doily. For what, I don't know, but we will see."

Crocheted doilies seemed to hold an important place in our lives. I too, had made many and loved to crochet. The doilies were given as keepsakes, to a certain person or for a specific occasion. They were a symbolic link to the other and kept for generations.

"Do you crochet?" Kaethe asked as her little helping hands moved busily here and there around her mother.

Susannah shrugged.

"Well, if I had a mother who didn't crochet, then I would quit!"

Susannah laughed at Kaethe's reasoning and choice of words as she turned her attention toward Klara.

"Will God keep us alive?" Klara grabbed her father's arm.

"Such a direct question," he raised his eyebrows and glanced at me. He turned toward Klara. "What is important is often not seen. It is in the heart and it must be willed. With God's help, choose a journey with hope."

I appreciated how his convictions shaped his life. He was a truly gentle soul.

"Everyone prays but still dreadful events happen over and over, Papa."

"This is war. People get killed. There are bad people. That's the way it is. The leaders know. You listen to what the government tells."

"That is exactly what you said about the Russians! And now you say it –"

"Quiet!" Klara's father grabbed her arm. "No! People hear, Klara. Keep your mouth shut."

The Russian government only told you what they wanted you to know, I thought.

Klara's family was so full of empathy that her father's sudden behaviour shook even me. He had never ever raised his voice. He was not quite himself.

In confusion, Klara ventured, "Maybe God is not listening to us. Maybe we are not important enough."

"Don't be foolish," I said with annoyance.

"Everyone knows that God cares about all his people." Her father hurriedly regained his composure. "God will provide."

"God doesn't care too much about the Jews," Susannah interjected.

"Now what do you know about that?" I queried.

"In Kutno, there were camps everywhere, Mutti," Abraham said. "There was a Jewish camp right in the middle of the village. I visited the camp."

"What were you doing in the camp?" I asked him sharply.

"I wasn't in the camp, but, you know, by the camp. It was another camp. The gate was open. I played there with *die Juden*, marbles, coins, and ocassionally, ball. They have big yellow stars. I played with the children," said Abraham. "They're not any different from us, so what is the difference to God?"

"The Jews are in a camp. We are in a camp," Klara's father shrugged.

I nodded in agreement. "Everyone is in a camp. They are behind a fence and when you leave, they close the gate. At our camp, we can take our papers and we can go when we want. That's the difference. Who knows what else?"

"There is another camp near here too. My aunts used to go there to sew. It's not far. They went on the train." Klara forced the lump in her throat down. She did not let her eyes meet Susannah's.

"What was the sewing for?" Friedrich asked.

"In these times, when you ask too many questions, you get too many answers. You had best stay away." Klara's father stood up with a huff and shot a worried glance in his daughter's direction. He waggled his finger at her, "Stay out of trouble. There is nothing you can do about anything. We don't even know what will happen next. There is nothing any of us can do. No one listens to refugees."

"It is enough for us to stay alive." I gave my advice emphatically.

I had seen hundreds of these people in striped suits and matching caps in the trains travelling by Zator. Some were children.

They were as thin as parchment delicately covering protruding and angled bones, barely able to lift their arms and legs. Many wrapped themselves in whatever they could find; empty bags hung on their bodies. I could sense the villager's shock at the fearful sight of such an enormous tragedy.

"It's called Auschwitz. The Polish Name is ... *Oswiecim*?" Klara said.

"They wear those stripes like convicts. They must have done something bad, mustn't they?" Susannah was puzzled.

It was a prevalent thought left over from the oppressive mosaic of threats, terror, and paranoia created by the Great War. The murder of the mind needed to transfer the culpability of its death elsewhere. The lurking need of Hitler, the master of death, along with a contingent of Nazis, readily found a target, the Jewish people.

"May God have mercy on our soul when the wheel turns again," Klara spoke softly.

"Enough!" hissed Klara's father in a low tone. Casper jumped at the noise and moved away.

But Susannah continued, "Abraham, you were told by an

ugly guard that the next time you looked through the hole in the camp fence to see your little Jewish friends, you would go inside too!"

Abraham shot Susannah a worried look but refused to look at me.

"We don't know what they will do!" Klara's father was near panic with insistence. "If you go in, you don't come out to tell about it! They make you disappear!"

Ultimately, the majority of German people were afraid. They were proud, passionate, and even careless in their choices, and as individuals lay blame, nations in trauma project blame upon others, a phenomenon that should never be disregarded or minimized.

"Enough!" I added.

Our epoch was a new edition to old and traumatic conflicts, and the German nation unconsciously fled from terror to safety, but it was a perceived safety. They were forced to flee towards the deceitful father figure of Adolf Hitler.

Friedrich ventured a comment, "From every direction there is such an apocalypse of noise and haze in the air. From the West, there is often a foul stench in the air — but not today. The tension at this camp is intolerable. There is so little to do."

The German economy only held its own due to captive foreign workers and the exploitation of prisoners. The failure of the democratic movement, the intrigues of industrialists and landowners, and the drive of the Nazis all played a part. Yet, no nation lives in a vacuum. Nations propelled into economic crises defend their interests. Economic nationalism can deviously transform into political nationalism. Without a doubt, nationalism assumed a more virulent and destructive form in Germany than anywhere else. All the eastern workers, the fugitive foreign workers, and Jews were brought by the quickest means to the nearest concentration camps to bolster the economy.

Klara's father nodded and replied, "Even though there has been an immense manpower shortage since 1941, work is hard to come by."

In fact, there was no longer employment at Auschwitz because sewing military uniforms required material that was almost impossible to come by. Yet, the trains to Auschwitz continued. Auschwitz was in the process of closure, but not before a suicidal uprising would blow up one of the crematoriums.

"Listen." Friedrich held up a hand. "It's like the grand procession of the recent national funeral for *Generalfeldmarschall* Erwin Rommel." Friedrich winked at me.

We stopped talking. There was an eerie silence from the bombing. Even the occasional bird chirped hurriedly, as if it knew that soon the cacophony would swallow them. A crisp cold winter wind blew across the river, through the forest, and ran over the field of tall dead grass. It touched and fumbled at the bushes, the last obstinate petals loosened, laying the dead pale reds and yellows on the snowless soil and across the trodden paths like a beckoning march to a grave-yard.

Friedrich launched into his appraisal of the status quo. "I have heard about these Nazis." He loved to dabble with politics.

Typical. He has a stupid opinion about everything, I thought. However, every so often, oddly enough, he was right.

"Possession of the streets is the key to their power in the Fatherland and for this reason the Nazis march and fight in the towns and villages," he began with satisfaction. "Agitators. Within the battle song of the Nazis there is always a smidgeon of truth and a relentless criticism of the former government." Friedrich loved to criticize the government and mimic its leaders.

A dangerous game to play. Klara's father looked on with consternation, motioning to Friedrich to stop talking.

"Friedrich," I cautioned. He ignored me too.

He continued, "The miniscule truth the Nazis latched on to has conquered public opinion and dictated the law for conflicts." Friedrich pointed his index finger. "They use physical attacks and create disturbances to agitate! The Nazi party is the future, and those people are idealized who silently obey, fight and bleed, doing only their duty."

Klara's father spoke. "We know how terror works, only too well."

"There is nothing new to talk about, Friedrich!" I felt uncomfortable.

"But they are fascinating," Friedrich enjoyed his audience and continued with relish. "People talk about how they arm themselves with blackjacks, brass knuckles, rubber truncheons, walking sticks, and beer bottles." He crouched forward toward the girls as if to pounce. "They are a walking evil," he whispered.

The girls shrank back from him. They had heard enough.

"It is time you left us," Klara's father said directly to Friedrich. Evening descended with a chill.

Friedrich came to a dangerous conclusion, "The Nazi conspirators appear to threaten their opponents constantly with organized reprisals and terror. They are thugs."

"Enough talk, all of you! You don't ask. You don't speak," snapped Klara's father. His love and concern to keep his daughter safe overrode his usually gentle demeanour.

Klara and Susannah are learning, I thought. "I have to leave. Susannah come with me. Dinner will be in a couple of hours," I said. "Abraham?"

He shook his head. "I will stay for a bit, Mutti."

"Fine."

For decades the Russians lied and terrorized us; the German people were terrorized by Nazi brutality. Yes, first it had been our turn. Now, it was the turn of the Jews. I knew the Germans were no different from the Russians.

****

Klara's mouth had clamped shut at her father's stern words. She knew the story of her cousin. He lived in a village where half the population had been Jewish, and he had married a Jewish woman. They had two lovely sons. Had. After the German front line had gone through and "liberated" the Ukrainian villages, the SA came, the *Sturmabteilung*, the paramilitary organization of the Nazi Party. The Mennonites called them the *Goldverzagen,* literally, the golden hopelessness. They shot the two boys and forced the mother, the wife, into hard labour working on the road. Someone from the village had seen her ravaged body in the chain gang begging the soldiers to shoot her. The Germans did.

The husband, Klara's cousin, her pacifist cousin, had been forced into the German army. He was branded with the tattoo of the SS on his arm. If caught by the Russians with that tattoo, he would be tortured and killed. Therefore, all the SS soldiers fought like maniacs. He could not escape the irony of fighting in the German army. The price of liberation.

Klara hung her head. That is the way of governments. In her experience, all the Jews had disappeared, all six men in Tante Ella's family, and in Tante Yust's, and Tante Agnes's, and … she could go on and on. All the young men had disappeared. Her crippled father, old Friedrich, the old men, and the young boys were spared. She pondered why things are done, or not done, the way they are — or the way they are not.

Klara grabbed her head with both hands. "I don't believe it. It's not possible. It is not what one can even think about."

In her mind, she could find no place to make sense of the horror and terror. She was not even sure about what she saw and heard anymore. It was a struggle to keep her wits about her. She searched inward to find composure, some inkling of herself. Her characteristic insight was absent.

Holding true to compassionate wisdom was almost an impossibility. Perversion and projected hatred weakens people, leaving them frail and gasping. The capacity to resist evil has nothing to do with intelligence; Hitler had a surprising number of enthusiastic followers among the intellectuals. Resistance to evil has to do with the degree of access to one's true Self. Indeed, intelligence is capable of innumerable rationalizations when it comes to matters of survival. For Klara, it was a vehicle for self-knowledge; she would figure it out. The wrong doings she experienced would be acknowledged, confronted, and healed instead of covered up, in time.

Abraham, however, knew if he thought too much, he would be afraid, deathly afraid. He could emotionally snap. "I, I ... have to go ... ah, now," stammered Abraham.

Abraham was off before another word could be spoken. He saw Gerhard across the camp and without understanding why, he felt a panic rise within him. Even from a distance, Abraham could tell Gerhard was in a fury. He wore a scowl, a thick dark frown creased his heavy brow, and he strode in Abraham's direction with a clear and unambiguous intention.

Zator, Upper Silesia
Friday, January 19, 1945
The Month of Violence
Chapter Twenty-One

A hard cold man seldom, if ever, looks inward, and certainly only arrives at a twisted form of self-knowledge through the loss of property, reputation, or power. Gerhard was the type of man who in an intimate conversation would agree with sentiments of love and relationship, and later would reframe everything, making it manipulative, harsh, and mean. Gerhard's pattern would not change. He controlled and pressured all those in his sphere of influence to do his bidding and to submit.

Gerhard strode with a menacing purpose. Abraham realized with alarm and shock that Gerhard was heading straight for him. Abraham had no idea Reiner had disclosed Susannah's confidences and to throw Gerhard off the scent, Reiner had told Gerhard that Abraham had stolen the satchel.

Abraham raced into the forest.

Soon, he heard running steps and heavy breathing behind him. Abraham's panic escalated. He lacked the composure to think of making his way back to the camp. In his panic, he felt there was no chance to evade Gerhard. He continued deeper into the woods. His initial burst of energy abruptly faded and a feeling of futility poured in. He came to an abrupt halt.

Where was Gerhard? Abraham couldn't hear. All his senses seemed to be malfunctioning. He couldn't think.

A rough hand clutched his shoulder, and Gerhard gasped, "I've got you. I've finally got you."

He was a powerful character willing to pursue selfish ends through evil means. His purpose would not be altered. An idea once planted would be like trying to wrench an oak tree out of the ground. There was no mistaking the threat in his actions and words.

Gerhard caught him by the edge of the river. The water mockingly slapped against the pebbles. It excited him to violate the young boy who had caused him so much trouble. Gerhard felt his own hatred and Abraham's fear, but that made the pleasure even more intense. He wanted to abuse him, to tear his insides, to shame him. He pushed him face down on the pebble beach.

When Abraham stifled a cry of pain, he felt victory. Abraham made a slight helpless upward gesture with his hand. He could feel the boy go rigid.

"You must relax," Gerhard whispered wickedly in his ear.

The icy particles from his breath made little clouds of fog. Gerhard cruelly punished him, using him as roughly as he could. He could feel the pain he inflicted, but Abraham was silent. His fingers made marks on Abraham's arms that were already reddening. The agony for Abraham seemed to go on and on.

"Stop. For the love of God, stop," gasped Abraham as tears covered his face.

"Nay, nay. I have not had my pleasure yet," panted Gerhard. He felt elation as he had never experienced before. It was part hatred, part surprise, part revenge and a physical release. He howled in exultation.

"Where are the papers?"

Abraham could feel his thickness inside him and the ooze of semen escaping.

"Do you want everyone to know you are a whore? You'd better not say a word to anybody." Gerhard spoke evenly. "Where is the satchel you stole from me?"

Abraham struggled to think. *What's he talking about?*

"You stole it from me, I know!" He thrust his hips forward.

"It was when I came to the camp!"

Susannah. He means Susannah! "Ah, ah, I gave it to Vater, to Peter. Peter Wiebe."

"Ah, yes. Peter, but the satchel was thrown away," Gerhard said sharply. "Keep talking or would you like some more, the way sluts do?"

No, no! Abraham began to cry. "He still has it."

Gerhard pulled back. Abraham gasped as he covered his face with his hands.

Gerhard laughed brutally as he stood up. "Don't cover your face. Your face is basically unblemished. Not a mark on it. I did you a favour. You should thank me." He stood over him. "Now we know," he sneered while his thumb stroked his chest.

Abraham could hear Gerhard's footsteps rapidly fade away. He whimpered as he rose, groping at his dishevelled clothes.

The watching eyes did not turn away from the unholy sight. In the gloom of the forest, the eyes glistened with delight, never feeling ashamed for witnessing the private loss of dignity and the victory of evil.

Dietrich knocked him down with a slap across his face and

fell on his back with a thud. Abraham struggled to stand but Dietrich's ferocity blocked any possibility of escape. He could feel Dietrich was roused.

"Shall I howl too," Dietrich whispered in his ear, "like my uncle?"

This time, Abraham's shock did not prevent him from struggling, but Dietrich's brute force pinned him down on the pebble beach near the river.

"Yes, little boy, I watched it all. Now, how does it go again?"

Dietrich laughed as his hand moved between Abraham's buttocks, pressing his full weight upon him, urging his naked member into his body. "And what did he whisper to you?" He made a brutal thrust on each word with a force that made Abraham moan with pain. Dietrich responded to Abraham's cries of anguish with youthful vigour by releasing his own moans and inarticulate cries with pleasure until he was done.

Abraham's world whirled around him. Yet, Abraham realized Dietrich was not going to let him live because Dietrich began to drag him toward the winter river. The water would be deep enough.

Abraham pushed his feet into the pebbled ground as Dietrich jerked him toward the river. He could see how it gurgled and jumped over the well-worn rocks. He fell onto the rocks to resist Dietrich's strength. He was not going to let Dietrich drag him in.

Dietrich never knew. He never saw the rock in Abraham's hand as his skull was smashed in. Abraham saw the blood on Dietrich's head and the strange look in his eyes as he fell over, off the bank and into the river. Abraham realized, with satisfaction, that the look had been a barely conscious fear just before the entire head went under the ice-cold water. In a surreal moment, Abraham watched Dietrich try to recover and flounder. Abraham imagined himself leaning all his weight on him while entwining his fingers in Dietrich's hair to keep a firm grip. Abraham struggled to stand still.

"Not this time!" he screamed.

The shock gave Abraham a depth of emotion that felt fabulous. He marvelled at the power he possessed. It was a feeling of rebirth. He watched the freezing water whirl around Dietrich's body. Abraham braced himself and waited. Dietrich's escaping breath made little bubbles and the sound of a long sigh finished as a gargle when his throat filled with water. He floated prone on the surface before going under as the current pushed him down the brown icy river. A circle of ribbons marked the spot where Dietrich went under. Abraham realized it was over. Yes, it was done.

His eyes followed the lazy leaves and twigs in the current sweeping past in the sinuous river. A false sense of calm and serenity surrounded him. Downstream, the resurfaced body caught in the growth by the soft water's edge and the dappled dying light played across it. The air grew colder as the sun began to set but he took no notice, stunned at what had happened to him. His ravaged body was as violated as his ravaged soul. Treetops captured the last of the sunshine thrown across their tops and beneath those silent sentinels, Abraham covered his face and wept harder than he had ever before. Another memory with dark and troubled edges had been created, already begging to be forgotten.

He staggered back along the river's edge where the rock bed was broad and dry enough to allow walking. In places, the frosty pools near the river edge were dark, deep and the colour of peat. The forest cleared to show sky, a darkening empty sky. He became aware of the chilling wind on his skin. The sun was almost gone, every passing minute morphed the woods into a gentle obscurity, drowning everything in the passing and still glow of a white evening sky that was innocent of his tragedy. The wintry trees and shrubs became more picturesque and impressionistic, charmed by darkness and romance. A thousand secret senses whispered about what had happened beneath their needled canopy. The illusion was absolute.

"All my life, I have waited for a huge disaster to strike," he whispered to himself bitterly, "and now I know I live one every day."

He laughed with a sharp sense of inevitable doom. Although his experiences up to this point in his life had been horrific, he had still been innocent of many. Yet, innocence is not synonymous with being safe. No amount of encouragement could have stopped him from positioning himself among the unworthy. The shame cascaded down on him. He embodied the toxic guilt of being raped.

His hands grasped at his clothes and clutched them to his chest. His slight frame shook with fatigue. He sat down while the tears streamed down his cheeks and he began to rock back and forth, moaning. The thoughtless motion gave him a place to exist and he stayed there until midnight. To be associated with evil is a heavy burden. He felt dirty as if the traumatic national conflicts and the personal atrocities were all his fault.

As the two clutching fists on the clock clasped each other, he heard, in the dark distance, frantic screaming.

"The Russians are here!"

Chortitza, Ukraine, 1789
Chapter Twenty-Two

Bernhard broke the news to Katharina. "The lands we chose are no longer an option."

Katharina was dumbfounded. She dove into their papers, pulled out the Manifesto and read from it. "We shall allow all foreigners to come into Our Empire, in order to take up residence in all provinces wherever it is agreeable to each of them!"

"It's no longer agreeable to the Czarina. The flatlands of Berislav chosen by the Mennonite emissaries to the Russian government could have accommodated a thousand families!" Bernhard exclaimed.

"Those lands are located east of the Dnieper River, the river they call the Nippa, aren't they?"

"Yes, they're across from Kherson, including several wooded islands. They're no longer available. Instead, we will receive other land."

Katharina's relief was evident, but her suspicions kicked in. "What other land?"

"It is near a place called Chortitza. That's all I know." What

Bernhard didn't know was that the manifesto issued by Catherine the Great contained lies.

The Russians viciously fought the Ottoman Empire until the signing of the treaty in 1774. The Zaporozhian Cossacks, instrumental in that victory, were wiped out less than a year later by the Russian Army under the orders of Catherine the Great who regarded their power as a threat to the Russian Empire. The Cossack stronghold, the Sich, was located on the island of Chortitza. Catherine the Great announced the Russian Empire had eradicated the name of the Zaporozhian Cossacks forever. The territory was distributed among Catherine's favourites, the nobility and foreign immigrants, notably pacifist Mennonites who would cause few political difficulties. Their supposed religious freedom and opportunity came dearly and at the expense at the decimation of the existing population. The lands had lain fallow for a reason.

When the group of Mennonites arrived at their destination, the bleak low hills near Chortitza stared insolently back. The sandy soil was far north of the promised rich tracts near Berislav. Chortitza was flat land riddled with wide steep-sided valleys, cutting through a countryside threatened yearly with spring floods and tormented with a cold east wind.

"Look how difficult the land ..."

"There are no trees."

The wind sent their teeth chattering in their heads. Nevertheless, the pitiless blast caused them to shake more in spirit than in body. Katharina and Bernhard, eyelids raw from the lack of sleep, gaped at their new home.

A place of desolation. How was this possible?

Terrible and unexpected events occur all the time. We should let them happen and accept what cannot be changed, for questions that don't answer themselves at the moment of their asking are never really answered.

Bernhard looked down at his hands and mumbled. He had carefully gathered all available information to make the decision to leave Poland. His desire to follow God's will was foremost. He surmised ironically that his capacity for Godward growth was great, for he had truly experienced good and evil in accepting Catherine the Great's offer. He felt he had made an informed decision, but he had been lied to and mislead.

A common and imminent threat of starvation in an

inhospitable foreign land linked the families together. The outcome of the entire venture caused an overwhelming and not all that unexpected intense emotional upheaval.

"This is impossible."

"It is a barren wilderness."

"There are no houses."

"Do you have any idea how ridiculous this is?"

"There's no lumber waiting."

"Reach out, take a risk, and ask for help in a daily act of courage. Be at peace with your journey and where you are now." Jutta spoke out loud to the group. "The future is new."

Some stared at her in disbelief. "You're an idiot."

"There is no help."

"No medicine."

It was easier to be pessimistic. A hush descended over the group. They had been pushed out of the common way of life. They desired nothing more than to reclaim that past life once again. They wanted to go back, but the past can never be revisited. They stood and quivered; their world was an illusion.

"The guest I will be inviting to my table is death." It figured.

The final comment came from a dull woman who lacked depth of character and confidence.

Katharina could feel the insipid turn in the group to an atmosphere of lethargy and ill-will. "Get to work and stop that nonsense talk!" Katharina directed.

She refused to allow melancholy residence and sidled around the wagon, threading her way through the families and their few hand-held provisions toward Bernhard. He stood alone, shivering, in the sudden blaze of sunlight looking thinner than he ever had. Their eyes locked and they stared at each other. As she gazed at him, she knew when the sun streams into the mind and you venture to peek in, only so far but no more, you are on hallowed ground. A solitary bird flicked over the grassland casting a kind of wavering spell over the steppe, making their tribulations fall away.

"*Borgen macht Sorgen*," he whispered. Oh! How they had borrowed to finance the expedition! There is nothing quite like being in someone's monetary debt to add insult to injury. Bernhard's mouth twisted into a barely perceptible smile at the incomprehensible enormity of the circumstances.

Katharina's face lit up. She savoured the small triumph and

attempted a laugh. "And Bernard, I am pregnant. The child will come in January."

"If we have a daughter, we will call her Susannah," he said.

They were tremulous as leaves on a tree, but they hung on. Katharina kept her resentment hidden in her own breast along with the feelings of obscurity and destitution.

She snapped at the group. "There is no point in being downhearted! It is not going to get us anywhere!"

She was determined not to forge a link in the chain of yesterday. She beheld an almost genetic belief that she had the right to make a claim for a better future. This caused her, the poorest member of the human race, to persist in the belief that she could inherit a kingdom.

"The world might appear to have changed for the worse, but this is a much better place with freedom and a future to make our own!"

Katharina had strength and integrity but she did not always choose them. The uncontrolled thoughts that come into her mind with happy abandon and ease were hers. If despicable, she cast them aside. She fought with the mirror image of her character in whose shadowy cave dwelled supreme thoughts of selfishness, violence, and excess. Instead, she chose to live with intention. She believed in herself and she chose quality. Where others would waiver and make different choices, she inevitably conquered her sour temperament and told herself her feelings were great liars.

Granted, the careless ones in the group swiftly dropped into a sluggish dependency, stupidly waiting for dreams to come true almost by accident because they felt it was owed to them. Fortunately, few exhibited this pathetic lack of self-effort and sense of entitlement, the two elements of failure. Those characteristics were not in the majority in this particular Mennonite group.

None of us is immune to catastrophe. It can summon us under the guise of disastrous adventure. *Come.* We desire the chance to create belonging as an exciting place for ourselves. Their personal and collective dream beckoned and they had gone. *Come to the fertile land of the Ukraine and have the freedom to worship and live the way you dream. You and your children's children will have a better life.*

However, true freedom is freedom for the oppressors as well.

In fact, the Mennonites were pawns in a game of political chess, like their descendants to come, Eleni and her daughter, Susannah. Over the following generations, every promise would be broken until even the ruling aristocracy itself would be broken and replaced by a Communist regime that in its turn would break every promise. A stark and challenging life awaited the descendants of Bernhard and Katharina. There would be no celebrations on birthdays; Christmas would be illegal; only New Year's Day would be noted under the future Communist regime as an orchestrated day of false hope.

Bernhard rose to the occasion of this day. His character threw an ideal grace over the hardness of life and preserved its quality. Both Bernhard and Katharina had the admirable character and the delusion of a family of importance. They did not enjoy flights of fantasy. Instead, they understood efficiency. The Mennonite committee had made the best directed plans and had tried to accomplish a dream, but God is the sole director of reality. They understood.

Mennonites could never be criticized for a lack of effort. Bernhard and Katharina were unstoppable. They would always succeed. In the morning, they arose from their little enclosure of arranged boxes. The ground was ice-hard and the snow came in the smallest flakes driven to the ground by the wind. There was a lucidity and transparency to the cold that made Katharina and Bernhard stare out from their makeshift shelter and do what people like them do over and over. They made new plans. Katharina would never call it a dream. Dreams were for dreamers. Dreams were nonsense. They would simply get working.

The landscape was slick with ice over the expansive bog. The wind whipped through their clothes sucking at the moisture of their heart. In that desert, their spirit took on a life of its own, full of risks and somber reminiscences. Katharina and Bernhard bowed their heads and prayed together like a rustic couple in a Jean-Francois Millet painting.

"We will make a good life here, Katharina."

"Do you swear?"

Bernhard looked up and saw a little smile on her lips. "Very funny." They had struggled long and hard for their core beliefs: not to swear oaths and remain pacifists. "How about this one? *As he desires that God should deal with his soul, so true is all that he has said.*" It was the formula Mennonites had used in Prussia when called to the legal court. Bernhard took her hands. His genuine gaze sought her eyes. "As you nurture us, the family, and others, I will care for you, Katharina."

Every success belongs not to one but many. Helping others helps us. She responded by pressing his hands. "We will heal our wounds and endure our suffering because what hurts or heals us can hurt or heal our relationships. We will nurture each other."

His unconditional love valued her. He pressed her hands in return. "Yes, we will depend on God. It is essential we are transformed by God, not transformed to the pattern of this world. We cannot let this beat us down. We will survive. All will see that we have integrity. It will be crystal clear." Bernhard shook with intensity. Those who exhibit gratitude, generosity, kindness of spirit and those who welcome their fellow beings with open arms, thrive.

Katharina nodded.

Bernhard continued the dedication. "Our lives will be characterized by an increasing love for each other and God. We will live vital, passionate lives. We begin today, now. We will grow in ourselves and in God. This promise with God will result, in the long run, in a life worth living."

That day, they chose a location to dig a shelter. Unknown to them, the lumber for houses would not arrive for another year, forcing them to live their mud hut mansion for more than a year.

One night, Katharina spoke thoughtfully, "Saying, 'Fine, let God do it and we will see,' is not as genuine as saying, 'Please Lord, your will be done and lead the way.' They are worlds apart. The second is humility and acceptance; the first is defiance and a way to rebel against God, one last time. God has been trying to teach us."

"We have chosen humility and acceptance," agreed Bernhard. "Many of us may become what we want but not what we can be. We will become what God wants us to be."

In possessions, they had little. Many of their belongings had already been stolen early in the trip. The theft was cleverly disguised. The locked trunks they had been transporting were filled with rocks. Any remaining goods had spoiled in the dreadful travel conditions and the rain. Yet, they did not let those moments of despair become permanent parts of their character.

The Mennonites continually reconstructed, mended, and

solved painful and divisive issues while always building a base for meeting challenges ahead. At the heart of this was actively doing and Bernhard and Katharina began work immediately. For them, work and grace went hand in hand. There was no time to dwell on petty behaviours. They worked from the morning light to the setting sun. To be stagnant was to die. They worked. They worked hard.

Perhaps Katharina and Bernhard were selective in their moral outrage. Perhaps their morality lacked a consistency. They did not treat their friends and strangers in the same way, an action seen as exclusive and counterproductive or convenient, depending on the viewpoint. They clung to their group, and they clung to their ideals. Life became their one cherished possession. It was not to be carelessly looked upon. The loss of a life sent people into spasms of grief. You survived no matter what.

"Surviving is a matter of dignity!" Bernhard would say.

As a people, the Mennonites had earned a respected place in international communities. They were a group of refugees who epitomized a brave and freedom-loving people with moral integrity and a well-developed sense of justice and purpose. The Czarina, however, wanted their backbreaking work to help Russia. Where are the leaders who light the way with compassion?

"We have lost many things. It may be we will lose more. We have suffered many humiliations. Dignity can be the first attribute to be stripped off, and yet, even that loss can be survived and restored." Bernhard would say.

Contrary voices would speak up and suggest they should protest these crimes to the Czarina. Bernhard would shrug his shoulders. What did he know about the crimes of tyrants and Czarinas? For all he knew, this was the Czarina's plan.

"I do not know," he would simply say.

Certain experiences can have a tremendous spiritual impact, and similarly, spiritual experiences that should transform us to be nobler can have no consequence at all. In an atmosphere filled with a fragile reality, blaming others made some feel better. When opportunities rise to see another person or a situation in a bad light, unfortunately, some revel in it and are ready to believe ill of another.

"They have no right to treat us this way. Someone is to blame for this!"

"We have lost everything."

Bernard would step in. Not everyone wanted to hear Bernhard. Pessimists were worried his optimism would make matters worse. Nevertheless, Bernhard would say it anyway. He could see the greenish-tinge of ill health and the sharp collarbones of malnourishment. Eyes with bluish shadows underneath would turn to him to listen, most eager to hear encouraging words. The arguing would stop.

"Your will to survive cannot be taken away by anyone. Only you can give it up. It would be the last surrender."

Friday, January 19, 1945
The train from Zator
Chapter Twenty-Three

The Russian canons boomed in the distance on the eastern horizon. Every evening the canons had hummed, but now they were constant and filled with urgency. The Soviet army was on its way to Zator after 'liberating' Lodz. The parents of the precious children sent to Lodz for safekeeping realized their treasured ones were either dead or shipped to Siberia.

The sound of the canons contaminated Abraham with a creepy ominous slime. At its most basic level, Abraham's human spirit wanted to expose his invisible wounds caused by repeated violence. His essential inner humanity screamed to be released and desired to be healed.

Yet, it was too much, too soon. Instead, he buried it. Deep.

Extreme violence pushes aside everything of beauty and peace, and lodges its story in the niches of world history. Even though ordinary experiences and daily tasks continue in front of a backdrop of trauma, attitudes and behaviours are defined by a new ugly and savage story. In this context, neighbours, acquaintances, and friends become enemies. In the long shadow of time, reality becomes a chimera with concealed mysteries, some of which are truly evil in origin.

When you have to survive, someone else lives inside you.

Survive. Just survive.

****

I had frantically searched for Abraham. I saw him standing at the edge of the forest. His breathing came in huge gulps and gasps.

In the distance, Mika yelled, "We have to flee!"

The cry had a rippling impact. Instant decisions. "Now. Do you hear? Move!"

"Where will we go?"

"To the train station!"

I waved my entire body at Abraham, gesturing him to make his way toward me. A single military train was going to leave from the tiny Zator train station. With few words, the swarm of people fled to the station, the waxing moon gave enough light to see the way. At the station, the throng begged to be allowed to climb into the final empty boxcar but to no avail.

"How many can it take?"

"Where is the train going?"

"It doesn't matter as long as it is away from here!"

My children pressed themselves close together. Heinchen stood stockstill and listened to the exchange. In Heinchen's arms was Casper. He couldn't leave the cat behind. We loved Casper who made us happy and always made us smile. I didn't have the time to argue with him.

The conductor refused to open the boxcar. "I apologize for not giving you an answer," simpered the conductor. "I am just the conductor. That is all I am. I am sorry."

I nearly lost my head. "I do not want you to keep apologizing — I want you to open the door to the boxcar! There are forty-three of us!"

Others chimed in. They became desperate and clamoured again to be saved, but no one was rescued. Heinrich squeezed Casper so tight the normally docile creature reacted with great alarm.

"I will eat my hat if you are allowed on that train and out of this train station alive," enunciated the conductor.

The group was laced with heightened anxiety and impatience, on the verge of chaos, but everyone treaded cautiously, not bumping into each other emotionally, not wanting to ignite the situation. Yet, the throng pushed nearer to the stationmaster. I could see a military officer approach and I pushed my family in the opposite direction, closer to the boxcar door.

"Mutti, Mutti"! Heinchen screamed, his empty hands grabbed frantically on my sleeve.

"Not now, Heinchen, not now!"

"Mutti, the cat!" Heinchen screamed.

I turned my head to see Casper skitter away and at that second, he was hit by the wheel of the cart. The crunch and squelch made a sickening sound. The woman driving the cart did not even stop.

"Look there!"

"Gott sei Dank!"

"They are opening the final boxcar!"

I fell into the car, pulling my children after me. Peter scrambled in after me. Before families had finished hauling themselves into the boxcar, the train abruptly pulled away from the station, heading west. The final boxcar swung and swayed on the tracks as if it was going to flip off. The door was still open and the last entrants clung to the sides of the car in frantic attempts not to be thrown off.

One was left behind. She watched the train ricochet down the track. Forty-two had made the train. One had not. The Russians would make sure Margita didn't miss her connection to Siberia.

In the boxcar, surprisingly, Abraham spoke evenly without distress, "I hate being squished." No one noticed his disheveled clothing.

I stood, packed into the boxcar, beside Abraham.

"I am hovering in a mist," Abraham said simply.

"What?" I turned to look at him.

"A mist, I float above everyone, waiting for mayhem to set in." He stared at me.

I did not even try to respond to my son.

The speed of the train made the air a glacial punishment as it whipped through the open boxcar. The wind tried to yank off scarves and hats. Even the cold could not hide the rank odour of the person next to me as we pressed on each other. The more modest tried to shift their position. I was no longer embarrassed about anything. I was so grateful to be in the boxcar I didn't care. Small children whimpered. Yes, someone had urinated in their clothes. The warm musty smell drifted and vanished in the bitter cold.

"The Russians are coming!"

"The Russian front is advancing!"

"The devil himself has come to Silesia."

The train slammed on the brakes and the side door flew open. In the distance, I could see Auschwitz. There were no SS soldiers visible, and we found out later the SS had already left the camp, forcing the inmates on a death march.

"Lieber Gott ..."

The crematorium would operate for five more days before the Germans would blow the whole complex up. The Russians would free the remaining 7,600 prisoners at the end of January but right now, above Auschwitz, the upside down Christmas trees fell from the sky. Success depended on split-second timing. The first primary marker planes dropped green parachute flares and green indicator bombs to mark out the general position of the industrialized areas around the camp. Right on cue, the wind picked up and the cold rain began to pelt down on us.

"The Russians are bombing us!" That rumour was wrong; it was not the Russians, they didn't have that many resources.

"Those are not the Russians. It must be the Allies, the United States of America!"

"They have flown here since July."

"Yes, they have bombed this area repeatedly."

A few minutes later, eight Mosquitos appeared guided by the green markers. They dropped their red indicator bombs on the target.

"Bombs are falling!"

"Now we are getting it from both sides!"

The main force located the target area outlined in red. Within ten minutes, the sky blazed in vicious colour. The bombs exploded right on top of the shuddering train. Fragments and bodies flew through the air. Everywhere, people, spattered in blood, shouted and careered madly in any direction. They dashed and leapt over the inert and the injured on the ground.

We ran. I dodged around deformed shapes crawling in the mud, but froze when I beheld a small child covered in an oozing dark crimson red. The child's upper torso was strangely propped against the train, exposed intestines sagged to the ground; the child was not crying, but the eyes held a glazed freakish stare. The remaining arm was thrown out to the side, and it moved eerily back and forth as if beckoning for assistance.

Someone screamed beside me and the sound jolted me back to reality. I charged up the slope of the hill away from the train. My children followed close behind me. I tensed myself against the wind that seemed to want to hold me back. I couldn't hear the falling bombs and was filled with alarm.

"Run! Run!" The gusts snatched my breath. "When you can't hear them, the bombs are right above you!"

A person scampering next to me made a bizarre yelp and collapsed headlong into the muck. Another, just ahead, abruptly buckled over and lay still, a child still in her arms. The freezing rain beat on my head. I stopped and looked back. People ran. Hands were raised toward heaven in that slight protective motion of people who ultimately have no control over their own fate. A man with a lobster-coloured complexion staggered over the debris. Another woman, square-mouthed with pain, sprinted past me with determination. A fat middle-aged woman, swollen feet bulging over lace-up shoes, tottered about in confusion.

I laughed, a short bark, and ran clumsily along the brow of the hill towards a distant clump of trees. My sister, Anika, rushed after me up the hill, but was sent sprawling. Immediately, she was up again and running but the trees were against her. Roots tripped her and sharp twigs tore at her.

Susannah had picked up Heinchen before jumping out of the boxcar, and stumbling toward the woods after me. She sprinted around the shapes in her path. The soft ground made strange repetitive noises. The steady rhythm of the machine gun noise seemed to be right next to us.

There was a dull thud beside me and a body smashed forward on to the earth. The people squealed like dying pigs at slaughter. Heinchen called out for Casper, the cat.

We kept going.

She sucked in her breath so hard when we finally stopped running that I thought she had been shot.

I looked up through the tracery of branches at the grey and scuttling clouds. Around me, I could see my children, my sister, and my mother nearby. I was filled with both a profound rage and an immense relief.

I looked back at the train wreckage and watched Peter sitting on the ground, his fingers spread over his shattered face, trying to scream but gurgling instead. I was consumed with a desire to question eternal life. *Is this another scar? Does this prove that I have fought the Lord's battle closely? Death where is your sting? Grave, where is your victory?* The poetic lines taunted.

I stared at Peter. In the most unpredictable moments, God can distill in every human breast a quest for meaning and self-understanding, making faith a real possibility. Was this a possibility for Peter? I knew he would challenge God to see how benevolent, forgiving, and fair He was. *Will Peter be saved?* Perhaps not, perhaps he would be remembered on *Totensonntag*. I didn't have long to wait to find out.

A flicker of intense light found the whites of Peter's eyes turned toward heaven. The remainder of the train exploded like the screeching groan and cracking thud of death when a felled fir tree hits its grave. For some, suffering is a passage and a transition, even though particular experiences might burn for what feels like a lifetime and transfix the heart — but not for Peter. Suffering did not claim him and transform him. It was too short. The fragments of the blast were all that was left from where he had sat. An entire life was gone, all that learning, all those struggles, all the questions, trying to find the path, the right way, the spiritual dilemmas, the physical pain, the labour, and for what?

Gone.

Beyond the bombing and wailing of the air raid, outside of the boundaries of this catastrophe, time moved forward, seconds died and minutes disappeared. Some moments are lost forever.

My hands fell by my side, and I simply stared. Small things in life mattered so much to me because those things were mine, but this ... *This* was enormous ... and it could *never* be altered ... *never*. I had a sense of one of the most difficult adjustments to make. When someone dies, the present tense slides away and is abolished, and an odd transition into the past tense occurs. How swiftly the coin lands with the head of calamity face up and the face of happiness hidden in the dirt.

Trancelike, I felt the roughness of the bark against my hand. I became aware I was leaning heavily against a tree with plenty of hysterical screaming beside me. I turned to see my sister, Anika, frantic with pain. There was a twig stuck in her eye! She had been so unnerved she had run right into a branch of a tree.

I reacted with disbelief and moved toward her.

"Shut up! You are ... a ... wienie! You would be dead without me!"

Brutal honesty in a relationship can be over-zealous. It may be honest but it is not necessarily the truth.

I yanked the protrusion out. Anika howled with pain. I grabbed her face hard and smeared the tears running down her cheeks. *If tears are you, Peter, then you are with me forever.*

I felt as if the whole spectacle had not happened, and later I would have difficulty remembering the episode. My mind went numb as it raced to halt the flood of emotions. I was guided by the recurrent history and forced dispersions of my people who wandered far to live in peace and had developed their own culture according to their beliefs.

I steeled myself to survive catastrophe. Reliance on my strength and conviction to start anew, to be pioneer labour in strange lands, to make it happen, had been hardened within me by the struggles of thousands of inherited adversities.

In the distance, the obliterated railway line vanished behind an ominous glowing sheet of sleet. As if in reply to events, Mother Nature delivered her opinion, for the weather turned particularly virulent. Picking my steps in the dimmest starlight, I felt rather than saw the way to the thicker shelter of the trees. My family followed.

Yes, calamity was piling deep upon my head, but I would use its shards as tools. I was determined we would survive.

"You just do," I said out loud.

****

Anika moaned all night long and in the morning, her eye was swollen shut. The crimson lid was stuck together and the eyelashes stuck out like little spider legs. I examined her eye and announced her fit enough to travel. What else could I tell her? "If your tears were hours then we would have banked an eternity of time to figure everything out. Do you have enough tears, Anika?"

Anika whimpered, "Shut up! You always talk about tears and crying. You don't care! My tears are endless. The world will cry forever."

I took a step back and stared at my sister. "Then the world will never end. Stop being helpless," I commanded.

Anika whined, "I am hurt! I am frightened here all by myself."

"You are not alone." I said sarcastically. "There are miles and miles of distance ahead of us to keep us company." Heading west and living a better life was what God wanted for us. It was clear in my mind.

Anika lamented, "Our world is torn apart. We are like villages severed from each other." Tears spilled down her face.

"You talk such nonsense," I spoke with conviction.

I was determined to sacrifice whatever needed to go, like pride. Begging, stealing, and grovelling would be necessary. And I would do it without Peter's help. A chilling realization descended on my group. The landscape lay brooding and the train wreckage loomed out of the mist. Except for our little hill, the land was flat and cold. The weather hinted at more freezing yet to come. The raindrops fell from the trees like big gobs of blood and ran down my neck.

We jumped at the screeching explosions. The bombing cacophony began again and lasted an entire hour.

When it was over, and silence descended, Susannah gestured and yelled, "Mutti! Look!"

Friday, January 19, 1945
The train from Zator
Chapter Twenty-Four

Furtive movements of striped cloth darted clumsily in the distance.

"They are prisoners from Auschwitz." Abraham kept his eyes on the figures. "Running to freedom … safety?" he speculated.

"There is no safety," Susannah stammered.

"I'm not afraid any longer." Abraham sounded dazed. "At any rate, not of death."

Despite circumstances, I thought Abraham was especially lucky. This last week, I had argued with other mothers to stay in the Zator refugee camp instead of joining the Germans in Hindenburg where they thought it would be safer. Safer! Ha! Those who left Zator were either dead — bombed to smithereens by the Russians, or captured and forced to dig anti-tank trenches for the Russians.

If that wasn't enough, the young and the old from the Zator camp were recruited by the *Volkssturm* and transported to Potsdam to fight the war. It was the final hurrah for the Germans. Luckily, Abraham had not been transported. The Germans didn't have enough vehicles. Those transported were housed in Potsdam, in an empty factory building, and were now dead — bombed to smithereens by the British.

"Luck. Fate. Bombed by everyone!" He jeered at the world. I could tell he didn't feel his luck; he felt anger.

He turned to me. "Is this God's doing to keep me alive? Maybe …"

First, the German bombing of the Russian train stopped his exportation to Siberia, and now the Allies tried to stop the Germans and end the war. In between, the Russians dropped bombs.

"Miraculously safe," he whispered and stared at the red and orange horizon. "Every explosion, every bomb fills me with the exhilaration that I am alive. It fills me with … Can I endure? If only this could go on for days!"

"Abraham." I moved toward him. Such crazy thinking could fill his mind. I knew he didn't wish it. He stood as if blind amid the drunken moment.

Not right now! Don't doubt. Not now. Not now! The thoughts screamed in my head. *This is all too much for him.*

"I know, I know. You don't understand." I tried to soothe him. "I don't understand either."

Don't lose control, Abraham. Not now.

The anger simmering inside him leapt to the surface the way a wild animal thrashes in a cage.

I watched as he released his anger. "I know you're trying. You're tired. You're tired." My hands moved up and down as if I were trying to push the emotions into the ground. I, too, desired to lash out. I wished his anger would flee and never return, but as quickly as it was vented, it rushed back with the force of a hurricane.

"Nothing matters! I don't matter!" he screamed. "Nothing makes sense!"

He seemed so lost. I felt the paradox of the moment in every feeling and every thought. I struggled not to vanish into the abyss with him. I had, at times, staggered aimlessly along and followed unquestioningly whatever stepped into my path, a dangerous moment for those who lose their way.

Heinchen took Abraham's hand.

It was the smallest of gestures. He slipped his small soft hand into Abraham's and stood there, not a word was exchanged.

Luckily for me, luckily for Abraham, the guidance that came

from a child, from Heinchen was a godsend and yes, it was preposterous and insane! His small wisdom was profound. Heinchen walked north as if he had a premonition, and everyone else followed.

We walked all morning along the railway track.

"I am surprised to find a railway track intact," grumbled Anika.

"*Gott sei dank!* There is an engine with a boxcar attached to it!" Oma pointed ahead.

Oma and Tante Anika, helping Heinchen, promptly climbed into the boxcar and collapsed onto the floor, thankful to be out of the cold and open wind. Abraham, Susannah, and I went to the farmhouse one hundred metres away to see if there was food. When we returned, the six of us travelled, by train, to the next station.

At that junction, I took Heinchen to get water from the tap on the outside wall of the station building. As I came back around the corner of the station building, I was astonished to see that the engine was all that remained.

The boxcar was gone!

"Where is the train?" I sputtered.

The conductor shrugged and waved in the direction of the track.

"What do you mean!" I shrieked as I mimicked his response.

Shocked, the conductor took a step back. I was severely traumatized by past and recent events and this new crisis made me let loose.

"Where is the train? Where are my children? My mother!" My breath exploded out of my mouth as if the conductor had struck my abdomen with a killing blow.

"The other engine needed the boxcar," he stated matter-of-factly.

I struggled to breathe. "What do you mean needed the boxcar? Do you mean to say another train took that boxcar and is now gone down that track toward Russia?"

The conductor nodded.

"You are going to get it back!" I screamed with such force and determination that the conductor vaulted toward the locomotive.

I kept gesturing him toward the engine car and harassed him to within an inch of his life. The more dramatic I was, the less shock

I suffered. I felt relieved to let it all out. I didn't care if it was a rehearsal for the next emotional crisis. I wanted it be effective and that was what mattered.

****

"Jump! Jump!"

Oma shook her head and pulled back from Abraham and Susannah.

They had all collapsed in the boxcar from exhaustion, unaware the train had pulled out of the station and had already travelled a few hours at full speed. When they woke, they were so shocked they ran around the inside of the boxcar in panic.

"Susannah, the train didn't even stop at that last station!"

"How many stations have we passed?"

"It is not stopping any time soon!"

They were frantic.

"Oma, you have to jump!" screamed Abraham. "The train is heading back to Russia!"

Susannah pleaded with her to no avail. She could see this

was one traumatic crisis too many.

"Oma! It doesn't make any sense to stay on the train!"

Oma shook her head with such force that Susannah feared she would strike it against the wall of the boxcar.

"You have to jump!" repeated Susannah. "The train is heading back to Russia!"

Another refusal.

In her dreadful confusion of horrible war experiences lay the nuclei of the actual and imagined. Her real memories created other memories of new events that had not even occurred. Oma refused to budge.

"You pull. I'll push," commanded Susannah.

Without hesitation she grabbed Tante Anika and pushed Oma out of the box car. The four of them flew through the air and smashed onto the hard ground. Susannah laughed at the daring and execution of the feat. Incredibly, no one was hurt.

"What now?" Abraham groaned. They looked at Susannah with expectation.

"The last station was not so far back. We can walk." She pointed. "That way! We can take turns climbing onto the station roof and from there we can see the trains coming. When we get there, I will take everyone and see if we can find food."

Anika began to wail again and collapsed to the ground, shaking her head.

"*Wie eine dumme Gans!*" Susannah yelled at her. "Stupid goose! A train will come and take us back to the other station, to Mutti and Heinchen."

Susannah ignored her aunt on the ground. No one argued. The chances of making up that great of a distance and reunion were ominous. Abraham prayed from sheer force of habit. To leave control of the situation in God's hands felt like a permanent defeat. Yet, he hung on to hope even though he had seen how swiftly the line of hope could snap like a whip and disappear.

They walked west and they did not look back.

I never do anything right, Abraham thought. He disowned the positive aspects of himself.

Don't be so hard on yourself! There was a subdued voice in his head that he barely heard. *You have accomplishments. Why do you always think it is your fault?* Abraham brooded. *Look at what has gone wrong. Look at all my mistakes.*

He looked down at his hands and remembered when they had been a mass of welts. *That had been a mistake!* On a special day off from school, he and his friends had gone swimming instead of attending the Nazi parade for youth. When the teacher had asked what they had done the day before, Abraham had shrugged and truthfully said they had gone swimming. *That had been a mistake!* The consequence was five whacks to his up turned palms with the ruler and pain for a long time.

Abraham stopped on the railroad track.

He looked at the vast distance ahead of him.

It was senseless; yet, he always tried to figure life out.

That's not a bad focus. Keep trying. The way you do things is different, not wrong.

Abraham looked at the remnant of his family. They had always given him a wonderful gift of love and acceptance. He felt loved, but his mind swung like a broken gate in the wind. He walked down the track because he had to move. All he saw as he looked ahead was an endless track. The black thoughts crashed into his heart.

Yet, at the core of every human being there is a dream.

Dreams die HARD. They explode. Deep in his soul, Abraham felt the shards slice him open. His heart bled until it was empty and stone cold, and that cold sorrow manacled him to a post like a prisoner, taking the place of joy and driving out hope. He remembered the German soldiers when they had come to his village in the Ukraine. They had all sat under the trees in the evening, smoking and drinking. Either they didn't know he spoke German or they didn't care because they never said anything to him as he listened from the shadows. Abraham had been surprised to hear one of them say that he thought the Germans were going to lose the war because it was hopeless. That soldier had been from Austria, Abraham recalled. He had said the Templar Knights, Napoleon, and now the Germans, would find defeat in Russia.

The tears rolled down his face. He tried to suppress his sobs but to no avail. His entire life had been wrapped up in a dream and Abraham felt exposed in a huge lie. He had dreamed how his life would be wonderful. The loss of his dream was a senseless act like chopping a head off with a scythe, swoop, and this time there was no blood, just a stupid decapitated noggin' bouncing down the hill making people laugh. *Oh! Look! What a shame! There it goes, another misconception!* Dreaming and hoping any longer seemed futile.

How could a dream realize itself when it involved other people?

There is certainly no control over anybody else or anything, Abraham thought. *People do not behave the way I would like. They make their own choices. They muck up the dream.*

He wiped away the tears with his sleeves and hung his head. He had struggled fiercely with rejection and being an outsider all his life. He felt its bite. To be physically separated from his family was more than he could bear. *Maybe I shouldn't think so much.*

How many times had he been at this crossroad? How many times had he dreamed and hoped? The grief and time ticked away. The lost hours dug a hole in his heart. *Use this time to listen. Wait ... just wait.*

"Abraham, there's a station," Susannah said.

When they got there, the station master wanted nothing to do with them and disappeared from sight. Abraham climbed up onto the roof. Hours passed. When the others returned from scrounging around, all they had was tea. Their grimy clothes were a mess. Torn and tattered, they waited.

"Tante Anika can't remember what has happened," Abraham whispered to Susannah.

Susannah nodded her head in agreement. "Yes ... no wonder. Here we sit alongside the station hut having cold tea."

Abraham peeked at his aunt. "At least she does as she is told."

Tante Anika sat quietly. Her lifelong difficulties created a nest of submissiveness and helplessness where she hid her anger and fear.

Back on the rooftop Abraham spoke to Susannah in a trembling voice, "I have been watching. There are no trains. There probably isn't regular service." Around midnight he noticed a small light in the distance. He stood up. Searching.

"There," Susannah shouted. "There, Abraham! Yes, I am sure. There! There is a train coming!"

"It looks so small."

Abraham's heart raced. It was definitely a train. He and Susannah clambered down and ran onto the station platform. It was essential the train not go through without stopping.

"Wait until it comes closer," Susannah instructed, "and then wave! Wave like a lunatic so it will stop!"

On the platform, they shrieked, leapt, and waved with all the energy they could muster. It halted. It couldn't have heard them, but they could see the light of the train engine a few hundred yards down the track. Abraham hopped down onto the tracks and ran towards the train. What was wrong?

Susannah shrieked at him to come back. Abruptly, the train advanced again. Abraham nose-dived out of the way as it passed him by. As he was sprawled beside the track, he saw it was merely the locomotive. No train cars were attached. He sobbed in a desperate panic and paid no heed to the din coming from the locomotive, which had paused on the track again.

"Abraham! Abraham!"

It was implausible. He listened dubiously. Yet, there it was again. What a trick to make it sound like his mother's voice!

He heard Susannah's voice yell, "It's them. It's them. It's them!"

****

Abraham ran to me. "You are all here!"

I was covered in coal dust from sitting on the coal pile. He started to cry violently while he embraced me and Heinchen.

"Why didn't you get the conductor to back the train up?" I demanded.

"I am not you! And we were asleep. We didn't know," Abraham replied with exasperation. "We thought we had lost you!"

I had managed to persuade the train conductor, who had yielded and said that the world was in an upheaval anyhow so he might as well drive the locomotive down the track. I had badgered him for an entire hour before he succumbed to my wishes. As the train approached the station, I had hit the back of the engineer with panicked relief and joy because I saw Susannah on the platform.

"Lieber Gott!" I had gasped. "Stop! Stop! There they are!" I had pointed wildly.

"There is Susannah on the platform!"

Heinchen wailed as the conductor stopped the train. I'm sure the conductor's emotions equalled my reunited family's relief. Out of the corner of my eye, I saw him shudder, and I ruefully surmised he must have been thinking about what I would have done to him if we had not found my family. The conductor thought it wiser to let us off before the station to avoid questions, for which I had been extremely grateful and slipped him five Reichsmark. I had then kissed his hand fervently, which he had brusquely withdrawn.

As the family was now reunited, we continued our journey via train, wagon, and on foot into a destroyed Germany. The Allied retribution was catastrophic. They attacked on land and sea. The Allied forces even used the German technology of Blockbuster bombs plus incendiary bombs. The Soviets sank the refugee ship, *Wilhelm Gustloff*, in the Baltic Sea. Nine thousand refugees drowned. Likewise, the British would sink the *Cap Arcona,* crammed by the SS with over seven thousand prisoners.

Any German city with industry or near a concentration camp was targeted by the Allies: Aachen, Aschersleben, Berchtesgaden, Berlin — 22,000 people would die there. Bielefeld, Bochum, Bonn, Bramfeld, Braunschweig, Brüx, Chemnitz, Dessau, Dortmund, and Dresden, where 35,000 people would die in an air raid that ignited a firestorm. Duisburg, Düsseldorf, Emden, Emmerich, Essen, Flensburg, Frankfurt, Hagen, Hamburg, Hannover, Helgoland,

Herbouville, Hüls, Kaiserslautern, Kassel, Kiel, Koblenz, Köln, Krefeld, Leipzig, Leverskusen, Ludwigshafen, Lüne-Merseberg, Lützkendorf, Magdeburg. The American forces targeted German government centres and railway stations filled with civilian refugees. Of all the people killed by the RAF and the 8th Air Force bombers, over 95% of them would be civilians. Mainz, Mannheim, Mariensburg, München, Münster, Nürnberg, Ostfriesische Inseln, Peenemünde, Pforzheim, Posen, Regensburg, Schleswig-Holstein, Schweinfurt, Solingen, Stettin, Stuttgart, Wiener Neustad, Willhelmshaven, Wuppertal, and Zeitz.

The aerial bombing demolished the German nation. The German leaders spoke with resentment: "We believe we are a master race, which must remember that the lowliest German worker is racially and biologically a thousand times more valuable than any other individual. What happens to a Russian, to a Czech, does not interest us in the slightest. Whatever a nation has we will take, even including the kidnapping of their children and raising them here with us."

And the Russian leaders of the East echoed in hatred: "Whether nations live in prosperity or starve to death interests us only in so far as we need them as slaves for our society; otherwise, they are of no interest. No one is exempt. If 10,000 Russian females fall down from exhaustion while digging an anti-tank ditch against Germany, then so be it."

In the face of this horrific backdrop of terror, my little group staggered on toward Kutno. I was clearly the head of the group, for I appeared outwardly composed and was successful in devising options when situations became difficult. I was driven by my cherished belief that safety was to the west. Yet, I was not exactly sure where we would find safety, as we had, unfortunately, detoured far enough east to still be in the path of the Russians. On the third day after our reunion, Susannah became feverish with constant diarrhea.

"Not now!" I was almost frantic. "Not now, when we are so close to escaping the Russians!"

I pushed the group on faster and when they could not carry on, we stopped to rest. By early afternoon, the group made it to the next village, one step closer to the refugee camp in Kutno, the ultimate destination.

"Oh, God, *lieber Gott,* don't let her die. Please don't let her die," I walked faster. My dream of a better life for my family in the west was seriously threatened. *I've badly miscalculated and now Susannah will die.* The shock of how misguided I might be in pursuing that dream was as devastating as the possible death of the dream itself. How could stupidity override good judgement? What folly! So much time and effort wasted, such precious time, pursuing my dream!

When someone dies, when dreams die, a canoe plummets over the waterfall edge and crashes into the spray at the bottom leaving no evidence it even existed. There is no debris, no sound — nil. That is what the demise of my dream is like, silence, total visual and auditory silence.

Why hadn't I seen that people and nations never co-operate? It was like burned cake falling through my fingers, shapeless.

Burned. Only ashes left.

The pieces remaining in this silence were my consuming feelings of bitterness and futility. No direction to turn toward. No distance to cover. There is a hush of grief. What an end. What a demise.

I pulled one foot forward and then the other. Dismal.

My body ached as I carried my daughter in my arms.

Losing a dream is a tragedy and tragedies are often re-enacted. With each occurrence, the sadness is felt as deeply as ever. *Yes, dreams die.*

I had no words to speak eloquently about the flight of dreams departing. I couldn't create a lyrical song to cleave the heart in two, for the death of a dream creates its own type of dis-reality. Dreams can be complicated. Even the surreal creates a belief that the dream is possible, but many dreams are not attainable.

Survive. How?

Because dreams live in hope. Dreams come true. Certain dreams can be wonderful, for everybody involved, and other dreams are vile and vicious, revenge really, ending badly.

Stick with the dreams of a better life and a better world.

The shadows enveloped me, and all I could feel was a strange blanket swathed around my naked body. Someone had stripped me of my clothing. I opened my eyes. I knew I had dragged Susannah ahead of the others, who had lagged far behind. I didn't remember when or how I had reached the house. I had a vague picture in my mind of lying crumpled in a heap on the front steps with Susannah in my arms.

I scrambled to the door of the room hollering, "Susannah? Where is Susannah? Where is my family?"

"Peace," the current homeowner's German voice greeted me.

The house had formerly belonged to a Polish couple, conveniently relocated when the area was declared German.

"It is late and everyone is asleep. They are exhausted." The woman handed me hot tea. "Your daughter is still sick, but do not fear. There is nourishment, sleep and rest. Come, see for yourself."

She opened the door to another room, and I saw Susannah asleep on the straw-covered floor. She had a slight flush on her face and was breathing easily.

"Before long, she will be well."

****

When Abraham rose, it was already a bright and clear day. The old woman, Susannah, and myself were sitting in the kitchen eating breakfast.

"My clothes! What is going on?" he blurted out while standing there draped in a bedspread.

Susannah turned and looked at him with amusement. "You have a new outfit, I see?" she teased.

The old woman said, "Your grubby clothes are soaking before we wash them. Your family is sleeping; they have stomach aches, no doubt. One must eat slowly when one is hungry, but, ach, that is difficult."

"My stomach feels like it is dancing around far too much! Sugar!" Abraham put five heaping teaspoons of sugar in his tea. "Black bread!" He wolfed down an extra thick slice.

The old lady laughed. "Soon you will grow to be a man. *Guten Appetit!*" She turned to Susannah and patted her on the leg. "Wash. There is hot water and there are sunflower seeds to scrub your feet."

Susannah went with the host while Abraham finished his tea.

He stared regretfully at the food. "I am tempted to eat more, but my stomach is warning me with a definite no."

A wistful melancholy fell over us like a mist. It was a

penetrating feeling and the longing to be home encircled its wings around all of us. Home.

"I miss my village," Abraham's hoarse voice filled with sadness, "and my friends. I doubt I will ever see my village or my friends again."

"What did you say? Did you speak?" Oma had come into the kitchen.

Abraham turned in his chair, "*Guten Morgen, Oma.*"

"I want to go back to Russia," Oma whined. "Opa and everyone are still there."

"Old people can be so stubborn, so stupid," I mumbled to myself. I adjusted the old house robe my host had given me and turned in exasperation. "They are *not* there. Opa left. We do not know where Opa is, where he is hiding or even if he is alive. We are *here* now," I snapped.

"The Russians will bring us all back together." "The Russians will send us to Siberia!"

"Everyone born in Russia is supposed to go back."

I knew, I just knew, if we went back it would be death. Abraham and I had a difficult time talking to Oma, but she insisted we go back to Russia.

My family carried the scars of recent events, now recent memories. Some were still too close to the surface and other memories were already buried in dark chambers. All the memories were now a past that no one could change. I wished the outcome was different! Every incident now carried such terrific weight and I wondered if each new happening would be the straw that would break the camel's back. I stared at my mother. A piece of gravel in her shoe was a catastrophe.

We could stay here in this house. Stick with the dreams of a better life and a better world. My dream was a beautiful dream. It filled my life with purpose. Surely such a goal God would deliver. I felt my goal was attainable. But, dreams cannot be made to happen. Success is never sure.

Try, Eleni, try! Oh, there is much to gain from the journey toward your dream! It sounds cliché, but it is true.

Life is made of beauty and ashes.

I didn't want my familiar world to end. The grief of loss emptied my soul and wrenched itself from my body, and nothing seemed to take its place. The effervescence and passion of life had been snuffed out and my recent actions became automatic.

This is stupid thinking. Trivial.

There was no fresh gloss of intellect or imagination endowing brilliancy on my situation. There was only a naked shock like cheap garments that cannot stand the rain from perpetual washing and shred from their own weight. A noble dream brings either sorrow or accomplished joy and when looked at closely, a trivial or mean act will always be found alongside, reminding us of the agony, the imperfection of our world. No matter how it is argued, war, traumas, and dramatic life experiences, do not mature people. Chaos fixates them where they are in that moment.

We could stay here. I saw this sojourn was simply another moment. *We have stayed too long in this house.* I refused to link recent happenings with longings for the past. If I chained them together, I would be chained to the past.

I had to move on to expand the edge of reality, but how I longed to stay!

I choose to dream. I must.

I left the room. I changed into my clothes and just like that, I changed my mind about our future, about staying in here.

Obviously, we could not stay.

After another day's rest, and I moved my family on.

As always, following close behind us was the foul breath of fear.

Wednesday, January 24, 1945
Chapter Twenty-Five

Abraham exclaimed, "Mutti, bicycles! How is this possible?"

"They are in pieces," I pointed out.

"I can fix them. All the parts are here!"

"Try," I urged him. "We need to rest anyway. See what you can do."

The weather was still cold, but it would be better than walking. Since leaving the old woman, everything was scarce. We needed to scour for food. I waited until Abraham had put the two bicycles together adequately enough for us to ride to the next village.

"Only three potatoes, Abraham. We need to get back to the family. We have been gone for hours." I could feel the worry deep in my chest.

"Mutti! Look there's a soldier at the end of the lane!"

I peered down the road. "He's arguing with the man over his bicycle!"

The sound of the gunshot made us jump with shock. For a split second, we were riveted on the soldier riding the bicycle away.

Abraham and I pivoted and rode out of the village and across the field.

"There are more Russian soldiers here too! There, in the distance ... " I stopped pedalling and strained to see what exactly was going on.

Abraham had plenty of admiration for me, but this time he was blunt. "*Dummkopf! Mutti, wir müssen gehen!*"

"Abraham! Abraham?"

"Mutti! No! Don't be an idiot! You can see they're Russian soldiers! What are you wasting time for? Keep going! Keep going! Back to the road!"

He led the way.

"Abraham, look! There is another group of people behind that old fence ..."

There was an opening, a clearing extending down from the road to the edge of the forest. Amongst the trees, a makeshift fence of broken wood kept a group of people corralled like helpless prey.

"Mutti, ride as fast as you!"

"Eleni, Abraham!" a call came out from the trees! That cry!

"Papa! Opa! How is it possible you are here? *Papa! Opa!"*

we hollered to him from the road.

Miraculously, he had seen us riding by. "Eleni, Abraham," was all he could say. There he was, sobbing.

We dropped our bicycles and scrambled toward him, down the small incline toward the edge of the woods. We ran through the tall dead grass in the clearing, falling over the holes and debris on the ground. The small group of people the Russian patrol had rounded up looked pathetic.

Papa and the others yelled in panic when they saw us coming towards them. The outcry brought the guards out of the woods, and they too screamed at us. There was no way to get Papa out. Abraham darted back to the road where he had left his bike, and I ran after him. Unbelievably, a Russian convoy of trucks had stopped by our bicycles.

I was terrified that they would take Abraham.

"No, no!" I shrieked and halted with my palms face up to the heaven beseeching God to stop the world. I was caught between running to my father, running to my son or running away from the Russians.

"NO! NO!" I shrieked again, unable to move in any

direction.

"Go! GO!" Papa wept and waved me away.

I ran frantically to the road. The Russian guards were in no mood to give chase, and the convoy had moved on by the time I reached Abraham. The Russians wanted both bicycles. They took them. As usual, they always took what they wanted. Thankfully, that was all they wanted. Abraham was furious his bike had been taken, but I was euphoric we were still alive and free.

I struggled to breathe. Papa was trapped and the Russians were all around us, hunting. I thought it was over. We bolted down the road.

Without any warning, a Russian soldier came out from behind a tree. He walked directly up to Abraham, grabbed one of his torn ragged mitts off his hand and viciously kicked him in the shin. There was an unnatural crack and Abraham yelped in pain. Like a bullet, the young soldier ran by us. Abraham groaned beside me, shocked by the suddenness of the attack.

All I knew was to move. I fled, Abraham limped, away from the group, away from my Papa. I was aghast. My sorrow and despair did not register immediately, but before long I was emotionally dragging myself through mud. My body heaved with an explosion of grief tearing at me from the inside. I fell to the ground and placed my head in the crook of my arm. I sobbed loudly and uncontrollably. The torrent felt unremitting. I turned away from Abraham and was grateful the rest of my family was not around to see me cry. I could not speak. It seemed irreverent to even try to express a word out loud. It was too cruel. I felt silly for the embarrassing display of emotions and wondered why I should mind if others saw me crying but I did mind. My feelings were so deep, I have no words to express them.

In my mind, there came a hush, signifying the final embrace of remembrance that I could give Peter and Papa and all the others. As suddenly as the emotions had come, they were replaced, for there was no free second of time to dwell on what had already passed. My mix of grief, anger and relief refueled my resolve. I recaptured my fury at the world and poured it back into my heart, pushing away the feeling of abandoning Papa.

"Come, Mutti, the others are waiting."

My family was where we had left them. A terse retelling of the chaotic Russian advance ensued, without mentioning Papa. We escaped beyond the village, along the road and out to the countryside.

****

Abraham fretted. "Something's wrong with my leg, Susannah. I got kicked."

Susannah raised her eyebrows and shook her head. "It will be fine."

"Susannah, I am hurt!"

"Abraham, you're walking so it can't be that bad. Stop getting hysterical."

"War, it's so awful," he gasped as if he had been skinned, and stifled a scream.

"Calm down. You are going to upset Heinchen." She gestured toward their little brother ahead of them. "There are other cards to play, Abraham — joy and laughter. You do not have to live with the angst."

He looked like she had slapped him in the face.

"What I mean is that stupidity, selfishness, a real meanness of spirit ... all those can be replaced with kindness and compassion," Susannah said quickly. She was trying desperately to hold off the raging red thoughts fueled by their situation and the fear that there was something wrong with Abraham's leg. Her voice sounded contrived but she needed to capture those thoughts of good, not the evil ones.

"You don't think I hurt my leg, do you?" he sneered at her. "Do you think I kicked myself?" He shook his head from side to side.

"It will not always be this way, Abraham. Stuff happens! That is the way things are now, but not always. You'll see," she continued. "I am grateful for this and I'm hoping for that ... see ... that's how you do it!"

Abraham turned to her with a look of hopelessness. His eyes were slightly red-rimmed. He threw his head back while pressing his lips together. "It is too much. It is too much to ask," he said contemptuously. "So, you want me to be reflective and speak softly? I'll just limp along and do that."

He shrank from her. His voice had dropped and taken on an ominous tone. He was surprised, however, that her voice was steady.

"Am I to love much, laugh a lot, also?" He was goading her now. His face twisted into a snarling sneering grimace.

Susannah gazed at him. She felt she was trying too hard, being too wise, too adult. She shivered as if to conceal her thoughts and hissed, "What do you want from me?" She moved her hands outward.

His voice was sullen and he spoke hesitantly. "Maybe, just be kind." Abraham didn't know what else to say. He was close to exhaustion.

"Kind? Maybe you could give something freely too?" Susannah said.

"Oh, that I have already done!" he said scornfully. His breath shortened, and he suddenly appeared absent.

Susannah stroked her fingers and wrists as she walked. She made various attempts to continue the conversation but Abraham limped along beside her and refused to speak.

****

I heard Susannah turn on the spot and struggle for breath. *"Ach!"*

Tante Anika stood still and begged, *"Halt. Halt, bitte!"*

As usual, I was the one who immediately strode toward the Polish farmer and his cart. He had no wish to argue and merely nodded his head. I piled my family into the cart behind his seat and climbed up in front with the farmer. He uttered not a word.

Relief put a slight curb on my escalating fear. It turned out to be a great thing to be with the farmer, a person of generosity, manners and kindness. As it does with many people, it elevated my own personal qualities. However, sadly, the reverse is often too true as well. We met the opposite around the bend in road as three errant Russian soldiers stepped in front of the cart.

"Show me your papers!" The leader spoke in broken Polish. The soldier's meanness swelled into action. "We are the security patrol!"

The threesome paced around and inspected the cart. This wayward patrol strode with the importance and arrogance of victors. They were lying hounds.

I slowly put my hand into my cloth travel bag. Although I did not understand Polish, I knew they were asking for our papers. I felt for the *Personalblatt* with its city of origin, Chortitza, Soviet Russia, written on it. All the information was on the document including my husband's name and birth date. Underneath on the left, beside the birth village, was his religion and to the right, where he had died. For Heinrich, in that box, there was one word: *verschleppt.* dragged off, taken away, disposed of like garbage. *Verschleppt.* The one word on that document that stood for our tremendous catastrophe, and to these Russian soldiers, it would mean traitor.

But it was not that document that I pulled out of my bag; it was the *Deutsches Reich Einbürgerungsurkunde,* the certificate of naturalization stating we were German.

I handed the document over.

I dared not turn to look at my family behind me. As an object of prey, I struggled to remain calm and do as I was told. I prayed my family would do the same. The Russian soldier barely inspected our papers but eyed us curiously.

"Sie sprechen Deutsch?" His German was as bad as his Polish, but I understood he was asking if I spoke German.

"Natürlich," I replied. The others were too terrified to

speak. I decided to explain our presence and our need to travel if need be. I took a slow breath.

"Good," he replied as he took out a notebook from his breast pocket and began writing.

"You are German?"

The farmer did not reply.

"Were you born here?" the Russian soldier asked in Polish.

The farmer nodded.

"You are travelling to Kielce?" the soldier addressed himself to the farmer.

The farmer shook his head with apprehension.

"Not to Kielce, but close by ..." His voice trailed off uneasily at the look on the soldier's face.

The soldier eyed him mischievously, "You must know of the ten commandments?"

The other two soldiers sniggered. "The first commandment is that farmworkers no longer have the right to complain."

The farmer sat still.

"The second is that there is a curfew from 2000 hours to 0600 hours."

The farmer nodded rigidly.

"The third is that the use of bicycles is strictly prohibited. Exceptions are possible for riding to the place of work in the field if a relative of the employer or the employer himself is present."

"We have no bicycles," the farmer said.

"No, no, just this family outing," the soldier toyed with him.

Abraham sucked in his breath sharply. One soldier moved toward the back of the cart.

"Where are you going? All of you, hmm?" he poked Abraham's leg. "The visit of churches, regardless of faith, is strictly prohibited. However, individual spiritual care by clergymen outside of the church is permitted. Are you a minister, too, farmer?"

"We are on our way back to the farm," the farmer ventured cautiously.

"Perhaps they have been out cavorting?" sneered the one behind the cart. A regular soldier whose hair sprouted from his ears, his nostrils, and beyond the cuffs of his sleeve jumped onto the cart. He was unmistakably fleshy and crudely potent as a goat. His sweaty clothes clung to his filthy skin. His fumbling hands threw our meager possessions about the cart.

The soldier raised an eyebrow. "Is this so? Visits to theaters, motion pictures or other cultural entertainment are strictly prohibited for farmworkers. Also, the visit of restaurants is strictly prohibited except for one restaurant in the village, which will be selected and only one day per week. The day, which is determined as the day to visit the restaurant, will also be determined. This regulation does not change the curfew regulation I have already mentioned."

The farmer's forehead broke out with beads of perspiration giving an odd glow to his flushed and frightened face.

"The use of railroads, buses and public conveyances by farmworkers is prohibited. And permits to leave the village may only be granted in exceptional cases, by the local police authority or the mayor's office. However, in no case may it be granted if he wants to visit a public agency on his own, whether it is a labor office or the District Peasants Association or whether he wants to change his place of employment."

"Perhaps it is not that which interests you," taunted the other one. The three began to laugh.

"Sexual intercourse with women and girls is strictly

prohibited, and where it is established, it must be reported. Do you have anything to report to us?"

The soldier moved closer to the cart and placed his hand on my thigh. They were ready for hard drinking and women.

"Gatherings of farmworkers after work are prohibited, whether it is on other farms, in the stables, or in the living quarters ... or in carts," he spoke and made a lewd gesture.

Abruptly, the soldier dropped his hand and quit his banter with the Polish farmer. He finished writing and spoke emphatically in Polish as he directed the farmer, "You will take this note to the Russian Commandant in Kielce. You will make the effort to do that." The soldier looked him directly in the eye as he handed him the written note. The illiterate farmer barely nodded, and with shaky hands, placed the dreadful paper in his pocket.

Although I didn't understand the conversation, I knew well enough the danger. The soldier handed me back my documents. He had only glanced at the header on the document, *Deutsches Reich,* and underneath the eagle with the swastika. At the bottom of the document was the signature of *der Reichsführer SS, Reichsminister des Innern.*

"We want to make sure that this family gets the assistance they need," he said in Russian to his comrades. The soldier's icy smile barely allowed the words to leave his mouth. "After all, the farmers feed the soldiers," he laughed "even if they are as dumb as this one. We will get to the women later." The soldiers snickered in anticipation.

I could barely breathe and made sure to give no sign of understanding.

"But not right now."

The cart rolled slowly forward.

Keep your head, I recited silently. *Get through this.*

The cart bumped on.

I was mute and gazed out over the landscape. I did not want to be here. I didn't care about the miracle that had just occurred. Instead, I recalled the beautiful Ukrainian countryside with its gentle autumn hills and meandering rivers under a large blue sky, where the land stretched endlessly into the distance, bathed in mists that arose from the shallow valleys. Here the sky to the east was fiery red and the few clouds that lingered had bright orange linings.

The cart bumped on. The hours fell away as we travelled the

distance in silence. Too soon, we reached the edge of the next village. Feigning indifference, I made hand signals to the farmer to indicate Kielce was far from the road.

The farmer grunted at my observation.

With measured detachment, I motioned to the Polish farmer to give me the paper and indicated we would walk into the village, and he could continue on his way. I did not look at him, but gazed with outward casualness at the ears of the horse. I tried to breathe evenly.

I waited.

The farmer was delighted and relieved at the suggestion. He wanted naught to do with the authorities. As quick as he could, he disappeared down the dirt road, and we pretended to go the few remaining miles to the Commandant in Kielce. When he was out of sight, I opened the folded note. The throbbing in my chest made me place one hand upon my heart and press hard to keep it from jumping out. The note was written in a barely legible Russian script.

"Mutti, what is it?" Susannah asked with agitation.

Afraid to say the words, I whispered, "It is for the Commandant, the Russian Commandant. It states we are enemies of the state. It is an order to send us back to the East, to Russia." I tore the note into shreds and buried it in the dirt. "Quickly, this way! Not to the town! Keep walking," I directed.

"Our enemies are everywhere!" Oma wailed. "They are wicked and angry. O God, give me wings of a dove to fly away from here, to flee from this wasteland, this desert, far, far away from this tempest. Confuse them God. I see violence, strife, and despair. It prowls day and night with malice and abuse, full of threats and lies."

Susannah stopped and stared at her grandmother.

"Why did they not arrest us?"

"They cannot arrest everybody on the spot! What would the three of them do with us? Besides, we were supposed to go to the Commandant!"

"It is a miracle," Tante Anika cried out, "they didn't figure out you are a school teacher of the Russian language!"

I was rather an anomaly. Most of the Ukrainian villagers only spoke German, despite having lived in the Ukraine for generations. I was a teacher who could read and write Russian. It was not a fact I publicized.

"Hush!" I retorted and grabbed her arms. "Never speak Russian or say that! Do you understand? They would have shot us on the spot!"

I shook Anika so hard she grabbed her wounded eye and cried. I pulled the document I had given to the Russian soldier out of my bag with shaking hands. It *had* been a miracle. I could hardly believe our luck. Indeed, the document had our birthplace in Soviet Russia, in the Ukraine, clearly stated.

He had not read the final statement in the document either. They all had *mit dem Zeitpunkt der Aushändigung dieser Urkunde die deutsche Staatsan gehörigkeit (Reichsangehörigkeit) durch Einbürgerung erworben. Die Einbürgerung erstreckt sich nur auf die vorstehend aufgefürten Familienangehörigen.* The Russian soldier could not read! He could not read that our German naturalization extended only to the family indicated on the document. Although he could speak Polish and Russian, he could not read German. He had not understood we were what the Soviet Russians combed the countryside for. We were displaced persons, D.P.s or ethnic Germans from the Russian Ukraine! He must not have known what he was looking at and was too arrogant to pursue the matter. What luck! I was incredulous.

"Mutti," his voice shook with pain, "my leg …"

I looked over to where Abraham sat on the ground holding his leg just below the knee.

"It's broken," gasped my son. "Where the Russian kicked me … I am sure it's broken."

"*Donnerwetter!* Get up! We will help you. We must get away from here!"

MIKA'S DREAM
Chapter Twenty-Six

No great mistake, whether suffered or inflicted, is ever set right. The passing of time and the immediacy of death renders that, quite literally, a dead end. Psychological mutilation is shattering. The irreparable ruin of the train wreckage and the bombing needed to be left far behind; yet, the landscape whispered unintelligible predictions. There was so much winter.

Mika lay on the damp ground. Small sounds escaped from her as she dreamed.

"Oh, how I loved him. I would drive to his house as soon as I could."

A small house that had once belonged to an old-timer. One storey. An Oma house with the gabled roof line. Cracked and peeling white paint. Lived in. Loved in. There was one room inside. You never ran out of room in that tiny house. That is what love does.

I would stroke his smooth hair. Soft beneath my caressing hands as he smoked and chose the next winners on his tote sheet. What would destroy us? His smoking, his gambling, his drinking?

Or my moods, my depression, my despair that was yet to express itself? I gazed at him.

I laughed. "Have you ever won?" I looked at the sheet on the kitchen table. He smiled and looked up at me with love.

"I won last week," he swaggered, "sixty-six Reichsmark!"

How little I knew him. I knew I loved him with a longing that would break me if I was not close to him. He put his arm around me and pulled me tight. The kiss was long. It filled me fully but only for that moment. More. I embraced him gently and pulled him close. Out of his chair and on to the floor. Sandwiched between the table and the wall. We broke out laughing.

"This is not going to work," we unanimously agreed.

I remembered how he came to me the first time. I would never lose that memory. Gentle. Beckoning. I moved into a world where I belonged, my total being. There was no doubt that this was who I was. This was where I belonged. I was home. Safe. Complete. He embraced me fully and pulled me to him. I lost my oneness and merged with his.

Later, I gazed at him in the car. Did he know I went to church on Sundays? Would he go with me? Could I even dare to ask? Oh, my God — I didn't think he could meet my parents. I could imagine the conversation over the dinner table. Who are your parents? What do you do? What is your last name? Well, if that ever happened, which I doubted it would, I would certainly know a lot more than I did now. I didn't know anything. Not knowing is a theme.

We continued the drive in the car to the school. The building was empty. But somewhere down the halls and the empty classrooms there was meaning. Memories. That was it. Because we had been here together because we had loved here together. And that meant that we had belonged here together and always would belong here. Here in this place, this empty building of remembrance.

Remembrance, love's last kiss.

I stared at the briefcase on the car seat. Papers are so important and they were tucked safely into his briefcase. The drive back up that hill seemed so long. This driving took such a huge chunk of time out of my life. It was as long as it had been in my childhood. The car drifted into the memory. The road back then had been lined with massive cedars on both sides and the road had seemed to disappear, up and over, to a place so vast and distant that my child brain could not fathom where it could possibly go.

This time, we, not only me, drove not to the house but to a boxcar. Parked beside an empty park, the boxcar seemed to be waiting for us to return. We unlocked the boxcar from the curbside and stepped in. Yes, it was ours. Battered and abandoned for a time. We now returned to it because we had need of it. I noticed as we walked toward it how much shorter he was than I. Someone pointed out what a nice couple we made. How was that possible? He's a full head shorter than me. How could that ever have been possible? How was it that I had never noticed the height difference? We stepped into the boxcar, the way one gets into an automobile.

We were in the boxcar when it slid down that muddy hill in the park, a park suddenly full of people. Sunny, picnicking, laughing observers. My boxcar and my love slid down steadily in the mud, a world apart from the onlookers, and all the people could do was stare and comment to each other. At the bottom, he got out, or was it me? Immediately, the boxcar was pushed back up by an invisible force from where it had come, all the way back, and placed on the same track.

Now, we stoked the fire to reheat the boxcar and watched as the fire turned and consumed the paper like it was reading a book. We were safely back up on the top of the hill. The location had a breathtaking view, but we had no windows! It did not matter, for the inside of the boxcar was glorious. The décor was unique. It was full of oval tables on their delicate single pedestals. The elegant support legs curved gracefully away from the single posts with capped brass feet, well, brass toes I guess. Those toes made the tables alive and living. Gorgeous legs, feet and toes. It doesn't count if they are not brass toes.

And of course, to top them off, to top everything off, in the entire room, everywhere there were doilies. Over everything. White doilies. Stitched. Handmade by the women from the village. You had to have doilies over your tabletop because ... well, because you did. That was the way it had to be in your life. You had to have white hand-stitched doilies on your furniture. I cannot stress the importance enough. The doily will connect you to the person who made it. You will then belong to each other. That was the belief. Was it a lie? I clutched at the lie as if it were a dream, for it would keep me out of the abyss of depression a little bit longer.

I looked from one table to another. All the furniture in our rectangular world was along the four walls. One oval table after another. All with doilies. An endless vista of white crochet. Was there no end? The door opened, and I came home with another table, or was it he who walked through the door? I could no longer tell us apart. Had I been waiting at home, or was I coming in? The next wooden victim was proudly placed in the centre of the room. There! And with a new doily too! I screamed or was it his voice? The attack came swiftly, but oddly it still retained that gentleness of affection that we once had.

"Don't wreck the hair," the sob came as the hands went up.

The massive salt-and-pepper hairdo was a foot high above the head, pushed back with a hair band. We stopped and stared at each other. Who was who? We were two impersonators looking at each other in our garish clothing and costume. The transformation was complete. How was that possible? The intention had been to ...? What had our intentions been? We were lost in ourselves or was it lost in our relationship? I could not tell anymore. Somewhere along the way I lost myself totally that was for sure. I could no longer tell who I was or where I belonged.

I was lost in a boxcar of oval tables, memories, doilies, and memories connecting to another Self I had never known, and certainly did not recognize now at all. The change had happened quickly, effortless. How trite and pointless this seemed. Even the memories seemed to have lost their great meaning.

How sad.

Mika peeled herself away from the wet earth and sat up, wide awake. She blinked into the dismal grey morning. *I seem to have been having a shared moment of great loss.*

In the chaos of the bombing of the train, everyone had run in different directions. Mika and Gerhard, too shocked to move any further away from the scene, had spent the night in a clump of trees close to the train. Reiner had disappeared, and Gerhard did not even know if he was alive.

"It was a ridiculous plan," Gerhard muttered with animosity. "How could stealing those blueprints of Riese achieve anything? What a fool! What a dreamer!" He yanked Mika to her feet. He looked northwest to Riese, to the location of Fürstenstein. "If Reiner is alive, that is the direction he would have gone."

He turned Mika in the direction Eleni had gone yesterday.

"We will follow the others," Gerhard commanded. He envisioned himself a sage, white-haired respected leader. He had assumed that position as head of the family and of the village he had left behind in the Ukraine but, in truth, he was nothing of the sort. His actions lacked honesty. He was a liar, fraud, and rapist. He was a fool with a lack of intelligence that would ensure he would never succeed or earn any type of true respect.

"I have a plan," Gerhard announced.

"Always," Mika mumbled, "you always have a plan, a dream. I had a dream last night, a dream …"

"What!" he spun so rapidly that Mika fell to the ground in shock. "That letter …" he sputtered. He swung his hands back and forth. "You lost that letter," he screamed and pointed his finger at her.

Nearby, fallen trees close to the blasted train rattled their aching branches against the metal like the sound of machine-gun fire. Mika covered her head with her hands.

"We will follow them! That is our future." He pointed in a northwesterly direction. "I have carried that letter out of Russia. Do you know what the Russians would have done to me if they had discovered that letter written in the German language?"

"Your brother would not have left the Ukraine if he had known."

"He did not need to know! Our fortunes and glory will be restored here, in Germany," was his haughty reply. "My letter and the documents exist. We will follow the others."

Mika had a revelation. He had a pitiable dream and she recognized in him her own pitiable life. Every face and every action of the past transferred like a series of photographs in the album of her life before her. There was the hovering mist of her youth! There were the forgotten moments! There was the traditional wedding photograph where she was standing stockstill, unsmiling. There was another photograph, years and years later, registering how her soul had been sapped of its spirit. All of it captured in black and white, and grey. Mika gave Gerhard a furtive glance.

Gerhard spit out angrily, "Ask me! Ask me then!"

She ventured cautiously, "First, I would have to think of a question." She had remarkable depth to her character, but she had felt hurt all her life and came across as shallow and feeble, the result of living with shattered dreams.

She felt totally lost.

Unexpectedly, the culture of cruelty and violence exploded before her eyes. He went after her with both hands aimed at her neck. Her breath shortened and her face flushed with the remembrance of previous violence as she dodged his advance.

The need to attack her emerged in a blast of anger. Gerhard beat his wife and spanked children because it was for their own good, a contradiction a small child or a wife cannot reconcile, therefore leaving a devastating effect. Hitting, spanking, beating, whatever it is called, is always degrading. Those who physically hurt and inflict mental cruelty often give it the honorific term of child rearing. A small child or a beaten wife is defenseless and in return is often expected to show gratitude and respect to the abuser.

"Where am I?" she screamed. Both her hands came to her face as the tears rolled down her scarlet cheeks. The emotion overwhelmed her.

Gerhard stopped as abruptly as he had started. The belief that beatings were not truly harmful surfaced to mask the consequences. He looked at her with irritated curiosity. He would certainly beat her if she continued to speak.

Mika had never been her true self. She had no idea who she was, but she knew it was now time to stop pretending. There was an entire lexicon of memories between her past and the present. The unexpected catharsis and abreaction hit her hard.

"It's difficult to breathe." She felt like she was being pressed with gigantic slabs of stone as if she had been condemned. She waved her hands wildly in the air around her head. "There is no escape." A sadness engulfed her. "Every time I hear your hateful opinion of people and … I lift my chest as high as it will go to fill it with air, but I cannot breathe. The pain is excruciating." She spoke with despair.

Shocked that she did continue to speak, Gerhard looked at her with tremendous annoyance. His thumb stroked his chest in a deliberate slow motion. He hated this kind of talk. The beatings he had endured as a child had made him dull to anguish. His posture straightened and his eyes narrowed. His anger was like the incinerating heat in a forest fire that travels underground and launches into action. Gerhard's pride cursed him, and this time he did beat her.

She gasped as his backhanded slap hit her across the face.

Her eyes welled up with huge tears of sadness.

"How, how can you be so angry with me, Gerhard?" Mika pleaded with passion. But, she knew why.

His response was resentment as he averted his eyes. He would deny access to truth about himself for all his life.

"How is it that you are filled with so much hate?" she asked anyway and put her hand on her cut lip. "I know there is a war, Gerhard. I am not stupid. Me, the family, we are not the enemy. How is it that you see us and everyone near with such contempt?" She wanted to hear it explained. The rules of her life were based on what should have been and not on what was. She wanted him to say it. "It is always us, us, who are at fault. *You* are never at fault."

"Oh, so it is always about me, blaming me, and this is my fault," Gerhard shot back, waving his arms around. The stone wall rose. There are specific types whose lack of character thrives on the excuses they make for themselves, the type who never knows when they have gone too far in their own selfishness, the type who never knows when to stop. The more allowances made for Gerhard, the more he presumed.

"We have been bombed Mika, or did you not notice?" he

snarled at her.

Forced by her life's continuing and terrifying ordeal, the burden of years poured out of her. She directed all of it at Gerhard. "I hate this bleak place. It is a place of anger and hopelessness. I hate what I have seen and heard." She lifted her head in uncharacteristic defiance. "I dread your ways. I hate the way you refuse to see your own disgust. I hate your dreams. Do you not realize that? It is hard enough as it is. The way you live matters. The end does *not* justify the means."

Gerhard stared. I am at fault was all he heard; his disbelief trailed off into silence.

"There was a time when you spoke gently, never nasty. You did not threaten, and there was no anger," she pleaded, turning her palms up. "It was beautiful." She believed what she said, but it had never been true.

Her splintered reality took hold of the past by the neck and thrashed its head to the ground making it unrecognizable. In truth, she was overlooked by her husband, by her brother and her sister-in-law. All those years, even the children, the nieces and nephews, had never spoken to her beyond salutations and had never been interested in her. It is always worse to be overlooked than looked over. Yet, to cope, she had denied her own personal tragedy and idealized the past. "I feel so sick that I cannot sleep. You have murdered the child within my own breast."

"I did not kill the children." The words twisted slowly between his teeth. Gerhard had never been kind — ever, and after the death of their three children, any possibility of kindness had expired.

Crushed, Mika gasped for breath. "It is the child in my own heart that was murdered. I tried so hard to find a hope to hang on to …" She struggled with her fear. "I want the way you speak at people, at me, and that awful tone you use to stop. I want you to stop saying everyone is a liar, a shit …"

He turned to glare at her.

"Stop it, stop it, Gerhard! I am tired of feeling alarmed when I am around you. I am tired of telling myself that I don't have to feel that way, that all I need to do is hope. I am tired of hearing you say my opinion does not matter!"

His response to Mika's emotional outburst was a menacing stare, but even that ominous sign was not enough to make her stop.

"I am tired of feeling afraid." She shifted into high gear. "I have had enough of you telling me there is something wrong with me. It is too hard. This is all too hard!"

She slumped further into the inhospitable ground and carried on. "You are like a stranger who spits at God. Any hope of having a heart full of faith is ..." She stopped to take a deep breath and looked at him. "You're defective, that's what it is. The anger and the hate that you spread, I can't bear it. I can hardly breathe."

She grasped her chest with both hands. "I feel like it is raining inside my heart and I am sliding down in the wet dirt in a storm, everything slithers down, black and callous, and the muck and the uprooted roots and the leaves of the trees glisten in the light, but the gleam sheds a reflection upon the mess of despair and hopelessness. It is a nightmare. The canopy of creation is falling to pieces around me."

Catastrophe lay all around on the cold ground. The rising sunlight sent tiny glimmers through the rain and softened one side of her face. Behind her, little rays of light jumped along the train wreckage, and as suddenly as the sunlight had appeared, it disappeared into a barely perceptible hint behind the grey clouds of a chilling winter day.

"I try to master my thoughts and feelings. I try to guard my heart, and I am immersed in this task *all* day. I feel such grief that I do not know how I can see the light of this day or tomorrow with any kind of hope."

Her gaze wandered around and over her surroundings informing her cognitions and shaping her decisions. Everything was a mess. "It feels so cruel. It's too difficult. Soon it will snap inside me and there will be such sorrow to witness because down is the only direction to go. I wonder how God can be so absent." Mika tried to tuck herself into a ball against the weather. She could hear how the sharper gusts of wind blew the rain against the railway car and the shattered supports of the boxcar. A mist of freezing rain was beginning to blur the bombed landscape, dissolving sky and hills together in a wash of grey.

She gritted her teeth in frustration. "I am drained and worn-out with how severe life feels. All I want is kindness. Even now. All I want is for the people near to me, my family and others in my life, to be kind to each another. You say that kindness only takes you so far and that it's not enough. Your asinine irrational thinking is a persistence in stupidity."

Gerhard's head snapped up with intensity.

Mika looked down at her hands and exclaimed, "Look! I am literally shaking with emotion. My hands quiver. Is that what old age is? Shaking because you have had enough?" She reached out to touch him.

Gerhard looked at her hands. The dilemma for him was whether or not to accept, this touch and become vulnerable. The gesture affected his humanness, and he quaked at the opportunity to accept the good side of himself. He would have to stare at his evilness and look into the night. It was daunting.

All he saw was Mika, the traitor.

There is such a thin line between compassion for and horror of people. The graveyard of his childhood triumphed.

Resigned, Mika dropped her hands. She no longer separated the evil deed from the doer, and in that loss, she was unable to embrace the slim fragment of Gerhard that might possibly have shown any positive element of compassion.

She spoke to herself; Gerhard no longer mattered. That was done. He was just plain nasty. "I tremble because I am trying to escape the world that travels with me wherever I go. I shake and fight to keep my wretched life inside me, but let it pass through your soul, Mika ... I have to let it happen."

She raised her clenched fists and thumped the air. "It's not that I need to let everything inside me go," she shrieked. "I should never have hung on to it in the first place! I cannot do this. God! You do it! Now, now, let your time be now."

Was she expecting a great manifestation of God? Nothing happened around her.

Gerhard stared at her.

He was lost in who he had become. His response consisted of a practiced and profound detachment designed to keep out the edge of fear. Yet, the potential for a further enormous loss of self-control hovered, waiting to explode within him. Strangely, Gerhard waited in silence. He waited for her to make her point, but she already had.

He hissed, "Are you done yet? This is quite tiresome. You think this is necessary to say, now?" Malevolence seeped out of Gerhard. "You talk about yourself. You want people to be nice? You are crazy. You, you, you. You are a bitch." He turned his back and walked away without a word.

The immediate past hung her head, for Gerhard did not see where love lay even when it had been right before him for years, asking to be invited in. Insight can be so discerning and every so often wears a sordid garb. Hatred distorted him and made his path crooked. He would have had to redefine his life, his values, to move on. It was too vast a project; instead, he felt he had two choices: his usual range of angry responses or avoidance. His pattern of consistently picking these two behaviours had become his character, and his character was his sad destiny. He was a cage looking for a bird.

The breeze of the Spirit twirled through the loose strands of Mika's hair. Did she notice?

Metamorphosis relies almost solely on a willingness to look at the not so nice features that are inside; defects everyone pretends are not there. Despair, fragmentation, and human longing says a great deal about what it means to be human. Her attempt at healing was a quest for ultimate meaning, and it came to that vacuum in her heart that was no longer filled with hate.

She was not perfect. She was annoying, arrogant, and she

had picked the wrong dream and found out she was dreadfully wrong. Dreams die. It was like having her face dragged along the pavement, bloody, crushed and broken. She was shattered beyond recognition. It seemed unbearable.

Mika felt the pressure behind her eyes that comes before crying starts, but the tears did not fall. Those barren tears signaled her anguished response, and she held it close to her heart for a second and then further emptiness rushed in.

She had no one to comfort her. There was no one to tell her to stop punishing herself. She felt she needed to berate herself for not having been more aware. *My fears have kept me imprisoned. My awakening has not been sudden.* Indeed, it hadn't been. It had occurred in stages. She had meandered down the side paths and dead-end corridors. She had experienced a collapse of understanding.

Yet, her newfound insight showed her where she was in her life's journey. Earlier, she hadn't known … she hadn't. If she could have, she would have. It was that simple. Not being aware of that failure to be a Self is despair. Not being conscious of despair is precisely a form of despair. Now, she had a hint of what it would take to be a Self. The barrier of silence disintegrated, and truth could not be held back. Now, she could make better choices because she was aware and awake, but not in advance. Her true feelings were acknowledged, and now true change could happen.

However, certain barricades are monstrous and thick. This is the wall of fear. *I have hidden behind a huge wall and I have paid for each mistake.* This was true, yes, and unfortunately, so had others. She nodded as she watched the back of Gerhard's retreating figure.

To know I have finally found a better way does not make the journey over, thought Mika. It was only beginning. Even the wrong turns and side roads had had meaning and purpose ...

... if only to teach her which way the path does not go.

****

I stopped in Pabiance, where Abraham's leg was tended to by an olive-skinned, almost Mediterranean-looking woman. He had cried silent tears the entire way there. She laced a tall leather boot up as tightly as she could and smiled at us with her pleasant crooked mouth.

"It is a small fracture. The little one, here on the side," She tapped the tall boot lightly. "It will heal. He can walk. No problem."

"May I read your newspaper?" Oma asked the woman. She took the paper to the corner of the room.

"What are you reading?" I asked Oma when I heard her gasp. I turned to see Oma sitting on the chair with a hand over her mouth.

"This paper, I have never seen anything like it. It is about the horrible activities the Jews do …"

"*Ja*, those kinds of abusive behaviours are written in that paper!" the woman interjected. "That is *Der Stürmer* published by Josef Streicher. It is astonishing what …"

"What's this?" Susannah asked the woman.

"What?" Tante Anika glanced at the leaflet in Susannah's hand.

"Let me see," Oma snatched it from Susannah.

"Ach! That came with my brother from Berlin. Two days ago, the RAF dropped those leaflets from the sky, and then they attacked the city!" The woman pulled at her upper lip with a self-conscious gesture to hide her prominent front teeth.

"But how did he …"

"Where did this leaflet come from?"

"The English dropped them from the planes of course! I just told you!"

"Why would they drop paper from the sky?"

"They mean to torment us. They are from the devil himself!"

Oma's hands shook as she read out loud, *"Du kleines Dreck, in ein paar Stunden bist du weg!"* You little piece of shit, in a few hours you will be annihilated!

We stared at the women in disbelief.

Tante Anika whispered, "What other news did your brother have?"

"My brother did not have any more news, isn't Berlin being bombed enough? But others say the Germans have left Wolfschanze, Hitler's headquarters, and the entire Eastern front scheme is abandoned."

An injured Hitler had lashed back at the German people since the disastrous failure to assassinate him at Wolfschanze. The Nazi state was unravelling, yet Hitler demanded the nation never surrender. The old and the young were called upon to throw their bodies into the slaughterhouse. If they refused to die in battle, Hitler cursed them.

I was shaken by the news but not wanting to delay our journey any longer, I found a transport truck leaving Pabiance, heading north to Kutno. The truck rumbled along like it had a broken back, and behind the truck, hooked on with a chain, was a Mercedes car. The driver agreed to take us as far as Kutno if Abraham would sit in the car and steer, making sure the Mercedes stayed on the road. I readily agreed. It was bad luck for Abraham though, but necessary. I am sure he was convinced he would die of cold as the freezing wind blasted through the broken and fogged windshield.

Once in Kutno, we went directly to the train station. The waiting area was already crowded but we found a small space on the floor. I noticed how Abraham's face had taken on that other-world-dream look that dissociation so distinctly gives. *He smiles and nods and keeps dying inside. It is all so routine now.*

"I am going to see if I can find any food." I encircled my shoulders with my shawl. Oma and Tante Anika were sleeping.

"Keep an eye on Heinchen. Susannah! Abraham! Did you hear me?"

****

They both looked at her and nodded. Susannah smiled and shrugged at Abraham who sat on the floor. "She is always so grumpy. Does your leg hurt?"

Abraham lifted one shoulder.

"Happy, sad, and heartache frequently come from the same source." Susannah sat down beside him. She watched how he nervously tapped the tip of each finger on to the tip of his thumb.

"It is an evil we must bear." He pressed his lips together and snorted. There was a part of him that doubted whether that was totally true. He knew facing the evil within himself would not be particularly difficult but he doubted whether he could come face to face with evil in other people, now that he knew what they could inflict. It would be easier to just give up. "Yup, I remember it all."

"Recalling every last detail has nothing to do with a good memory, Abraham; it is called holding a grudge."

He glanced hastily in her direction, but she was looking out the window. He followed her gaze. The *Bergfinken* flitted with incredible speed in and out of the broken windows. He studied the birds. It was a relief to have his eyes freed from the ache of the grey town.

"They are a blur of energy," he said to change the subject. Not speaking about his experiences was a way to take cover.

"They are amazing! They are tenacious and ferocious in their quest for seeds in the winter," Susannah said with passion.

"The tiniest ray of balmy sunshine reflects the mellow rust of the downy breast in the cool mist of the morning air." He smirked. "Tender sunshine."

She looked at him with curiosity and raised one eyebrow.

"See, I'm a poet, as good as Goethe!" His expressive language revealed the conflict between his deepest longings and the raw aspects of his inner self.

She snorted. "Next, you'll recite the Bible."

"Has God revealed, amid the tears, a way to tread, a path to follow? At times, I felt there was no way. I was not sure, and I did fall. God picked me up and held me fast, and now I see the Sun at last."

"That's not the Bible."

She noticed how blank he looked, unfocused, like a new born babe.

"Maybe the sun is a source, a type of secret wisdom that beams into your heart, your true heart." Susannah held her breath.

Abraham could abruptly change the pace and direction of their exchanges without explanation. She wanted him to be introspective. Conversations with him were like hanging onto the back of a sea creature, alternating between the deep death plunge and coming up for air only when absolutely necessary. It happened too often.

"Papa loved Goethe," Abraham said wistfully. "Papa was a kind and gentle man. I remember when we cultivated sunflowers together. I rode the horse and Papa walked behind the cultivator shouting instructions."

Abraham's emotional core was by its very nature spiritual for the yearning came from his heart. Abraham needed to talk about himself and where he was in his life journey. He needed to be encouraged to talk more about his earthly father than his heavenly father.

"Use your heart, Abraham."

The birds hovered, pulsating and warbling outside and inside the building, then hovering again, like Susannah who waited attentively, willing Abraham to judge the emotional climate safe enough to speak.

"My heart," he snorted again, "all my heart wants to do is to pump blood through my veins every day. This is what people live with ... Maybe caution is wise," he spoke with a flat affect. The first eagerness to speak faded. He knew he had the potential to be Gerhard. He knew he had the potential to be as compassionate as Irmgard. In the Zator camp, Klara had often said how much she admired Irmgard and strove to be like her. There was a little voice inside him that questioned from where his humanity would come.

"You know what I mean," she gently ventured. "We can be better than everything that has happened. We can concentrate on what is ahead of us, not the pain behind us."

Abraham clung to the little bit of humanity Susannah offered him and he tried to focus on her lead. His erratic speaking struggled to be sincere.

"Yes, I think so…" his voice fluctuated, and died away. He could no longer speak.

She loved Abraham so much and through that she fostered a sincere atmosphere of empathy. God had answered her prayer to keep them all alive. She had not bothered much about God, so, she made a deal with Him. God would continue to keep them all alive and she would help Abraham change.

****

When I returned, all of them were asleep with their heads on their rucksacks. The midday meal I scrounged up was meager and silent.

"We need to head towards Berlin." I tried to open a conversation with Abraham. There was no acknowledgement that Abraham heard me because he turned and walked away. Never could I remember Abraham behaving this way. He seemed depressed, unable to concentrate and forgetful. He had moments of frightening intensity. I followed him out to the street. The pavers leered at me and the windows strained their ears to eavesdrop.

"Are you following me?" Abraham's pale face abruptly

turned toward me. Purple shadows had taken up permanent residence beneath his eyes. His blank dog-round eyes were empty and devoid of hope.

"I wanted to speak with you," I spoke tentatively, "without anyone else around."

The pause was agonizing. I thought to myself in frustration how young my son looked compared to how old he must have felt. Abraham was scarcely aware of what youth was and even less aware of how fleeting a prize it was. If lucky, he might experience a second sense of youthfulness and joy. But not today, not Abraham.

Finally, Abraham replied, "What are you doing here?"

"I want to talk. What are you doing?"

Abraham's foot pushed at the dirt. He screamed with rage, "I will break every plate in the cupboard!"

"But, Abraham we don't have a cupboard, and even if we did you know you would not do that," I reacted. I felt the weight of worry push down on my shoulders. There was a sense of not being present, of standing alone in my mother's kitchen, and staring at the nearly empty shelves. The light streaming to the ground behind Abraham seemed to avoid him.

Abraham folded his arms across his chest and screamed for me to stay away. "Don't you tell me what I will and will not do!" His arms flew in the air and then he wrapped them tightly across his upper body again.

Silence.

The gap widened. In bewilderment, I spoke, "Abraham, I don't know what's going on. I don't even understand what we are talking about."

Abraham's body slumped. "I don't know either. It is like I am all these different people inside, and they all want to go different ways. I end up going nowhere. We are always running away, but it feels like we are stuck."

"This situation is not your fault, Abraham."

Abraham glared at me suspiciously.

"There is little we can do or have control over, but we must do what we can. We must stick close to one another."

"I do not want to be close to anyone!" he spoke evenly, stressing each word. "I don't want to be close to you!"

"Don't say that. You either ignore me or you lie to me. Stop making up excuses so you do not have to be near me. You're such a liar. One minute you say and do one thing, and the next minute you say and do something else! Then you seem all right, and at other times I can see that you are upset with me, that I irritate you. I want to know what I have done," I pleaded.

Abraham appeared totally disillusioned.

"You need to think better of yourself," I advised.

"Stop interfering!"

"It sounds like you need someone interfering! Let me help you work it out. It's distorted. Maybe together we can …"

Abraham's rage flared. "You don't get it, do you?" His face was unrecognizable. I moved back with shock at his distress.

The expressionless look that I found uncontrollable when suddenly confronted with a strange twist in events slipped over my face. On the outside, I appeared in control but in reality, alarm filled my entire body. Who was this person in front of me? Not my son. Where did this person come from?

"I have to protect myself from you and hide from you. Don't you get it? Get out of my life! Leave me alone!" Abraham burst passed me and ran down the hill.

Stunned, I followed. "My God, my God. He is not himself.

What is so terribly wrong?"

Abraham stopped halfway down the hill and hid himself under a bush. He was incredibly stirred up and ready to defend himself against any onslaught. Poorly concealed, I could see he lay down in the dirt, his legs stretched out to the side.

"Abraham. Abraham, what are you doing? Stop being ridiculous. Stop acting like a child!"

Abraham jumped up and marched up the hill toward me, his mother. "If you would treat me like an adult, I wouldn't have to act like a child!"

I felt as if Abraham's whole identity had changed. Who was he? He truly did not know himself. *His life and his world were shattered beyond recognition. He wants to avoid everyone and everything — but surely not me.*

It didn't occur to me at the time, but Abraham was vigilant because he felt it was an absolute necessity to protect what little bit of himself he had left.

"I treat you like an adult. I treat everyone like this," I tried to reason with the unreasonable. He was only fifteen, after all. "What can I do for you?"

"Perhaps you could leave me alone. Totally alone!" Abraham screamed.

It's the emotions that he can't stand. He needs me to help him calm down. "Abraham, do not say that. You do not know what you're asking. It does not have to be like this."

"I can fix things, lots of things," boasted Abraham triumphantly.

I nodded with confusion, the change in the conversation caught me off guard. *If he can't convince me then confuse me?*

But he could not erase horror and shame with a detour. It does not work that way.

"Okay," I said. "Great, that's good." *What are we talking about?*

I waited.

Even though unintentional, both of us had chosen to go further in what was turning out to be a totally irrational argument, and now I did not know the way back. Destructive emotions are self-limiting.

Silence.

Abraham attacked in the only direction open to him for

escape. He rebounded from the silence with his teeth clenched together.

He spat out, "Get out of my life! You never did anything that mattered anyway. You are not the person I thought you were. You, yes, you embarrass me. I thought you were kind and caring, but I can see that you are nasty and inconsiderate. I don't ever want to see you, talk to you or have anything to do with you ever again!"

He hurt me, deliberately.

"Abraham!" His name was all I could gasp.

But Abraham had turned his back on me, and I was staring at his retreating figure. "You don't actually believe that!" I called after my son.

Abraham was totally bereft of reason. Yet, with all my experiences of the terrible in the world, I was ill-prepared for those words from my son. I often wondered what cross I would have to bear in my life. I never ever thought it would be this. My whole world stood vacant, stunned. I starred at Abraham's back.

"That is such an infantile, coping mechanism!" I shouted.

"You mean I'm acting like a baby!" shrieked Abraham at the top of his voice. He continued to walk away.

I struggled to articulate a point of view but abandoned it even before it matured. It didn't occur to me to move. This was the only place I could be. The feeling of absolute despair made me mute. My shoulders sagged and the weight of anguish made it hard to breathe. I felt incinerated.

I sank to the dirt to keep myself together, and sat there, like a pile of ashes, staring at nothing.

Rejection on this scale was a feeling I did not even know I could have.

I felt I had lost the love of the only person in the entire world I had ever truly loved. The love my son shared with me seemed to disappear as if it had never existed, as if it didn't matter, as if it had never mattered. I could not understand how that could be.

I did not understand that Abraham had to risk the loss of love to regain his lost self. The mist of a massive defeat hovered around the fringes of my mind, and it clung like sweat. I needed to love him. I needed something or someone to love ... everyone does. It can be an idea, a country, an object, a person but to lose that love is catastrophic.

My spirit sent out a cry that was low and inexpressibly sad as my dream died. It was like opening the door to dreariness and perpetual rain outside and just not caring.

Once a dream is gone, a part of our soul is gone too.

What do you want? A small voice questioned in the far recess of my mind.

I want to be at ease. I want people to be kind to me, always. Yes! I want to be in a perfect world where happiness flourishes, where forgiveness thrives, and where my mistakes are trifles.

I wanted to live in a world that didn't exist.

Come on Eleni, search for yourself. Remember who you are in your best moments. It's too hard to continually struggle with what I don't feel. Think of the ideal Self. Be loyal to that person.

In the past, I would have talked to Peter about it, who would have sworn, "Schweinehund! To heck with him if he treats you like that!"

No, no, remember, loyalty turns betrayal into a love that is then repaid. I clenched my fists. *Be loyal and one day Abraham will be.*

I pressed my lips together to foster conviction. *Be*

courageous — life changes. Let me feel the intensity of my sorrow and loss, and not be burdened by it. Let me have strong passion for life. Let my family thrive!

I looked around with sightless eyes. A layer enveloped me, a dark shroud, a sharp blade of emotional hurt worse than physical pain struck me.

Self-pity perfected.

My thoughts were empty. Along with the world falling apart, my world had fallen apart. Pandemonium. I stared down the street and watched a starved cat creep by, both ears shredded and tattered by conflict.

The air raid sirens wailed.

The Russians came.

Saturday, January 27, 1945
The Night and the Fog
Chapter Twenty-Seven

It was too dangerous to stay in Kutno. Dealing with the Russians was a lesson already learned. The native Germans would learn the hard way. The Russians came with big trucks into the county of Hohensalza to load up with loot. Cigarettes hung from their lips, and their trucks smoked as well. The soldiers were promised booty and plenty of licence.

Anika wailed, "We must flee! The weather is turning bad, I can tell. We have no clothes for travelling in this winter weather."

I looked out the window of the train station where former lawns and flowerbeds, rank with straggling weeds and dead gladioli, stuck out from under the accumulating snow.

I spoke sharply to Abraham, "There is a winter storm coming. Go! Get the clothes from where the soldiers are fighting. Now! Run!"

Abraham understood what he needed to do. He left without a word.

"Where are the trains?" asked Anika

"There are no trains from this station," I replied.

"What! What have we been doing here!?"

"I just found out. I can't make them come here!"

In an hour, Abraham was back with clothes covered in blood.

"Give them to me just like that."

My mother stared at me, "You think there are choices you will never make ..."

"But you do," I finished. "You need their extra warmth. Put them on." I pointed to the grown-ups.

They looked at me strangely as I lay down the thick grey blankets we had found in the train station. "Here, lie down. Quickly. The clothes will not be enough." I motioned to my children.

After I had cut out their shapes in a single piece, I handily sewed the two sides of the coarse blankets together. I hoped these new outfits would keep the children warm.

That is how we managed.

The foreboding of the oncoming Russian reprisal chased us toward the next railway station located slightly west of Kutno. A freak winter blizzard hit us with such force I thought we would die on the spot. We had to get to Berlin. The time to quicken the pace happened when we could no longer hear the sounds of fighting.

The only conclusion I could come up with was the sheer excitement of pillaging German villages in a snowstorm had prevented the Russian military from harassing our little group. Our luck would not last. The silence told me the Russians had gotten through, and sure enough, we observed German soldiers retreating via Kutno.

"The Russians are coming," snarled a small German soldier with brown teeth and fish lips who bolted crossed our path. "Watch where you are going! Do not come close! You're in my way!" he lashed out recklessly.

Abraham was jolted back to the present. "You do not know what the Russians are like," he hastily spat back. I could scarcely see him through the falling snow.

"The Russians are coming." He had a secretive smile. He held his hands up by his shoulders, rapidly bending and straightening his thumbs as if to repeatedly give an affirmative thumbs-up signal. After which his hands rapidly clapped together compulsively and then found their way back into his pockets.

Murder was written all over his face. He smiled again, wicked with delight, and moved on.

"Stay close, no matter what!" I grabbed Abraham, pulling him along. When we reached the next train station, it was mayhem. Everyone rushed out to the platform. "Stay together!" I screamed to my family. The heaving crowd nearly forced me onto the track. Susannah thrashed madly to stay on her feet and keep hold of Heinchen's hand. The crowd went riotous when a train edged its way into the station.

"Get inside the train car!"

"I can't Mutti!"

"The doors are closed!"

"I am freezing!"

"Mutti!"

The storm battered at the shut train cars. I could hardly see. Susannah held Heinchen in her arms as we banged on the rail cars. Someone yelled from inside the train, "Let that woman with her children inside the car."

And they did.

Just like that, the doors opened and we tumbled in. People

were already crammed tight. On the outside of the train, people jumped on the rungs. They hung on everywhere, people clung like hoar frost.

In the dead of the night, the last train pulled out before the Russians came.

But the train travelled for only a few minutes when the car door was thrown open despite the bitter freezing weather. A German *Hauptman* stood outside the car. This captain was an imposing, floridly handsome man with startling blue-green eyes under thick brows that slanted down at the corners.

"*Raus, raus, Meine Soldaten brauchen ...*" He told the civilians to get out of the cars and let his soldiers in.

I could not believe my ears. "I need the car," I frantically pleaded with the officer. "Please, for the sake of the children!"

"We need the car, not you!" Oma shrieked.

The night was arctic and the *Oberleutnant* snapped into action on command, yelling, "I do not care! My soldiers are commandeering the train. They have been without shelter for days in this icy weather." I'm sure he was thinking it was like the Battle of Stalingrad, where the temperatures had dropped far below zero.

The light from a lantern cast a shadow across the lieutenant's thick neck and jowls, rising from broad shoulders in a single column. His countenance displayed an expression of utter and callous disregard for others, a desire to hurt, a deliberate, chilling perversity. His men pushed and hauled us out of the railway car.

It was a dreadful winter, like Stalingrad in 1943, when General von Paulus was ordered by Hitler to take Stalingrad; surrender had been strictly forbidden. Ironically, the Russian army had also been ordered by Stalin not to take a step backwards. Every soldier was expected to hold his position to the last man, and by his heroic endurance make an unforgettable contribution towards the establishment of a defensive front and the salvation of his nation! Folly. Hitler pursued disadvantage after disadvantage, rejecting common sense while communicating his irrational directive to General von Paulus. It was stupidity.

Hitler promised the conquest of Russia in six weeks. Propaganda in Germany was a huge lie bolstered by newsreels showing one German victory after another. German soldiers were shown eating hot food and frolicking in the snow. It was a lie. After an entire year of brutal siege and hand to hand combat, Paulus, obviously a more rational man, surrendered Stalingrad, but the failure of the German Army was a disaster for the Nazis, a monstrous defeat. A complete army group was lost when 91,000 Germans were taken prisoner. The Battle of Stalingrad was a turning point.

After this defeat, the Germany Army retreated using every means to pull their troops back. Such a massive loss of soldiers and equipment made it impossible for the Germans to cope with the Russian advance to Germany. In his fury, Hitler ordered a day of national mourning, not for the men lost at the battle, but for the shame Paulus had brought on the Wehrmacht and Germany. Hitler commented that the God of War had gone over to the enemy.

Perhaps the memory of General Paulus strengthened the resolve of the German soldiers to commandeer the train. This train, at least, they had control over.

"Friend or fiend? In war, there are only fiends!" I spat and gestured at the German soldiers who were now inside our train car.

"They are wicked," someone else muttered.

"I can't believe that it is German soldiers who kick us out of the train!"

"They think only of themselves."

"The captain came and threw open the doors. The sins of the forefathers have appeared with their past written upon them, and it is the children who suffer! I can't believe they shoved women and children out to get into the boxcar."

"They have lost, lost to the Russians," came another bitter reply. "The soldiers were ice cold. Can't you see their hands are frozen and fingers are missing?"

"What about us!"

"They kicked us out! All of us, into the cold!"

"I could scratch his eyes out." Filled with anger, I hissed under my breath. "But what good would it do? You can't do anything. Arguing would not make one bit of difference." We watched the train rumble off.

We were afraid to turn back into town because of the lack of law and order. The government officials, the police, and military were all in flight. Most of the public buildings and vacant private houses had already been looted since the departure of authority. Ironically, we had been evading any government authority for days, and now we were alarmed because those very people were absent.

Like an isolated grove of spindly trees, the group of twenty outcasts from the train stood mute beside the tracks. Silhouettes of bombed buildings showed gritty gaps in the landscape. An icy yellow stench filled the air. It was already a cemetery. A dark angular caricature of a cat sneaked by with its mustard eyes and barely pink nose raised to sniff the air.

I was worried about Heinchen and Anika. Both were sicker than I would like to admit. The little one had been having bouts of diarrhea since the day before. There had been so little food. We were exhausted.

"Here, here!" a woman with a small child motioned to us. "Get behind this." It was the remnants of a former doorway.

"Mrs. Doerksen!" Abraham exclaimed when he recognized Klara's mother. "Where is the rest of your family?"

She made a faint motion with her hand.

"Mutti, I am cold," moaned Heinchen. His small frame was limp.

"It's no good to think about it now. You get through this night now. Do you hear me?" I gently shook him. "You survive.

You live! You just do. You get through it!"

"*Ja, ja.* That is true little man, you get through it." I nodded with gratitude to Mrs. Doerksen, who spoke quietly, "I have been fleeing the Russians for seven days. My family got separated. I do not know where they are …"

Her voice quivered with fear. "We have barely eaten. Kaethe is so weak."

I looked at the limp child in her arms.

"The Reds have followed us relentlessly, pillaging everything German." Mrs. Doerksen did not even cry. She did not have the strength for it.

The strangers in the group began to entrust their stories to each other. We were not strangers now, not now — for we had a moral obligation compelling us to listen. We are ourselves but we are others too. Each one in the group owed the other a terrible loyalty, for we were bound together by the horror of war.

"People lay in the farmyards and at the edge of roads. There was evidence of systematic murder."

"Everything and everyone German is the target of the Russians. Women and children were squashed flat. Their ill-fated souls were rolled over by Russian tanks along with wagons and teams of horses."

We listened, mesmerized by revulsion.

"Never underestimate the power of hate."

"Anger is the means. Destruction is the objective. Although I may be an unimportant person, I will use my voice to say that it is *wrong*. Wrong!"

"Russian vengeance."

"Women were stripped naked and crucified onto barn doors. Babies had their heads bashed in or sheared off with an axe or spade."

"Stalin wants the Germans to suffer."

"They destroyed everything, even what they could use. Wagons were hurled into the ditches on top of the entrails of horses."

I visualized the terror. It seemed as if all the suffering of humanity were outside my window and if we could not get on to another train to Berlin we would sink into the ground and be consumed.

"Mutti," Abraham whispered to me, "Little Kaethe is very

ill. Will she make it to Berlin?"

"Hush, Abraham, God have mercy!" The picture of that darling child in the camp at Zator was a painful memory. "Don't even question such a thing!"

On this very day, the Russian army finally descended upon Zator and nearby Auschwitz, along with several feet of snow that covered western Poland and eastern Germany. In the grim darkness, my group whimpered and shivered like dogs that have been shut outside in the cold. We dug down into the debris to huddle together and keep warm. In those hours before daybreak, we could not shake ourselves loose of the vile images and nightmares. During the night, little Kaethe died.

In the morning, Mrs. Doerksen sat there holding Kaethe in her arms. "She stirred in my arms and then stopped breathing." This memory would haunt me for the rest of my life. "I can't leave her here, Eleni. I can't."

Unbelievably, almost immediately, the morning temperature rose. The morning sky was fine, but down below the rapidly melting snow transformed the ground into a quagmire. Everything was bogged down in the morass. All day long, the snow melted and the ice dripped. Miraculously, German trucks, churning their way west as they fled the Russians, appeared. They halted on the roadside to refuel at the only gasoline depot within miles.

The Germans had been there for twenty minutes when Abraham said to me, "We will need passes to get in those trucks, Mutti. It is our only chance." Abraham watched the trucks forlornly.

"Yes, I know. I got them."

"How?"

"I got them." I did not look at Abraham but headed for the trucks.

The selected survivors were loaded onto the truck beds. We sat wordlessly as the open trucks bumped and jarred laboriously along. I was almost paralyzed after the hardships of the last two days. Abraham did not sit near me.

The coming evening sent a cold and colourless light over the landscape as we approached Krustryn. The roads ran with liquid mud and small tuffs of fog came to lie softly in the hollows so that sounds were muted and distant. We would cross the Oder River bridge at Bernbaum.

Abraham sucked his breath in sharply, "Mutti ...!"

I stared mutely at the two rotting corpses hanging from the rafters of the bridge. The bridge to freedom. They had been stripped of their German uniforms. The rain dripped off their remains and landed on our heads as we drove underneath. It was the mark of the devil.

"Deserters," someone whispered.

We bent our heads and turned our eyes away. You cannot kill a yearning, a body yes, but a longing, no. Out of the thousands of deserting soldiers, here were two soldiers the German army had caught and shot. The bloated corpses swayed and shook from the vibration of our trucks moving over the wooden bridge as if they were trying to come back to life. The bridge to freedom, spanning the Oder River.

Life is so sad, like a manic dog that shakes its prey to death by snapping its neck.

March 30, 1945
Tribben, near Berlin
Chapter Twenty-Eight

Specific misfortunes can harden the heart — if we let them. Susannah watched Abraham out of the corner of her eye as he pointed to himself with a little nod. He seemed to be emotionally hanging on and letting go at the same time. Even though Susannah understood the tacit agreement with her brother, she could not make eye contact with him. They were both like little steam trains in a toy room puffing on their own tiny circular tracks, only aware of the other so that they would not collide in the crossing.

Once they had reached Tribben, Abraham was astonished how events had turned out. He wondered if God had anything to do with it. He was not convinced but how else could they have survived? Abraham felt an earnest desire to dispel his substantial amount of guilt about having ignored God and the church in the past. Many times he had not paid attention when his father had read the Bible. He had disobeyed his mother. In fact, he had downright doubted the existence of God. He leaned a little closer to Susannah, who was sitting beside him.

"What are you thinking?" Susannah asked. "Tribben isn't bad. We've been here for two months but you hardly talk to me. You could at least share what you're thinking with me."

Abraham's body radiated an intensity that screamed to be explored.

"What are you thinking," she asked again, moving her hands as she spoke.

"Wie kommt es, daß es so ist?" He forced the words out in a husky voice. He was searching for the intersection that would mark a change of direction and not a collision. He shared, a little bit, but not enough for Susannah to really understand what had happened to him.

"Abraham," Susannah said curtly, "Abraham, I don't know why things have come to be the way they are, but the way you see life now … it's the way you see what has happened … and that is important but remember your perception is not the truth. It is the way *you* see it."

It wasn't that she didn't believe the little he had told her, it as that she wanted to shed a different light on it and move on. She could see where he needed to go. It was agonizing for her to slow down. She tapped her foot and smoothed her dress with her hands. Everyday, it is war. Sometimes I think I am a nonentity."

Abraham quietly responded, "What a blessing it would be if I could think only of myself and not care about anybody else, then no one could hurt me."

Susannah's face flushed. Her hurried tone became elevated, for she did not want to lose this opportunity. She risked pressing him for more.

Abraham seemed disoriented and sucked in his breath as he babbled away. Susannah used his intensity to generate positive responses, the pieces that would remind him he was a good person, and ignored everything else pointing to a different conclusion.

Abraham couldn't tell her everything. He just couldn't.

As he withdrew and slouched back into the chair, Susannah realized how vulnerable he was to loss and shame. She knew something had happened to him, but did not know what. How she wanted him to continue speaking! How she wanted a discussion where healing was the focal point!

"Will you be alright, Abraham?"

He did not answer.

"Where is Tante Anika? She is going out all the time."

"I have to go to work now." His voice was laced with frustration.

For the last few weeks, Abraham no longer went to German school, a circumstance he was elated about. Back in the Ukraine, Lieutenant Strauss had said there would be German schools for German children, like in the Reich. Strauss had stood at attention when he had lectured Abraham on the honour of being an ethnic German and stated that Abraham would have to learn to appreciate it!

Abraham had not been impressed. The Lieutenant had then told him he should be careful about what he said about being a *Volksdeutscher* and had gone on to say that Abraham was a child and would have to be watched. To which Abraham had replied, *Das ist mir scheißegal* as far as the Reich was concerned. The reference that it was all shit had not sat well with Lieutenant Strauss.

Initially at school in Tribben, Abraham had put up his hand to say that he wanted to take the German high school test. The principal of the school had responded that the high school test was not available to damned Russians even though Abraham was academically at the head of the class. He had further insulted Abraham, calling him a communist, a Jew, and a factory worker. At the time, Abraham didn't know what to think about the ostracism, for he had never been considered a factory worker.

So instead of going to school, Abraham found a trade job with a printer. He had shown the employer his carefully forged school report, number 322, his *Schulentlassungszeugnis* stated he had completed the 8th class. He had always behaved at school because he loved learning and Abraham was attentive; therefore, *Betragen - gut, Aufmerksamkeit - gut.* Eleni had left *Fleiss, Ordnung und Sauberkeit* blank, to make the document more authentic. Truthfully, it had been difficult to be totally compliant, orderly, and clean.

As a mother, Eleni thought the grade of "good" for those categories stretched belief a little too far. *Schulbesuch - Regelmäßig.* Of course, Abraham loved to attend school. *Deutsche Sprache - gut und Schriben - befriedigend.* He was a bit of a talker in the right circumstances. His German language was good and his writing was satisfactory. *Zeichnen, Rechnen, Geschichte, Staatsbürgerschaft - alle sehr gut.* Abraham was smart and, of course, the comments were very good for arithmetic and the citizenship mark would be looked upon as the foundation of a good student. Abraham was also good in physical activities such as swimming and gymnastic exercises, like any true German. Obviously, there would be no grade for needlework or housecraft, and tactfully, another category was left blank, religion.

Only in one class was Abraham graded deficient, *mangelhaft,* and that was in music. Eleni couldn't hide that; although, he loved music. Susannah had never even heard Abraham sing, not ever. It was a believable report, stamped with the eagle and the swastika, and inscribed with *Der Leiter der Volksschule in Christinendorf,* the official seal Eleni had accessed to craft the forgery. The final touch on the bottom left hand corner was *Nachdruck verboten,* a directive to forbid reprinting.

And so, with his forged report card, he had secured his first job. He felt lucky.

Lucky. Ironically, Abraham was lucky. He was not the target of Rosenberg's Top Secret memorandum for the occupied Eastern Territories, detailing how to apprehend vast numbers of youth, transport them to the heart of the German Reich, and assign them primarily to the German trades. This action arranged through the Organization Todt was welcomed by the German trade since it represented a decisive measure to alleviate the shortage of apprentices. Susannah was grateful that Abraham was allowed to stay with his family. She was thrilled with the new challenges of employment for him. She confidently believed any idiot could do the job and since he was not an idiot, he would be successful.

Susannah was incredibly resourceful and supported Abraham any way she could. She was on her way to becoming an emotionally healthy adult not driven by childhood conflicts. She held a realistic and optimistic view of life. Current events and her future plans influenced her more than her painful past. She took conscious control of as much of her life as she could.

"I am going now," he repeated to Susannah. "Mutti has gone for an interview. You have to look after Heinchen."

"We can talk again when you get back?" Susannah spoke to the back of Abraham's head.

****

"Eleni. Your name is Eleni." He was interviewing me for the school position. I refused to look directly at him. "I am *Oberscharführer* Manfred Kerrem."

"Yes," I replied. "I have papers from teaching in the Ebenfeld refugee camp in Colony Memrik, but in January 1943 we had to leave for Waldheim and join the retreat of the German troops."

He said steadily. "You mean the relocation of the troops?"

I nodded warily in compliance. In 1943, Lieutenant Strauss had told me there were only a few Germans left in the area, scattered over several villages and when the Germans pulled out, we should too. The Lieutenant had not made it back. On his primary deployment to the Eastern front, he had met with a bullet in the middle of his forehead.

"*Alles in Ordnung.*" The senior squad leader finalized the application. "It's a good thing I am here in Tribben as a ... substitute this morning. This is not how I usually spend my time." He nodded superciliously and shrugged in reply to my questioning glance. "It is war. We follow orders." He gave a slight shrug again. "I will assign you as the teacher in our little school, not here in

Tribben, but in Christinendorf."

"Thank you. Thank you, *Oberscharführer*." My relief and joy were evident. The children could stay in Trebbin, and I would work in Christinendorf. I got up and then prudently sat down again.

"You have come quite a distance," he continued, pretending not to notice my eagerness to be away.

My hunger to stay alive made me more defensive, cagey. I ventured, "We almost didn't make it from the camp at Zator. We travelled through Pabiance and Kutno."

He exhaled slowly, forcing a smile as he met my gaze. "Where is your husband?"

He must have seen me hesitate even though it was a mere second, not even. "My Peter was killed in an air raid."

I sensed him start, the type of reaction one has when bits of life spring out like unruly hair that will not stay put. It was the type of response that made me wonder if the emotional fabric of life was loosening a touch. Was it possible … that our stories were braided together somehow? I ignored the thought.

"I am sorry to hear of your loss," he spoke automatically. "You have a family?"

"Yes, two sons. Abraham and Heinchen, and a daughter, Susannah."

"Ah, yes ... that is good, yet it is difficult when all you are left with are a few meager possessions, a satchel maybe or various letters and papers, that sort of thing."

I should have been more alert for it was a curious statement. "We had walked so far already, and we weren't able to carry much! We were desperate when the blizzard struck. I thought we would freeze." I stood up self-consciously, holding the chair's backrest.

"Was that when you lost Peter?" He tried to make the question sound as nonchalant as possible.

I shrugged. "You have been to Zator?" A small bell of memory and warning tinkled in my head, way in the back, trying to get my attention. I ignored it.

"Zator is a difficult area. You must have been in agony there." He tried again to steer the conversation.

I looked at him sarcastically "No. Agony is lying in a shell hole with your legs shot off. My sister said she would rather starve than beg. I said to her, 'Go ahead'. We are accustomed to living in fear." I stood taller.

Manfred nodded. I interpreted the look on his face as approval and imagined him thinking, *Yes, this woman has spunk.*

I spoke more confidently, "Yes. I went out onto the streets in the villages we passed through to beg for food. I would come back with three potatoes. That is how we survived. I could not afford to be proud. I was desperate. I had a small child who cried, *'Mutti, ich habe Hunger.'* "

I thought his man, who doubtless could be hard in his heart, understood.

"We were starving. Even though we are hungry here too, it was different. That kind of thing stabs in your heart. I will never forget the small voices of my children."

"You have a place to stay here, for you and your family?" His newly developed empathy made him shift in his seat.

"Yes, the old schoolhouse building here in Tribben." I paused. "I will be on my way now. Goodbye." I wanted to hurry to relay the good news to the family. I was elated to have the position at the school in Christinendorf, which was ten kilometres away. Eager to see where we would be living in Tribben, I took a detour to the vacant schoolhouse.

Nevertheless, it took me a while to reach the old building that would be our home. Tomorrow, we would move from the cramped single room we had been living in. The yard was filled with the struggling shrubs and bushes reclaiming their lives after the winter season. Inside, I looked around the unused room contemplatively. It was in good shape, surprisingly. I inspected the small building, even going down to the basement to check its condition. When I returned upstairs, I saw him.

He stood in the doorway and peered into the room. The painted plaster walls held a soft wash cream colour imparting a luminescence, the final caress of evening sun. It was a moment of peace. The wave of his lips broke into a fleeting smile. "Hello." The pleasant tone caught me by surprise. "You forgot your papers."

I snatched the papers from his outstretched hand. Despite completing his errand, he did not leave the doorstep. "Good," he said.

"Are you staying to see how I am doing?" I retorted. I glanced up, caught him looking at me, and flushed with confusion. His need was too blatant to be a total compliment, but it elicited memories of an unencumbered girlhood with youthful fantasies, bringing me a flash of pleasure. He caught my eye, daring me. I looked away. His reticence was annoying; yet, I felt connected to him in a wistful sort of way.

My thoughts came in a hurried muddle. *You cannot live your life as you lived it in the past. He's not your past. Not him. Not with him. Decide how you will live today. This isn't working. I can't go back. This will not work. He is very handsome.*

My spoken voice had a catch in it, out of nervousness, but the next thing I said was only "hello".

I know it happens. People are attracted to someone as diametrically opposed to their life as can be. Perhaps we both wanted to make a point of independence and trigger a fond memory. If we belonged to each other, even for a moment, we belonged to the creation of a memory, a connection. Doesn't that matter? Wouldn't I then be important?

Maybe, it was none of these ideas. I wasn't sure. I found it difficult to think.

He grasped the bush by the door and broke off a twig to mask the awkwardness of the moment. He seemed somewhat lost. The sun was going down but still tinting the clouds at a high point in the sky. The bright hues lingered with the sunset. The mutual attraction was obvious.

"Shut the door."

"Yes," he replied. "We don't want to let the heat out."

How swiftly we both became entangled. He was already beside me, shaking. I could barely see him in the dim light of the room. He touched my arm. The feel of his hot hand made my blood stir. Like seconds of golden sunshine, all the burdens fell off my shoulders. I was suspended in a perfect moment. Bliss. All I was aware of was the eagerness of my body. He clasped me intimately and kissed me. His entire body burned with an earnestness that endeared him to me. We sank to the floor.

"In a few moments, we will have a wonderful secret together," he whispered in my ear.

I stretched and arched towards him, guiding him to me, feeling the heat of his skin and the pressing of his body. I felt the pulsating hardness slip into me and my body moved of its own desire. I encouraged him on with my escaping little noises. I felt his powerful thrust as he moaned incoherently. He surged into me. I clung to him.

The speed of the encounter astonished me as I cradled him in my arms, holding him with a sleepy tenderness. He kissed my exposed breasts. I kissed his hair and cheeks in a natural gesture that thrilled both our hearts. We lay together in the quiet of the room. Under that spell, he brushed his lips on my skin and caressed me again.

Outside, the sun had gone and a contrasting wane before the darkest indigo night sent silvery soft moonbeams falling into tight angles and hidden places lingered. The shuttered and bombed out windows in the buildings were like blind eyes. Even so, I saw my world.

Peter had not been a romantic adventurer but a misguided fool. I saw how the horrors of the recent years had affected my children. I felt how perilous the situation was; yet, I continued to dream of the West. I felt hope in the vision of a different life.

A week later, when he left for duty, he pressed a piece of paper into the palm of my hand.

"My family address," Manfred emphasized, looking me straight in the eye. "They will help. Write to this address if we are separated. The Russians are close, and I am with the *Waffen SS*."

I nodded, speechless. I knew the gravity of the time we were in, but I fought to keep the influence of the collective drama of war, occupation, and constant struggle to a minimum. I accepted the paper with the Elsterverda address.

****

Two days later, I found him on a cot in the military hospital.

He spoke with animation, gesturing to accentuate a point. "They caught our patrol by surprise." He reached forward and grabbed my shoulder. "Not many soldiers were lucky to escape the assault." I moved sideways as if to shrug him off, but he held on with a vice grip. "We should have died … I am the senior squad leader. I should have died." My hand went up to pry off his fingers, while I tried to smile reassuringly.

"You are alive." I tried to calm him and myself. "I won't be going far."

"You will come back?" His angst was apparent. He seemed to be broken. Unmendable. "It was chaos. The Germans are … How is this even possible? I don't want to die … You will come back …"

His eyes brimmed with tears that were as far from happiness as you could get. I was struck by his appearance. I felt like I was encapsulated in his desperate love with no way out. I had known how gentle he could be and had known how his love caressed me. It had been warm and comforting, yet I knew his pain. The tears of his anguish captured me, surrounding me and molding me into an equally imperfect vessel to be filled. Being there was enough.

"Of course, I will," my heart replied. "I must speak with the doctor." The sunlight scattered across the floor as it caught the fragmented window glass. By the time I returned, Manfred had written me a note containing a poem, *Das Mädchen unter der Laterne,* composed by a comrade who had been in Hamburg with him.

Vor der Kaserne,

vor dem Großen Tor

stand eine Laterne,

und steht sich noch davor,

so wolln wir uns da wiedersehen,

bei der Laterne wolln wir stehn

wie einst, Lili Marleen.

In front of the barracks, at the large entrance gate stood a lamplight, and it is still standing there, so we want to see each other there again, by the lamplight where we stood before, Lili Marlene.

Unsere beide Schatten

Sahn wie einer aus.

Daß wir so lieb uns hatten,

das sah man gleich daraus.

Und alle Leute sollen es sehn

Wenn wir bei der Laterne stehn,

wie einst, Lili Marleen.

Our two shadows seemed as one. That we were so much in love, one saw at once. And everyone should see it when we are standing by the lamplight as before, Lili Marlene.

Schon rief der Posten,

sie blasen Zapfenstreich,

es kann drei Tage kosten.

Kamerad, ich komm ja gleich.

Da sagten wir auf Wiedersehen,

wie gerne wollt ich mit mir dir gehn,

mit dir, Lili Marleen.

Soon, the sentry called out, they are sounding curfew, it can cost you three days. Comrade, I am coming right away. Then we said goodbye, how much I wanted to go with you, with you, Lili Marlene.

Deine Schritte kennt sie,

deinen zieren Gang,

alle Abend brennt sie,

mich vergiß sie lang.

Und sollte mir ein Leids geschehn,

wer wird bei der Laterne stehn,

mit dir Lili Marleen?

It knows your footsteps, your graceful walk, every evening it is burning, but forgot me long ago. And if harm should come to me, who will stand at the lamplight with you, Lili Marlene?

Aus dem stillen Raume,

aus der Erde Grund

hebt mich wie im Traume

dein verliebter Mund.

Wenn sich die späten Nebel drehn,

werd ich bei der Laterne stehn

Wie einst, Eleni Marleen.

Out of the still place, out of the earthly ground, I am lifted as if in a dream to your loving lips. When the evening fog swirls in, I will be standing at the lamplight as before, Eleni Marlene.

"Oh Manfred," I laughed. "Nice touch at the end with my name. Too bad I don't have a second name. This song is lovely. It is one of my favorites."

"Here," he insisted as he hastily pulled a gift for me from under his pillow with effort. "Keep it in here." He flashed a shy smile that meant *we understand, don't we?*

I accepted it meditatively. It was a round metal music box. The hand painted porcelain lid showed a 17th century woman sitting on a bench and a man on his knees before her. When the porcelain lid was lifted, the *Donauwellen* tune tinkled beautifully.

"How ...?"

"I have ways," he hastily whispered. "I knew you would come. I had to have a gift for you. A gift you deserve, not this." He gestured with disgust at his body. "I am afraid that my memory will fail. Everything is mixed up in my brain," he whispered and grabbed his head. "Don't leave me. Don't leave me! I long to remember you. It is what I need. Does love fade too when we no longer remember?"

There was so much I wanted to remember, and even more I wanted to forget. Yet, the more I could remember of the good and the bad, the more divine my life would be.

"Shh, shh, Manfred." His frantic endeavours shook me. He had been shot in the lower leg, not his head. His tremendous angst didn't make any sense to me. "It's all right," I soothed him. "You will be safe here. They will move you to another hospital. You must sleep."

"My foot. Eleni, my foot is the worst. I cannot walk."

"It will heal. It needs time …"

"There may not be the time!"

I could feel the urgency in our lives and pressed my lips together. I didn't have many comforting words left. His panic was unnerving because the Russians could come to the hospital any time. I took a deep breath. "We are not victims, Manfred. We will take what comes and survive." It was not what I was feeling.

He gulped the air, "We will not stop striving for ideals, Eleni, for us, for each other." He held my hand in a vice grip.

I looked deep into his eyes. "I will make room for you and keep you in my heart, Manfred," was my response. "Being loved by you, Manfred, makes me feel like I am capable of even more love. Grace lives through action, the action of love."

Manfred threw my hand away. I could see how he hardened at the thought. "This is war, Eleni. Stop talking nonsense. You sound like you are ready to forgive everybody!" He waved my response away with a flourish of his hand. "Loving in these times is difficult … what if …?"

"Hush, Manfred." I shook my head. "What is happening in the world now are events that are too weighty for us. I only meant … God have mercy on my soul."

"You're not angry with me for this, are you?" he gestured violently at his leg. The indignity of the wound made him flush. The dishonour of having survived taunted him.

"I couldn't be angry with you. I'll never be angry with you — ever." I implored him with searching eyes. "Oh, Manfred, I am here. I will always be here. You can always come to me, my love."

The tension of the war bound us together. However miniscule our shared moments of love, it felt like we would love forever, no matter how cliché that sounded. Without the connection of love, belonging, every human existence is a void. Love is the bliss that makes all things true.

"What is done is done. We make huge mistakes. Our failures are common to all of us," I stated with a practical finality. "We must try to head in the right direction."

"For you that direction is west!" Manfred blurted. We both broke out in uncomfortable laughter followed by an abrupt and long silence filled with Manfred's hurt.

I nodded quietly, encouraging him to speak.

"We thought we were invincible." His hand waved toward the window. "It was like the wind appeared in that cobalt blue and darkening sky and I was harried along to become a storm, Eleni." Tears came to his eyes again.

"It is a type of insidious regret, making me feel the need to hide myself where I could never be reached," The brine on his cheeks made meandering stains down his drawn face. He stifled the moaning of his rediscovered soul.

Previously, his tears had been the symbols of excitement and loyalty. He had unashamedly pursued his pleasures, his lust for Nazi supremacy, and desire of a promised future. Embraced, that dream had pulsed for a while. A wave of shameful realization left him now with tears of surprise that what he had held dear, what he had pursued, were tears of illusion.

"Eleni," Manfred confided. "There is much to regret."

His former provocative smile became tight lips of regret. "All these years, I followed and obeyed. Right now, I can tell you, the monster of regret is seizing my soul, without regret, without warning, and leaving me with a single question, 'Do you realize what you have done?'" Manfred hung his head and stared into his upturned palms.

"I am still a German soldier, even here, on this bed. No matter what prison I may physically end up in. My earlier life is like a prison too, but I promise you my heart will escape to be free and true, and to love you, Eleni."

"I promise to love you, Manfred."

"You must leave and go west. I will find you." He grabbed my hand, crushing my fingers and placed it on my chest. "This is where I live, Eleni, in your heart. This is where I belong. It is where my heart is and where I am happiest. I will not apologize for that."

I knew so little about him. "This is the way it has turned out. I did not know it yesterday, but I know it today." I was sure.

Tomorrow, the Russian swarm would arrive.

April 20, 1945
Escape
Chapter Twenty-Nine

Abraham needed silence as a witness to the degradation he had experienced in his life, but now, another need, a need to begin the healing process, emerged. He needed to tell his story. He chose Susannah because the love she had for him would be his shield against judgment; however, he never found a chance to speak with her and by the evening, he was pent up with emotion.

There was an overwhelming feeling of irritation. He wanted to be loved, not aggravated. Every minute he wanted to know that he mattered. He didn't want to feel ignored. He needed to be treated gently and indulged. He longed to have a fuss made over him all day. He desired to be enmeshed in pleasure. The goal was to be happy and have all his desires filled immediately.

It was infantile.

For him, it was too bad that it couldn't happen. It would have helped him, at the very least, to feel a little bit better about himself. Instead, he brooded, his inner dialogue fighting between what was sensible and right, and what was plain wrong.

I would like to have days and days with a true friend to see what it is really like, but the truth is I would grow to hate it. I like to have time alone, yet, I need to know someone cares about me. I need someone to tell me that.

His despair crushed his confidence.

It doesn't work to say it to myself. I can't do it. I know that. Why do I doubt myself when I am not around people, when they are not praising me and telling me what I love to hear?

This thought made him feel worse, of course, but he couldn't seem to stop it.

I question myself all the time. My faith in myself is so shallow. My faith in God, so ... thin. I wanted a beautiful life .... that past dream is gone.

His guilt at feeling so bad was taking over.

I held a dream for the future. How futile! I haven't been able to get over my bad experiences. I can't forget any of it. Most of my life has been a life of misery.

As he began to work it through, his story looked ugly. The fading light of the day and the incoming darkness of the night seemed to parallel his emotional descent. He rallied. A glimmer of light appeared.

Hope for better life.

For a second, illumination, and then it was shut out only to reappear elsewhere!

His mind, like the leaves of the trees stirring in the slight breeze, flicked the silvery white light to and fro upon the chaotic pile of twigs on the dark forest floor.

Does anybody care how dreadfully lonely I am?

He kicked his foot on the floor.

I detest stupidity. I detest weakness. I detest that cowering submission life clearly beats upon my head. I detest it! I do! I am exhausted. I am angry at being full of fear.

His family ignored his mutterings and had settled down to sleep for the night. He swore a blue streak. His venting rehearsed every fault he could find in himself. It solidified his unhelpful self-perceptions through each repetition.

It bothers me that people do not say what they think. It bothers me that I am intolerant of people's struggles. What do I care if they cannot speak up? Yet, it annoys me immensely when someone does say what they think. I can't have it both ways. I am fed up with compromising. I am!

He laid his head on his blanket and begged irritably for sleep to come. The wood floor beneath his blanket was as hard and unforgiving as he was to himself.

I am sick and tired of sneaking around, of running, and everything else that goes along with it. I have had enough!

He lashed out loudly at Susannah, who was already fast asleep, "You know what else? If you ask for my opinion, at least listen to it without getting incensed that it is different than yours!"

Oma turned to tell him to be quiet, to which Abraham hastily replied, "If you are going to roll your eyes every time I speak contrary to what you say, then go get yourself shot! Seriously, I am so sick and tired of your eye rolling!"

When a spirit is crushed, one becomes peevish at small offences, forgets the great ones, and sadly, fails to distinguish between those who love us and those who do not.

****

I burst in through the door. I had covered the ten somber kilometers from Christinendorf while it was still dark. War is a hard schoolmistress. There would be no more days to teach reading and writing. I found Abraham, Susannah, Heinchen, and Oma crowded together in the dark basement of the old building.

"Where is Anika?" I asked in disbelief.

"Tante Anika has already left."

"She …"

"She has an address." The rest was left unsaid. She carried the child of a German soldier and now she was going to his hometown. She would need all the luck in the world.

"They are here!" Abraham was on his tiptoes peeking over the rotten window sill. Through the smudged basement window, I watched a German soldier running by and the Russians close behind. They formed stark grey shapes against the dusky morning sky. The shadows stretched behind them in a tunnel of endless and colourless death.

The gunfire made sharp loud notes and peppered the schoolhouse. We jumped at the sound.

"Put the light out!"

I took Heinchen in my arms. His pasty wet forehead flopped

on my breast. "Heinchen! You're sick!" I was frantic. This was supposed to be our most western destination, but it was clear we had to move further west toward Helmstedt, to the British army. "We must leave tonight. *Lieber Gott, sei mit uns.*"

All day we huddled in the basement. When it was dark again, we crept out along the dirt road.

"Mutti," came Heinchen's little voice.

"Yes?"

"Mutti, look at the moon. I guess he didn't eat well."

In the light cast by the half moon, the houses hugged themselves tightly as if to give themselves courage. Panic stifled our ability to breathe and made our limbs resist movement. The rising wind flapped at the new poster boards as if they were swings with phantom riders. I sucked in my breath as I read the Russian slogans on the feeble posters. Red Army Soldier: You are now on German soil; the hour of revenge has struck!"

"What, what is it Mutti?" asked Abraham. His eyes followed mine. Although his Russian was not as good as his mine, but 'German' and 'revenge' were words he could make out. "Life has instantly become very complicated," Abraham said.

Susannah stared at him in amazement.

"Make haste!" I yelled to everyone, even though no one needed prompting.

The blood on the sick soil was old blood from old wounds, not new, but ancient conflicts, conflicts remembered by the Russians and now categorized as injustices and betrayals. How memory can be so accurately inaccurate is astounding.

Perception is not the truth.

The grim reality of being trapped between the Russians and the Germans set in. We hid and scrounged for days. Curtains of rain came. At long last, on Friday, we slipped onto a train that was slinking into the countryside, heading west. It seemed to take forever, but; finally, it crossed the Elbe River.

"We are trapped in this box," Oma said. "This is wrong … conditions should be better."

"It could be worse, Oma," Abraham ridiculed her.

"Abraham!" I said. I was astonished that his rage had such a savage tone to it.

"All I want is for it to be better," whined Oma.

"This is better. Get out of the train. You can see how much

better it is getting," Abraham said sarcastically.

"Now, we walk," I interrupted.

"Where is this?"

"This is the last place on the line. The gauge of the railway track has changed."

"Look," cried Susannah, "we can take the *Schmalbahn* the rest of the way. We won't have to walk!"

But that railway track did not take us far enough. I had no desire to draw attention to myself by arguing with the engineer. No amount of arguing would have taken one single person any further, anyhow. We walked on in the dark.

"I cannot walk. I do not want to walk anymore," lamented Oma, stopping in her tracks.

I turned on her with all my exasperation and frustration. "Wings open, wings close. The bird flies and the bird walks. We don't fly. We walk!" I bellowed.

Following the railroad or the road was too dangerous. Our way to Helmstedt was barred by a slack wire fence that twitched in the wind. A lonely snag of fabric was caught on one of the barbs. I pulled two strands of wire apart and eased myself through, catching my sleeve. I struggled to free it and broke into a sweat even though it was cold. I helped the others through. We picked our way carefully over the countryside.

"I want to go back to my home," Oma cried.

"Your village!"

"Yes."

"It doesn't exist anymore," I said, brutally honest. "There is no village. You cannot go back. Be quiet!"

Ahead, there were waterlogged crusty fields. The scene looked anemic. Here and there were pallid fallen bodies, corpses drained of blood, clutched by the earth and sucked into the ground. There was no going back to before.

"This is different," Abraham sneered. "How disappointing that there isn't even a road." The chilly rain plastered his hair to his head and ran in rivulets down his face. "I thought each day was a new day."

"Shut up!"

"Why, is happiness just around the corner? Afraid, that if it hears me, it might disappear?"

"We have a chance," I urged my family. "Hopefully, no one

will see us."

In the distance, we heard the rat-a-tat-tat of the machine gun.

"I want to go home," chattered Oma. She cried, the tears streamed down her face. She smeared her face with both her hands. "If tears were my thoughts, then I would have so much, and my life would be full."

"You talk like you're on the stage. Don't you know no one is listening?" Abraham whispered a reply. "I know my life is empty. There is no village ... Get it? No place to go! There is no home!" Abraham sniggered. "This is a journey Oma. You know at the end of this you will be a better person. You are on loan anyhow, travelling to the golden gates. I can see them up ahead." Abraham hooted, his finger alongside his nose, pointing across the field into the wood.

"Stop it, Abraham!" I yelled at him.

Like falling dominoes, his emotional state was on the precipice of being a series of fatal emotional collisions. He ignored me. "Remember the Ukraine, Oma. Remember the way the Russians engaged in terror to make us German-speaking Mennonites succumb to a collective way of life — the Russian dream of a better world! Isn't that what you want now, Oma?"

Oma was too terrified to respond to an attack from her own grandson.

"Remember how grateful those German soldiers were to hear their mother tongue! And us too! The arrival of Hitler's army brought euphoria and all our dreams back! All those years, decades, we Mennonites had spent building a viable economic system, only to have it wiped out by the Communist revolution. Do we stay? No! We didn't stay, we decided to flee! We flee because in 1943, those bastard German protectors sneaked out of the village in the dead of the night leaving us Pacifist Mennonites to defend ourselves against the Russians with word and deed alone! And here we are doing the same thing over and over again!"

Abraham could not keep back his laughter. "Terror approaches, the dreaded Red Army, and a future spelled out in the word 'misery'."

His behaviour alarmed me. I wanted to instill hope not promote mania.

How does one keep hope?

Susannah said, "There was no life in Russia for us, Oma.

The war brought an end to life in Russia." Retreating with the German army to the West seemed like an obvious thing to do to people of a winged nature like the Mennonites, but some were like the fruit trees they had tended all their lives, with roots they would not tear up. "Those who refused to leave. What were they thinking? Did they honestly believe they would be allowed to stay in their homes? Oma, you know they were shipped to Siberia."

Susannah stared at her youngest brother. Heinchen had shat himself.

"Abraham, grab Oma! Susannah! Move! Stop standing there!" I yelled. I could see the shivers consuming Oma's body.

The rain halted, but the soaked ground was now like mucus. The mist rolled in, adding another eerie layer. The light sent a hazy gleam, revealing spindly dead-looking trees in the distance. There was no shelter from the spiteful wind. I felt like a lizard in a surreal world, slithering through fleshy and slimy mud that filled in every single one of my footprints.

I mumbled to myself, "Hang onto the invisible with your heart."

Heinchen had even stopped whimpering in Susannah's arms.

"Love what matters, never loosen your grasp on where you belong — that place is in a heart, in a spiritual heart. Not here, not this." I forced myself forward. The others would follow. "We are beings, stumbling around on two legs … but we are spiritual beings." My mumbles sounded like slurs I was tossing at myself. "Keep moving." I knew I was alive because death would not bring that punishing feeling of heat and cold.

The barely perceptible bluish glow from the late frost underfoot throbbed into my stone-cold feet. I was close to panic. We were drenched.

"Honesty has been replaced by cunning. Decency has been replaced by coarseness," I mumbled on. "The Russians hate us and call us *gryaznyye nemtsy*, the dirty Germans."

"Mutti, why does everyone hate us?" Heinchen's small voice squeaked out.

"The Germans hate us because they say we are the *verdammten Russen*, the damned Russians."

"The German soldiers told me I was not a true German but a *Volksdeutscher*," recalled Abraham. He had responded by saying he liked it in the Ukraine and besides he would rather remain a

Mennonite, like his father.

Their bitter voices echoed in my head. Trembling, I led the way over another barren field attempting to reach the cover of the forest. We scrambled and slipped, our muddy feet like death weights, pulling at the muscles of our thighs. I feared we would disappear in a pronouncement of it all being too much to bear. The rain from the pasty-coloured sky sent a pressing hand down. I saw that my hands bled from where I had torn away fingernails. We crawled on our knees through the quagmire of mud.

When at last we reached the trees, I was too exhausted to continue. I had walked for hours and no longer knew east from west, north from south. The moon was not quite full, and the shadows played on the ground like a game of hide n' seek. Here and there a clearing night sky shimmered in the puddles of water. I was lost in a house of mirrors because it all looked the same. My drenched shoes cried for warmth as the slushy gravel underneath pained both my feet.

The world drifted far away into a place that belonged to other people who lived in distant lands. Above my head, the restless birds had a sense of foreboding as they flew from tree to tree to find the right place to spend the impending night as darkness shut the door, but my clutch of souls did not know. We were bereft of direction, surrounded and engulfed by a mass of boughs. The rain began to weep again.

I got up and told everyone else to get up. We staggered through the wood, adrift in a land of wooded chaos. I harkened the gusts of wind as homeless as myself. It sighed and rallied against me. Now, it was a sturdy tussle and then a breeze. Next, it became a blast, a rude wind rumbling and blustering into our lives with an unruly gust. We tramped on, staggering forward. The tree stumps we tripped over lamented in torment. The twigs snapped with cries of desolation at being misused. It went on and on and on.

I ceased moving. I didn't even wipe the night rain from my face or the drops from the tip of my nose.

I thought I saw a soldier looking straight at me.

**July, 1945
Bremerhaven
Chapter Thirty**

The tortuous path of war is on the continuum of life. No matter where, disaster hammers down. He awoke with a cry and lay there, sweating. The anguished expression on his trembling, glistening face became faint like a struggling flame among the dark embers of a fire. His spirit had snapped, the way trees swoop in a black storm, breaking, snapping their twigs and scattering their remaining leaves upon a path on the ground. At the head of this path, Reiner found himself.

Lonely is when no one cares to hear your story and it is when you no longer care to tell it.

He spoke to no one, "A precious dream is what I had and now it is dead. I cherished that dream. Now, it is gone, and I am dead."

But the remembrance of the carpet-bombing of Dresden remained. The non-scorched areas of his skin had a greenish pallor like the dense grey-white of inedible codfish. Tens of thousands of bombs had burned for seven days. How many months since the thirteenth of February, 1945, when he had been in Dresden?

Now, he lay here, on his cot of straw, full of nervous defiance, and a fragile senseless pride. The late evening sunlight of July, the colour of apple cider, poured into the room, seizing him with sadness for today and all the past summers.

Each generation thinks the world of their youth has been altered beyond recognition. For my generation, all sense of belonging ... all sense and common sense, in fact, is gone. Gott sei Dank, he thought.

But what did he have to thank God for? It was a fleeting moment, replaced by a profound awareness of being alone. There was no one who had a sense of his history, his life, no one who would have known him when he was a little child, no one who had watched him grow up. There were only those strangers he spoke to ... and they were lonely, too.

The rejection of life hurt. It was like a daughter telling a mother to leave. It was like a son saying to a father that he did not need his guidance. It was like a husband telling a wife not to come home. He struggled to reach his wooden chair. Flicking his tongue over cracked lips, he gazed fretfully around the bare room. Outside, the sun was swollen and red, sinking toward the horizon. The brutal bloody disc struck the steeples and factory chimneys behind the obscure haze of drifting smoke from the train station.

The sun set.

The breeze sucked the curtains through the gap in the broken window glass. Despite the heat, he felt bitingly cold and puckered his lips. A tremor flooded into his hands, his left eyelid fluttered with a slight twitch, the pathos of a strong body broken. He laughed. A slightly alarmed sound. There were phantoms everywhere, even the living were simply spirits in the making. To survive he would have to learn to ration his allegiance to the living. He would create distance and stand apart. Dissociate. He felt like he was looking sideways out of his head. Time taunted. The moment already had the quality of becoming a memory.

He felt like he was far away as he reached across for the knife lying on the dirty floor. He drew it across his skin, again and again. The stinging was delicious. The ability to be in control of the feeling was exhilarating. No one would hurt him again. He would hurt himself. So there! How relieving. He touched the blood seeping over this white skin and it stuck, making his fingers stick together like glue. He felt odd. The moment hung.

And then it was over.

He felt dreadfully old, tired, filled with a wretched torpor. Tomorrow would come. A hard chunk of dismay lodged in his throat creating a great bitterness in his voice.

"I see you," he spat with a growl to the walls. He became dramatic. "I see the moon drifting clear from the gauzy wreck of clouds over this ugly place."

He threw out his blood covered arms and hands and stood like a crucifix.

"Your shadow is coming. The edges are as sharp as this knife. Darken me again. I have nothing left."

Desperate is when you open the door to a grey and cold day, and it is raining outside, again, and you no longer care.

Outside the window, a black smoke drifted across swaths of dark greenery struggling to grow in the rubble and a line of hedgerow white in the dark with a summer blossom. Further on, the country side stretched in front of him, grey striations of lanes and roads, and the distant twinkling reflection of a pond near a field of wheat.

In the other direction, he could see into the decrepit Bremerhaven train station. Every rafter in the train station was lined with pigeons. The roar of the approaching train startled the birds, making them clamor together and stream out from under the roof in one great flap. The pigeons wheeled, beat their wings, banked and swooped in chaos as the black smoke filled the sky. He sensed the vibration of the rails. The train shivered into the station. He could see the people in the pale electric light waiting by the barrier, sick with anxiety as they hopped about and craned their necks. Inside his soul, a cacophony sounded as the train slid to a halt like a victim collapsing into a final rendition of disgruntled mutters. It was so final.

He leaned against the window frame and took out his packet of cigarettes. He twirled the pack this way and that way in his hands. He grunted at the script on the pack. *Handgepackt. Really?* Hand-packed cigarettes. Was that supposed to mean they cared? He nudged the cigarette out and inspected the fine printing on the paper. *Sturm Zigaretten, Dresden. How ironic.* Storm Cigarettes manufactured in Dresden. A fellow survivor of the firestorm! How fitting.

He turned back to the window and recognized the man standing on the platform asking for money. He and that fellow had done exactly the same thing the other day, but not too close to each other, for he did not like the man. Yet, for all his faults, the man had, at least, bowed his head and said thank you for the coin he'd received. It was the simple gesture of gratitude with submission to what could not be changed, not right now anyway. Reiner had also received money, but he had muttered good, not thank you, and his ingratitude glared back at him even today. He surmised that the man's meager life had at least a shape and definition that his lacked. One more thing that was wrong. It was too overwhelming.

He collapsed onto the straw mat on the floor. He couldn't sleep; he was far too hot. The cuts burned. The dry blood pulled where it stuck to his skin. He simply lay there and let the sensation open his mind's eye. He let the ghosts of exhaustion come and inhabit his wakeful dream. The first thing to enter was the crunch of gravel under boots from beneath his window. The next was the view of the ragged lace curtains hanging limply in front of the cracked glass and then the view of the one unbroken window directing the glimmer of moonlight across the top of the chair.

After a while, he rose and looked out at the buildings again. In the empty street, the exhausted lanterns were like souls that have no acquaintance with melancholy but nevertheless send out their sporadic glows specifically void of the presentiment of metamorphosis. He had to travel through the dark night of the soul to find the light. It was the universal theme of transformation.

Should I choose to be transformed into an imaginary existence, a journey away from reality, where there is a type of freedom? Hmmm ... isolating ... No. Perfect freedom does not exist. There must be an answer somewhere ... Ah! I could focus on a cause or a purpose outside my own pitiable needs! No. Fixing someone else's problems is a diversion and more harmful than facing up to the skeletons in the closet. How to cope with the world? How will the world cope with me?

He stared at the feeble lanterns and raised his hand to fiddle with the lace curtains stiff from grime and rain. The cuts on his forearm split. The aching sensation of life made him gasp. He stared at the cracked plaster ceiling where the house had bled silently from its cuts. Outside, the ruins stood stark in their darkness, silhouettes with their jagged edges touched by the gentleness of white moonlight. The contrast was confusing. Still dazed from lack of sleep, he wrestled with the shock of seeing how quickly a torrent of rain and wind swept into the scene.

The song sang in his head. *Underneath the lamp post, by the barrack gate, darling, I remember the way you used to wait ... bei der Laterne wollen wir stehen wie einst, Lili Marleen.*

The quiet persistent knocking of the trees on the window got his attention. He heard their beseeching tone as if the trees were talking to him. *Reiner? Reiner? Are you in there?*

Reiner returned the question, "There?"

The urgency of the knocking of the trees was apparent. *Reiner, listen to us. Can you hear us? You can make it there and back again.*

Reiner snorted in derision. "I know I can make it back. I know that." He stared at the window. "I don't know if I can make it there!"

He wept. His past mourned its departure. Those days with their shaped memories of delight and disappointment disappeared. He let out a massive sob. His present days dripped with anguish. His future was filled with wailing winds. He was truly afraid.

"I had a dream. It was a good dream!"

Yes, it was, the trees replied. *Acknowledge your pain. Look at it. Stop isolating yourself! You're making your suffering worse. Remember hope. What you did mattered. You matter.*

"My dream was to help! I was going to stop the evil!" yelled Reiner. He felt foolish about his failure. Dreaming did not make him a fool and neither did the disappearance of the dream, but he couldn't accept that. "My dream was to help people with their lives ... to have good lives. There is nothing wrong with that!"

Your intention was noble, but you have no control over anyone else. You cannot control what happens. The trees bent their boughs to weep alongside him. The music of the boughs tapped into the depths of his unconscious. The tears knew what reality was.

"I only have control over myself." Reiner said sadly. "That is selfish ... I had a dream for others ... for others!"

Reiner paced the floor. "I can't define happiness for others. I can't walk their journey. I know that!" Reiner fell, sobbing on to the floor. "It's just that ... my dream was good! I was going to stop Hitler! I was going to stop him at Riese! I was going to ..."

The savage rebuttal, where his doubt lived, emerged. *Stop him? By doing what? Blowing the entire place up? With what? You're an idiot!*

"It was a plan. I stole the blue prints. It could have …" His finger traced a pattern in the dust on the floor. "There's my dream. A fantasy …. a real dream is about yourself, Reiner." He mimicked himself savagely, "A real dream is about yourself."

He spat at the floor. His anger got in the way of his reasoning making it difficult to recognize his limits. He had not been promised a life without suffering.

"With eyes to heaven and on God, I plead for release. I have seen with my own eyes hell on earth. Everyday, like a massive charge of the starving toward food, like herds of beasts stampeding in panic, I have carried those visions. They have destroyed any ideal and hope I had. Now, I am done."

No. It was not done.

Terror orchestrated by those who seize power always attempts to extinguish all the forms of beauty found in the human heart. Far, far inside Reiner was the tiniest bit clamoring to stay alive. He had beauty. He had a heart. He had a story. Those who tell their story enter a violated ground to reveal the flaming passion of the human spirit at its best.

"I have a story ..." Reiner whispered.

It was the only thing left that belonged to him. Stories inspire; they preserve and prevent the destruction of the good. The trees tapped the affirmation that he was alive and ready to continue to live.

Hesitantly, he murmured, "I look over my lifetime ..."

Instead of condemning, he was curious at how much wasted time and stupidity had dominated his youth. In his lifetime, he had done many different things and, in a sense, he had lived many different lives. He could look back on his life, which had, for the most part, been blessed with health and lack of want, and declare that he was miserable for most of it. Those luscious moments of delight and happiness had been fleeting. A soul can be so sick when the body has never suffered and sometimes it is the solution that creates a bigger burden than the problem itself.

He was full of regrets about his life.

He remembered his aunt who had always prayed. *Herr, bleibe bei uns, denn es wird Abend werden.* He prayed now, in the night of his darkness, that God would stay near him. His aunt had been truly kind. True kindness mattered. Gratitude mattered.

Sighing, Reiner tilted his head to the side. Nodding, he listened to himself instead of arguing. *You can live where you belong, Reiner, that is where you really live.*

Persevere. Endure. Risk.

This time, instead of going to despair, Reiner would choose differently. *You are a tree replanted.* The curve of the branches swayed. Reiner waited. He listened in the silence for guidance, for the tap dance filled with cadence and rhythm. In the quiet of the room, he listened to the music of his soul.

There were those who believe in chaos, who believe that we should have no sense of who we are, who try to define us, who place us and determine what we can and cannot do, even telling us what we owe to each other and how to value it, those who decide and those we decide to follow; we bond to them. They are people who hate. They hate the sense of identity that people possess. They hate the small countries. They hate individuals. They want to reduce everyone to the level of unquestioning anonymous servility. They wish to live in expansive impersonal *Reichs* and be governed by so-called leaders on personal quests for vast glory and power. They try to convince everyone of it.

Let them think that! I will not. Reiner decided. He would no longer be ashamed of loving, loving his home, loving life, loving his culture and his people, the segments that continued to give sense to life. Those things did not need apology. Reiner looked at the trees outside his window.

We are like a grove of trees in the same field. We bask in the same sun and are nourished by the same rain. We are swaying our branches and curious about what the other tree is doing. How are you growing over there? I'm fine. It's good. It's a bad spot. Leave me alone. I can't take it anymore! These are the replies. I know I will have to come to terms with all that has happened, but right now is now and that is what we deal with. That's the way trees are.

"The leaves of the tree are for the healing of nations," came his whisper.

He would survive. He would believe. He would fashion a new dream. His tears were acceptance; they would be like the morning dew transforming the harshness of the landscape into beauty even while fear was still near.

Life is hard. Take the easy way, the hard part that comes all by itself, and to heck with them, those people who don't care about you. That is what his Oma would have said.

Rework. Choose to have courage. Make life intentional. Plan. The end of a dream is for yesterday, not tomorrow. Hope.

Another day passed by in the giving and taking of light. Would he lose the flow of this new dream? In the morning following, the sunlight streamed into his room and renewed his joy of living between sunrises. *I have made it to this city. I will leave this God forsaken land.* In the grey-blue harbour of Bremerhaven, the same sunlight sent morning flickers over the ship christened *Die Tabintha*.

July 1945
Schäferhof
Chapter Thirty-One

As usual, and far away, decisions were made that affected individuals, families, and significantly, me. The American army had moved us south from Helmstedt to Sharfenbrück, north to Hamburg and then to Schäferhof. Adequate shelter was scarce and there was a relentless stream of refugees. During the war, I had found work in Christinendorf, but I was idle in the American camp. *Now, Eleni, you sit and wait.* It was a thought I had everyday.

Germany was desperate in 1945, and it witnessed extraordinary hostility burdening the lives of survivors. German cities were heaps of debris. Human aggression scars individual memory and generational collective memories. Governments use aggression, fear, confusion, and our childish credulity. History shows that once exposed, a regime will collapse and change is inevitable. Unfortunately, the replacement is not always better.

I felt a distinct disappointment that life events and Abraham, in particular, were not co-operating with my vision of the way things should be. *Why do my dreams never come true? My dream is of a perfectly enclosed utopia, of living happily in the village with my family and with a multitude of friends around me. My dream has value and truth. It's a good dream to have.*

I shook my head sadly. I could not turn back the clock to when we grew up in the village, nor could I control the behaviour of people. *You live in an altered world, Eleni. You shed far too many tears. Oh, if all those tears could be collected to keep me safe ... to give me courage ... I would have much of what I need ... If. If is only a word.*

Twisted individuals in government where not unique to Germany. The two leaders of Russia and the United States divided Germany into East and West. The Morgenthau Plan, devised in the United States, was psychopathically anti-German in its philosophy and its effect. It provided a measure of vengeance, making sure there was no strong state left in the Russian orbit for Josef Stalin to be concerned about. The concentration of Communist sympathizers in the Unites States Treasury Department is a matter of public record. The Morgenthau plan was politically aggressive and emotionally, socially, and economically punitive. If German industrial power was throttled, the economic recovery of Europe was delayed, creating an always politically dangerous situation.

Here you are Eleni, thinking about the way the world should be. "Should"... what an awful word. All that word does is stop you from living fully today! My longing for what is past is huge, but I can't keep manipulating the past, demonizing or immortalizing it in my memory. It's not a guide for the future.

On a personal level, my dream of family bliss would never be true, because that perfect life in an idealized past had never existed. It was actually a past whose dreadful family stories of suppression had been drilled into me, making me fear the future. My parents prepared me to expect the worst and to have more than one plan for the future, but in reality, I lived with a constant anxiety and dread of duplicating the errors of history.

I realized with a shock how my entire emotional life was in the past, and I was depleted. I found it impossible to live in the present. Yet, my skillful anticipation had contributed to my survival, no question, for I had navigated each yesterday skillfully. Now, the yesterdays appeared cold, sunless, and stagnant.

The lengthy days of summer sunlight tried their best to gladden my soul with tender gentle beauty; yet, the sun's rays seemed to grow melancholy and philosophical with the effort. I felt lost. I thought about Casper who was dead, run over by a stupid woman with her cart. I could see his black fur and his guts spewed out in the dirt. It was a vile and senseless waste. I had always thought if one were to err, it was better to err on the side of generosity, but now I wished I had retaliated and gone after that woman. It would not have brought that dear creature back. Still, even now, when I thought about it, the loss was almost enough to make me resort to senseless violence. It would match one meaningless act with another meaningless act to somehow create a balance at least.

Eleni, you're obsessed with that one disgusting event. To have a thought is one thing, to say it out loud is another, to tell someone is yet another and to actually follow through with it is absurd. Don't let it go ... you should never have hung on to it in the first place!

I was spent. I grieved everything and everyone that was gone. It hit me hard and I pressed my lips together to hold in the emotion. The lessons of the past were lessons for the past. I would need to learn to stop trying to apply them to today.

But how, how could it have been different? Is this not what we go through? Is this not a journey, my journey? I desperately wanted a clear and simple answer of how to keep my family together.

I wanted the formula for happiness.

Life is what it is.

I spent much of my time with Irmgard. Surprisingly, several of us from Zator had come together in the American camps. Each one of us had arrived with our own incredible stories, but many did not know what had happened to family members. Despite this, Irmgard had the courage to delight in the commonplace, and for her, life was bursting with a sense of wonder. There was meaning, and even beauty, in the smallest object or interaction. Irmgard alternately inspired me with her conversations of hope in discovering where the heart of God lay and annoyed me in her determination to avoid the alternative because, according to her, that was where the Devil resided in evil.

On one of those days, she had said the most amazing thing. I can still hear her voice. "I believe there is a heart of goodness in all of us. Even the Nazis had moments of tenderness with their own families before behaving like crazy people. So, in those good moments, is that who they were?"

I had looked out to the landscape because I didn't buy her argument about nice Nazis. Our countries had been engaged in a decimating warfare. If she wanted it simple, so be it. "Maybe particular people are just born that way, ya know, nasty."

Irmgard ignored those kinds of comments. "We know about women beaten by their husbands and those who in turn hit their children. Then we all go to church on Sunday. Yes, we are imperfect."

I had bent my head to look at the ground. Imperfections, manipulations and guilty pleasures, we all have them.

"Mennonites have a history filled with struggle and yet we constantly turn to God in faith. At times a varying faith, it is true, but we give true credence to the belief that sin does not win." And with that, I guess, she had won the argument.

Today, when I observed her making her way over towards where I sat with my mother, I spoke before she had a chance. "The war is over, Irmgard," I said with finality. "Stop preaching."

"Good people must fight the bad and not let them get away with evil."

"How are you going to do that?" Oma came up behind her.

"Resistance!" Irmgard said.

My eyebrows shot up.

"Not that kind of resistance!" exclaimed Irmgard. "Kindness fights the evil."

I gave a little sniff and helped my mother sit down.

Irmgard spoke earnestly, "Forgiveness. Friendships, brotherhood, family, and faith are connections that cannot be ignored. People look instinctively to the other when they meet someone new. We always search for mutual acquaintances to play the Mennonite name game."

I smiled inwardly. The conversation of who was connected to whom could continue for hours. My name was the link to the person I had been and the person I now was. My common struggle and my common history were honoured in the names we gave our children. Everyone was named after someone else. Our names were living remembrances of connections filled with love.

I met Irmgard's eyes. "I know, Irmgard. It is as reassuring as talking about the weather."

"Oh, how we need these connections!" exclaimed Irmgard,

glad that I had finally made a positive response.

"I am afraid they will send us East if they think we are Russian," Oma whispered. The thick green foliage surrounding the camp provided a canopy of leaves under which we sat.

"Well, then stop talking about it before somebody hears you!" I chided.

"I hear there is another camp near Chelb."

"If you keep this up, they will send you there and one step closer to Siberia!"

"The last place I saw my daughters was in Kiev. Olga was there with Maria," said Oma.

"We do not even know if they are still alive," I replied to my mother. "It is impossible to know. We must get to Bremerhaven."

Manfred had been shipped to the Gulag, to a Russian labour camp in the Solovetski Islands. I yearned to hear from him. I had considered moving to Hamburg where Manfred had first begun his training as a police officer, but my family had urged me to come to this camp and from here, hopefully, make it to the coast, to Bremerhaven.

The smells of the wet earth from the recent rains, of the tree leaves dripping moisture, and the sound of the constant trickle of water contrasted with the first mass of insects buzzing merrily in the welcome sunlight filled my senses. I wanted this fragile day to be a blessing; it could still go either way. I needed gentleness, patience, and rest, rest for my body and for my mind, so my soul could love. I felt lost and hurt … maybe it was the other way around. I didn't know

"Oh, Eleni!" I turned to Irmgard with a questioning look. "What do you think of everything that has happened?" Irmgard displayed her universal eagerness to hear what I had to say without ever feeling attacked by a different perspective. She was open and interested in hearing people's stories, to hear the stories in all of us.

"This topic of conversation is a huge risk, Irmgard! You might have to change the way you think when you hear what I have to say," I laughed.

Irmgard had the knack of gently reframing responses and letting the conversational process take them wherever it needed to go. "Think of the best in the people around you," Irmgard encouraged, exhibiting her usual ease of mind.

"Oh, Irmgard." I marveled at how my friend's heart lacked

the criticism and the stonewalling necessary to be nasty. She must have laid those aside years ago, and replaced them with a heart gently cloaked with respect. Nevertheless, I was sure I looked somewhat flabbergasted at Irmgard's lack of contempt, the beginning of being, for me, quite irritated.

"Today is a day to be particularly thankful for, Eleni."

"I'm trying," I said under my breath.

"It is strange how people can manipulate meaning. They turn it around when it suits them." Irmgard's soft voice ached to heal me.

I spoke a little sharper than I intended. "History evolves, accumulates wounds and the longer the injustice, the more deeply felt the resentment." My dreadful experiences were buried deep but not deep enough. "That is the same anytime, any day." I shrugged.

"Good relationships that's the key! They nurture us with appreciation and understanding. Good relationships teach us about belonging."

"Irmgard! Honestly! Right now, we don't belong anywhere!"

She shook her head. "That's where you are wrong."

I make mistakes, and I am not always right, but I am never wrong. My father used to say that and then laugh with amusement. It brought a small smile to my face.

"Eleni, we teach each other to distinguish between the horrors of the past, the influences of the present, and the fantasy of the future. If we do not understand the impact, if we do not understand the problems of our human existence, we cannot understand how God can be the solution." She looked at me beseechingly.

This is exhausting. I spoke concisely, "Well, I look for an answer, and there it is!"

"Eleni," she reached out and took both my hands, "we are who we really are when we are in the heart of God. That is where we belong."

"I'm not God. I don't know who's in his heart or not. Amen." I laughed to hide my irritation, dropping her hands. "Thanks for the sermon."

I tried to sound as light-hearted as I could. I didn't want to hurt her. I really didn't, but I was annoyed. I hate being told what to do or what to think. *Thank God, she's not talking about the end of the world and damnation because it would take more than this conversation to foster my existential growth. Devotion is not going to occur solely due to intellectual insight.*

Irmgard waited for a better response but none was forthcoming. "What's wrong with you, Eleni?"

"Oh," I stared ahead of her. "Funny, I noticed a satchel on the person who passed by … that once was … that I had, but it's not possible …"

"Well, I do not know about that but I am blessing this day from the first breaking of the bread."

"Yes, each day," I agreed looking back at her.

Irmgard was amazing or … simple, I didn't know for sure. She could sit at a table with the dullest person for hours and be content with prosaic conversation. I shook my head with disbelief at the mindless waste of time small talk is, and how it's designed to drive the sanest person crazy. Irmgard's altruism forever astounded me.

"What to do now? What choices to make? How will we live, Irmgard? Kindness or selfishness? Them or us?"

"I know the dilemma," Irmgard consoled. "No one can make

you love. No one can make you hate."

"True."

"We navigate life."

"I have tried to do the best I could, Irmgard."

"Yes," she replied, honouring the memory of the days gone by. "I will let happiness touch me, lift me up, and I will be exhilarated." Irmgard generously threw both hands in the air above her head.

I laughed too, letting my anxieties drop away. Irmgard had that effect on me, too.

"I feel like I am being tickled, Eleni! No more worries. There will be joy and amusement. We will have fun, and ease of mind. It will be like stroking a soft plush fur."

"No, Irmgard, it is knowing that you can eat as much platz with ice cream as you like. It will never be bad for you and never make you fat, only happy!" Like a little child, I imagined asking if there was any more. True contentment brings lasting happiness and fulfillment. I let the little child in me take over. Indeed, for that split second, I felt like giggling as if I were experiencing a real Christmas in summertime, not like the barren Christmas seasons I had known.

I moved away from Irmgard and sat myself down on the wooden bench tucked into a quiet corner of the yard.

"So, you are out and about too," Irmgard beamed her ever-present smile at Susannah, Abraham, and Heinchen, who had walked into the yard. Energy and bubbliness escaped from Irmgard, who continued talking to Oma. "I nearly forgot! This morning, a small group of us heard about a ship off to Canada from Bremerhaven. We sang *Gott Mit Euch Bis Wir Uns Wiedersehen*. It was lovely!" Irmgard giggled with pleasure.

The mixed emotions churned inside of me. Soon we hoped to sing the song of God being with us until we met again.

Irmgard continued, "Yes, I am excited too. We have come far. The ship can take thirty of us. Did you know that? It is a miracle that we have ended up here in this camp and when I get to Bremerhaven, I'll find passage, too! Your turn will come. Your family will soon get a booking on a ship to freedom."

Oma shrugged. "Help me to the house, Irmgard. I'm tired."

The children smiled politely at Irmgard as she left with Oma. Abraham and Susannah moved in my direction, but they hadn't noticed me sitting on the corner of the bench surrounded by foliage.

Susannah said cautiously to Abraham, "You see how life change. One minute we live this way, and the next minute it is different. What you told me ... maybe you didn't ... I mean, maybe, you felt ... imagined?"

He made a little snorting sound. "That doesn't make sense, Susannah! I did not imagine things. It was real! On the train when we tried to get Oma to jump, I knew I never wanted to go back, not to the Ukraine, not to the past. I want to go forward but you cannot imagine what has happened, Susannah. It's too ... it's impossible."

"Stop hiding. Stop teasing me with bits and pieces! Why do you want me to guess? Just tell me!"

He was startled by his response I could tell. *Yes, he does block conversation. Yes, he does want you to guess, but when you guess wrong, he gets even more upset. He likes to be vague. He thinks that's safe, but it really is a lack of trust. How sad. He needs to defend himself and resist if need be, even resist Susannah.*

His introversion often made him appear like a blank wall, but behind that thick wall was a curiosity, a creativity trying to find a way out. "Is it not strange the way life continues on?" Abraham changed the conversation, looking at her quickly "I mean people die and babies are born."

What do you think, everything stops! Children are so egocentric. Months ago, we were near death, and now you are still amazed at life!

Susannah shrugged her shoulders and quickly shook her head back and forth. She waved away the bee that buzzed around her head.

"But, they actually got married!" Abraham said in disbelief. "Can you imagine? In this place! It's too much to even believe ... but life keeps going on. It is strange."

"Are you worried?"

Of course, he's worried. The answer came immediately to me.

He looked up quickly. "No, no, not much now." He was not convincing. "I am only worried about having enough food to eat!"

Abraham made a swipe at the bee. "It's like this thing is waiting for me." He threw his hand out and knocked down the bee and stomped on it. He looked up in shock. "I squashed it dead. I lost my head. I didn't mean to do that."

Susannah ignored the incident. She stared at him intently. "Listen to me! Stop being a ninny! We can make today for us," she asserted with passion. "That is possible." She manoeuvered around to stand in front of him. "I too felt the same way sitting on that roof after we had jumped off the train. It was like something happened. I … I decided I was not going back to Russia, too. I did. I miss my home. I do. But I realize that I am never ever going back to the Ukraine either. I knew I had to change."

My heart felt heavy for my children. I wanted to get up and walk away, but I was caught between embarrassing them with my presence and hoping they might never know I was there.

Abraham stared, but not at her, not at me.

Susannah continued anyway, "People think being vulnerable is the way to achieve growth by enduring suffering, but that doesn't make any sense to me. You can't keep cowering and hiding. Be strong. That's the way."

Good for you, Susannah! Come on, Abraham, why do you always take so long to figure things out?

Abraham was an introvert. A behaviour that was as

frustrating for Susannah as it was for me. He made several faint remarks that Susannah considered fair game and when he refused to self-disclose, she felt he was unfair and she told him to stick to the conversation and stop changing the topic.

"How are you doing?" Susannah asked. "Seriously, be honest."

"Oh, don't worry, Susannah. I have given up the hope of having a better past!" He attempted a carefree tone, but it was not convincing.

"There!" she affirmed him anyway, to validate him for what she imagined he could be — independent and original. Abraham gave her a little friendly smile.

If only it were that simple. I watched Abraham tap the tip of each finger one after another on to the tip of his thumb and wait. I sensed the conversation going deeper. It was like standing on holy ground. I silently thanked God for the honour of being present.

Abraham flung his arms wide open. "You want me to joyfully embrace everything that is new?" There was the slightest hint of enthusiasm behind his little smile.

She smiled too.

I wanted him to be the way I knew he could be if only he would be more flexible, more receptive to new values, warmer to new people and more confident with making decisions. If. I had no idea what he had to overcome.

"I want you to forgive yourself, Abraham."

"When it comes to forgiveness, doesn't it matter I might not have anything to be forgiven for?" Abraham pretended and looked at her.

"Forgiveness is a gift you give yourself. You forgive yourself for what you did or what you didn't do! You forgive yourself, Abraham."

He gave a little shrug with one shoulder.

"If we do not forgive, Abraham, we are chained to the unforgiven."

"Long after events are gone and even forgotten, I remember." Abraham hung his head. "I am chained to those feelings. There is a lasting powerful feeling of being wronged and doing wrong."

"Yes, I know it is true that long after the slight is remembered the hurt burns long and hard. Hours and hours. Days.

Years. Is that what you want?"

"It was not a little slight!"

"It no longer matters that somebody was hurt or not. It is done. Whatever it is will destroy you until you forgive, Abraham."

"You do not know what you are asking of me!"

"I think I do."

Oh, my darlings, you are not to blame. None of this is your fault. What has happened ... I felt like jumping up and embracing both of them, but Abraham's quiet voice made me stop.

"My heart aches for Papa. I feel such remorse about our last time together when Papa was taken by the Russians."

No, no, no! Not this! It serves me right! I had no business listening to their conversation. Now, I will hear what I don't want to hear!"

"Mutti was sleeping ... I don't know where ... because she had been granted the divorce she had asked for ..."

Susannah gasped.

Ahh ... he knew. No! Now Susannah knew!

"There was nothing I could have done to change anything."

Oh, Abraham. It was not your fault. The shame is mine.

"Papa knew I knew. He told me to take care of the family, Susannah." Abraham looked at Susannah. His eyes filled with tears. "I was scared. The Russians were in the room. They had come to take him." Abraham pounded his fists on his chest. He was crying now. "It was in the middle of the night. I was scared, but not for him, for me!"

Oh, Abraham. You were a child! A child worried that dinner will not be on the table, concerned that decisions will not be made, full of anxiety about the future.

"Do you know what I was afraid of, Susannah?"

"The Russians, the …" Susannah guessed the obvious.

"I was afraid that there wouldn't be enough money! Money!" Abraham's confession broke my heart.

"I feel so guilty that I couldn't even have the right feeling, that I didn't do anything to help Papa. How I wanted to tell him that I loved him, how I wanted to feel for him, how I wanted to ask Papa to forgive me."

"Oh, Abraham," Susannah whispered.

"I wanted Papa to forgive me because the only thing I said to him was, 'Papa, is there enough money?'"

Oh, Abraham. I can hear your child-voice speaking to Papa. No, Abraham, no. There is no shame there. None.

"You can't alter the past," The words caught in his throat. "I asked him about ... money. It was the last thing I said to him ..."

Susannah pleaded, "You have to forgive yourself. It does not matter that the forgiveness is accepted or even known."

"Acceptance is impossible."

"You do it for yourself. If you forgive, the past loses its power to hurt."

"I have done the unforgiveable and the unforgiveable has been done ..."

"Abraham, there is no voice to defend you and there is no voice to accuse you, but nothing is unforgiveable."

A huge truth.

Susannah said, "I know. Forgiving yourself is the hardest thing to do. Maybe let God forgive you, Abraham. We carry burdens around for all our lives, unable to share, unable to acknowledge them, unable to speak about them even if only to ourselves. It's impossible to change if we keep doing that."

Violations are never acceptable, never, and they must never

be repeated but they are forgivable. Susannah extended an invitation to Abraham to traverse the gulf of the horrific into the world of the forgiven with him.

"You are saying forgiveness is possible. How?" Her clarity was helping him navigate his confusion.

"By looking at someone with a little less hatred than you had before," she said. "Even if that person is yourself."

Forgiveness is the re-humanization of perpetrators of atrocities. When Susannah and Abraham were ready to surrender, mercy would be granted at last and the experience of forgiveness would come alive.

"Well Susannah, you have done all the talking for me." He pressed his lips together and slapped both hands on his legs. "I have nothing more to say until tomorrow or the day after that or maybe not even the day after that. It has all been said."

"Faith in Christ turns suffering from a problem to a myste

"Honestly Susannah, enough with the rhetoric!"

"Suffering makes fools of us and other people."

"Enough Susannah! It is enough," Abraham snapped. He patted her hand.

"I know I go on and on. I can see what would help. I desperately want you to be happy despite everything. It is possible!" Susannah stopped talking. She gave a small nod, indicating with her hand that she was now going to walk away.

Abraham followed a few steps behind her.

Oh, Abraham. How much we must forgive. There is so far to go before I am well, before we are all well. I must live with what I need. Love? Happiness?

I was at the threshold of self-forgiveness, but I could already feel it slipping away as I watched Abraham walk away. I tried to begin to construct a reality of truth connecting myself to what was beautifully human within me and within my children. I acknowledged that their truths would be different from mine.

Try, Abraham. Breathe in the spirit of Blessings.

Gently now. Go gently with yourself.

Gentleness goes a long way, and courage can be as infectious as fear.

July 1945
Chapter Thirty-Two

It broke my heart to hear what my daughter and my son had said. There was little I could do for them. We were safe in Schäferhof. My immediate family was alive. The most I could hope for was that due to the thorns in their feet, they might be able to jump higher than anyone with sound feet.

My children had never met Manfred, and I was grateful. I knew Abraham would not have wanted to be that close to a German soldier. He had had enough of Lieutenant Strauss when we relocated to Ebenfeld. Every time Abraham had seen him, the lieutenant made a stupid remark. Abraham concluded German soldiers were idiots. I had done what needed to be done to survive. I would no longer second guess it.

We had small huts in the Schäferhof camp and little garden areas where my family and I sat to make small talk. Most often we talked about family and friends, who had died and who might be alive.

"Mutti! Look! There she is!" Susannah exclaimed.

How speedily things change! A sweet-tempered breeze sent

the thousand leafy tongues jabbering all at once. Tante Olga, my sister, stood before us! We were instantly, so happy.

"Unbelievable! We were just talking about you …"

"There you are, standing in front of us …" I whispered.

"I found out you were here!"

"We do not know if anyone else is alive!"

Olga was like that, if she wanted to or needed to do something, she just went and did it. She had searched the perimeter of the camp fence, found a hole and crawled through into the camp. She was a bit of an adventurer.

My legs shook with the emotion of the reunion.

"Look at your weepy eyes. They're shining!" Olga laughed at me. "Your face is so flushed!"

In amazement, I asked, "You have walked all the way when you heard we were in this camp because of the letter we sent to that German address?"

What people can give to one another because of love is truly amazing.

Olga nodded with self-assurance. "Everyone in our family is alive. Can you imagine?"

I embraced her with the gratefulness that comes from realizing how easily my loss could have been irreversible. The harshness of life thawed, releasing brilliant smiles and enormous sighs of release. The light became brighter, giving everything an exceptional clarity. The grass seemed freshly verdant instead of worn and tired as it crept along the bases of the fences around the camp. It was a miracle! My family had survived intact. Even Opa had somehow managed to reach the West.

I experienced such true joy, not the kind of happy one gets when the weather is good. This was unfathomable in its breadth, a transcendent source giving a profound blessing. It was a memory to keep, a memory to keep in the treasury of my heart forever.

How important family is and how easily it is taken for granted. We say "keep those you love close, stay together." Yet, we can spend the least amount of time with those that are closest to us. Time together. That is the best gift we give to each other, to those we love.

Olga brought not only news for us but for others. She eagerly shared that she knew so and so was alive or that a letter had been received at the same address in Germany. "What a time of joy for us!"

"But not for everyone."

We continued our conversation quietly, for many around us received news their loved ones were dead. It was painful. Olga could not answer everyone's questions.

"Who is in the camp with you here?" Olga asked.

Yesterday, the Meiers had buried their son. No one from the camp was allowed to go to the cemetery, only the parents and one aunt. It was a somber affair. They had hoped that now, with the Americans, things would be different.

Only a few months ago, in April, I had had that same hope the night in the forest when I thought I had seen a soldier step in front of me. I recalled how I had blinked away the hallucination, and dragged a wet sleeve across my face. The world's bleakness descended. I was ice-cold. I felt I would never move again; I was already part way into my grave. All I had to do was lie down and freeze, and the winter in my body would change into the sleep of death. There no longer seemed to be the need to hurry, for I would soon be motionless through what remained of my life.

As if forcing me to succumb, the clamor of the gale had

swept the sky clear to give a glimpse of the starlight through fluttering remnants and forest foliage, and then the wind became a sledgehammer. It tore at my bare bloody fingers. The high wind sang its sighs, sobs and shrieks through groaning trees; I heard sobbing and realized it was myself. Shivering on numbed blue feet, bruised from stumbling through the forest, I pushed myself forward, clumsy, moving as if drunken. If I fell I would never get up again. I saw footprints in the mud! My hair hung in limp strands. My clothes had clamped themselves onto my body like a second skin as the rain lashed against me. Mud washed down the slopes, pouring into the foot prints I had discovered. Someone was nearby!

Drops of rain had struck my cheek. I recognized those footprints as my own. Not again! We had done the same thing in the snow, and now it was happening in the mud! Not again! We had lurched our way to nowhere between the Russians and the Germans. We had not been moving west, we had been walking north and south the entire time. The potential meaning of my actions and decisions was too dangerous to even consider. I had no strength left to make the best of it. I was struck dumb.

I was too afraid to try anymore. What if I couldn't? What if I could not see the silver lining? What if I could not survive on my own strength? What if? "If", such a small word, a word of taunting and dangling hope. Hope was dangerous. Hope gave the situation a shimmering pain.

It would be better if I slid into oblivion, into the depression where I could embrace the sleep of despair. There I could float between nothing matters, what is the point, and no one cares. Those familiar companions of giving up screamed and stretched out their long arms and their clutching filthy hands with their pointed fingernails. They sucked away my breath with howling noises.

Deep down I knew the most important part of life were those facets I could not see. I was stuck in a wasteland. What made this wasteland beautiful, although I no longer cared, was that somewhere, out there, hidden, was a well and a place of refuge. But, platitudes are for those who are safe. Panic filled me. *Time was running out!*

From long ago, in another life, I heard the recitation of Goethe's poem in my ear. There was no freedom in despairing, but I could not control or change any of the feelings overpowering me, like a gust of the chilling damp wind out of a long-closed vault where the door is accidently set ajar, a cowardly whine escaped.

> *Feiger Gedanken*
>
> *Bängliches Schwanken,*
>
> *Weibisches Zagen,*
>
> *Ängstliches Klagen*
>
> *Wendet kein Elend,*
>
> *Macht dich nicht frei.*
>
> *Allen Gewalten*
>
> *Zum Trutz sich erhalten;*
>
> *Nimmer sich beugen*
>
> *Kräftig sich zeigen*
>
> *Rufet die Arme*
>
> *Der Götter Herbei.*

My affirmation to survive and my lingering bits of tenacity escaped in a rather desperate pitiful sigh, and I had painfully begged to any God or person who might hear, "*Hilfe.* Help."

It was the kind of hurt that was the edge of oblivion, but

there was enough of an awareness of the knife poised to slash, of the raised hand for the back slap, of the cutting tongue to inflict irreparable damage; there was just enough of the suggestion of the end. I felt it mutilate. It was too much to think about, not now, not ever. I did not know what to do, so I waited, hoping my feeble appeal for Grace would be answered.

A man wearing a trench coat and a hat appeared before me.

I knew I still had a desire to live, but I no longer felt inside. I observed with numbness the entire scene between myself and the man.

I breathed deeply. A tear escaped from one eye. If we are quiet and content with ourselves tears become a time of quietude and contentment. But not in that place, not in that moment. I had prayed frantically that he would not be someone who would shoot us. I prayed I would not be dealing with one of those people with whom there simply could be no dealing as he quietly stood in front of me.

He had simply said, "I walk the border land. Follow me. I help people across."

And we did. We stumbled, maybe, a hundred metres and

there were the British guards, sitting in their hut, playing cards.

I will never forget. Abraham had commented that the soldiers hadn't even looked up at us as we passed by. They hadn't even raised their heads. Heinchen had asked what was wrong with their throats. He had motioned toward the soldiers and then to his own throat, and asked again what was wrong with them because they made funny sounds.

I didn't even have the strength to laugh.

"English," I said to him.

The wonder of it struck us with incredulity! The United States and the British armies had been waiting west of the Elbe River since the eleventh of April. The very next day, the Russians began cutting down the entire forest to the makeshift border so they could see who tried to escape. That was how much their dear citizens meant to them. The Russians couldn't let us go. The Red troops entered Warsaw and Warthegau, and the tank divisions drove people back to the East. They surrounded Berlin and captured the city on April 25th.

Unchecked, the Russians combed through the border areas of the supposedly safe West Zone and took everyone East who could not prove beyond a doubt an Old German nationality. They sent them back, not to familiar villages and homes, but to labour and perish in the Russian North or in Siberia. The tragedy and our luck in escaping makes my heart beat frantically, even now. The saying is that people make their own luck. Maybe, but not always.

We had escaped into the western zone.

The allied victory called for the destruction of the German nation. President Roosevelt stated that there was no reason why the Russians should not get two million German labourers as restitution for war damages in Russia. It was not punishment for a crime but simply solving a problem — as if the problem was a shortage of machinery, for example.

A few people challenged the creation of a compulsory German labour force as treating millions of people as slave labour. The United States Treasury Secretary, Morgenthau, reminded opponents that the whole issue of compulsory labour had already been decided upon at Yalta. He argued the Yalta agreement in effect and if anyone was going to protest, they were against the Yalta agreement.

Luckily, we were refugees and even the President left us

alone. The excessive and fatal attraction of Hitler was finished. Hitler's invincibility was shattered. The division of a tainted Germany was his legacy.

I recognized the Germans and the Russians committed the same horrible acts. When people ran to freedom, they sent a spray of bullets into the flock of sparrows. No man, no problem is what Stalin declared. When they protested, they terrorized them. When they refused to cooperate, they made them vanish to camps in Siberia. Every victim, every brutality, is a crime.

Every one of those people lived, loved, and hoped. The spirit of everyday people, their desire for freedom, their brilliant ideas, war or prison cannot murder, a fact that often escapes tyrants who by their very nature oppress and govern with little wisdom.

Even now, I shook my head to think that one month before the end of the war after fleeing the environs of Berlin, my family and I had been heaving ourselves through the forest toward the British border near Helmstedt. I later learned that during the time of our escape, Manfred had been captured by the Russians. The news had broken my heart.

The thoughts of our terrible flight to freedom flooded into

my memory, constantly. I was still amazed how lucky we had been.

****

The next day, in the morning, our luck continued.

"I spoke with the authorities and have given them the German address. We have all been given passes to leave," I told my family.

Democracy is not perfect, but it is the best thing we have come up with so far and my introduction to it was convincing. Freedom to the West! "We leave in three days. Olga, you are coming with us!"

We laughed but capped our enthusiasm. One did not want too much revelry here. Perhaps in the nightclubs of Berlin but not here in Schäferhof, not in this camp. We agreed not to go to the German address, that distant relative whose address had shaped our destiny. Instead, we planned to leave from Bremerhaven, sail to Halifax, then to Quebec City, and then take a train to Sardis, British Columbia where Uncle Ernst would welcome us.

Standing at the edge of the camp, by the wire fence, I

noticed Irmgard gazing back at us. I knew she was glad of our good fortune.

****

Irmgard's hand moved to caress the twirled wood bead necklace she wore. There had been surprise and pleasure for her when she had found it on the ground in the forest near the camp at Zator. The necklace around her neck felt familiar, and that emotion brought the feeling of safety. The vivid colours, the blues, yellows, whites, reds and especially the greens reminded her of the vividness of life, freedom, and faith, like a genial sunbeam for every care and a soothing pity for every separate need. The necklace was a comfort to her, a caress, to see her through all the lonely nights and dreams that were untrue. She was so glad she'd found it. Although she had not always been its possessor, when she wore it she had knew she could be quiet like a sweet bird resting on a bough of a tree.

    She watched a rustling paper skip along the broken pavers. It met with another scrap and blossomed into a creation made up of all those mistakes made in distress, all her past unhappiness. Now they were gone and there was a new creation. She believed she was where she was meant to be, even if it did not mean this was where she was meant to stay. Her faith faced reality. Irmgard breathed a deep sigh of gratitude and let it flood through all the pain she had known and find rest in her soul.

Above her head, like friendly hands, the round tree leaves rustled by a summer breeze in the trees sounded like a pocketful of pennies. Listening to the leaves of the trees and the voices around her, reminded her of those happy stirring sounds in a household when another beautiful warm summer day has peeked in through the bedroom window. In her heart, she had a solitary prayer.

I want my life to be a simple story where good triumphs against cynicism and melancholy. I pray to be blessed with that life. What is the point of ridiculous complexity and dysfunction where there is no room for joy, celebration or even pathos? Where is the life in that?

I yearn to understand how I am a gift from God. I yearn to know what task God is setting before me so I can find out exactly what I should become. Show me how to do that Lord.

Irmgard had been born generous, seasoned with suffering

and marinated with sorrow. She had become what she never would have been in a careless life full of pleasure and self-indulgence. Irmgard had been blessed with a strong affection for life, a type of conviction widely admired. She thought often about how much she loved being alive.

She loved what she knew the world could be. She loved it because it renewed itself; it was green and alive, and the sky was an ongoing concert of greys, pinks, and mauves with slashes of white, and it was so heartbreakingly beautiful in all its moods. She loved the people who were striving, and interesting, and full of joy and expectation, and sorrow.

What we love dearly with all our hearts will bring understanding, in time.

She loved the connection an intimate circle of people can bring, of people who find time to love one another and celebrate in song and dance and music despite other people who are constantly frustrating and scheming. She loved those who lived inside the wonderful history of culture and beauty, who spoke a multitude of languages, who wrote poetry and stories. She loved those who adored the outdoors, who tended their gardens full of rhododendrons, and gathered the leaves of the trees with care to place them where they would become the nurturing soil for tomorrow.

She loved life for all of that.

Bremerhaven, 1945
The Letter
Chapter Thirty-Three

Heinchen came into the room and spoke softly, "Mutti? The man said there is mail."

"Thank you, *Liebchen.*"

I grabbed my shawl and made my way to the Bremerhaven train station to collect the mail.

Manfred. I gazed at the hurried script on the letter that had come via Elsterverda.

I felt thrilled like a child blessed with a packaged gift even without knowing its contents. My hand trembled as I caressed the letter. His tears had made little splashes on the creased paper. The marks were promises, a pledge that his love for me was constant, but the letter itself told me little even though its voice sounded like Manfred.

The letter began: *"Wo Du auch seist, im Herzen bleibst Du mein. Was Gutes in mir lebt, dein ist's allein."*

Yes, it was true, no matter where I was, I lived in his heart and whatever good there was in him, belonged to me. In that first kiss he had stolen and held my heart and soul.

I took a brisk walk down the street to the sea to be alone. The ground was a thick dusty brown and my footsteps showed up along the path, an indication of where I had come from, but not where I was going.

The street was dim but not cool. When I reached the footbridge, I opened the package that had come with the letter. It was a book with a quick note instructing me to keep both letter and book close to my heart or at least on my bedside table.

"Auf den Nachttisch zu Legen," sagte er. *"Eine kleine Bettpostille zusammengestellt von Dr. Owlglass. Für schlafloser Stunden!"*"

"Manfred, ich habe keinen Nachttisch." I laughed at the thought of having furniture to lay the beautiful book upon. I had had a night table once. It had been the only striking piece of furniture I had owned, lovingly crafted by my dear father. He had made two, one for me and one for my sister, Anika. Those beautiful night tables had to be abandoned. It was one of those recollections that breaks your heart, making it weigh twice as much.

He spoke with deep meaning. *"Da drinnen gibt es eine*

kleine Note. Wünsche ich meiner lieben Eleni von ganzem Herzen und wünsche mir sehr, dass diese Zeit endgultig die letzte sein möge, die wir getrennt verleben. Ausliegende kleine Gaben sollen Freude bereiten und Dir ein Stück Deutsches geben. Von dem Geschenk erhoffe ich dass es Dir sehr viele sonnige Tage anzeigen möge! Grüß und einem sehr festen Kuss!" Manfred.

He wished for me what I wished for myself. He hoped, as I did, that time would pass quickly and we would soon be together. How had he managed this communication from the prisoner camp?

From the bridge where I stood I saw the harbor and *die Tabintha,* the ship my family would sail on. The emotional journey had been a longer journey than the physical one. I felt the need of a voiceless person, the breaking feeling of impending exile.

The receiving of the gift did, as I imagined he would wish, bring me pleasure. It was a little bit of the Germany I loved. I gazed out at the beautiful German landscape with a heavy heart. I made an imprint on my memory of the scene to keep it close for I did not know when the opportunity to see it would come again.

I wept.

When I was done, I felt replete and moved into the

welcoming shadows to walk back to the house. A stray cat moved out of my way.

"When I dream of you, Manfred, I will dream all night long."

Chapter Thirty-Four

The seedy little place we inhabited in Bremerhaven had a yard of straggly plants dying in a great variety of containers. The summer heat beat up from the pavement into our faces. It was an entire town sweltering in sticky heat. On the horizon, the thunder began a desultory grumble. A warm wind whistled through a gap, disturbing the trees, whipping up the litter into whirlpools that ran down the street. The sun blazed in through the windows, turning the far side of the square into a wall of fire like those seen in Dresden.

I re-entered the house and got a sense something was different. Slowly, I took off my coat and peered around the corner. I tiptoed down the hallway.

Someone was in the kitchen.

As I entered the room, I was sweetly greeted with, "I have tried to make you tea. Would you like a cup?"

On the table was white bread, butter, cheese and marmalade.

"Yes, I would," I replied in surprise.

It had been a long, long while since Abraham had spoken to me in that wonderful tone. It was a bird-like melodious voice, cheerful and clear. Abraham smiled when our eyes met. It was a genuine smile that went all the way down and through and around.

The tea was luke warm but I held my tongue. All tension left and a restful feeling took its place. I felt validated and smiled in return. Abraham felt forgiven or was it that he felt like forgiving?

"You seem ..." I stopped. *Damn it, why do I always have to go to that personal let's-take-a-deep-look-inside-spot?*

"It is okay, Mutti."

Abraham reached across the table and briefly laid his hand on top of mine. The squeeze brought tears of gratitude and relief to my face. It was such a small gesture of empathy at my mistake.

"I am sorry," I moved to wipe the tear off his cheek. I was relieved he wasn't angry.

"No, Mutti, it's okay. Don't be sorry ... I am sorry too ... I find it impossible to look forward to tomorrow. Thoughts keep creeping into the little corners of my head, waving a red flag, and I can't ignore them. They plague me like the bad boys in the school yard."

I peeked at my son, wondering if we were talking about the same thing.

He heaved a great sigh and looked down. "I don't even know what I am confused about. This world is too chaotic for the rules I try to apply. Life should be different. I want it to be different."

I, too, wanted things to change!

I spoke, "I want everything to be perfect. I want others to behave the way I want. I want others to be loving and wonderful. I feel like writing a book so I can make everything just the way I want it."

We both laughed.

"What would you write about us?" Abraham asked.

"Oh," I paused. "I want us to have that perfect relationship. Not possible, I know, but I would at least like it to be friendly. Friends. I would like it to be without the disgust at my mistakes. I make mistakes! That does not make me a horrible person!"

"You are not a horrible person."

"I know, but why do I have to keep on telling myself that?"

"I don't know. I don't tell you that."

"Well … you ask me to leave or you stop talking to me altogether or you ask me to leave you alone!"

There was an awkward pause.

"And you don't do it," Abraham's voice became hard and exasperated.

"Why would I leave when things are upsetting or bad? That's when you stay, not run or sneak away. That's when you figure it out!"

"Okay, okay. Don't get excited."

"Why not? I hate it when you tell me to calm down. Why should I calm down?"

Abraham shrugged. The exchange was following the old pattern.

"This is vital, and I am saying it with emphasis. Should I pretend I am falling asleep and this does not matter?"

"Maybe if you were not so intense. We all know how intense you can get."

"Nothing I do or say is okay with you."

"That's not true."

"You are always able to criticize. There is always something that is not right."

"What did I criticize?"

"You tell me to calm down like I am a hysterical ninny. You insinuate I am so lacking, so incomplete. Why don't you think about yourself?"

"I refuse to become what others think I should be. I am not upset."

"You are so superior."

Abraham stared at me.

"As if *you're* not intense, Abraham! I say what you don't like, and all you do is get angry. You literally run away! You are not perfect, you know."

"I know." Abraham clipped the words out and sat waiting, fuming inside.

"Oh, are you putting up with me now?"

"Yup."

"You are so condescending."

There is always tension from conflict when sparked by intensity, the underlying tinder of frustration expressed in a harsh and intimidating voice speaking the wrong word.

"You know what, I will leave until you can ... I don't know what ... get over your insecurities, I guess."

"No wait. Please. Sit down again." I reached out for his hand.

Abraham hesitated.

Try. Try, Abraham. Listen to your heart. Let it show you the way, let it show you how you can bring yourself home. Please, please, sit down.

Choice.

He sat back down.

I let out my breath. "I do not like the way you talk to me. I feel like you always point out what is wrong with me. I don't even think you like me."

Abraham made a noise.

My exasperation increased. "Please, let me speak. Let me say everything until I am done, totally done." It is generally recognized that people do not respond well when confronted by a steamroller. A fact I have difficulty remembering.

Abraham raised his eyebrows.

"You asked what would I write? I would write make-believe because, sadly, I know our relationship is not the way I want it to be and I can't find the key to change it."

"It is what it is."

"That sounds final, defeatist."

"No, it is realistic."

"Stop interrupting! I don't want it to be this way. I want it to be better!"

I grabbed my forehead with my two hands as if to squeeze clarity into my head. It did not work. What could I say? How to speak to him with confidence when he was waiting for every misstep and once discovered, would point it out? How could I speak to him when he already had his mind made up about who I was?

"Mutti, our connection is the way it is because you are you and I am the way I am. Maybe you should accept that. I do not want to be around you all the time. Quite frankly, you get to be a bit much. Yes, you have done so much, and, okay, we must be together, but that's it. I have my life and you have yours. This is not all about you."

I looked at Abraham and thought about how much I hated that damn speech. I rarely thought about myself first! How was it possible I had given that perception?

"You are interfering," Abraham snipped.

"No, I am sharing, keeping us together, bringing us together."

"I don't see it that way." The mask on Abraham's face reappeared.

"Try to see it that way. Try," I implored as I took his hand. Abraham let me; he did not withdraw it.

"I am afraid you will hurt me," he said blankly. "You expect so much. You are so aggressive and always, always make things ..."

I didn't know what to say. There had been times when I had hurt him. Times I fiercely regretted and would take back, but not everything was my fault. Abraham's sweeping generalizations and perceptions astounded me. I could tell he tried to make sense of it all in the aftermath, but as he transferred his anger and his despair onto me, it reinforced his false perceptions and distorted view of reality. In the horror of the passing war, Abraham's traumatic transference contained the heart of our relationship.

"I want you to remember I love you ... more than anything." I sought Abraham's eyes but he just stared at me. "How much I want to have a son I can love without judgment for how that love is expressed. Just remember I love you."

I felt like an imperfectly decorated Christmas tree twinkling in the corner of the room. Every year, I lovingly placed those handmade ornaments on the tree. They were beautiful to share, a symbol of giving. How painful it was to have others see their imperfection and not their beauty. Each ornament had a special meaning and was not a superficial twinkle. They shone with depth, like me.

I always go to the meaning of everything. It is what I do. It is how I survived. It is what I had to offer.

I raised my eyebrows. "I'm not perfect and I don't always get it right."

Abraham barely nodded.

I importuned, "I have ... we have much to learn. Our love and the way we love each other is imperfect. There is nothing that has happened, that could happen or will happen that will make me love you less." I began to cry.

"You don't know ..."

"I do know! I know life is cruel, difficult. I know that! I don't need to know exactly ... I just need to know you love me!" Unmentionable and undisclosed failings are a great drowning weight. Yet, they can be easily removed, but not by me.

Abraham seized the opportunity to take a risk and threw his arms around me. "I love you so much, Mutti."

"I have always loved being your Mutti." His touch filled me with hope.

The genuine words came easier now. "Thank you for being my mother. I have always wanted you to be proud I was your son, but …"

"No. No buts."

Abraham closed his eyes. "No buts. You are my Mom. I will talk to you—not about everything — but enough." He paused.

I could tell he was making a big decision.

"I had a dream last night. There was a hallway. The hall was empty. Strange. You would think there would be people about; after all, there were people in there, a building, a type of clinic. There were small rectangular windows in the double doors revealing another hallway. I could see through to the other side but there was no one there either. *Could I make a break for it? Is it locked? Do they do that anymore?* That's what I thought to myself in the dream."

Abraham peeked at me to see my reaction. I sat still, listening, not wanting to betray my inner turmoil at this unexpected sharing.

He continued, "I see myself dashing out of the ward. A crazy escaping from the ward would be a nostalgic headline. Then, the way it does in dreams, the grey walls slid into the grey floor. I turned the corner and went down the side of the quadrangle. No one was there either. No sound. There was another door, a single door with a small rectangular window, on the left. I peeked in but no one was there."

Abraham recounted without a pause. I wondered if he remembered I was there.

"*It's a prayer room,* I thought to myself. *Prayer? They have a prayer room here?* There were mats on the floor. I leaned back to look at the sign. *Hmmm. Muslim?* Yet I imagined a Sikh woman, veil over her body and head, rocking back and forth. *Hmmm, yes, she would need prayer.* I don't know where I got that image from ... I looked down the hallway. Grey and smooth. In the corner, there was an object hanging on the wall. It was a Mission Statement. Funny, in the dream I distinctly remember thinking to myself.

Seriously, I hate those things.

I turn the corner. Two full sets glass doors. One after the other. There was the unreal world outside. I looked at the short grass, the tree. Leafless or was it budding? I couldn't remember what season it was. The world outside the building looked like the unreal world. Not this. *This is the real world*, someone in my head said and I turned my head back toward the hallway."

I wanted to take Abraham's hand to comfort him but I didn't dare move.

"Grey," he said. "I turned my head to look through the outside doors. Grey ... there was a late evening sky. I kept walking. What else could I do? I was in a dream."

Abraham gave a funny laugh and shook his head.

"It was such a vivid dream. On the final side of the quadrangle, parallel to the hallway, there was a radio room. Yes, the radio room, but the walls were glass and I could see into it. The nurse's station was across from it, behind glass. The radio room had people in it. I remember thinking, *so, this is where everyone is. Of course, it's the prayer room that is empty.* I looked into the radio world from the hallway. Someone asked me if I was new here? I turned. He was tall. Thin. Dark hair. Faceless."

Abraham's breathing came a little bit faster as he stared off into the distance. He pressed his lips together.

"I thought, *what the ...? Am I new here? This isn't a bloody resort.* I stared at him. I looked. He looked back. His face came forward. He shifted to the other foot. I could see that he could see there was no talking to me. Nope. He knew he had come up against someone whom there was just no talking to. He disappeared. *Good,* I think to myself."

I thought he was finished. "That's quite a dream." I bit my lip.

"Oh, it went on. It was like I was there with the busy nurses, but they didn't look up as I moved by. I went to the next door and told them my sleeping medication wasn't working."

My eyebrows must have shot up because Abraham smirked at me. "Mutti it's a dream."

"What happened next?"

Abraham took a long pause. I held my breath.

"The nurse silently looked up and I had a thought. *Are you going to stare or are you bloody well going to speak?* He doesn't.

My, my, you are looking sullen tonight. If you are that angry, why do you work here? You shouldn't be a nurse when you are such an asshole. Hmmm, someone else whom there is just no talking to."

Abraham seemed to take satisfaction in that, but didn't know what to make of it.

"But I keep moving on. My toes are swollen and my ankles ache. I look." He stopped. Tears came to his eyes. "It's the pain, trying to get out. The skin keeps it in."

I sat silently.

"My legs shuffle slowly like it's a void, a chasm. The last bed was mine. It was by the window. The window was full length. Rectangular. What was it with that shape? I sat on the bed. Yup, it was rectangular too. You need to change your clothes. Here's a hospital gown. She placed it on the bed beside me. I looked. She looked. I'm thinking, *you know, I am laughing on the inside.* She was not amused. Angry? No. She waited. *You're a patient one and you're not going away I can tell.* I refused. Because I could. After all, I was the crazy one. In my world, I get to refuse. So there."

"Abraham!"

"Oh, she left but she came back. Every few minutes, she

chirped as she went out, you're on suicide watch."

"Abraham, no," I whispered.

Abraham barely nodded.

"I was not sleeping in my dream, just lying down in the void. Dinner was untouched on the tray. What did I need to eat for? I could see the parking lot through the window where I could watch people come and go. There was no one out there though. It was dark. I heard someone say, damn you. Get out of here! I can't even repeat the tirade that came after that introduction from the hallway."

He shook his head.

"But in my dream, I must have dozed, because I remember thinking *I am wide-awake now. Why does she have to stand outside my room and do that in the middle of the night?* Her imagined domestic war continued. Over and over. On and on. *You shut the eff-up! Where are the nurses? Why don't they do something?* I stared at the ceiling. That voice carried the agony of longing to be heard. I didn't want to hear it. Finally, she moved away. Good.

In the morning, there was a check-in, early. He must have wanted to get it over with. I need to go back to the village, I told my psychiatrist. The psychiatrist nodded with understanding or was it relief? It sounded like a conclusion. He liked it. Yes. Good. He wrote in his notes.

It was a lie though.

There was no village.

There was no place where I belonged. I couldn't go back. I couldn't recreate it for the future. There ... was ... no ... village. I didn't know that then. But I do now. The last thing I remember in that dream, was that I looked up to see a piece of paper taped over the face of the wall clock. It said, Now."

The final note of hope in Abraham's tone of voice embraced my heart with such true feeling.

I nodded. "Now," I said. "I want to be part of your life. I have so much to share with you, so much love to give you, so much joy in being with you."

I didn't want to be someone he made time for.

"Mutti, know that if I don't always share or speak that ... we are fine. I need ... space."

I nodded. "Okay."

"I thought many times I would lose you, that death would claim you and I would be alone. I am thankful we have survived —

together." He stroked my face with his fingertips.

It was what I was really thinking and what I had hoped for, yet I needed Abraham to utter the words I could not, even though they seemed brilliantly obvious.

Abraham was my voice just as Susannah had been his. He had doubted his words could ever be spoken outloud, and now they had been. Each time, now, would be a little bit easier to speak of what was inside. Abraham was trying to forgive himself, now he could do. He could love himself that little bit.

For me, the expression of love created a place to belong and grow wondrously within, especially when there was forgiveness. A burden diminished. Yes. A sense of wonder. Yes. What was in the past and what was in the future, did not compare to what was in my heart now.

I kissed him on the cheek. "I love being loved by you, my child, my son."

Abraham smiled. "I will speak gently with you because I know how touchy you are."

We both laughed.

"I will respect your boundaries because they are not walls

against me," I said.

"I will always let you in … eventually," Abraham said, "because I do trust your love for me. You have wisdom and courage for me to draw on."

"As do you … "

"Mutti, I promise I will not turn my back on you, drive you away, ask you to stay away or ask you to leave. I will never run away from you. I would not do that to you. Not now. There has been too much of that in this war. I do not want that for us. Our time together is precious. I want you to listen and stop trying to fix everything."

A tall order considering the circumstances.

"It means so much to me to hear you say this with kindness and mean it," I gratefully disclosed. It was a relief to finally get a conversation out of Abraham instead of a report or a list of wrongdoings.

"We share this moment. We will share many more," Abraham said simply, "let's finish our tea. It is getting cold."

I laughed quietly to myself about the already cold tea.

He smiled gently at me. "And then I have to take Heinchen

out to play."

I gave him a little nod.

****

After Abraham left with Heinchen, I marveled at the wonderful conversation. A true conversation, not an argument! It fulfilled me to realize it was never possible to give too much. Abraham's unexpected response embraced my soul in a calming way.

I knew it would not last, the next time had a good chance of being imperfect, and I would have difficulty with that and my almost uncontrollable fear of disaster would kick in. Life doesn't give you closure, you make your own.

Yet, I now knew what the world had destroyed, only grace could heal.

I realized what I had undergone and suffered, I would never get over it ... but I will get through. Once through the fear, I will marvel and be amazed at what I have survived.

And right now?

The same goes for today. Each day. I will manage. I dream

of a labyrinth of happiness, devoid of fear, that welcomes me, for the ultimate task set before me is to be whole, and to live, by knowing what no angel in heaven knows —— what it means to live, to belong, and to dream in this world.

THE END

My parents fled, with their families from the devastation of World War II. My mother boarded a ship called "Die Tabintha", sailed across the Atlantic and docked in Halifax. It was the middle of winter. January. She and her sister stood outside the train that would take them across Canada to British Columbia. She recalls standing in her short dress, thin coat and knee socks with a candy in her hand! A new land. My father's family left from Bremerhaven and sailed to Quebec City. He too, boarded a train to British Columbia, where sponsors awaited them.

Their life was, initially, beyond my true comprehension — until I wrote this narrative.

The more I researched WWII, the more horrified I became. If I were confronted with the physical evidence of what occurred, I would have to say my eyes and ears are lying! I am absolutely consumed with disbelief. Today, I have the luxury to close the book, turn off the computer and avert my eyes from those grotesque photographs. I can create distance and safety. I am unbelievably appalled by what people did to each other.

My ultimate reaction to the terror of the Past was to discover that there exists an abyss in my being so silent that not even tears can reach it. This I experienced when visiting Beaumont Hamel, a WWI memorial: the sacrifice and the pain are enormous. The loss of even one person has such far-reaching sad consequences and affects many people. I believe the opposite is also true: that the survival of one person and the telling and receiving of their stories can begin to heal us. The story of my family coming to a new country is a story of success; it is the defeat of fear and trauma.

Thank you to my family, my ancestors, for your stories. I love you all so much. I love your courage. The way you face every day. I love your true love, your generosity, your forgiveness. I love your laughter, and although I hate to be teased, I love your kidding. My life without you physically close is lonely. I miss you so much. For those now absent, I am filled with such longing for yesterday, I sometimes think the Past is the only place I can truly live and feel; yet, you have given me a better life. Now.

You are all such a part of me—my Past, my Present, and my Future—all these are with you ... all of you ... you are the Spirits of my existence.
I love you all.

Wo Du auch seist, im Herzen bleibst Du mein.

Was Gutes in mir lebt, Dein ist's allein.

Meiner lieben Leni zum Weihnachtsfest 1948

Hermann

Photo aufnahme von 31.X.1948

Made in the USA
San Bernardino, CA
09 June 2017